STANDING
BEFORE HELL'S GATE

The Showdown Trilogy, Book 1

The Last Brigade, Book 4

William Alan Webb

δ
Dingbat Publishing
Humble, Texas

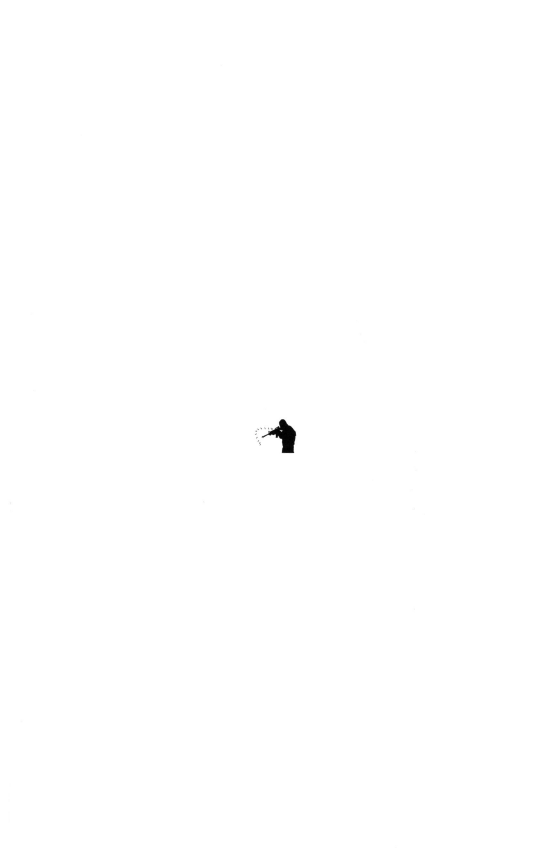

Author's Foreword

If you're reading this, then chances are good you've read the three and a half previous books in *The Last Brigade* series, and maybe the independent story *The Hairy Man,* which means I am grateful to you in the extreme. You've helped make a lifelong dream come true, to write books that people enjoy reading.

If you're reading this foreword well after the book's publication date, my subsequent apology may seem odd. See, the previous volume in the series, *Standing At The Edge*, came out in January of 2018, well over a year before *Standing Before Hell's Gate.* For the readers who finished book 3 and have been patiently waiting for book 4, I'm very sorry to have made you wait so long. During 2018 I finished writing *Jurassic Jail*, which I started in 1988 and which has a special place in my heart, and then spent the rest of the year finishing a non-fiction book on World War Two entitled *Killing Hitler's Reich: The Battle for Austria 1945.* Since it clocked in at nearly 300,000 words, it took a bit of work to finish. It is the definitive work on a heretofore unreported chapter of that horrible conflagration.

I also finished some shorter stories, notably *The Hairy Man, A Story From the World of the Last Brigade* and *The River of Walking Spirits* for an anthology coming out later in 2019, which stars the Snowtiger sisters' great-great-great-grandmother. All told, I wrote about half a million words in 2018, which I hope to double in years to come. If that sounds like a lot, it's only 3,000 words a day... not so many, really.

Anyway, back to my original point. I remain grateful to all of my readers and want this series to be as much yours as mine, so please join my Facebook groups and give me feedback for what you'd like to see in future books. Much of what is in this book comes directly from suggestions by readers. The two groups are:

facebook.com/WorldsofWilliamAlanWebb/ or
facebook.com/keepyouupallnightbooks/
and my website thelastbrigade.com

Lastly, the scope of the series has reached a point where the cast of characters is growing quite large. I'm aware of this, but it's the nature of the beast. Trust me that I only introduce new named characters with the greatest reluctance; I really am not trying to overwhelm you. I'll keep the count as low as I can, I promise, but as George R.R. Martin says of his books, they're a complex story and complex stories are complex.

Enough already. Let's go blow something up.

A note on tech in this book

These books contain references to a lot of military hardware and *none* of it is made up. In some cases, I have taken existing technology, such as hovercraft, and imagined it as it will be. The same was true of the AH-72 Comanche gunship, which at the end of the day is just a beefed-up AH-64 Apache. It doesn't exist, but it could, and the same is true of the tech in this book.

You might be tempted to see something and think it pushes the bounds of willing-suspension-of-disbelief, but if that's you, then remember, DARPA is working on some pretty amazing stuff. We're getting into an era of smart decals, after all, so as an author I'm going to use that kind of thing for my own purposes, which is to say, for making mayhem.

#

CAST OF CHARACTERS

The Angriff family

Nicholas Trajanus Angriff — General of the Army. Nick the A to those who fear him. Idolizes George Patton's tactical genius and persona, but not as fussy as Patton about personal appearance and decorum. Like another hero of his, Winston Churchill, Angriff is sometimes accused of courting danger. As a three-star general, he led tactical missions more suited to a captain or lieutenant, usually against direct orders not to do so. His career survived because of his popularity with his men and the public, and his record of success.

Janine Marie Jackson Angriff — Nick's wife, a victim in the Lake Tahoe 'incident.'

Lieutenant Morgan Mary Randall, nee Angriff — Oldest of Nick's two daughters. Lieutenant in the U.S. Army, executive officer First Platoon, Alpha Company, 1st Tank Battalion. Call sign Bulldozer One One Two. Married to Captain Joe Randall. Nicknamed Tank Girl.

Cynthia June Angriff — Nick's youngest daughter, caught in the same attack as her mother.

Nicholas Trajanus Bauer (Angriff), Jr. — The real name of Green Ghost.

Nicole 'Nikki' Teresa Bauer (Angriff) — Real name of Nipple.

The Americans

Lt. General Norman Vincent Fleming — Executive officer of the 7th Cavalry, also the Brigade S-3, Operations. Norm is Nick Angriff's best friend, dating back to their days in OCS. Both men enlisted and worked their way through the ranks, an almost impossible feat. Fleming is the man Angriff trusts above all others.

Major General Dennis Tompkins — Survivor of The Collapse who did not go cold, but instead lived fifty years in post-Collapse America, leading his team of five survivors.

Captain Joseph Daniel Randall — The best helicopter pilot in the brigade. Married to Morgan Randall. Call sign Ripsaw Real.

Lieutenant George 'Bunny' Carlos — Joe Randall's best friend and co-pilot.

Sergeant Lara Snowtiger — Marine sniper, a full-blooded Choctaw. Snowtiger embraced her heritage and is versed in Choctaw lore. She is considered as good as any sniper in the 7th Cavalry, including Zo Piccaldi.

Sergeant Major of the Army John Charles Schiller — Trusted subordinate who runs the day-to-day routine for Angriff's headquarters. Angriff often asks Schiller for advice.

Colonel William Emerson Schiller — Brother of Sergeant J.C. Schiller, he is the brigade's S-4, Supply Officer, and is considered a savant at supply chain organization and utilization.

Lt. Colonel Roger 'Rip' Kordibowski — Battalion S-2, Intelligence Officer.

Colonel Fitzhugh Howarth Claringdon — Former executive officer of the tank battalion. Imprisoned for the assassination attempt on General Angriff.

Lt. Colonel Astrid Naidoo — Temporary S-9, Civil-Military Cooperation.

Colonel Khin 'Chain' Saw — Brigade S-1, Personnel.

Sergeant Howard Wilson Dupree — Communications specialist and computer whiz.

Sergeant Frances 'Frame' Rossi — Crew chief for *Tank Girl.*

Major Alexis Iskold — Deputy S-3 and Norm Fleming's right hand.

Major Edward Wincommer — Commanding officer of the 7th Cavalry Regiment, 7th Cavalry Brigade.

Major Samuel Ball — CO of the 1st Airborne Battalion.

Colonel Robert Young — CO of 1st Mechanized Infantry Regiment.

Major Dieter Strootman — Executive officer of 1st Mechanized Infantry Regiment.

Captain Martin Sully — Commanding Officer of Dog Company, 1st Marine Recon Battalion, First Marines.

Lieutenant Onni Hakala — Sully's executive officer and commanding officer of 1st Platoon, Dog Company.

Captain April Jones — Commander of Echo Company, 1st Marine Recon Battalion, First Marines.

Captain Ted Wang — Replacement pilot for *Tank Girl*.

Lieutenant Pra Sakoya — Captain Wang's co-pilot.

The crew of Joe's Junk

Staff Sergeant Joe 'Toy' Ootoi — Gunner and boyfriend of Nikki Bauer.

Task Force Zombie, a/k/a 'The Nameless'

Green Ghost — Nick Angriff's only son. Longtime subordinate of Angriff's and currently his S-5, Security.

Vapor — Original member of TF Zombie. Wise-cracking member of the team. He and Green Ghost have known each other since childhood.

One-Eye — Original member of TF Zombie. Nickname refers to his personality.

Wingnut — Original member of TF Zombie. Taciturn, a specialist at explosives and chemicals.

Glide — Replacement addition to TF Zombie, Glide is an ultra-dangerous computer specialist. She is gorgeous, and an 8th degree Krav Maga.

Nipple — Green Ghost's twin sister. Most think she is psychotic, but like her brother, her reflexes are off the chart.

Razor — Replacement addition, the newest member of the team.

Frosty — A veteran member who started out in Third Squad and transferred to First Squad after the Congo operation.

Zeus — Original member of TF Zombie.

Claw — Former commander of Second Squad, Task Force Zombie, and an original member.

Other Americans

General Thomas Francis Steeple — Disgraced and imprisoned founder and driving force behind Operations Overtime and Comeback.

Colonel Amunet Mwangi — Norm Fleming's first cousin and formerly second in command of Operation Comeback. She was Tom Steeple's closest advisor and confidant.

Norris McComb — Construction foreman at Overtime Prime.

Creech Air Force Base

General Jamal Kando — Base commander.

The Scrapers

Junker Jane — Jane scrapes Northern California, Nevada, Utah, and into the Pacific Northwest.

Jingle Bob — Bob scrapes the area north of Idaho Jack and east of Junker Jane.

Nuff — Nuff isn't actually a scraper himself, but his father was. Now he lives alone in a small shack in the desert.

Kodiak 'Kody' Kate — Built like a bear, Kody scrapes parts of California and Nevada.

Shangri-La

Johnny Rainwater — Elected leader of Shangri-La.

Abigail Deak — Leader of the Jemez Pueblos and Johnny Rainwater's de facto deputy leader.

Mohammad Qadim — Muslim member of Shangri-La who infiltrated the Sevens as a spy.

Billy Two Trees — Young scout from Shangri-La.

Operation Evolution

Györgi Rosos — Billionaire who used his money to undermine capitalist republics around the world, in addition to financing part of Operations Overtime and Comeback, as well as his own independent operation. He believes in communist totalitarianism and greatly admires the North Korean Kim family dynasty.

Györgi Rosos, Jr. — Sometimes derisively called *ketto* (an Americanized version of the Hungarian word *kettő*, meaning *two*) by the rank and file at Evolution, the eldest son and namesake of Rosos Sr. is a naturally affable man who is constantly vying with his younger brother for their father's affection.

Károly Rosos — Only their father matches the younger Rosos' ruthlessness and ambition.

Adder — Former member of Task Force Zombie. As dangerous as Green Ghost but ruthless and cares only for himself.

The Sevens

Nabi Husam Allah — The Caliph of the Caliphate of the Seven Prayers of the New Prophet, self-proclaimed prophet of Allah. In truth, he is Larry Armstrong, a criminal conman. His adherents are fanatically loyal.

Abdul-Qudoos Fadil el Mofty — Emir of New Khorasan. His original name is Richard Lee Armstrong, brother of the Caliph, Larry Armstrong. He bears the title of Superior Imam, second only to the Caliph himself, who is the Supreme Imam. These titles were created by the Armstrong brothers to elevate them above all imams in Islam. He is also second in command of The Sword of the New Prophet, the military arm of the Caliphate.

Sati Bashara — Senior Aga and oldest nephew of Emir Abdul-Qudoos Fadil el Mofty, appointed head of the province of New Khorasan, a region of the larger Caliphate of the Seven Prayers of the New Prophet, encompassing parts of Arizona, New Mexico, and old Mexico. He is the second most powerful lieutenant in New Khorasan.

General Ahmednur Hussein Muhdin — Primary military commander of the Caliphate's Sword of the Prophet.

General Tracy Gollins — Daughter of Abdul-Qudoos Fadil el Mofty and commanding officer of the Mecca Regiment in The Sword of the New Prophet.

The Apaches

Govind — Chief of the Western Apache.
Gosheven — The middle of the three brothers.

Ma Kelly's

Dave Weiner — Proprietor of the trading post known as Ma Kelly's.

Hoover Dam

Lulu, aka Dr. Louise Repperton — Head of Hoover Dam.

The Chinese

Generalissimo Zhang Wei — Commander of all Chinese forces in California.

Captain Chen Yi — Chinese liaison officer to 1st Mechanized Infantry Regiment.

Captain Xiao Ki — Chinese intelligence officer also attached to 1st Mechanized Infantry Regiment.

Groom Lake Air Force Facility (Area 51)

Major Jonathan Cane — De facto commander of the remnant garrison of Groom Lake Air Force facility.

Winfrey Butler 'Bondo' Cane — Brother of Jonathan Cane and his deputy at Groom Lake.

The Devil looked down with a snarl and a frown
As I stood before Hell's gate;
"Where have you been, my wayward friend?
You're very, very late."

"Now fall to your knees and worship me,
"Give the Devil his due;
"Belief in me will set you free,
"Denial will bring your doom."
  Oscar O'Connor, from "Standing Before Hell's Gate"

PROLOGUE

In the eyes of god, an infidel is not considered fully human until they accept the New Prophet as the true voice of Allah. Until then they are as the beasts.
From The Revelations of Nabi Husam Allah, Chapter 6, Verses 11–12

The Blue Hole of Santa Rosa, New Mexico
1347 hours, April 21, ten months after initiation of Operation Overtime

The midday sun warmed the dripping wet limbs of Abdul Qudoos Fadil el Mofty, Emir of New Khorasan. At word of the arrival of the Caliph, Nabi Husam Allah, el Mofty climbed out of the refreshing sixty-two degree waters of the Blue Hole and shook himself like a wet lion. A slave handed him a thick cotton towel. It had once taken half an hour for his thick hair to dry, but those days were long gone. Aside from just turning gray, his once-black locks had thinned considerably in the past decade.

His nephew, Sati Bashara, followed him out of the water, and paused to examine the young woman nailed to an X-shaped cross fifty feet to the west. El Mofty noticed him staring and followed his line of sight. The woman's rolling head meant she still lived, even if they couldn't see her face.

"The day promises to be a great one," the young man said.

"Do you know something I don't, Sati?"

"I don't understand why you say that, Uncle. Already today we discovered an infidel in our midst." He pointed at the woman. "The army is in the field and ready to fight, we have refreshed ourselves in cool, clean water found in the middle of the desert, and now our blessed prophet is among us. What more can we ask for?"

How about a cold beer? el Mofty thought, although what he said was quite different. "You have the optimism of youth, Sati. It's why I value having you near me. Come, let us welcome my brother, your other uncle."

In the nearby parking lot, a knot of his officers and counselors surrounded a faded green International Harvester Scout. As with most pre-Collapse vehicles, it had been heavily modified and used an aircraft engine in place of the original V-8. A dozen other vehicles surrounded the Scout and armed men in green uniforms kept the crowd away.

The Emir pushed through the high officials and stood beside the right rear passenger door. Seconds later, the stocky figure of the Caliph climbed out of the car to a round of applause. Clothed in loose white cotton pants and a white shirt, wearing sandals, he smiled and nodded and hugged his brother, and then shook the hand of every man there. After a few minutes of back slapping and well-wishing, he invited his brother to join him away from the crowd for a private conversation. Both men smiled and laughed as they strolled fifty yards from the others, far enough they couldn't be overheard.

With no one to hear them, the Caliph reverted to his real identity of Larry Armstrong. "What the fuck are you doing? You move ten thousand men into hostile territory, with a definite target in mind, and then stop and go swimming? What the hell, Richard!"

"Fuck you, Larry, but I'm not gonna make the same mistake I made last year. You goaded me into moving west before I was ready and look where it got us. I'm not doing that again."

"I didn't goad you into anything."

"The fuck you didn't. Look, I've got patrols out doing recon all the way into central Arizona, because this time I want to know what's in front of me before I fight. I'd think you'd want that, too. Let me wait on their reports and then I'll move on Shangri-La. It's not going anywhere. I've spent all winter training this army to fight and it *will* fight, and this time it's going to win."

"I hope like hell they can, but honestly, they don't look much like an army to me."

"If I say they can fight, they can fight."

"All right, Richard, I'll let it slide for a while. But we're not getting any younger and by the end of summer I want southwestern Arizona in our hands, got that? By the end of summer."

"Phoenix, too?"

"No, we avoid Phoenix until we learn what happened there, but the rest of it, all the way to the California and Nevada borders, that I want."

"Don't worry, you'll have it."

"I'd better. Who were all those people I saw in the field beside the driveway to this place?"

"Christians, Jews, Mexicans, even a few Muslims, everybody who wouldn't convert. Instead of stoning them this year, I brought 'em up here to use as human shields."

"There's a fucked-up idea. How much did they slow you down? And how much are they eating on this march? Damn it, Richard, if you had a brain, you'd be dangerous."

"I'm getting tired of you picking on me, Larry. I sent them ahead before the main column left, so they haven't slowed us down at all. And we're not feeding them one more crumb than they would have gotten anyway. You got no cause to be pissed off."

"Fine, just stop whining. Now that they're here, we might as well get some use out of them. But not the Muslims. Punish them some other way. It looks bad."

"What does our beloved New Prophet suggest?"

Larry Armstrong shrugged. "You can't crucify a Muslim, so cut off a head. That's always popular."

\#

Chapter 1

Fools don't hunt deer, fools hunt tigers.
Xiang Weh, circa 600 B.C.

Overtime Prime
1410 hours, April 22

For Tom Steeple, the worst part was the boredom. There was absolutely nothing to do except stare at the rough-hewn stone walls of his cell. No TV, movies, books, music, nothing. Nick Angriff could have given him any of that, but hadn't. It wouldn't have cost him anything, but Nick the Asshole wanted to make him suffer. The lack of mental stimuli was maddening, but he would never give that prick the satisfaction of showing it.

The latter part of Steeple's career had been spent as a man in the center of a whirlwind of activities, all of which had had grave importance to the world. Whether writing and coordinating reports during his time in Personnel at the Pentagon, or making decisions on new weapons systems or talking to Congressmen or briefing multiple presidents on military matters and recommending courses of action which had had profound impacts on human history... for more than two decades, he'd been someone of utmost importance. A man could get addicted to wielding such power, and Steeple had. But all of that was gone. Now, he could only lie on his bunk and stare at the shadows cast by the bare LED bulb overhead.

He had managed to calm his mind into thinking about nothing when scratching at the door roused him. Getting up on one elbow, he craned his neck. The door swung inward and a man in wrinkled denim work pants and a coarse light blue shirt entered his cell. He wore scuffed black work boots.

"Do I know you?" Steeple said, swinging his legs off the bunk and sitting up straight.

"We've never met," the man said, extending his hand. "But you put me here. I'm Norris McComb, I'm a foreman in Jamaya Diloub's construction group."

"Of course," Steeple replied, shaking hands. "Jamaya's a good man." He stood up, smiling, trying to remember everything he could about Jamaya Diloub. It wasn't much. "How is he doing?"

"He's fine, General, but look, we don't have much time. The guard changes in thirty minutes and I've gotta be long gone by then. There's not many of us left now and we can't risk being found out."

"I understand... may I ask, who is *us*?"

"*Rabota sdelayet vas svobodnymi.* We shorten it to RSVS."

"The Stalinists..."

"Stalin was a great leader."

"I'm not sure all the people he killed would agree."

"He didn't back off doing what needed to be done. Russia was a medieval country that he turned into a modern world power in less than thirty years."

"Angriff said you were here."

"I was Bettison's backup for flipping the switch to connect the comms with Comeback, only he got there first."

"How many of you are left?"

"Five, counting me. That bastard Green Ghost and his crew got the rest of us. Rita almost got Angriff on day one, but... well, look, there's time for that later. What I need to know from you is, if we get you out of here, are you with us?"

Steeple had assumed his familiar posture when listening to proposals brought to him by people asking for his help. Head tilted slightly down, narrow shoulders squared, hands clasped behind his back. "I don't know what that means."

"It means we need a strong leader who realizes that rebuilding America can't be done the way it was the first time.

No democracy, no republic, none of that crap. It doesn't work."

"You're talking about a dictatorship," Steeple said, his voice rising with genuine surprise. "You're actually suggesting that."

"Call it what you want, but initially it's the only way. Maybe later we can reconstitute some sort of republic, but in the meantime, we need a leader who's not afraid to build a better country, a man with strong organizational skills and the drive to finish what he starts. Operation Overtime is a testament to your ability to do exactly that... that's why you're the man for the job. But I need to know right now, the guards could change at any minute, and getting you out of here will take some planning. What d'ya say?"

"Angriff will never stand down for this. As long as he's here, it'll never work. It sounds like you don't have enough resources to fail again, so we've got to be very careful."

"You're in?"

"Of course I'm in."

"Angriff's leaving."

"What? When? How long will he be gone?"

"Tomorrow. He was supposed to go today, but they couldn't get everything together that fast. He's going along with a relief column heading up to Sierra Depot."

"This is all news to me. What's at Sierra? That's a long way from here."

"There's no time to fill you in now, General."

"Is Fleming in charge while he's gone?"

"Fleming is at Sierra." Despite the lack of time, McComb gave Steeple a thirty-second run-down of the latest events at Creech and Sierra.

As he spoke, Steeple tapped his front teeth again and started pacing in a circle. "Who's in charge while he's gone?"

"Colonel Saw."

Steeple stopped circling and grinned. "Chain Saw? Perfect. You're right, McComb, this is the time to act."

"I've gotta leave now, General, but I'll be back as soon as I can to get you out of here."

"No!"

"The guard could change any second now."

"I don't care. I'm in charge now, so listen! You said you have access to sub-floor eleven?"

"Yeah."

"On a shelf in the far left corner, there's a wooden box marked *flares*. Take the top off and look for a small sliding bit of wood underneath it. Inside you'll find a key. Take that key into the shaft with the switch, the one you had to climb down to link Comeback with Overtime. Do you remember how to do that?"

"Yes, hurry!"

"Right beside the switch, there's a dark little hole. It doesn't look like much, but it's a keyhole. Use that key to open the door there and bring me what's inside."

"What if I get caught?"

"Bring it!"

"At least tell me what it is."

"It's a satellite phone. To pull this off, we're going to need help."

"Should I tell Colonel Saw?"

"No, not yet." *Not until I have a backup plan,* Steeple thought. *Saw might like being in charge too much to give it up.*

#

CHAPTER 2

The Dark Man returned on a moonless night.
His black form drank the wan starlight;
"I know your spirit as I know your might,
"And despite your might, and your will to fight,
"To no avail you'll fight for right.
"In the end you'll fall and feel death's bite."
Sergio Velazquez, from "The Dark Man"

Operation Overtime
1932 hours, April 22

"I have never seen anything like your office, Nick," Janine said. They stood on the catwalk on the side of the mountain, accessible from the small door at the right side of the Clam Shell. "It looks like you are commanding a space ship in the movies, not a cavalry brigade."

"It takes some getting used to, that's for sure." Angriff eyed her as he could only eye his wife. She leaned against the restraining lattice work and shivered from a sudden wind. He came up behind her and wrapped his arms around her waist, burying his face in her neck. "But some things you never forget."

Her voice dropped an octave. "Mmm... so I see." He started to kiss her neck but stopped when she started coughing.

It went on long enough for him to let go and turn her around. "You all right?"

"Oh, yes," she said with a tiny laugh. "Who knows what I am allergic to in this infernal desert?"

"It's getting a little chilly out here, too."

"Nonsense, Nick, I'm fine. I probably inhaled some cactus pollen, that's all. Now, where were we?"

He kissed her once on the cheek and then patted her shoulder. "I was about to go inside and go over a few million last minute details, and you were about to go back to our quarters and lie down."

"Oh, I was, was I?"

"Don't make me make you," he said, smiling and looking deeply into her face. She looked tired, and... frail. One thing Janine Angriff had never been was frail. "I want you to see Dr. Friedenthall while I'm gone, okay?"

"I do *not* need—"

He cut her off. "I know you don't, but humor me, just this once."

She coughed again but stopped herself with a visible effort. "I'll go, but you cannot make me like it. Oh, Cynthia said she might drop in later."

"Oh. Sure, great." He tried to remember when his youngest daughter had ever shown up at his office, anywhere, by herself. "Did she say why?"

When his wife smiled, Angriff again saw the girl he'd fallen in love with at first sight.

"Nick, I know you are a general of the finest sort, but when it comes to being a father, you are downright blind."

<hr />

2109 hours, April 22

Dennis Tompkins saw Angriff rubbing his eyes and debated going in or leaving without saying anything, but it wasn't in his character to just run off and not tell his CO. Especially not now. "Got a minute, Nick?"

"Sure, come on in. Want some coffee?"

"No, thanks, I'll be up 'til next week if I have coffee this late. And at my age, it's hard to get rid of it again. People say you only rent coffee and beer, but I think I've signed a long-term lease."

That drew a chuckle. "What's on your mind?"

"I know you're fixin' to head out yourself..."

"Yeah, 0600 hours on the dot. I'm already worried because we had to push it back a day. Why?"

"Nick, I hate to bother you as you're headin' out the door, but, well..."

"Whatever it is, the answer is yes, unless it involves you getting shot at."

"Me and the boys need to get out of here for a while. We're thinking about borrowing some of the spare horses and riding up north into Utah. There's some pretty country up there."

"You're just thinking about it?"

"Now that you mention it, no. We're pretty much decided on doing it."

"May I ask why? I'd think after fifty years in the wilderness, you'd never leave civilization again, so why do it?"

"Now that's a harder question to answer. Don't get me wrong, we're all damned grateful to you for saving us and we're all in on Overtime. But I'll be 82 this year and a couple of the boys are a little older than me. We ain't gonna be around too much longer and I reckon we just wanna go for one more ride while we still can... plus it won't hurt to have eyes on what's going on up in Utah."

"No, it won't hurt a bit. I just wish the timing was different, what with me pulling out in the morning."

"I'll stay if you need me to."

"I hate the idea, Dennis, but I'm not going to forbid it. Sure, since Norm is gone I'd feel a lot better if you were here at Overtime, but I get it. Take whatever you need, including a long-range radio. I insist on that. That way, you can let us know if you're in trouble, or if you run into something I should know about."

"That's a deal, Nick."

"And plenty of ammo."

"That you ain't gotta tell me."

"How many Humvees do you want? Two?"

"We're, uh... we're gonna ride."

"*Horses?* You mean you were serious about that?"

Tompkins' chin dipped. "Yeah."

"You're out of your mind."

25

"Probably."

"What the hell, you don't need me to hold your hand… go on, then, before I change my mind. Or before I stick you behind this desk and I take off for Utah with your buddies."

2251 hours

"Hi, Daddy."

Angriff looked up from his computer screen. "Cynthia, your mom said you might drop by. Sweetie, is everything all right?"

His youngest daughter looked a lot like Morgan, but where Morgan had an athletic, tomboyish quality, Cynthia carried herself more like a dancer. Her upturned nose had the same pixie quality as her sister's, and the line of her jaw was delicate, like her mother's. Unlike her sister, Cynthia didn't have to fit her head into a helmet, so her blonde hair spilled halfway down her back.

She sniffed and gave him a chastising frown. "You've been smoking." She started coughing and he was instantly on alert.

But then he realized she was faking it to protest his smoking. "It's *my* office. So is everything all right?"

"Yeah, sure. It's just that the way Morgan described this place made it sound so futuristic, I wanted to check it out for myself. Look. At. That. View!" She wheeled and nearly ran into the side of the office glass, staring out the blast windows onto the moonlit desert below.

"It's amazing, isn't it? There's also a small platform outside, on the face of the mountain itself. I'll take you out there sometime."

"Now?" She was barely out of her teens and still had a childish charm to her smile.

"I'm a little busy right now. How about when I get back?"

She stuck out her lower lip the same way she'd done as a child. It was a playful exaggeration of a pout that he'd rarely been able to deny. Both of his daughters knew how to play him. Just as he was about to cave and take her out to the platform, Corporal Diaz appeared in the doorway with Corporal Dupree behind him.

Cynthia arched her eyebrows in a pouty expression that her sister had never mastered. "Did you send him a signal?"

"I swear I didn't, sweetie."

"I can come back," Diaz said when he realized he'd interrupted them.

"No need, Corporal. We'll do it when you get back, Dad."

"Hey, before you go, one more thing. I told your mother I want you both to see the doctor about those coughs."

"They're just allergies, Dad."

"That's an order, soldier."

The lower lip protruded even farther this time, but then she spun, wiggled her fingers goodbye, and headed out the door. As she left, she smiled at Dupree and Angriff noticed. Was she simply being polite? As her mother's daughter, she'd learned to smile and greet many people at once, and how to make each person feel that she focused on them specifically, so when she extended her hand to Dupree, he extended his in return. Angriff was amused by the shy young man's nervous smile. What surprised him was the grin she gave back to him. He'd seen it before.

Oh, no, he thought, and understood his wife's cryptic remark from earlier.

#

CHAPTER 3

Coffee puts you to sleep, unless you drink it.
attributed to various comedians

Overtime Prime
0109 hours, April 23

"J.C."

Corporal Diaz appeared in his doorway within seconds. "Sir?"

"I'm sorry, Juan. I forgot J.C.'s back in the hospital. How's he doing?"

"He overdid it is all, sir. He'll be back again tomorrow or the next day."

"Good, good. Could you get me some coffee, please?"

"Coffee, sir?"

"I've got a watch, I know what time it is." Angriff stopped himself and apologized. His close relationship with Sergeant Schiller had become second nature, but he couldn't treat Diaz that way. The corporal was already intimidated by him. "Again, I'm sorry, Juan. Please make a note to schedule a call with General Schiller for 0530."

"Pardon me for saying so, General, but won't you be getting ready to pull out?"

"Yeah, but this is important. Wait, no, you're right. I forgot the internal network is connected to Comeback. I'll write him an email... but schedule the call anyway." Leaning back, Angriff rubbed his eyes. Massaging them felt so good. "I can feel it again. It just started, but I can feel it. Swirling all around us."

"I don't follow, General."

"Events." Angriff made a twirling motion with his index finger. "They're circling around us, faster and faster. I can see it in my mind, spinning like a tornado."

"Uh, yes, sir."

"You think I'm crazy."

Diaz shook his head. "No, sir, I don't think any such thing."

"Then you're in the minority. The few people I've told that to all think I'm delusional. But I get these feelings every now and then, usually before a battle, always have, with the most recent being right before the Chinese showed up."

"That doesn't sound good."

"No, it doesn't. Damn, damn, damn... something's about to happen. I just know it."

Emboldened by having an unexpected personal conversation with the C.O., Diaz ventured to say, "Maybe you should cancel your trip to Creech?"

"Because I have a feeling? No, I haven't left this glorified tomb since last year's battles. I need some fresh air, I need to put eyes on Creech to judge the man in charge there... I really need to see what we've got at Sierra. But mark my words, Juan, something's coming." When the corporal turned to leave, Angriff stopped him. "You're doing a fine job, son. Like you said, Sergeant Schiller shouldn't be out too long, and in his absence I know you'll perform your duties well. And since Colonel Walling won't be back to full speed for weeks, and Colonel Saw will be in charge of Overtime while I'm gone, he's going to need your support. I know you can do it."

"Thank you, sir. That means a lot coming from you."

"Now... about that coffee?"

Operation Comeback
0519 hours, April 23

Colonel William E. Schiller settled into the desk chair that had once belonged to General Thomas Steeple. When he took temporary command of Operation Comeback and first entered the office, he'd removed the pillow on the chair's seat. It had made the chair too comfortable, and Schiller believed a commander should forever be uncomfortable. But he had to admit that otherwise Steeple's desk suited his tastes perfectly, with everything arranged in precise fashion and nothing extraneous on the polished wooden surface.

Upon sitting, and despite the 40-inch computer monitor having a digital holographic clock in the upper left corner, Schiller checked his wristwatch and felt disgust with himself. The precise time he wished to be seated for the day's work was ten after five in the morning. Reveille was 0400 every day. After ablutions, he ran for fifteen minutes, showered, ate breakfast, brushed his teeth, and dressed at precisely the same time every day. This would all be accomplished by 0500 hours, which allowed him to be at his post by 0510. Taps was 2000 hours.

But today he was nine minutes late. That was unacceptable, regardless of having gone to bed after midnight. Work had to be done for as long as it took and fatigue was not allowed.

However, everything else was correct. His Army Combat Uniform had the crispness he expected of himself, put there personally with an old-fashioned iron. After-shave lotion, part of his personal baggage allotment, stung his freshly shaved cheeks. Despite the late start, everything else proceeded on schedule and as expected. Earlier in life, a Lucky Strike cigarette would have burned in an ashtray on his left, and he still felt the cravings. The morning's first cup of coffee cooled on the desk by his right elbow, as it always did, and he would take the first sip right before opening the morning's email messages, as always.

That is, until he saw the message outlined in red on the first email, and the sender's name, General of the Army Nicholas T. Angriff.

Effective 0320 hours, April 23, 2077, Colonel William Emerson Schiller is elevated to the rank of acting Major General in the United States Army. General Schiller will continue as commander of the facility known as Operation Comeback until such time as General Angriff relieves him of this duty or he is re-assigned by General Angriff. In this capacity, he is solely responsible for the assets and personnel assigned to his command. His acting rank will be reduced or made permanent solely at the discretion of General Angriff.

In addition to duties outlined in previous communications, General Schiller will prioritize the earliest possible deployment of Operation Comeback's allotment of Fairchild Republic A-10 Thunderbolt II aircraft. His authority to place these aircraft into service includes any and all necessary requirements, including but not limited to requisitioning any materials and equipment, ground crews, pilots, or other personnel deemed by him to be essential to the completion of this mission. Additionally, he may request any materials needed to construct an airfield from which these aircraft will operate.

Extraordinary measures taken to complete either of these missions are approved in advance, excepting any measure which impacts upon missions given other 7th Cavalry assets by General Angriff, including but not limited to Operation Overtime. For all purposes including the chain of command, Operation Comeback is to be considered a separate command organization reporting solely to CINCUS, ergo, General Angriff.

Schiller blinked and read the first part of the message again. With a trembling hand, he reached for his coffee and spilled some on the desk. He didn't notice. Nor did he feel coffee dripping onto his ACU blouse. He put the coffee to his lips and drank from sheer reflex, not blowing on it twice per his daily habit, nor even tasting the dark liquid. All he could do was stare at two words in the message... *Major General.*

After a career of loyal service, helping lesser men achieve higher rank, he'd finally made it. When he closed that email, another one outlined in red was next in the queue. He had a brief panic that maybe General Angriff had changed his mind. But a far more prosaic message awaited him.

It took you long enough. Congratulations!
J.C.

"Corporal Duglach!"

Mikhail Duglach had barely managed to beat his C.O. into the office and worried he'd overlooked something. General Steeple shared a lot of personal similarities with Colonel

Schiller, but Steeple didn't expect his staff to be on duty until 0800 hours. As far as Duglach was concerned, 0500 was the middle of the night.

"Good morning, sir."

Schiller's lean face wore a stunned expression the corporal hadn't seen before. The blue eyes seemed watery and unlike his usually precise manner of speaking, his response seemed distracted. "Good morning, Corporal. Please request a full set of major general's insignia from the Fabrication Shop."

"Major general? May I ask, is this for the colonel?"

"Yes, it is," Schiller said with a faraway look. "It is."

"Then let me wish you congratulations, General. And I was about to tell you that you have a call from General Angriff at Overtime."

"Thank you, Corporal." He *had* changed his mind, Schiller thought, but at least he had enough class to call and break it to him personally. Schiller waited for Duglach to leave before picking up the receiver. "Schiller here. Good morning, sir."

"Good morning, Bill. Call me Nick. Have you read your mail?"

"I have, General... uh, Nick. I appreciate your confidence in me."

"Any questions?"

"Questions?" he said, unable to keep the confusion out of his voice.

But instead of demoting him back to colonel, Angriff laughed. "Yes, questions. Why did you think I called, to bust you back to bird?"

"Ha-ha, no, sir... ummm, no, Nick. So do you still want me to ask you about any significant decisions?"

"As long as we're in contact, yes, it can't hurt to keep things coordinated. But if something happens and you can't get me, do what you think is best. Your orders should cover any situation that might arise. Oh, and you need a strong second, so be thinking about that. Let me know who you want."

"If I may, Nick, I already have a candidate in mind. Major Iskold."

"Alexis Iskold? Norm Fleming's deputy? Sorry, no can do. She's the acting S-3. Anybody else?"

"Lieutenant Colonel Naidoo."

"Astrid... good choice. She's the acting S-9 while Colonel Minokawa is working in Prescott, but she's got excellent organizational skills. All right, you've got her. I'll have her orders cut right away. Anything else you need before I leave?"

"No, sir."

"No, *Nick.*"

"No, Nick. Except thank you again."

"See you when I get back."

#

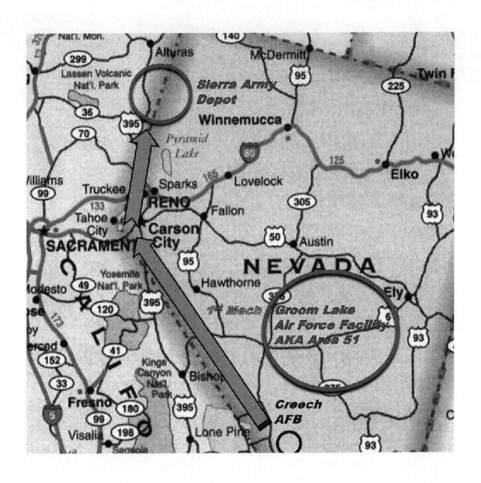

Chapter 4

I love the smell of carbon monoxide in the morning.
Apocryphal, sometimes attributed to George Patton.

Operation Overtime, Motor Bay D
0523 hours, April 23

The noise of powerful engines echoed through the cavernous space of Motor Bay D, their exhaust fumes sucked away by powerful fans. Colonel Bob Young stalked among the hundreds of vehicles assembled, preparing to depart in less than 37 minutes. As commander of the 2nd Mechanized Infantry Regiment, he couldn't show the men and women of his command that this was anything more than just another mission. But in truth, Young grinned through worry. A long-range drive through unsecured country with known hostiles on the loose was dangerous, and while he had a lot of confidence in his regiment's ability to adapt and overcome once in the field, his biggest concern was being tied down by the supply column they were escorting all the way to Creech.

Still, he'd led them through the Battle of Prescott the previous year and earned the personal praise of his C.O., Nick Angriff, a man Young had never thought much of in the past. He'd always been a protégé of Tom Steeple. Along with that distinction went a built-in dislike for certain officer types and even a few officers in particular, with Nick Angriff at the top of the list. But Angriff's handling of that battle, and his subsequent praise of Young's regiment, had modified his feelings. The regiment was his first major combat command and it changed his views on everything.

Surrounded by his staff, Young eyed each vehicle even as he waved to his men and wished them good luck. One Stryker commander gave him a thumbs-up and Young paused for a second of banter, something he'd learned from Angriff.

"You loaded up with ammo?"

"Every round we can cram in here, Colonel."

Young smiled and patted the armored vehicle's side. "Go get 'em."

His executive officer, Major Dieter Strootman, was standing by the regimental M1130 command vehicle near the head of the column. Right behind that was an identical one for the commanding general, who was accompanying the regiment as far as Creech Air Force Base. It was Strootman's job to oversee the details of such an immensely complicated move.

"How we lookin'?" Young asked.

Strootman didn't look up from the sheaf of papers clamped on his clipboard. "We're good to go. The only glitch is a flat tire on one of the HEMTTs." *Heavy Expanded Mobile Tactical Truck.* "But that should be fixed before it's time to move out."

"Excellent." He paused for a few seconds and turned around, taking in the whole environment. "I've been in the army a long time, Dieter, but during all those years I never really understood the *smell* of a large-scale operation."

At that, Strootman looked up. "I guess I never thought about it."

"Exhaust, gas, sweat, grease... it all combines into something unique. I understand General Angriff much better than I did a year ago. Speaking of whom, have we heard from the general?"

Before Strootman could answer, a Humvee came toward them past the column of trucks and armored vehicles, with the familiar figure of Nick Angriff standing in the gunner's hatch and waving at the troops. It pulled to a stop next to the general's own command vehicle and the first person out was a black-haired female major, followed by Angriff and a petite corporal. Young couldn't help noticing the puckered scar on the corporal's throat and something about her name, Santos, was familiar.

"Good morning, Colonel, Major. We ready to roll?"

"Right on schedule, General."

"Outstanding. Gentlemen, this is Major Iskold; she's Deputy S-3."

"We've met, sir. Nice to see you again, Major," Young said. They shook hands all the way around. When they were done, Colonel Young pointed at the corporal. "Why do I recognize her name, General?"

Angriff turned around, saw who he was talking about, and smiled like a proud father. "Corporal Santos won the Silver Star for her actions at the Battle of the Highway last year. She stood right beside me and kept fighting even after she'd been hit in the throat. Docs only cleared her for active duty last week, but that's the kind of person I want in my headquarters. Believe it or not, she's my bodyguard."

"If I may ask, sir, why the change in route of march? The map shows I-40 being a much more direct route, through Flagstaff and then directly west to Hoover Dam. The way we're taking adds more than fifty miles."

Angriff shrugged. "We thought we could take I-40, but the civilian engineers found issues with some of the bridges out of the mountains, and rock slides blocked the road in multiple places. We couldn't wait for them to clear the road and shore up the bridges. That'll take weeks."

"It's time to form up," Major Iskold stage-whispered in his ear, loud enough that Young could hear.

"Let's get this show on the road," Angriff replied. "And Corporal? Don't take that comment about being my bodyguard literally. I had to promise Colonel Friedenthall you'd only be my driver."

Colonel Young watched him slide back in the Humvee, this time into the back seat. Now that he had a combat command, Young wanted to emulate the man that even Tom Steeple admitted had no equal in the modern army, down to the last detail. He even thought about smoking cigars, except he didn't know how to get any, and besides, he hated the damned things.

As the regimental commander, Colonel Young's M1130 command vehicle led the column. Based on the Stryker armored personnel carrier platform, the M1130 variant had all the necessary equipment to run a large unit in the field and would double as Angriff's headquarters while he was with the regiment. Directly behind Young's vehicle came an M113 fire support vehicle to direct any combat the regiment might become involved in, followed by a Bradley filled with a squad of guards for the fourth vehicle, the Humvee carrying Angriff.

The Humvee had been shot up during the Battle of the Highway the previous summer. While it was in for repair, the maintenance shop had fitted the interior with an armored cage, surrounding the occupants with an inch and a half of steel in the roof, doors, front, and rear, and three inches in the floor. This greatly increased fuel consumption, so they upgraded the capacity from 25 gallons to a 35-gallon self-sealing tank with half an inch of armor.

Angriff sat in the back seat with Major Iskold. Santos rode shotgun with an M-16 across her lap and skinny Corporal Donald H. Imboden drove. While Santos had stood beside him during the Battle of the Highway, Imboden had manned the GAU-19 50-caliber Gatling gun mounted in the cupola through the roof. The gun's mounting barbette interfered with Angriff's leg room, but in his mind firepower always trumped comfort.

For once he had nothing to do other than observe, which was at least part of his reason for coming along. If he was going to restore the United States, he needed to know what was left, and while he trusted his subordinates, there was no substitute for seeing things with your own eyes. Major Iskold sat beside him with microphone-equipped headphones slipped over her ears, papers scattered in her lap and on the seat beside her. She pressed down with her left thigh to keep the papers from spilling onto the floor.

Engineers had spent the winter building a true road out of the western gate. Although unpaved, the low points where water might stand were reinforced with rock and crushed gravel. Bridges over deep arroyos cut time to the main roads leading south, and existing bridges had been inspected and reinforced. Angriff had gotten reports on the work's progress, but that was no substitute for seeing it for yourself, and he was impressed.

A newly erected farmhouse near the road on his left caused him to sit up. Two people on a covered porch waved as they drove by, an old man with his arm around a woman of the same approximate age.

"I know those people!" he said. "That's Joshua!"

Major Iskold looked up and took a pencil out of her mouth. "I'm sorry, sir, what did you say?"

The farmhouse had slipped behind them, so Angriff pointed backwards with his thumb. "Those people back there, we rescued them last year. I remember Captain Sully's Marine company saved them from some of Patton's men."

"Oh, yes, General, that's correct," she said. "I thought you knew. We're settling refugees on the west side because it's a shorter distance for the irrigation pipes."

"I did, but it didn't sink in until right now. What are they growing?"

Iskold's eyes widened in fear. His voice had that commanding quality his usual staff knew better than to take seriously, but Iskold hadn't been around him all that much. "I don't know, General... Ummm, if that was put under Operations, I didn't know it."

Angriff realized what he'd done and patted the air. Norm Fleming wouldn't have been intimidated by his gruff manner, but his young deputy didn't know him that well yet. "My fault, Major. I'm sorry. You're right, it's not a job for the S-3; it's under civilian relations. Don't be afraid to tell me something I need to hear." He smiled what he thought was his most charming smile, the one that caused his daughters to roll their eyes.

Iskold stared at him for a moment, blinked, and then nodded. "Yes, sir. No fear."

"Anything I need to attend to right this minute?"

"You've got orders to approve for the construction crews working on those small refineries, but they aren't drawn up yet."

"Good. I'm gonna take a nap. Wake me in two hours."

#

CHAPTER 5

Let me remember the touch of my love as I remember the touch of the wind on my face.
Lepidus Manius Sulla

Overtime Prime
0825 hours, April 23

"You didn't want to see your dad off?" Joe Ootoi asked.

Nikki Bauer snuggled her head further onto his shoulder and pressed against his right thigh and hip. "He'll be back. Besides, how often will you be here with a day off to sleep late? I don't plan to let you out of this bed until you're due back on duty."

"That's two days from now."

"Yeah." She licked his cheek and kissed him. "I know."

"I don't know if I can keep up with you for two more days."

She propped up on one elbow and lifted a stray hair away from his forehead. "Well, if you die, just think of what a great way it will be to go."

"Can I at least get up to pee?"

She pretended to think about it. "I guess that's better than the alternative."

He nodded. "It is to me."

0827 hours

Bumps in the road woke Angriff before the two hours had elapsed. Blinking, he looked around, but it took a moment for him to recognize his surroundings. Corporal Santos turned in the front seat and handed him a half-full cup of coffee that nevertheless sloshed from the rough road. High overhead, caught in the light of the morning sun, a prairie falcon spiraled in search of prey.

"Where are we?" he said.

"Arizona Highway 89, sir," Iskold said. "Ten klicks north of the Prescott airport."

Despite the Humvee's upgraded suspension, they all bounced when it ran over a deep pothole. Coffee spilled straight up in the air, but without thinking Angriff caught most of it in the cup.

"Sorry!" Imboden called from the driver's seat. "This road's pretty rough."

"I thought—" *Crump!* They'd hit another hole. "I thought the engineers got this road fixed."

Distracted by trying to keep her paperwork from flying over the back seat, Iskold shook her head without looking at Angriff. "You prioritized the city's infrastructure first, General, then the airport. The runway's patched up and ready for aircraft, but Prescott's taking everything they've got right now. You ordered the engineers just to get this road passable. They'll get back to the road once they're done in Prescott... should I change that priority?"

"Negative," Angriff said. "It's just annoying. What about Colonel Young's engineer company?"

"It's my understanding they're ahead of us, checking on the structural integrity of any bridges we've got to cross."

"As they should be. All right. Imboden, do your best, son."

"Yes, sir, I always do."

The brief nap refreshed him, but the warm sunshine pouring through his open window made him drowse again. Angriff hated the feeling. Once upon a time, he'd been able to stay awake for three days straight, but lack of sleep in the preceding week had taken its toll, making him painfully aware that he was no longer a young man.

They passed the wreckage of the Chinese convoy, destroyed the previous summer. He'd seen it before, right after the Battle of Prescott, and was gratified to see that the smashed trucks and vehicles had been stripped of anything that could be reused — tires, doors, seats, batteries, wiring, and tools. The remaining shells reminded him of the empty cicada exoskeletons he'd seen every summer while growing up in Virginia.

The town of Chino Valley had been abandoned when last he saw it, but now people roamed the decrepit houses and stores and appeared to be clearing the streets. And if he didn't know better, he'd swear that a bar and grill had people inside cooking. At the next town, Paulden, both roads over the highway had collapsed, with the debris moved to either side to allow two lanes of traffic to pass. He saw no signs of humanity there. On the north edge of town, a large sign declared the local water company was right down a road off to the right.

"Alexis, make a note to see where they got their water," he said, pointing at the sign.

"The Big Chino aquifer, sir," she said without hesitation. When he lifted an eyebrow at her, Iskold said, "I anticipated your question and did some research, General."

"Good job. Make a note to see if we could get that machinery pumping again. If so, this could be just what the doctor ordered for resettlement of refugees."

Empty desert passed on both sides until they came to a causeway marked Hell's Canyon Tank on the digital map on Iskold's tablet. A dry river bed showed signs of having flooded the roadway in times past, cracking the pavement and leaving one slab of asphalt canted at a twenty-degree angle. The column slowed to avoid it until weakened asphalt showed spiderwebs at the sudden influx of weight. Iskold made a note for the engineers to repair it.

Thirty-five miles north of Chino Valley, the column stopped at a tiny place called Ash Fork, at the juncture of Highway 89 with Interstate 40. The four tanker trucks began topping off vehicles according to a detailed schedule, with one starting at the front, another at the back, and two in the middle, working their way toward each other.

Angriff got out and stretched his back, then followed a knot of other men behind a collapsed billboard, including Colonel Young. Once finished, they had a chance to inspect the ruins of the little community.

Angriff pointed to a building with a caved-in roof, where a sign on top was still partially visible and he could read the words *Best Barbeque.* "I could use a pulled pork sandwich right about now," he said.

Young smiled and nodded. "With slaw?"

"Hell, yes, and extra sauce."

#

CHAPTER 6

The truth always gets out, but sometimes it takes a few millennia.
Archaeologist Jacques L'jeune

Groom Lake Air Force Facility
0832 hours, April 23

Major Jonathan Cole used both middle fingers to rub his eyes, leading Joe Randall to wonder if there was something more subliminal at work than merely massaging fatigue. Randall had drained the one dented metal cup full of water Cole had given them and wanted more, but the major explained that would only come with more honest answers.

"I've told you everything there is to tell," Randall said.

"If there was anything else, I'd spill it just to get out of here," Bunny Carlos threw in.

As if expecting all of them to say something, Cole turned to Jingle Bob.

"I ain't got no idea," he said. "All I did was lead 'em to where all those people jumped outta that airplane. The rest of it I don't know."

Cole's sigh wasn't theatrical. Instead, it was that of a tired man who wanted only to go to sleep. "So let me see if I've got this straight. In the years before the Collapse, America's armed forces dug a huge base out of a mountain and filled it with surplus weapons and people it froze for later use. The commander of this force is none other than General

Nick the A Angriff, and you two," he pointed at Carlos and Randall, "fly helicopters—"

"Helicop*ter*," Randall said. "Singular. We fly one helicopter, an AH-72 Comanche gunship to be specific."

Cole turned his head and squinted in thought. "You said that before and I thought it sounded familiar, so I looked it up. The AH-72 was called the Golden Eagle, not the Comanche. That was a different program, the RAH-66 it was called, a stealth attack helicopter the Army spent seven billion dollars developing but subsequently cancelled. How do you explain that?"

"Technically, you're right. It's the Golden Eagle. But that name sucks and nobody who flew or maintained them ever called them anything except Comanches."

"Uh-huh..."

"Are you a professional asshole or something?" Carlos said. "One little cup of water and no food and you with this whole bad cop act..."

Instead of reacting with anger, Cole pursed his lips and waited. "Are you finished?"

Carlos nodded toward the two men holding rifles, who stood behind Cole's chair. "As long as Larry and Moe over there are pointing guns at me, I guess I am."

"That's music to my ears. Now, you," he pointed at Carlos, "flew the C-5 because you once had fifty hours training on it, even though it's an Air Force aircraft and you're an Army helicopter pilot."

"Like I said—" Carlos started.

Cole interrupted him. "Right, it was punishment by a base commander in Kuwait. I heard you the first time. So let's say I believe you on that. As part of a task force, you reached Creech to our south only to discover that another force you didn't know existed was under attack by the Chinese at the weapons depot northwest of Reno."

"Sierra Army Depot," Randall corrected.

"Of course. And the only way to help Sierra was to drop a battalion of paratroops, which is where the C-5 came in."

"That's it."

"Uh-huh, uh-huh... you *do* realize how ridiculous all of that sounds, right?"

"I can't help how it sounds. It's the truth."

"Sure, sure..." Cole turned to the third man seated on that side of the table, Jingle Bob. "You I've heard of." He pointed at the scraper. "What's your part in all of this?"

"I just met these boys, but the part about the army is real. I saw it with my own eyes."

"You saw this base... what was it you called it? Overtime? You saw that?"

"Well, no, but I was at Creech and I saw a lot of big machines in perfect condition and people in uniforms. I was only on that airplane as a guide, to show 'em where they could land up near Sierra."

"Did you see these alleged Chinese?"

Bob shrugged. "They looked like ants to me."

Without warning, Cole stood and turned for the door. "I'll let you know what I decide."

"Hey, what the hell?" Randall stood up and leaned over the table. The two guards aimed at his chest. Cole didn't stop.

Carlos shouted at his back. "At least answer one question!"

Cole stopped and turned around. "What?"

"Roswell, the UFO, that whole thing," Carlos said. "Was all that real?"

Cole's expression changed from that of a man in control to one of fear. "Don't ever bring that up again." His voice was half an octave higher than it had been. "Never. I command this facility, but there are places even I don't go. If you say that where they can hear, there's nothing I can do to protect you."

"*They*? Who is 'they'?"

Cole left without saying another word.

———

Overtime Prime
1408 hours, April 23

When the door to his cell rattled, Tom Steeple sat up on his bunk and said a silent prayer that it wouldn't be Nick Angriff. Then Norris McComb's voice alerted Steeple as to the identity of his visitor.

"Did you get it?" he asked when McComb was in the room.

"It wasn't easy, but yeah, I got it. Twisted my ankle a little."

"I'm sure you'll live," Steeple said, then shook his head. His escape stood on a knife's edge, McComb was the key, and here he was being arrogant to the man. "I'm sorry, McComb. Your first name is Norris, right? I'm sorry, Norris. Incarceration doesn't suit me."

"Don't worry about me, General. I've got a thick skin."

"Is Angriff gone?"

"Pulled out first thing this morning."

"Excellent. Did you get the phone?"

"I did." He patted the left breast of his jacket. "But you'll never get a signal this deep underground."

"No, I'm sure you're right." Steeple tapped his teeth while he paced. He was going to have to trust this McComb, but trusting anyone was something he tried never to do. By keeping all reins of power in his hands, he'd managed to build Overtime and Comeback, but now... was there another way? Not that he could see. "All right, Norris, I'm going to trust you with the future of Overtime. Do you understand? The future of everything, it's all on you now. Can I trust you?"

"I'm probably the only one in this entire mountain you *can* trust, General Steeple."

Steeple approached and laid hands on both of McComb's shoulders, looking him directly the eye. "Here's what I need you to do..."

#

CHAPTER 7

A man who surrenders makes a prisoner of himself.
Inscription in the ruins of the Palace of Knossos

Groom Lake Air Force Facility
1703 hours, April 23

"This blows," Bunny Carlos said, pacing the confines of the small room. It was cool because it was underground, and some sort of ventilation system pumped air currents through it, but the musty smell nauseated both men. "This really blows, Joe. Frame drops a baby bombshell right before I fly off into the sunset, and now these refugees from a B-movie tell me I can't leave because I'm a security threat. If I don't get out of here soon, somebody's gonna get hurt."

"Be careful it's not you," Joe Randall said.

"Maybe it will be me, but I'll guaran-fucking-tee you I'm not the only one going down. But what's up with you? How can you be so calm? Morgan must be out of her mind worried about you."

"I'm sure she is."

"So?"

"So what good does both of us ranting and raving do? You do it well enough for both of us anyway."

"I don't understand half o' what you guys are sayin'," Jingle Bob said. He stood with arms folded, leaning against a wall in the corner as far away from them as he could get. "All I know is, I've avoided this place all my life because people

48

who came here never came back. Now I know why, and I gotta tell you boys, I wish'd I didn't."

Carlos finally sat back down in the metal chair they'd provided, leaned forward, and stared at the wall. Randall had his own chair and put his head down on a steel table, careful to avoid a rusty patch. Despite the air flow, he felt sweat trickling down his sides.

Not long after that, they took Jingle Bob out of the room, leaving Carlos and Randall to sweat and grow hungrier and thirstier. Sometime later, it seemed like hours but was less than one, the door opened. Two men with rifles waved them outside. They were led down a long corridor, up two flights of stairs, and through a door into an area outside. Shadows stretched out from the building they'd exited, but the heat of the day still rose from the concrete, so Randall knew immediately it was late afternoon.

The short figure of Major Jonathan Cole stood waiting for them, surrounded by two more armed guards and a decidedly unhappy looking Jingle Bob. Cole stood with hands clasped behind his back, bouncing on his heels. Randall thought he looked like somebody off an old TV show, but he couldn't remember which one.

"You boys are lucky," Cole said. "I've had a chance to check your stories, your identities, and the rest of it. So far I believe you. Bob, too, although I already knew about him."

"Good for you. Bob, aren't you lucky?"

Not recognizing the sarcasm, Bob's left eye closed in a squint. "I ain't feelin' lucky."

"So can we go now?" Randall said.

The question startled Cole. "No! What are you talking about? You're lucky I didn't have you shot as spies, and I still might. Just because I have no cause yet to call you a liar doesn't mean I won't find one."

"You've got a funny definition for lucky," Randall said. He felt Carlos nudge him and heard a whisper.

"We gotta get out of here," Carlos said.

Randall didn't need prodding. Despite what he'd told Carlos, he felt the anger he'd bottled up welling inside him, burning his face and causing his hands to clench and unclench. Like a shaken soda, the rage all spewed out at once. "You stuck us in a room for the last day and only let us pee twice. You fed us some stale bread and now these octogenarian assholes are pointing guns at us. I've got a wife worried sick that I'm dead, Lieutenant Carlos has a pregnant wife waiting for him, and Bob didn't look too thrilled to be here, either. So forgive me if I'm not feelin' real lucky about now!"

Cole stepped back a pace, wide-eyed. It took a moment for his shock to wear off, and Randall realized the man wasn't used to being argued with. The folds of his face slowly changed from the ovals of surprise to the deep cuts of anger. "You flew the largest aircraft ever built into the most restricted airspace in the United States, and *you're* indignant for being challenged?"

Bob held up his right hand. "I didn't fly nothin'. I didn't really even wanna go." Nobody paid any attention to him.

"There *is* no United States!" Randall said, leaning forward a little.

"I thought you said that's who you fly for?"

"Well... it's complicated."

"So I gather. Go ahead and explain it... trust me, we have plenty of time."

"How 'bout you treat us like human beings and give us something to eat and drink? And maybe we get out of this oven while we're at it."

"This oven, as you call it, has been part of our daily lives for half a century. You should thank me for putting you underground. And while you seem to think we live in a world of plentiful food and comfort, none of us can remember such a world. Maybe *you* can, but we can't. To me, it feels like air-conditioning down there, or at least as much as I can remember how that felt."

"None of which is our fault."

Cole thought about it. "All right, let's talk over food. But you'd better find some manners."

"And then?"

"And then we'll see."

With guns pointed at their backs, the three captives were led back indoors, through a series of stairs, corridors and doorways, until they came out on a small patch of dirt. Across a driveway were a series of doors leading into what looked like a hangar.

"Inside, you first," Cole said.

"Where? The doors all say authorized personnel only."

"This place wasn't built for visitors. The one straight ahead."

Dinner wasn't what they'd expected. The two Comanche pilots wouldn't have cared if the food was dried lizard, they were so ravenous, but it turned out to be rabbit in a tangy tomato sauce over pasta, washed down with, of all things, wine. There was even enough for seconds. In addition to metal flatware they were given cloth napkins. Stains and ratty edges indicated long years of use, but Randall could tell they were clean.

The meal was eaten family-style in an empty hangar. A long conference table had been dragged in decades before and, from the chips and stains, this was obviously the main dining hall. They sat at one end on either side of Major Cole, with Jingle Bob on Carlos' right. Cole told the scraper he'd be put to work trying to repair some old hand-powered tools. Bob didn't look happy about it, but didn't say anything, either.

"What about us?" Carlos said.

"Let's see if food gives you some manners."

Randall counted seventeen more men at the table, all but four of them with gray hair, or no hair, and deep wrinkles like Cole's. The other four were much younger, and he guessed they flew the F-22s. Two men stood guard, obviously for their benefit, and halfway through dinner they switched places with two men at the table.

"Feel better now?" Cole said, wiping his mouth. "Ready to act like an officer?"

"I'd feel even better if people would quit pointing guns at me."

"The decision to let you eat with us wasn't unanimous. Only the decision to feed you was."

Randall nodded as if that made sense, but he thought, *Why does a commanding officer have to take a vote on decisions?* "You debated feeding us?"

"We don't take food for granted here. If we're going to feed a prisoner, there'd better be a damned good reason."

"I'm glad we passed the test."

"Just because we fed you once doesn't mean we'll keep doing it."

Carlos leaned into Cole's line of sight before Randall could say anything else. "Where did you get this wine?"

"It's made from plums. Do you like it?"

"I do, yeah. What about you, Joe?"

Randall didn't answer, he merely glared at Cole and chewed in silence.

For the first time, Cole said something in a non-accusatory tone. "Look, boys, I'm sorry how this has played out, but we can't take any chances."

Randall couldn't let that go. He swallowed and washed it down with a mouthful of the wine. It really was good. "Chances of what?"

The major frowned, missing the sarcasm. "You'd be surprised. Now, tell me your story again from the beginning. Don't leave anything out."

"Then we can leave?"

"Not telling me won't make that happen."

Randall glanced up at Carlos and their eyes met. He arched his eyebrows, which meant *should I humor this gasbag?* Carlos shrugged. Inhaling through flared nostrils, Randall scowled at his friend's non-help, which was another silent message meaning *thanks a lot.*

Randall told the table of listening officers all of it again, down to the tiniest detail. Recruitment to Overtime, details of the base itself, the battles with the Sevens and the Chinese, and finally the process of getting the largest aircraft ever built back in the air so it could violate the forbidden zone over Area 51.

"I told you once that we don't call it that," Cole said. The sudden tightening of his face made it clear he really didn't like that name. "We are Detachment Three, Air Force Flight Test Center. D-three for short. This whole area is Groom Lake Air Force Facility."

"Why don't you like the name Area 51?"

Cole ignored him. "You said you took off from Creech… Who's the commander there now?"

"Can you remember his name, Bunny? I can't, but he's a heavy-set black man of medium height, mostly bald with gray at the edges. Kando! That's his name, General-something Kando."

"All right, sounds like you've met him, at least. But while I tentatively believe your story now, Randall, you've got to admit it's a wild one." He turned to Carlos. "For example, supposedly you learned to fly a C-5 by accident, put in fifty hours left seat, and this was how long ago?"

"If you mean literally, I don't know... a long time," Carlos said, looking to Randall for help. Instead, he folded his arms and returned a smug look. "To me it seems like about thirteen or fourteen years."

"Right, right, the whole sleep thing... what did you call it?"

Randall answered. "Going cold. Once you're in it, it's called Long Sleep."

"Going cold, that's right. Did you hear that, Bondo?"

The man two seats down from Randall leaned forward so he could see the major. Randall recognized him as the sergeant who'd stuck a rifle in his gut when they'd first landed.

"Cold sounds good to me, Major. I could do with some of that cold about now."

"It's an expression," Randall said, annoyed. "Look, you asked, I told. Now it's your turn."

"My turn for what?"

"Sharing information."

Cole's demeanor changed. He laughed and pointed at Bondo, who shared the joke with the rest of the table. "When did I agree to do that? If you haven't noticed, those men with guns take orders from me, not you. Even though I think that I believe your story, I don't have to tell you anything."

"You don't have to be an asshole about it, either."

Carlos mouthed *shut up!* Then he stuffed in another mouthful of food. Cole turned his way to see if he agreed, but Carlos puffed out his cheeks and chewed, slowly. When it became apparent that Cole wouldn't fall for the ruse, Carlos swallowed and washed the food down with the last of his wine. "I've never seen this guy before," he said.

At that moment, Cole looked every bit the commanding officer of America's once most heavily secured military installations. Narrowing his brown eyes caused a spray of wrinkles around each one, but that only added gravitas to the look of an officer who was un-amused by a subordinate.

"This whole story about the C-5 sounds ridiculous on the face of it. And then you want me to believe that some helicopter techs put it back in flying condition in less than eight hours, after it had been laid up for fifty years, right? Then you come in here insulting me to my face. It wasn't me who landed on your runway, Randall. Now, you want to try that again?"

One of the guards took a step closer. Randall put down a forkload of rabbit, leaned forward, and crossed his arms on the table. It was obvious he was deciding how to answer. After a few seconds, he looked up, but before he could say anything Carlos spoke up.

"No," he said. "What I want to know is why, if you really believe that we're fellow American officers, why you're treating us this way?"

Randall expected Cole to explode, but after you'd been chewed out by Nick the A, some dumpy guy claiming to be an Air Force major from the old days wasn't overly worrisome.

Except Cole didn't explode. Instead, he leaned the chair backward and nodded. "So, feeding you two only makes you surly. I won't forget that."

"Just him," Carlos said. "When you feed me, I mellow out."

Cole went on. "I also won't forget rude conduct toward a superior officer, namely me."

Randall couldn't help himself. "You?"

"Of course, me. If you really are from the old United States Army, as you say, and which your uniforms and possessions seem to indicate, then would you have treated a major in the Air Force the way you've treated me? That's not a rhetorical question, by the way, because we both know if you had, you'd be in jail."

Randall's next remark died on open lips. Instead, he squinted in thought, and then arched an eyebrow at Carlos, who reached for thirds on the rabbit.

"No," Randall said.

"In those circumstances, would you have said *no*, or *no, sir*?"

"No, sir."

Now Cole let his anger show. Leaning forward, he pointed at Randall. "I haven't lived in this god-forsaken desert for fifty years by allowing disrespectful conduct from the people under my command, either military or civilian..."

Civilian? Randall thought, but didn't let the surprise show on his face. *Now we're getting somewhere.*

"You two say you're Army helicopter pilots, right? Well, I've met a lot of pilots in my life, and the only ones who are usually arrogant assholes are fighter pilots. Since the Army didn't have fighters and based on you two, I'm guessing gunship pilots are the Army equivalent of a fighter pilot. You think your shit doesn't stink, am I right?"

"His does," Carlos said. "I can testify to that."

Randall could think of no reason to lie. "We're hunters. It's kind of the job description."

"And you think that makes your dick bigger, but it doesn't. All it does—"

The *clang* of a metal door opening fast and hitting the hangar wall interrupted him. All heads at the table followed the progress of a man running toward them across the oil-stained concrete floor. His footsteps echoed in the metal framework high overhead. Randall noticed how much younger he was than anyone except the four men he assumed to be pilots. Panting, the newcomer leaned on his knees for a moment, cupped one hand around Cole's left ear, and whispered. Randall was close enough to hear some of it.

Riders... red scarves... too many...

When he'd heard enough, Cole nodded and stood. "Let's go, people, we've got a perimeter breach on the northeast. Zapboards and extra ammo. We move out in five!"

He turned to go, but Randall grabbed his arm. "Are these guys on horseback, red scarves around their necks?"

Cole stopped. "Friends of yours?"

"Not in this life. These are the Rednecks we told you about. At Creech, we shot 'em up pretty bad."

"With your helicopter."

"Her name is *Tank Girl*."

"Well, Captain Randall, I wish you had *Tank Girl* here now, but you don't." With that, he pulled his arm free and stalked away.

The two guards with guns pushed them toward the door they'd entered the hangar through, the door that led back to their room.

"Wait a minute, Major. If you need two extra bodies, we're pretty good shots."

Carlos tried to grab his arm and pull him back into his seat, but missed. Jingle Bob just shook his head.

Cole didn't bother to turn around, as if he'd been expecting that response. "Bring 'em!" he shouted to the guards.

"I'm a terrible shot," Carlos said, putting up his hands. "I'm good stayin' here."

"Bring him!"

Jingle Bob held back.

"Get going," one of the guards said.

"He didn't say anything about me."

"Bring him too!" Cole yelled over his shoulder.

#

Chapter 8

This is another fine mess you've gotten me into.
Oliver Hardy

Groom Lake Air Force Facility
1847 hours, April 23

Bondo ushered them out, M-16 leveled at their backs. "You two follow the rest of them," he said to Randall, Bob, and Carlos. Then he trotted to catch up to Cole, out of their hearing. "Major, a word, sir."

"What?"

"Is bringing them a good idea?"

"I don't trust those men as far as I can kick them. I think they might be in cahoots with these riders, but I won't know that until I can see how they react when they're face to face. And if they're not, you can learn a lot about a man when he's under fire."

"So you want me to keep a watch on 'em."

"Hell, yes! Watch everything they do. If they do *anything* to help the intruders, anything at all, don't hesitate to shoot first and explain later."

They didn't walk far in the twilight gloom. At a hangar two hundred yards from the first one, Randall saw the huge door slide open, and men dragged some flat-looking objects onto the tarmac. In addition to the dinner crew, minus the four young men Randall assumed to be pilots, another group joined to make a total of 26 people. Most wore one-piece Air Force blue coveralls.

Cole waved everyone into a circle. "We've got a perimeter breach in sector two. I don't know how big or how serious, but it looks like it's those riders with the red neckerchiefs again. I'd like to get some prisoners, but don't take any chances. Kill 'em if there's any doubt. Remember what happened to Rod. Let's move out. Bondo, find a place for our guests."

"I'm really okay stayin' here," Jingle Bob said.

Bondo jabbed with the gun. "Get on."

"Get on what?"

"The BatHoP."

"The what?"

Even in the dim light, Randall could see a bizarrely shaped machine lying on the ground ten feet away. "I think he means that," he said, pointing at what Bondo called a BatHoP.

Four metallic circles, each three feet in diameter, were arranged around a fifth larger central circle with a mounted platform. The smaller circles each had curved transparent walls around their outward-facing halves, with sturdy rods that looked like ski poles outside of those walls. Below the center lay a large round shaft extending about two feet downward. Eight struts mounted equidistant around the four exterior areas seemed like some sort of support system, with a center-mounted tire under each one.

Squinting, Randall realized what they were. "That's landing gear!" he said.

"Bright boy," Bondo said. They all heard his sarcastic tone.

Now it was Carlos' turn. "This thing flies?"

"Get on and you'll find out. There's a step by every station. Once we get going, hang on tight to the railing."

"What does BatHoP mean?"

"Get on now, or I swear I'll blow your head off!"

"Come on, man, just tell him," Carlos said. "It can't be some big secret."

Bondo curled his lip like Carlos had been sprayed by a skunk. "Battle Hover-Platform. Are you happy now?"

Four smaller machines were brought out last, each with a single rectangular platform, a curved handrail on two sides, and a small square housing on the underside, all held up by the same thin-strutted landing gear. The nearest was laid in the dirt four feet from where Randall stood, and despite the poor lighting he paid close attention to everything the pilot who stepped up to the hovercraft did.

Each standing space on the BatHoP had a bracket to hold a rifle, and the Air Force men also each carried a sidearm. As Randall squinted to make out what he was doing, the man beside him switched several levers and boosted what could only have been a throttle. The engine started with a loud whirring sound and kicked up a dust cloud, but the sound soon changed to what sounded like air hissing out of a giant balloon. Seconds later the five-man BatHoP vibrated as their pilot started its engine.

When it elevated straight up to an altitude of about twenty feet, Randall was surprised at how stable it felt underfoot. He'd expected wobble, at least a little, but instead it felt like he stood on solid ground. It was also faster then he'd thought it would be; he judged their speed at thirty knots or more.

What he needed most was goggles. Flying insects smacked his face, and then his arms when he tried to shield his eyes. Skimming so low over the desert wasn't a new sensation, he was a helicopter pilot, after all, but doing it without the metal skin of a cockpit was. He also hated flying without any controls. During the Battle of Prescott the year before, with Chinese and Sevens firing at him throughout the day, he'd never once felt nervous. Now he shook like a child terrified of the dark.

After flying for what seemed like an hour but was actually only fifteen minutes, he saw flashes ahead and realized they were muzzle flashes. As the BatHoP raced closer to what was obviously a firefight, he saw some flashes coming from atop a small hill, and a lot more from the surrounding desert. As they raced closer and closer to the circle of what he assumed were Rednecks, Randall began to wonder if they were going to slow down before engaging the enemy. If so he, Carlos, and Bob were sitting ducks without weapons.

All of the hovercraft and BatHoPs peeled off left and right, except theirs and the two single-person craft directly ahead of them. Instead they passed right over the heads of the Rednecks, aimed directly for the top of the little hill. Instead of taking evasive action, the pilot counted on darkness and speed to keep them safe. Randall heard the hiss of a bullet zip past his head and the metallic *kunk* of another one hitting the BatHoP, but then they were over the hilltop. There was a moment's panic as the leading gear deployed and the craft settled, then they all jumped off and ate dirt. The men on the two smaller hovercraft, known as *flitters*, had already landed and rolled to safety.

"Bunny, you good?" he yelled over the gunfire.

"I'm in one piece, if that's what you mean."

"Me, too," Bob said, even though Randall had forgotten about him.

The hilltop was concave, with a shallow bowl at the crest. Two men lay on the sides firing into the darkness, while two men lay still at the bottom. Despite being a cloudless night, the starlight and quarter moon weren't enough illumination to pick details out of the desert. Incoming rounds kicked up dirt on the rim of the depression, but the three new riflemen fell on their stomachs and returned fire.

It only took Randall and Carlos a few seconds to acclimate to being at the center of the battle. Carlos grabbed a rifle from one of the fallen and scrambled up the depression's side. Below the rim of the bowl, Randall was not under direct fire and had time to inspect the two wounded men. One lay still, but the other rolled back and forth, moaning in pain. Randall knelt beside him and felt hot wetness soaking the left shoulder of his uniform. The darkness was nearly absolute but he didn't need light to recognize the smell and feel of blood.

Leaning forward, Randall found the bullet hole and put both hands over it, pushing down hard. "I need something to use for a bandage," he called out.

"Leave him alone!" Randall recognized the voice as Bondo's.

"He's gonna bleed out. I need something to use as a bandage!"

No answer came right away.

"If he dies, it's on you!" Randall yelled, holding his fingers together as tightly as he could.

"Look on my flitter!" Bondo shouted down. "There's a bag with some rags in it hanging on the rail. Use those."

"Bob!" Randall said.

"I'm on it."

Randall kept glancing up to see if Carlos was all right, and then back down at his hands. Between them, Randall and Jingle Bob managed to shove the oily cloths under the injured man's shirt. Randall felt his arms cramping and showed Jingle Bob how to press down, hard but not too hard. Leaving Bob there to apply pressure, Randall wiped hands on his pants, felt around until he found the stock of an M-16, and climbed up next to Carlos. A bullet struck close to his left cheek and kicked dust into his eyes.

"Damn!" he said, rubbing his eyes. Even though Carlos lay right beside him, Randall had to shout to be heard over the gunfire. "I learned to fly so I didn't have to do this."

Carlos wasn't sympathetic. "It's your fault I'm here in the first place."

"Since when?"

"Since that night in Tel Aviv where you got me drunk and talked me into this."

Randall searched for targets, but the lightning-like flash of guns only served to destroy his night vision; it didn't illuminate anything. "How can I tell who to shoot at?"

"Hell if I know!" Carlos said, squeezing off a shot.

"What if you hit the wrong guys?"

Carlos cut him a sideways look that he couldn't make out in the dark. Leaning over, he spoke in a lower voice that Randall could barely hear. "I'm aiming over their heads, just making it look good."

Over the tumult of battle, they both heard Bondo screaming at them. "Hey, you two, put those guns down!"

"I'm not gonna sit here and get killed!" Randall yelled back. All he could see was a large shadow, with the strobe-like flashes letting him pick out details of Bondo's face twisted in anger. The bigger man stood, a dark shadow against the darker night, and then he vanished. It took Randall's brain less than a second to process what had happened; he'd been hit and toppled backward onto the hillside.

"Shit!"

Without thinking, he ran down into the bowl and up the other side, to where Bondo had been. Once there, he kept going. He dove head-first over the top and rolled down the bank to where Bondo lay on his back, stamping his foot in pain. Out in the open like that, Randall discovered the moon and starlight seemed much brighter than before. Bullets ripped into the dirt around them, but overhead he heard another rifle join in suppressing fire, and then heard Carlos' voice.

"Get up here, you idiot, before you get yourself killed."

"Can you walk?" Randall said to Bondo.

The words came out more as a groan than spoken language. "Hit in the left leg."

Randall tried to help Bondo to his feet but he was too heavy. As they wrestled around in the attempt to stand, Randall felt a tug at his left collar. Touching it, the fabric was hot; a very near miss. "Fuck me... Bunny, get down here and help me!"

Seconds later, Carlos rolled beside him and started trying to lift Bondo. Both remaining riflemen had moved to their side of the hill and shot at every flash they saw. It wasn't easy, but between the two pilots they managed to push, pull, and lift Bondo over the lip of the hill and down into the bowl, after which they followed him without either one being hit.

\#

CHAPTER 9

Never give counsel to your fears.
Lt. Gen. Thomas J. "Stonewall" Jackson

Great Basin Desert, northwest of Groom Lake Air Force Facility
2130 hours, April 23

There was no time to catch their breath. One of the two unhurt riflemen slid down to help Bondo, so Randall and Carlos had to take over shooting. Randall had just moved to the opposite side when he saw a man running up the hillside toward them. He fired instinctively into the man's chest, but then panicked at the idea it could have been one of Major Cole's men. The round struck somewhere near the sternum and knocked the man off his feet. He rolled to the base of the hill and lay still.

Before Randall could search for another target, an intense firefight broke out in the desert, interspersed with yelling and half-seen movement. Horses whinnied and at least one screamed in pain. Major Cole's group had obviously launched an attack, but it was ten minutes before Randall knew who won.

"Hey, it's Cole, don't shoot!"

Cole led four other men up the hill by the simple expedient of each man holding the back of the shirt of the man in front of him. Only when they disappeared under the rim of the bowl at the hilltop did he break out a glowstick. Seeing three of his men wounded, he knelt beside Jingle Bob. "How bad is he?"

"I ain't no doctor, but he needs one bad. Can one of your men take over, Major? My arms are crampin' up."

Cole directed a man to relieve Jingle Bob, and then saw Randall and Carlos holding rifles. He trained his own pistol on them. "Drop 'em, boys."

"No good deed goes unpunished," Randall said, and let his M-16 topple into the dust. Carlos did likewise.

But before Cole could do anything else, Bondo called to him. "Hey, Major, can I talk at you?"

They whispered for a minute and then Cole walked back to Randall and Carlos, picked up their rifles, and handed them back. "Thanks, boys. Bondo told me what you did here, so I guess I believe your story now."

"Thank God," Randall said. "*Now* can we leave?"

"We'll talk back at D-3 in the morning."

<hr />

North Dakota
0415 hours, April 24

Despite her heavy coat, with few aboveground structures to block the wind, its full force chilled Amunet Mwangi to her core. Later in the day it would warm to something approaching bearable, but with dawn nothing more than a hint on the eastern horizon, the temperature still hovered in the lower twenties. After a winter of unending arctic conditions, she couldn't wait for spring. Or, rather, spring that felt like spring.

She hated North Dakota.

But never before had she gotten a voicemail on the sat. phone, so like it or not, she'd rolled out of bed and hurried topside to get a signal so she could hear it. Only one man knew the number. She'd expected to hear from him long before this and was eager to find out the situation, because she'd trade the bitter cold of North Dakota for the blazing heat of Arizona in a heartbeat. Now, with her head tucked against her chest like a turtle, she turned the volume all the way up and shivered.

"This message is for Colonel Amunet Mwangi," it started. She paused it and started over. It wasn't Tom Steeple's voice, a voice she knew as well as she knew her own. "This message is for Colonel Amunet Mwangi. My name is Norris McComb. I'm a friend of General Steeple, who asked me to make this call. The general told me to tell you that he's imprisoned in the unfinished section of the base and there is only one chance for him to escape and take command of Overtime. General Angriff is away from the base right now, as is General Fleming. Getting him out of his cell is only the first problem.

"He needs a personal security team that can occupy key areas of the base, and he needs them fast. We anticipate General Angriff will be gone less than a week, so time is of the essence. I will call you again at the same time tomorrow. Please be expecting my call, and please have positive news. We're all counting on you."

And that was it.

Fuck!

Was this for real? And even if it was, what could she do in 24 hours? Overtime Prime was 1,500 miles from North Dakota and besides, she commanded no troops, no forces. She was a guest of the Rosos family and lately hadn't been getting the friendliest feelings from them. What did Tom Steeple think she could do?

But one flaw that Amunet Mwangi did not possess was self-pity. Her refusal to take no for an answer had pushed her up the ranks far beyond what her education should have allowed, and cursing herself for wasting precious time wasn't going to stop her now, either. Károly Rosos had flown to California with Adder and the old man hadn't been seen in months, but Györgi Junior was there. Mwangi got along better with Junior than with his younger brother anyway, and headed for the doorway leading back underground. Anything to get warm.

Great Basin Desert, northwest of Groom Lake Air Force Facility
0657 hours, April 24

One BatHoP returned immediately with the wounded, but the rest of them stayed until dawn. Three Rednecks lay dead in the desert, including the one Randall had shot as he charged their position, and blood evidence indicated they'd hit at least three more. One horse died and a second had to be put out of its misery. They recovered five Czechoslovakian-made AK-47s, nine empty magazines, and four full ones.

The men who'd been ambushed all rode horses, but since neither Randall nor Carlos knew how to ride one, they were given a crash course in handling a flitter so the flitter pilots could ride the horses. Although the propulsion system and controls were vastly different from those of a helicopter, they found that their pilot experience flattened out the learning curve. It took a mile or two of slow going for them to figure out how to handle the lightweight, ultra-responsive hovercraft, but after they did it was a fast return trip.

Once on the ground again, Randall slung his arm around Carlos' shoulders like it was a common gesture between them, although the lieutenant's horror-filled expression made clear that it wasn't.

"What the fuck?"

"Ssshhh... keep your voice down. Don't forget any of what we just did," Randall whispered when nobody was close. "Go over it in your mind, again and again. Those things might be our ticket out of here."

#

Chapter 10

The world is a dangerous place to live; not because of the people who are evil but because of the people who won't do anything about it.
Albert Einstein

0922 hours, April 24
Near Willow Beach, Arizona

Shadows stretched westward as the morning sun rose behind the column of riders. Major Edward Wincommer felt grateful that General Angriff had okayed his suggestion that his regiment ride on the column's northern flank to prevent potential ambushes. He loved being in the saddle and it didn't cost much in the way of supplies. Horses didn't drink gasoline like armored vehicles did.

At that moment, Wincommer had the strange feeling he was living someone else's life. He rode at the head of three troops from the Seventh Cavalry Regiment through desolate country that George Custer himself would have found familiar. The morning sun warmed his back as they traversed a valley between two rocky ridges leading to the northwest, but the day's heat hadn't yet burned away the coolness of night, making for a pleasant ride. The screech of a circling prairie falcon caught his attention and he smiled without realizing it; unlike most people, Wincommer loved predatory animals that benefitted man, like snakes and raptors.

Good hunting, he thought.

His executive officer, Captain Ron Lozano, interrupted his reverie. "Corporal Coco coming in, sir," the captain said with binoculars up to his eyes.

Wincommer followed his gaze and saw a dust cloud boiling in the wake of someone riding hard for their position. Then he turned in his saddle. The man directly behind Lozano wore the tactical radio backpack known as the Land Mobile Radio System. "Anything?" he said.

"Negative, sir."

He turned back to Lozano. "Thoughts?"

"They've either had radio failure or they're in close proximity to an enemy force."

Corporal Coconino reined in his horse on Wincommer's left, saluting with his right hand and holding the reins tight with his left. The animal's nostrils flared and its coat glistened with sweat. "Lieutenant Tribaldos sent me, sir. We have eyes on a party of Rednecks, two dozen or so, two miles ahead in a valley."

"What are they doing?"

"There's some sort of complex and it looks like they've been camping there."

"What kind of complex?" Lozano said.

"Hard to say, Captain. It's big, but made out of corrugated metal, old signs, cinder blocks... looks like somebody built it out of whatever they could scavenge. There's heaps of stuff everywhere, too, and pens for cattle, sheep, horses, goats... even a chicken coop. I think it's some kind of trading post, sir. And there's a big sign painted over the door, *Ma Kelly's*."

"Ma Kelly's?" Wincommer said. "I don't know why but that sounds familiar. Any sign of sentries or outriders?"

"None, sir. They look pretty relaxed."

Wincommer held up his hand for the column to halt and turned back to the radioman. "Get me Cherry."

0935 hours
ten kilometers southwest of the advance cavalry

Angriff stared out the Humvee's passenger side window in that hypnotized state halfway between being fully awake

and fully asleep. Arizona State Highway 93 had proved to be in reasonably good condition, just as Norm Fleming had reported the week before, and the drone of the engine left him fighting against sleep. Several times he caught himself when his head nodded toward his chest.

They'd reached the part where ridges adjoining the roadside rose sheer, like the interior of a cake after serving several slices. Some rockslides blocked part of the highway, but veering around them wasn't hard. The schedule called for a stop before they crossed the Valley of the Colorado River below Hoover Dam, and he knew they were getting close, so when the orange light on the M1130 command vehicle in front of his Humvee began to flash, it snapped him awake but didn't surprise him.

Once they'd pulled over, he got out and stretched his lower back muscles. He'd never let on how much they hurt.

The M1130 was built on the chassis of the eight-wheeled Stryker armored personnel carrier, but configured as a mobile command vehicle. The rear hatch folded down to act as a ramp into the interior, and it had no sooner hit the ground than Colonel Young stepped out and came over to Angriff.

"Major Wincommer's cavalry is in contact with two dozen Rednecks about ten klicks northeast of our current position. He's ordered his men to encircle them without engaging or making their presence known, awaiting further orders. Apparently there's also some kind of structure, a trading post maybe."

"I see. What are you going to do?"

"The cavalry's not under my command, sir."

"You're the tactical officer in charge, Bob. You make the call."

"Based on our previous encounters, I don't anticipate they'll surrender."

"Me, either."

"I'm going to send them a mortar squad and order they hold in place until the mortars get there. If they are forced to attack in the meantime, to do so at minimum risk with prisoners a low priority."

"I'm going with the mortars."

The colonel's face changed to an expressionless mask that virtually screamed *you must be kidding!* But he was far too savvy to say it. "As you wish, General."

Angriff laughed once and clapped Colonel Young on the shoulder. "I've seen that look before, Bob, but don't worry, I'm not gonna get myself killed. I want to see this trading post for myself."

"I'd be remiss if I didn't remind you about the schedule."

"No reason to change it. Go ahead and send recon to Las Vegas and get the engineers to work inspecting the bridge. I'll meet you before the main body gets to Hoover Dam."

"Should we wait before crossing?"

"Let the tactical situation dictate that."

———

1024 hours

Angriff's Humvee followed three M1129 mortar carriers armed with 120mm mortars, and two Stryker Dragoons armed with 30mm Bushmaster guns and carrying six infantrymen each. Despite the rough up-and-down nature of the desert, it only took about twenty minutes to cover the six miles until they found Major Wincommer.

He filled Angriff in on his dispositions while the mortar crews' forward observers climbed to the top of a hundred-foot-high ridge overlooking the bowl where the Rednecks camped. Twin doors in the vehicles' top folded back to allow the mortar tube to be raised and aimed. Other members of the crew stacked round green cylinders containing the actual shells forward of the tube and within easy reach.

Even as Wincommer spoke, Angriff's eyes cut to watch the performance, and he couldn't help comparing them to a NASCAR pit crew. "Sounds like you're ready, Major."

"We are, General. All we need now—"

"Major!" A stocky corporal half ran, half slid down the ridge. Covered in dust, he saluted and coughed.

"What is it, Coco?"

"I'm sorry to interrupt, but you need to see this sir."

"See what?"

"They're torturing some dogs."

Without another word, both Wincommer and Angriff went scrambling up the rocky slope. Once there, they lay down and looked over the crest into an oblong space surrounded on three sides by rock walls. Only on the north was it open. It measured about three hundred yards wide and five hundred long. Penned animals took up most of the western side, to their left. A sprawling one-story building abutted the stockyard, with heaps of materials scattered nearby, everything from copper pipes to bricks.

The Rednecks were mostly gathered around a large bonfire about one hundred yards distant from where Angriff lay. Several charred bodies lay nearby, still smoking, and he realized they had been dogs. Four people without red scarves stood guarded by three Rednecks and even at that distance he could see the rage on their faces as one Redneck laughed and held something over his head. At first Angriff couldn't tell what it was, only that it was black, gray, and tan, but then it squirmed and he knew it was a puppy. The Redneck had it by the scruff of its neck and swung it around before walking slowly toward the fire.

"That bastard's going to throw it in!" Wincommer said.

Angriff looked past the major to a captain he hadn't met yet, who held an M-4. He panted and blinked away tears, forgetting everything as rage took him. "Gimme that rifle,

Captain," he said, holding out his hand. The man didn't hesitate and neither did Angriff. "As soon as I shoot, Major, open fire."

He heard Wincommer's frantic radio calls to alert his command, but ignored them and drew aim on the man one hundred and twelve yards to his front. The man's right side faced him but he didn't want to risk hitting the dog, so he aimed below the armpit. Angriff had always known that if he was put on Earth for only one reason, it was to shoot a gun, any gun. His hand-eye coordination had always amazed those who saw him shoot, but it was more than that. Lying there, his breathing slowed without him thinking about it. The gunsights lined up as if they had a will of their own, and he knew precisely how long he could wait until the man got too close to the fire for him to risk it, and in that millisecond he squeezed the trigger.

The recoil wasn't like his beloved M-1 Garand, but the bullet flew just as true. It struck the man holding the puppy exactly where Angriff had aimed, shattered a rib and sent fragments into the left lung while maintaining enough velocity to strike his spinal cord and lodge there. With a gasp, the man took one more step, fell to his knees, and then pitched forward on his face. Nerveless fingers released the puppy, which scurried into Ma Kelly's.

A split second after he fired came the shotgun-like cough of the mortars, followed within two seconds by three explosions amid the knot of Rednecks gathered near the bonfire. Simultaneously the troop of cavalry opened up with small arms and cut down the enemy. Two men made it to the horses and tried to ride out the northern opening, but the Americans blocked the exit by stepping out into the opening. One man tried to ride through and slumped off his saddle, riddled with bullets. The other pulled his horse into a halt and threw up his hands. Neither of their mounts was hit.

The fight was over in less than a minute. The Rednecks managed to get a few shots off but didn't hit anybody. None of them were left standing, although one man dragged himself toward the horses as blood poured from the stump of his right leg. Angriff rose even before the last shots rang out, rifle at the ready and searching for a new target. Once it was over, he handed the rifle back to the captain, whose name he read from the man's uniform. "Thanks for the loan of the rifle, Captain Lozano."

"You're welcome, General. That was... uh, a fine shot."

"Yeah." His gaze drifted in the direction of the scorched dogs and a change came over his face, a tenseness of the jaw muscles, betraying the anger that earlier in life would have consumed him. He'd toned it down in recent years, but earlier in his career it had inspired the sobriquet of Nick the A. "I wish I'd gotten here sooner."

#

CHAPTER 11

The best thing about food is that it's food.
Bunny Carlos

Groom Lake Air Force Facility
1102 hours, April 24

The returnees ate lunch at the same table they'd eaten at the night before, only this time nobody stood behind Randall and Carlos with a gun. Major Cole was likewise different, treating them with gratitude, if not respect.

"Why'd you boys do it?" he asked after washing down a mouthful of cornbread with tepid water. Where the base got corn flour, he didn't say.

Randall chewed a lean cut of meat that tasted like deer, but he'd been told was antelope. "I can't speak for Lieutenant Carlos," Randall said, which prompted Carlos to give him a look that meant *since when?* "But I doubted I could explain the difference between us and you, it being pitch dark and all. I figured the Rednecks would shoot us out of hand."

"So we were the lesser of two evils."

"Something like that."

"I'm flattered."

"I'm not sure what else you expect, Major. Look at it from our standpoint. We thought we were dead. We're up there flying an unfamiliar aircraft through a combat zone, the largest aircraft ever built, for good measure. We've got thunderheads topping fifty thousand feet piling up between us and our landing field, and then suddenly, like magic, a long, beautiful runway presents itself for us to land on. Then a couple of F-22s with USAF markings show up as a fighter escort to sweeten the deal. Against all odds, we touch down safely and see genuine American military people waiting for us, only to have guns stuck in our faces and to be treated as enemies."

"If you're expecting an apology, you're going to have a long wait."

"Right now I'd settle for an explanation."

"All right... you've obviously heard of this place before..."

"Not under the name you called it."

"But you've heard of it."

"In the pre-Collapse world, everybody'd heard the name you don't want me to use for some weird reason. There were books, movies, TV shows, you name it, all about what was going on out here."

"UFO people."

"Not just them. When something's as mysterious as this place, people are gonna wonder about it. But yeah, for the UFO believers this was ground zero."

"And if an unauthorized C-5 Galaxy had violated the restricted airspace over that place, what would have happened?"

"I don't know, but I'm guessing they'd have been blown out of the sky."

Cole nodded. "That's right, and yet you weren't. At my command you could have been, those F-22s carried operational air-to-air ordnance, but you weren't. I allowed you to land safely, which wasn't a universally approved decision, I can tell you. Many people saw no reason to take a chance on you."

"So why did you?"

"The plane. That aircraft is now worth more than anything in the world, at least to me. But first things first. I'm in command of this whole base now. If this was the old world, I'd have to be at least a three-star general to hold this command, but those days are long gone. Or I thought they were, anyway. At its height, tens of thousands of people worked here, but now there's less than three hundred of us and most of us came here after the Collapse."

"You, too?"

"Yes and no. My father was stationed here when the earthquakes hit and we joined him some time after that, my mom, brother, sister, and me. I was three. Dad was ordered to stay here and safeguard the research projects, to keep them away from the enemy. As part of the deal, those who stuck around got their families flown in to join them. As the country deteriorated, most of the people left, a few like us came, but after a while flights and incoming traffic died away. At the end, only wagons and lone stragglers came here. One day they quit coming, too."

"So you grew up here."

"My brother and I both did. My sister died when I was still a little boy, stung by a bark scorpion, but Mom and Dad lived until about ten years ago. They died within a week of each other. It was my father who taught me about the base and groomed me to take over his duties."

"What happened to your brother?"

"You saved his life last night."

"You mean what's his name... Bondo?"

"That's him."

"Why is your brother named after a car body filler?"

Cole chuckled at that. "He's not. His real name is Winfrey Butler Cole. When he was a kid, he got teased about his name, so he told everybody to call him a name after the toughest man he could think of... James Bond. Except he thought it was Bond-oh. So that's the name that stuck. It's just a coincidence that he's a genius around engines."

With Major Cole more relaxed, Randall asked the one question he couldn't imagine an answer for. "America's been gone for more than forty years, so why are you still guarding this place?"

"That's easier to show than tell. How would you boys like a tour?"

"Hell yes!" Carlos said before Randall could answer.

"Remember you said that," Cole said.

#

Chapter 12

Truly the universe is full of ghosts, not sheeted churchyard
spectres, but the inextinguishable elements of individual life,
which having once been, can never die, though they blend and
change, and change again for ever.
H. Rider Haggard, King Solomon's Mines

Groom Lake Air Force Facility
1141 hours, April 24

The base was enormous, even when compared to Over-time Prime. Despite acres of solar panels and wind turbines, energy was precious, so foot power was the only mode of transportation. Cole explained that both the solar and wind generators had lost efficiency over the years and the base still required a lot of power for the functioning lights, refrigerators, and the like. In the baking heat, it didn't take long for Carlos to regret his earlier enthusiasm. As for Randall, as much as he itched to get back to Creech, like so much of the world he'd spent his whole life wondering what the elaborate security measures at Area 51 really concealed. Curiosity drove him to drink in every detail of what Cole showed them, although he told himself it was research for his father-in-law.

Cole started by showing them two cavernous hangars filled with non-serviceable aircraft of every make, type, and size. The only lighting came from huge skylights in the walls and roof, with slatted blast doors for protection that could be opened or closed at need. Opened now, Randall doubted they had been closed for decades.

Randall didn't know Air Force aircraft types all that well, but the plethora of F-22s was hard to miss and he mentioned it.

"They were collected here when the F-35 went into service. Apparently a lot of the Air Force commanders didn't like the F-35 and wanted, as my father used to say, 'to have a real fighter if the shit hit the fan.'"

"I thought the shit *did* hit the fan?"

Cole shrugged. "I was a little kid. All Dad ever said about it was that everything happened fast."

Cole let them stroll among the planes and waited by the door they'd entered through. Although outside it neared midday, even with all of the windows the lighting wasn't good. Wandering among the parked aircraft, Randall and Carlos could only shake their heads at the potential of the collected warplanes.

He had just rounded the nosewheel of yet another F-22 when Randall pulled up short and waved for Carlos to join him. "What the hell is that?" he said, pointing at an aircraft parked in a corner.

"Beats the hell out of me, but I'm in love."

It was shaped something like a cross between the F-16 and the F-22, but was much longer than either of those planes. Mounted on either sides of the sleek fuselage were swept wings, and instead of two twin engines mounted side by side, it had four, laid out in a square around a boom tail. The all-black aircraft's only markings were small white stars near four covered slots in the nose.

"Hey, Major! What's this thing?"

"Eh?" It took Cole nearly a minute to find them. "Oh, there you are. I see you found our *Rogue*. The Boeing XF-77, gentlemen. That's the prototype of the first orbital fighter jet."

Randall stood beside the nosewheel and pointed upward at the four grooves in the metal over his head. "Are those cannon?"

Cole nodded. "Yeah. Dad said the idea was that battle damage at the edge of space would be instantly fatal."

"Did he say why? I mean... cannon? Fighters haven't had onboard cannon for decades."

"He never explained about the damage, no, but those cannon were supposed to fire homing rounds. There's even a store of them here they used for testing. The shields over the tubes retract when they're not being used."

"I wonder if this thing ever flew..." Randall mused.

"Oh, yeah, I saw it fly half a dozen times when I was a kid. A lot of the design engineers didn't have anywhere else to go, so they stayed here and kept working on it up until about twenty years ago. This is actually the third prototype; the other two are underground."

"I wonder if it could still be put into service..."

"If so, nobody here knows how to do it."

They next headed for the parts and tools area, the machine shop, paint shop, power-generator plant, solar power collectors, and the water well and purification system. Power still flowed to the latter system.

As they walked through the quiet buildings, illuminated only by morning sunlight that seeped through holes in the hangar walls, both Randall and Carlos gaped at the dark skeletons of once state-of-the-art machines that had been crammed into every available space. Not just aircraft but forklifts, bulldozers, excavators, cars, trucks, gantries, cranes, and even an ice cream machine. None of the hardware remained operational.

Cole explained how the old-timers had passed on their skills to the younger people, but without the intense practice mechanics and technicians had in the pre-Collapse Air Force, their abilities had atrophied. Nevertheless, the Groom Lake Air Force Facility, the part of the Nevada Test and Training Range that he commanded, had been outfitted to survive almost anything.

After spending an hour aboveground, Cole led them to double doors marked *Approved Personnel Only* in faded red letters. Heavy double steel doors led to a stairwell, which Cole pointed to but didn't lead them down. He explained that while most of the base was underground, including vast hydroponics farms, research and medical facilities, barracks, laboratories, bowling alleys, nuclear bunkers, and a water processing plant connected to deep wells, the only way down was twenty stories of steps, or about 300 in all.

"I remember," Randall said.

Cole thought for a second. "Oh, that's right, you were down there."

"There's no elevators?" Carlos said.

"Yeah, of course. Lots. But only three that work, and those are reserved for emergencies. Take no offense, boys, but showing you around doesn't qualify as an emergency."

"What about the rest of it?"

Cole's convivial smile faded. "I honestly don't know."

"How can you not know?"

"Drop it, Randall. Just drop it." Cole's tone left no room for discussion.

So Randall changed the subject. "Why are you doing this? What's this place to you?"

Cole appeared genuinely surprised by the question. "It's home."

"Yeah, okay, I get that, but..."

"But?"

"But all this military formality, all of this loyalty to a country that no longer exists... I don't get it. I've seen it before, it's like this down at Creech, but I don't understand it."

Cole paused in front of double doors labeled *Bio-Hazard Area*. His middle fingers met at the point of his hairline and he ran them down each temple, pausing to massage the skin near the outside edge of his eyebrows. The two pilots' eyes met and Carlos mouthed *headache?*

"I don't *know* anything else, Randall. I've never lived anywhere else and this is how I was taught. D-3 has everything we need to survive, and from what I'm told, places outside of here don't, so why would I ever leave? As to protecting it for a country that doesn't exist... if what you've told me is true, then you grew up in that world, right?"

"Yeah."

"So you knew what you signed up for. I never knew that world. My dad said there used to be places called grocery stores, where you could get any food you wanted... that's true?"

"A little simplified, but yeah, it was like that."

"So you knew what you were protecting when you joined the army. I didn't have that, but a man's still gotta have a purpose to his life; otherwise he's not living, he's existing. At least that's what my father always drilled into our skulls. I know the country slid pretty far down before it collapsed, that's what all the adults told us kids, but from everything I've known in my life, it sounded like a helluva nice world to live in. From everything I know, there's some potentially powerful weapons on this base, so keeping them out of other people's hands, people who might use them to make this world even worse than it is, well, that just seems like a worthy goal, you know?"

"I do," Carlos answered, surprising them all. "Like me, I've more reason to live now than ever before. I'm gonna be a father."

"That's a good thing, Lieutenant."

"Not when I'm stuck here."

Cole looked over his shoulder at Carlos, but kept walking and didn't reply.

"One more thing. When we landed, you said you'd just gotten new orders from someplace in the east. Who was it?"

They pushed through a bulkhead door constructed very much as might be seen on a warship. Cole reached over and flipped a light switch and something happened that neither Randall nor Carlos expected; light flooded the vast room.

"This is the materials laboratory," Cole said, ignoring the question.

"More electricity," Carlos finally said. "I thought you didn't have much."

"I told you the base never lost it. The redundancy is amazing. These days it's mostly solar, since our power needs are so small, but the fossil fuel and nuclear generators still work. There's even a last-ditch steam plant if all else fails, although I've never heard of it being used. The big problems are replacement bulbs, LEDs, switches, fixtures, and wiring. We only use the lights when it can't be helped."

"This isn't that," Randall said.

Cole shrugged. "I don't get much chance to show the place off."

Odd machines took up much of the space. Randall recognized computers and their monitors, but the rest of them were alien to him. They spent more time wandering through various offshoots of the main lab, but eventually wound up back where they'd started. Three hours had passed.

"What say we eat lunch and then I find you boys a bunk?"

"I say to hell with that," Randall said. "What you need to do is let us go. Look, what's going on here, Major? What's with the sudden one-of-the-boys routine, the info-dump and the tour? I'll admit it was fascinating, but all we really want is to get back to our unit. A lot of people are wondering what happened not only to us, but to that C-5 parked in your hangar."

"That C-5 is right where it should be. It's Air Force property and this is an Air Force base."

"So was Creech."

"My father always said possession is nine-tenths of the law."

"It's not funny!"

Cole's heretofore friendly smile faded into a scowl. "No, it's not. And don't forget you're talking to a superior officer, *Captain.*"

"From what I can tell, you were never actually *in* the Air Force. You're not old enough."

A few men standing around the far end of the hangar looked up as Randall's near-shout echoed through the rafters.

But Cole's fleshy cheeks once again lifted in a grin. "Oh? Is that because there was no United States to have an air force?"

Only then did Randall realize he'd been trapped. "You know what I mean."

"No, I don't. You can't have it both ways, Randall. If there was no United States, then there can't be one now."

"I've explained all that."

"Not to my satisfaction, you haven't. Look, you've asked a lot of questions, so let me give you a couple of answers. Maybe that'll wet your feathers. Why do we need you here? Because most of the men here are old, and you're not, and you're pilots, too. Military officers, apparently, and yeah, I'm convinced of that. Moreover, the communication we got by radio told us to keep this place locked down tight, almost as if they knew you were coming."

"Coincidence."

"Maybe, but that doesn't alter the orders."

"I wouldn't know, since you won't tell me who sent them!"

Cole wiped away sweat on his forehead with his sleeve. "Fine... hell, maybe you can make sense of it. First off, you should know we only monitor communications two hours a week. We used to do it all day and all night, but when the equipment started wearing out, we decided to cut back, so it's possible this department, whoever they are, has been sending us messages for weeks or months, hell, maybe even years.

"The reception was bad and we didn't catch all the words, but they identified themselves as Something Time-Something. I think the first word was *operation* but I can't be sure. I reached over Rachel, she was monitoring the radio that day, and turned up the volume, and everybody within hearing gathered around. Whoever was talking to us said they were somewhere in Tennessee, we caught that much, and claimed to be a remnant of the federal government and I thought I heard the word *army*, although some of the others didn't. Then, for a minute or so, the signal came in stronger, and we all clearly heard them say to keep the base locked down and to await further orders."

Randall gaped, turned to Carlos, and then spread his hands. "Did they identify themselves?"

"All we got was Judge Gomorrah."

"Who the fuck is Judge Gomorrah?"

Cole pointed. "Watch your mouth, Randall. Second warning."

But Randall could only shake his head and turn in a circle to keep from striking the man. "You're keeping us prisoner because of some garbled radio message? Is that what you're telling me?"

"I believe it to have been real," Cole answered. His tone made it clear that his patience was running short. "But don't forget where you landed."

"On a U.S. Air Force runway, or so I thought."

"Through the most restricted air space in the world."

"Once upon a time, maybe. I can't believe you, Cole, I really can't. One way or another, we're getting out of here. You can't keep us prisoners forever."

"Prisoners?" At that he tilted his head back and barked a laugh. "You boys aren't prisoners. You can leave any time you want."

Randall started to reply, but Carlos put a hand over his mouth. "Is that for real?"

"Yeah. Go anywhere you want, and take any personal property with you."

"What about our jet?"

Cole scratched his temple and turned away, staring toward an open doorway at the far end of the hangar. "Now, that's not personal property, is it? That belongs to the Air Force."

Randall jerked Carlos' hand away. "What about loaning us a vehicle, or some of the hovercraft?"

"No, sorry, I couldn't do that."

"What about horses?"

"Nope. We can't afford to lose anything, machines or horses. But I'll tell you what I'll do... I'll give you a canteen of water."

It finally dawned on Randall what he meant. "You expect us to walk out of here? Through the desert?"

"No, I don't expect you to do anything of the sort, but if you want to leave I won't stop you."

"How far is the nearest town?"

Cole shrugged. "Hell if I know. It's about sixty miles to Las Vegas, but I got no idea what's there. You could try Creech. They might be sending out searches for you. Of course, there *are* all those riders you call Rednecks..."

His sarcasm didn't sit well.

"You're a bastard, you know that, Major?"

"Like I never heard that before." Again Cole smiled the irritating smile that drove Randall to purse his lips and ball his fists. "But if you're not leaving, then let's go see about those bunks."

#

84

CHAPTER 13

It is not enough for us to restrain from doing evil, unless we shall also do good.
St. Basil

Ma Kelly's Trading Post, southeast of Hoover Dam, Arizona
1150 hours, April 24

The Rednecks had totaled twenty-six. Eighteen had been killed, seven wounded, and one captured. When Major Wincommer asked Angriff what to do with the wounded, the general thought for a moment.

"Where are those four people they were holding prisoner?"

"Over there, sir, by the door."

"Let's see what they have to say about it."

Careful not to turn an ankle on the loose gravel as he descended the ridge into the bowl, Angriff veered to his right toward the man he'd shot. A combat medic had turned him over and knelt beside him.

"Is he dead?" Angriff asked.

"About there, General, but he's alive for now."

"Can you do anything for him?"

"He'd need a full trauma team and even then I don't think they could save him. I've got some morphine, though."

"Save it for our people."

As Wincommer stood by, Angriff knelt beside the man he'd shot. The powdery topsoil soaked up the blood pouring from the man's side. The man hadn't shaved or bathed for weeks, as grime caked his skin, washed away only by sweat. He stank of horse, body odor, and excrement. Like a rat's hind legs scurrying furiously when the brain died and no longer controlled its reflexes, so did near-death cause many men's muscles to relax and release their bowels. None of that even registered in Angriff's senses; he'd experienced it too many times.

Angriff leaned forward and whispered in the man's ear. Blood bubbled from his nose and leaked from the corner of his mouth. He made a sucking sound when he gasped for shallow breaths.

"If you can hear me, I'm the man who killed you." The man blinked. "If you believe in God, pray now while you still can, because I'm sure as hell not going to."

Then he stood. The dying man's eyes met his and Angriff stared into them for nearly a minute, until he saw life leave and death glaze them over. The medic announced the man was dead. Without another word, Angriff wheeled and followed Wincommer over to the four people near the building.

Three were young, two boys and a teenage girl. One of the boys, maybe twelve years old to Angriff's eye, couldn't stop sniffling, and kept glancing over his shoulder as if searching for something. The second boy appeared to be nine or so, and despite hiding behind his father, when he peeked around the man his face showed defiance. The girl stared at them with vacant, gray-rimmed eyes. She had a swollen mouth and puffy face. Angriff had seen the aftermath of enough battles to recognize trauma when he saw it. The children formed a tight semi-circle behind a stout older man standing in a protective stance, with legs braced wide apart and thick arms crossed. A matting of black and gray beard covered his wide face, and his posture made it clear that to get to the younger ones, they'd have to go through him first.

A sergeant stood beside them and took Wincommer aside for a brief private chat before stepping back out of the officers' way. Angriff let the major lead the talk.

"I'm Major Wincommer, commanding officer of the Seventh United States Cavalry Regiment, and this is General Angriff, commander of the Seventh United States Cavalry

Brigade. Sergeant Patel here says you didn't want to give your name, so may I ask why not?"

The man's eyes narrowed to a squint and there was no mistaking his suspicion, or his anger. Although standing with crossed arms, he clenched his fists so tightly they whitened. Every time someone walked by, the man tensed up even more, as if expecting a sudden attack.

"You having to ask my name is why not," he finally said. "Everybody knows me, so I've gotta ask myself why you don't, too. Those bastards didn't know me either, and that turned to shit real quick like. They fooled me 'til it was too late, but you're not touchin' my kids unless you go through me first!"

"We're not here to hurt anybody, sir. We're here to help."

The man snorted. "That's what *they* said. They were here to trade, not cause trouble. I'm not as educated as my folks were, but that doesn't mean I'm stupid, either."

"I never said you were stupid, sir. I only wondered how to address you."

"Just leave. That's all I want."

Wincommer started to become exasperated. "We killed the people that were tormenting you, didn't we? I've told you my name. Just tell me yours."

"You coulda killed them so you could have it all for yourself."

"Sir, I—"

Angriff took a step forward. All eyes immediately focused on him. "Major, do you mind if I speak with this gentleman?"

"Not at all, General," Wincommer said, with obvious relief.

Angriff extended his hand, but the man made no effort to shake it. "My name's Nick Angriff."

"I heard him." The man nodded at Wincommer.

"All right, then. We're not gonna stay long; we have other business to attend to. We call the people who violated you Rednecks, because of the red cloth they wear around their necks. We're not sure exactly who they are, but we do know they're our enemy, so we shoot first and ask questions later. We captured at least one of them. Would you like us to share with you what we learn from him before we pull out?"

Behind them, the girl groaned and held her head. Both men looked at her, and then locked eyes.

"At least let me have a medic look at her," Angriff said.

"What's a *medic*?"

"They're like a doctor, somebody who can help her."

Again he glanced back at his daughter. "If you're lying, I'll find a way to kill you."

"I wouldn't lie to you. I have a daughter, too. Three of them. Not too long ago, somebody tried to rape one of them, and then to kill her, so I know how you feel."

"Would you have died to protect her?"

"I took a bullet for her. Right here." He pointed to his right rib cage. "Hurt like hell."

"What'd you do to them?"

"They're dead."

Although the crinkles around his eyes still showed deep suspicion, Weiner nodded in obvious approval. "All right, go on, then. I guess I couldn't stop you even if I wanted to."

"I'll bet you could." Once again Angriff out his hand. "Call me Nick."

This time the man shook it, meeting Angriff's gaze. "I'm Dave. Dave Weiner. This is my place."

Weiner went with the medics who were attending to his daughter, ready to fight if they had bad intentions. He picked up a rusty pitchfork along the way and Angriff let him. For the moment, he was alone in one of the most remarkable places he'd ever been.

Ma Kelly's wasn't one large structure. It had been added on to at least a dozen times over the years that he could tell, with all material used in its construction being obviously recycled from other buildings. Corrugated metal comprised most of the exterior walls, with patches of gray-faded wood here and there. Two large cross-planked wooden doors made up the main entrance, the type of doors found on barns. Mounted over the entrance was the faded image of a woman with a cigarette dangling from her mouth. As she stared out at the viewer, her expression was that of a world-weary waitress in a run-down dive. Above that were the bottoms of some letters, the rest of which had been trimmed off to make the section fit in place. Angriff assumed the woman was Ma Kelly.

He wandered freely, moving through one doorway after another. Most additions connected via short covered hallways with windows cut to allow breezes through. Sweat rolled down his neck and chest and he could only imagine how it felt inside what was essentially a giant metal heat sink during July and August. The interior walls were lined with other materials, mostly wood, but also some fiberglass insulation and even a small section of cork.

Getting from one building to another wasn't the biggest problem in Ma Kelly's; walking through row after row of materials was. Shelves overflowed with everything imaginable, from nails and screws to cups of metal, ceramics, and glass. One section held nothing but cured snakeskins nailed to the wall, with 55-gallon drums of cured animal hides underneath them. A nearby worktable with a large window cut into the wall over it, various hammers organized in neat rows, and nails in jars, made him realize this was where boots were made to order.

By far the largest part was for food, which the Rednecks had looted and left a disorganized mess. Jars of desert barley flour spilled to the floor and boxes of a type of hard bread, a version of hardtack, had been riffled through. Angriff picked up a biscuit and tapped it against his front teeth, where the rock-hard bread made a *tick tick* sound. Scraps of jerky littered a shelf. He'd made it about halfway to what looked like the last building when he heard Weiner calling him.

"In here," Angriff yelled back, and wound his way among the rows until he once again stood in the main building near the entrance. "How's your daughter?"

"Beat up pretty good, as I guess you might've figured out. Your medics say she'll recover physically, except she can't stop crying. I don't know how to help her after what those animals did to her..."

Angriff waited for him to say more, but he didn't. Weiner's gaze went over Angriff's shoulder and he stared at nothing.

"We might be able to help her."

That snapped his attention back to Angriff. "Yeah, so who are you exactly?"

"I saw some chairs. Mind if we sit down?"

"Sure, my knees hurt anyway."

"For me it's my back."

Before they started, Weiner insisted on making tea. It wasn't much, he explained, but he felt the need to repay Angriff somehow, even if the gesture was small. At first Angriff demurred, having heard stories about what people now considered *tea*, but relented when he realized that to refuse was an insult. To the general's utter shock, the tea turned out to actually be tea.

"Where did you get real tea?" he said, sipping the hot liquid. Weiner had sweetened it with honey and Angriff had to admit it tasted delicious.

"Things like tea bags last forever if you keep them dry. I'm told they lose some flavor, but I wouldn't know what they tasted like before."

"Let me tell you, it's wonderful. Thank you."

"Some folks drink it with milk. I can get some if you want."

"This is perfect."

Weiner smiled, his grizzled cheeks spreading wide in satisfaction. He gave Angriff a short history of the trading post. In the time immediately following the Collapse, people fled toward Las Vegas, thinking there was safety in numbers, but within two months food supplies were gone and the local government lost control. No more trucks delivered food and the value of money fell. As the central government failed, the city became a shooting gallery. Starvation turned friend against friend and family against family. Sin City had always been run by nefarious organizations, everything from the Mob to the Mexican cartels, but when all authority broke down, it became an all-out war to see who ruled the ruins.

"Last I heard it was still going on," Weiner said.

"Still?"

"It's what I heard."

As corpses piled up in the streets, desperate refugees sought refuge at Nellis Air Force Base, northeast of the city, but were turned back at gunpoint. Gasoline became more valuable than gold as survivors piled food, fuel, and water into their vehicles and took to the roads, headed for anywhere there might be food and shelter. Thieves set up roadblocks on all highways leading out of town. As a rule, they killed the men immediately, raped the women before killing them, too, and stole whatever they wanted. A lot of the kids were sold as slaves.

A Colombian immigrant named Oswald Nuñez packed up everything he could and drove east with his family crammed into one Suburban — his wife, three kids, three grandparents, and the family dog. He also had two AR-15s, two shotguns, three pistols, and a lot of ammo. The highway gang that stopped them didn't want to shoot up the Suburban and ordered them all to get out. Oswald obliged them by blasting the man at his window while the two grandfathers and the oldest son came out shooting.

The thieves fled, leaving another of their gang dead on the highway, but Oswald knew they'd be waiting in ambush further down the road. Instead he pulled off and found the protected spot where Ma Kelly's now stood.

"There's a spring out back," Weiner said. "That settled everything."

People passing through the area found the secluded valley and begged Oswald for water. He gave it freely if the people had nothing to barter, but most had something he wanted. Those who tried to take it by force quickly discovered the bottom of a grave, and not always after they were dead.

"Brutal guy," Angriff said.

"Those were brutal times. Still are."

As the years went by, fewer and fewer people came by what had become a permanent structure, but the ones who did tended to be regulars who traded food for other things, including shelter. Slowly, some of those people became scrapers, those who roamed the ruins of North America looking for useable leftovers.

"I know some scrapers," Angriff said. "You ever heard of Jingle Bob?"

"O' course, I been knowin' Bob for a long time. Know Junker Jane, too, but only to hear tell. Bob says she's a looker."

"What about Idaho Jack?"

Weiner chuckled, a deep wet laugh. "He ain't such a looker."

"No, he's not." Angriff laughed, too.

"What about Nailhead Neil, you know him?"

"Never heard of him... So how did you wind up getting the place?"

"That's a really long story, Nick. Sure you've got time?"

"I'm the boss. I've got as much time as I say I've got."

Weiner made them a second cup of tea and his boys joined them, arms crossed and looking suspicious even after their father assured them all was fine. Weiner told how his family came to Ma Kelly's five or so months after Nuñez founded the place. His father had been a construction foreman and had not only the knowledge of how to build almost anything, but also brought a lot of tools with him in the family's camper.

"You can still see it around back."

Nuñez knew the value of a man like Weiner's father and welcomed him and his family. Over the years, the Nuñez family died out through illness and accidents, while Weiner's thrived. They finally took over the place when no more of Nuñez's relatives were left alive.

They were deep in a discussion about the details of Weiner's life when Major Wincommer came in looking for Angriff. "General, I've questioned the prisoner and believe I've gotten most of what he can tell us out of him. What should I do with him?"

"What about the others?"

"There's six other wounded, but they're all unconscious."

"We'll take the uninjured man with us. Let's let Mr. Weiner here decide what to do with the wounded."

"I can do anything I want with 'em?"

"They're murderers and rapists who harmed your family. I don't give a damn what you do to 'em."

———～～———

Angriff ordered Wincommer to leave half a troop at Ma Kelly's, in case more riders showed up. The driver had the motor running, but before he got back into his Humvee, he leaned against the roof and pointed west. "What's ahead of me, Dave?"

"Out there? You know about the lake and the river, right?"

"I do. Lake Mead and the Colorado River... I also know the bridge is still standing over the canyon."

"Don't know that I'd trust it."

"The engineers should be there right now, checking it out for structural integrity."

Weiner smiled. "I think I know what you mean by that. Are you going to the dam, too?"

"Yes, and into Las Vegas and beyond. Is there anything I should know about?"

"The dam... You're gonna have some fun there. It's run by Lulu and her crew."

"Dangerous?"

"Naw." He touched his temple. "Not quite right in the head, but that's what comes of keeping that dam running for too many years. Lulu's one of a kind, but she's harmless. Now Vegas, that's a different story. I wouldn't go there if I was you... although you might have the firepower for it."

"You mentioned there's still a war there."

"Has been ever since I can remember."

"You ever been there yourself?"

"Once, a long time ago, but I left quick. I never understood it, Nick. Just living's hard enough, you know? So like I told you earlier, I know the who and the where, I just don't know the why. From what I understand, there were a lot of gangs there when the Collapse came, and remnants of them joined up with each other to fight the rest. Every now and then, we used to get people coming through from the city, but I ain't seen any for years now. Maybe they all killed each other."

"That's a big help, Dave, thank you. I guess I'd better get going now." He extended his hand and they shook again.

Once he'd gotten into the Humvee and shut the door, Weiner leaned inside. "I owe you a pair of boots."

"I want rattlesnake skin."

"It's a deal. I should've measured your feet while you were here. You ain't got time now, do you?"

"Nope, sorry."

"Oh, yeah, one more thing. Wait here just a minute."

"Dave, I've really got to get on the road."

But Weiner was already walking as fast as his thick legs could move back toward Ma Kelly's. He came back carrying something and as he got closer, Angriff wondered if it could be alive. Then Weiner held out his hands and displayed a wriggling German shepherd puppy, which he put in Angriff's hands before the general could stop him.

"Her name's Kona. Those Rednecks killed her mother and my kids wanted you to have her."

"I..." He looked up. Major Iskold giggled behind Weiner. When she realized he was looking at her, she blinked and yawned and tried to put on a serious face again. Then Kona changed everything; leaping straight up, she licked him on the lips.

"Oh, hell," Angriff said.

#

CHAPTER 14

It is impossible to suffer without making someone pay for it;
every complaint already contains revenge.
Friedrich Nietzsche

Overtime Prime
1234 hours, April 24

By the time the guard pushed lunch through the cell door, Tom Steeple felt his stomach rumbling. He'd never been a big eater and until yesterday, his appetite after being thrown into a cell had been bad. But with hope rekindled, his body used energy at a greater rate and he needed to fuel it, so despite the bland nature of the food, he looked forward to each meal now.

The dented metal tray slid under the door through a flap made for the purpose. Steeple remembered the day when he'd signed off on that particular detail of the cell's design, thinking that anyone in a cell deserved their food served on the floor. He was self-aware enough to realize the comedic irony of his current situation.

As usual, the food was cold. A grayish meat with brown gravy the consistency of pudding sat between a handful of green peas and powdered potatoes, also with the congealed gravy on them. It was only while using the edge of the fork to cut off a chunk of meat that he noticed the gravy on the potatoes formed the letter I. More letters followed... n-m-o-t-i-o-n.

IN MOTION.
Suddenly the food tasted much better.
#

CHAPTER 15

Don't cry because it's over, smile because it happened.
Dr. Seuss

California Highway 70, west of Sierra Army Depot
1344 hours, April 24

Junker Jane shoveled dirt side by side with Green Ghost, trying to match his relentless pace to the point where the other paratroopers helping dig the mass grave started elbowing each other and pointing. She never looked up from the deepening hole, not even to wash dirt from her mouth when a water bottle made the rounds. After cradling the charred corpse of a man she'd identified as Bam Bam Bear, she'd thrown all of her energy and concentration into burying him and her other friends.

"If you start that foot bleeding again, don't look for sympathy from me," Green Ghost said. "You heard the doctor."

"I thought you said he wasn't a doctor," she said.

"You know what I mean."

"I had to come."

"I know, I get it, but you need to know when to pass off the mission to somebody better equipped to finish it."

"That's not how it works in my world." Panting, she felt lightheaded from the exertion. She'd lost a lot of blood and wasn't back to full speed yet. "But since we're in your world, I'll do it your way."

Their horses were tethered well away from the worksite, where burned-out vehicles lay scattered on the highway and in the nearby desert, mute testament to the battle fought there a week before by Bear, Jane, and their friends. Scavengers had since despoiled the dead, eating away all nutrient-rich organs, including the eyes. Jane had gone from one friend to the next, kneeling beside the body and closing her eyes for a moment, then moving to the next. Then, while she, Green Ghost, and six other paratroopers dug a shallow grave for the dead, others collected anything of value they could find and piled it in the bed of an old pickup truck pulled by horses — weapons, uniforms, knives, ammunition, papers, boots, bottles, and rations.

Once the hole was three feet deep, they gathered the bodies. Exposed for a week, they reeked of rotten meat, and several men vomited. Others stripped off their uniform shirts and tied them around their faces. Jane thought she'd be all right until she found the remains of the girl named Suzanne, who'd died fighting beside her in a ditch. The eyes were gone, along with most of the internal organs, but still looped around her neck was a leather strap holding an old-style cameo. Inside was the photograph of a young child. Jane had no way of knowing the child's identity, but that didn't prevent tears from rolling through the dust coating her cheeks.

Her foot had begun to throb again, so she mostly let Green Ghost and the paratroopers find stones for the cairn, only adding a few small ones herself as a token. By the time they'd finished piling rocks over the grave, it was mid-afternoon. The ride back to Sierra Army Depot would take the rest of the day and into the night, but Jane didn't move. She stood in silence, remembering her friends and trying to remember the words to a prayer, any prayer. It was only when she cocked her head that she noticed Green Ghost standing beside her.

"I haven't prayed in a long time," she said. "I can't remember the words."

"You don't have to. He knows. But if you want to try, just say whatever you feel."

A fly buzzed around her head as she paused. She swatted at it and missed. "These were loyal people. I thought of them like my family and they never let me down. God, please take good care of my friends." She bowed her head a moment and then looked up, feeling warm tears in her eyes. "Was that okay?"

"Best prayer I've ever heard."

"Thanks."

Without further comment, she mounted her horse and turned it to catch up with the group making their way east, back to Sierra, but reined the horse in when Green Ghost stayed behind. "You coming?"

"I'll be along. I've got something to do first."

"Like what?"

"Those." He pointed to a stack of rectangular, wire-bound boxes they'd hauled from Sierra. Each had a stencil that read M21. Two shovels lay beside them.

"What are they?"

"Anti-tank mines. I'm gonna enlarge some of the holes in the highway and leave them as presents in case our Chinese friends come back. With any luck, this will at least slow them down."

"You've got two shovels."

"Yeah, so?"

"One's for me."

"You sure? It'll be dark soon. And you can't hide that limp."

Jane half smiled. "I see better at night." She dismounted and joined him, trying to keep her steps regular. Electric pain shot up her leg.

Having never handled mines before, she let Green Ghost assemble and place them, while she dug out holes in the broken asphalt big enough for them to fit in. It was hard work, even where the pavement had been blasted out of the roadbed. By the time they finished, the sun had dipped below the line of mountains in the west. They moved half a mile from the battle site and stopped to eat in a patch of small trees, where the horses could forage on leaves and California meadow barley. Neither believed there were any Chinese stragglers left in the area, but didn't build a fire, just in case. As for four-legged predators, the quarter moon lit the desert well enough to see them coming in plenty of time, but they kept their rifles close by just in case.

They hadn't expected to stay out overnight and hadn't brought much food. Dinner was dried strips of mountain goat they'd brought from Sierra, plus a mushy orange and some hard squares of dark bread Jane had found in a discarded Chinese food sack. They washed it all down with tepid water from their canteens.

"I hope I don't break a tooth on this bread," Green Ghost said, more to make conversation than because of the poor quality of the food. He'd eaten much worse.

"The Chinese grow a lot of wheat in California. These are made from a type called hung-you-my. It's red and the bread you make from it has a strong flavor. I call it hard bread. I've eaten cakes like this my whole life."

"I didn't know you spoke Chinese."

"Huh?"

"Hung-you-my?" he said.

"Oh. That's not how the Chinese say it, but that's how my dad taught me."

"Seems like he taught you a lot."

"I wouldn't have survived without the skills he taught me. I had an older brother, but he died before I was born. That was ten years after the Collapse, and by then, Mom and Dad had built our house up in the mountains south of Lake Tahoe. I still live there."

"Is he gone?"

"You sure ask a lot of questions."

Green Ghost turned away and she knew exactly why. He thought the darkness would hide his blush, the unfamiliar sensation of his face getting warm in embarrassment, but it didn't. Not from her.

"Sorry."

For the first time that day, Jane laughed. "It's okay, I was joking. You're funny, you know that?"

"That's not something I hear very often."

"Well, you are." Her voice dropped lower. "My father died when I was twenty-two. He'd broken his leg during the winter, but was mending fine by spring. I had Tornado by then and we needed meat, so I went hunting. I got lucky and found a buck mule deer right away. It was so close to home I didn't even bother field dressing it. I just dragged it home. I was half a mile from the front door when I heard screams and gunshots from inside the house. I rode like hell but was careful not to make any noise going up the front steps to the porch.

"Through a window, I saw my dad rocking in his chair in the main room, with blood covering his face and chest. A Chinese soldier in a ragged uniform lay on the floor, trying to stop his own blood from gushing out of his thigh. Dad had gotten off a shot from a black powder pistol he'd made and defended his granddaughter before they killed him. I couldn't see Nado, until I opened the front door slow enough that it didn't squeak.

"She was under a table, holding a knife, and a second Chinese soldier reached down to grab her. She was about three years old. His hand touched the floor and she stabbed it so hard the knife drove into the wooden floor and pinned his hand. He was reaching for a pistol when he turned and spotted my rifle pointed at his head. Before he could say anything, I shot him twice in the left temple. I told the other man I'd save him if he told me about the rest of his group, but they were deserters. It was just the two of them."

"Did you save him?"

"I couldn't have even if I'd wanted to, which was good, because I didn't want to. He bled out within three minutes. The stain is still there in the wood."

Neither spoke for several minutes.

"It gets to be a lonely life," Jane finally said.

She glanced over to see if he'd reacted to the comment, like he had earlier, but this time he hadn't. She filed that away for later use.

#

CHAPTER 16

All fled—all done, so lift me on the pyre—
The Feast is over, and the lamps expire.
Robert E. Howard

Iron Horse, California
2156 hours, April 24

Rather than sleep in the open desert with no bedding or fire, they decided to head back to Sierra, despite the darkness. Highway 70 went northeast and then east before joining Highway 395 and branching north, so they picked a route that took them cross-country. Later they would get back on Highway 70 for a while and then cut straight northeast toward Sierra. They led their horses over the rough terrain instead of riding, because despite the brightness of the quarter moon, the danger of stepping in a hole was too great.

Green Ghost wanted to lead but had left his NVGs back at Sierra, so Jane firmly insisted he follow her. He argued but eventually gave in. She wondered if he'd comment on the view, half hoping that he would but also knowing that he needed to keep his eyes roaming for trouble, but he said nothing. Within two hundred yards, she had steered them around a Western rattlesnake that didn't rattle a warning, and giggled when Green Ghost jumped sideways away from a second snake.

"Watch it!" he said.

She pitched her voice low so it didn't carry. "That's a gopher snake, silly. Harmless."

"But its head..."

"They can flatten it to look like a rattlesnake. Now do you see why I'm leading?"

"If I get bit by a Gila monster, I'm blaming you."

Jane stopped and looked back over her shoulder. She didn't know Green Ghost all that well, but in the time they'd had together, he'd never done more than scowl and ask questions or bark orders. Despite that, or maybe because she was lonely and hadn't realized it, she found something about him intensely attractive. "If you step on a Gila monster, you'll be the first person ever in these parts to do it."

"Why's that?"

"They don't live this far north."

"Oh."

"They also live mostly underground. I've only seen one in my whole life, and it was dead."

"Okay, I get it. No Gila monsters."

She hoped he could see her smile. "Don't be scared, big boy. Junker Jane is here to protect you."

Green Ghost had to remind himself not to stare at Jane's backside as she led her horse along a trail he couldn't see, a distraction he'd never had to deal with in the field before, not with Glide, or Frosty, or Esther, or any of the other female Zombies. Somehow his brain recognized that while the Zombie women were all beautiful, or at least athletic, he was forbidden to see them in the usual way a man sees a woman, or vice versa. They were part of the team, and not someone you had romantic feelings for. Jane, on the other hand, wasn't a Zombie, so...

He'd just pulled his eyes away from her yet again when without warning Jane crouched and unslung the Kimber Mountain Ascent thirty-ought-six from her shoulder. Green Ghost immediately dropped to one knee and flipped on the IR scope for his M-4. He knew better than to speak. Scanning the desert, he spotted numerous small heat signatures, but nothing that appeared threatening. Then, faint but distinct, he heard screaming. Was it a woman? If so, she was being hacked to death with a butcher knife.

"Bobcat," Jane whispered a few seconds later. "Full-grown, probably a male."

"Do they attack humans?"

She spoke so quietly he had to strain to hear her. "Not unless you threaten them. They also don't scream without a reason... it's mating season, but that's not a mating call. That's a warning."

"What hunts a bobcat?"

"A starving cougar could, but there's too much game around here."

"Anything else?"

"Humans."

That was when a gunshot *cracked* over the desert in sharp echoes.

Seventy yards from the gulley, a campfire flickered in the center of a triangle of three wagons. Green Ghost had circled from a distance until he'd found the best angle of fire. Lying in the ditch, he propped elbows on the lip and aimed his M-4 at the laager. The fire washed out his IR scope, so he turned if off to conserve the battery.

"I count at least four adults," he said quietly to Jane, who lay beside him. "Might be some kids, too. No weapons in sight."

"That wasn't thunder we heard earlier."

"No, it wasn't. But I don't see any sentries." He looked away from the scope. "I think it's a family or families."

"What are they doing way out here?"

Instead of answering, he simply stared at her, in that way most people found so annoying. It was his way of saying *why are you asking me?* But Jane kept silent long after most people would have said something further, waiting him out, and after a long minute Green Ghost's mouth twitched. "How the hell should I know?"

"I thought you were some kind of super soldier."

"What is that supposed to mean?"

"That's what some of the men back at Sierra called you. Are you?"

"Am I what?"

"A super soldier?"

"Is this really the time to be talking about that?"

"Can you suggest a better time?"

He opened his mouth to reply, but the words wouldn't come out. Finally he said, "If you don't think those people are families, then who do you think they are?"

"Oh, I think you're right, I think they're families and they're running away from something."

His voice rose to a loud whisper in his exasperation. "Then what was all that super soldier bullshit about?"

Although she lay in the dark shadows of the ditch, he clearly saw her teeth when she smiled. "Just playing with you." Then the tone of her voice abruptly changed. "I'm going to go talk to those folks."

"What? No, you're not! What if they shoot first and ask questions later?"

"That's what you're here for. Assuming you know how to shoot that thing." But when she saw the confusion on his face, she stopped on the lip of the ditch. "Listen, a scraper has to know what's going on in their territory. I've spent most of my life alone in this vast country, digging through the ruins of old America, and to tell you the truth, it's been a pretty interesting life. But the only way to survive is to talk with people, find out what the latest news is and where the dangers might be. I've never seen travelers in this part of the high desert before and need to find out what they're doing here."

"I still don't like it, but I guess I can't stop you."

"No, you can't, and I'm glad you didn't try."

———

"Hello in the camp!" she called from behind a young pine tree growing in the scrublands, no more than twenty yards away from the nearest wagon. People often called the area south of the old Plumas National Forest a desert, but it wasn't. Instead it lay between the far northern tip of the Sierra Nevada Range to the south, and the Cascade Mountain

Range on the north — flat lands cut by deep ditches and covered in tufts of grass and scrub pines.

She heard scrambling coming from behind the wagon nearest her and saw shadows pass in front of the campfire. Alarmed voices spoke in low tones she couldn't make out, but didn't need to; clearly she'd panicked them. The metallic *click* of a gun's hammer being pulled back was plain to hear.

"I mean no harm!"

"Go away and leave us alone!" cried a man's voice. "I'll shoot you if you don't."

"My name is Junker Jane." She waited, hoping they might have heard of her.

"Don't care about that, don't know you, don't wanna know you!"

What could she say to that? As Jane tried to think of something to say, she heard more talking coming from the camp. She decided to wait and see if the man said anything more, and didn't have long to wait.

"How do we know it's you?"

"Have you run into a lot of people pretending to be me?"

That brought a laugh followed by a curse. "Don't mean you're you."

"I'm standing up. Please don't shoot me."

"Are you armed?"

"Of course I am. What kind of idiot doesn't carry a gun?"

"Leave it behind."

"Like hell I will! It's over my shoulder, but I don't go anywhere without my rifle, so if you're gonna shoot, then make sure you don't miss."

With her right thumb looped under the rifle's strap at her shoulder, Jane rose from concealment and walked straight toward the little encampment. Flickering firelight lit the way, illuminating the side of a lanky man pointing a very long gun at her. As she drew closer and could make out more details, it became obvious that it was a single-shot musket, probably made post-Collapse. Passing between two wagons, she entered the triangular campsite.

Two older women and an older man stood in front of seven children, all of whom appeared to be teenaged or younger. The man pointing the gun at her had the lean, leather-skinned look of someone who'd spent a life outdoors. A cook-

106

ing pot sat beside the fire and it was obvious the wagons were loaded with their possessions, but there was one thing Jane immediately noticed was missing: animals. Each wagon had a horse to pull it, but no cows, chickens, goats, or even a dog.

One of the women crept around the fire and came toward her. Jane noticed the muzzle of the musket shaking and a sideways glance showed the man's finger on the trigger, also quivering, as if he expected her to try and jump him.

"I'm going to raise my hands," she said. "Just don't pull that trigger."

"Don't you move!" His voice cracked.

"I'm not moving! But take your finger off that damned trigger!"

"If I shoot you, it ain't gonna be no accident."

"That's not what I'm worried about. I've got a friend out there with a scoped rifle centered on the side of your head, and I'm afraid if you don't move away from that trigger, he's gonna put a bullet in your brain."

"It's a lie. Keep that gun on her, Lem," cried the second woman, across the ring of stones enclosing the fire. Two small children hugged her, one to each leg.

"Ghost!" Jane yelled. It startled the man named Lem, the man with the gun, who jumped and almost fired.

Then a reply from the darkness caused Lem's head to turn. "I'm here." Jane could tell Green Ghost had gotten closer since she'd left her position.

"We're all friends here," she said.

"How do we know you ain't another commissar come to take us back?"

"Hang on, Lem." It was the woman who'd sidled closer to Jane. The deep lines cut into her cracked skin made her appear older than she probably was. "You look like Lyssa described you to be."

"Lyssa? The young woman who ran with Bam Bam Bear and the Enclave?"

The woman squinted with her left eye. "What'd she look like?"

"If it's the same girl, about yay high—" She held her hand about five feet above the ground. "Small frame, blonde hair, really pretty eyes, the color of the flowers on black sage."

After a brief pause, the woman turned to Lem and nodded. "I believe her. Put your gun away, Lem."

With obvious reluctance, Lem lowered his musket.

Jane smiled at the woman nearest her, unslung her own
rifle, and propped it against the wagon at her back. "Thank
you..."

"I'm G-momma Ellie," the woman said, spreading her
arms to hug Jane. Once all the introductions were made, G-
momma Ellie asked if the man in the desert might want to
join them. They didn't have much, but would share whatever
they did have.

"He's not very sociable," Jane said. "And thank you, but
we've got everything we need."

"You could use some tea, couldn't you? Everybody needs
tea."

"Thank you, I'd love some."

Tea had long since ceased meaning water poured over
the leaves of an evergreen bush native to East Asia. Now it
was any concoction made from roots and leaves native to
North America that could be collected to provide flavor to hot
water. Each region had its own variety. Even Jane had one of
her own, created by the elderly Indian named Tenuhci, who
looked after her compound when she was gone. It didn't have
a name, it was just *tea*.

G-momma Ellie handed her a dented metal cup filled
with a steaming liquid she ladled from a pot sitting in the
ashes of the fire. Steam rising from the cup smelled strongly
of pine needles, with a floral undertone. Sipping the tea,
Jane found it bitter, but smiled and swallowed anyway. Un-
expectedly, it felt like her sinuses opened up and she could
breathe deeper.

"Thank you," she said, surprised that she meant it.

"You like it?"

"I do. It's a little bitter but... I don't know, there's something about it."

"I'll teach you how to make it," G-momma Ellie said with
a grin. She still had all her teeth.

"Let's see if there's time first. Maybe you could tell me
why you're out here in the middle of the desert?"

"We knew it was comin'. We told Lyssa all about it. You
seen her lately?"

Jane waited to speak until the words had formed in her brain. "Lyssa's why we're out here, G-momma... her and Bear and a man named Artu and a brave girl named Suzanne... we... me and the guy out there in the dark, we buried them this afternoon. The Chinese killed them more than a week ago. I saw it with my own eyes, G-momma... Bear sacrificed himself to save me."

"Oh, Lord," G-momma prayed. Several of the children started crying. "Not that sweet little thing. Tell me it ain't true."

"I wish I could."

"Damn Chinese," Lem said. He looked over his shoulder, to the west, and scowled.

"I don't know why God lets such people walk his Earth," G-momma said. "They killt all them good folks and they ran us off our land. That's why we's out here — they took our farm. We figured it was comin' but not this quick."

———

When the U.S. armed forces were the mightiest in the world, the requirements for joining any special operations branch included superior physical skills as a minimum, but the best of the recruits also had top-flight mental abilities. That did not mean simply calculating a tactical situation in a dynamic environment, or thinking up clever ruses, or the ability to speak multiple languages, although each of those was also a highly desirable trait for those involved in special ops. The most critical mental discipline was patience, not just when operating as a sniper but patience to allow situations to develop and give your team member a chance to complete their mission before breaking cover and going in after them.

Green Ghost was about at that stage and had put one knee on the lip of the ditch when Jane finally emerged from the campsite headed his way.

Once there, she knelt down and extended her hand. "Come on, let's go."

"What are you talking about?"

"We've got a long way to go before dawn. We need to get started."

"It's pretty late now and we don't *have* to get back to Sierra tonight. We can wait until morning."

"We're not going to Sierra and we can't wait for sunup. The Chinese might spot us."

"What the hell are you talking about, lady?"

"We're headed southwest, twenty miles or so."

"I've gotta get back to Sierra. I have responsibilities. Never mind *why* you wanna go twenty miles to the southwest. I just can't do it."

"I guess I'll have to do it alone, then."

"Do *what?*"

"Save some prisoners of the PRC."

———

"Knock it off with the jokes."

Under the starlight, Green Ghost could read her confusion. "What jokes?"

"Calling it the PRC. It's a play on People's Republic of China, because the state of California loved oppressive government."

"Now what are *you* talking about?"

"You called it the PRC. I assumed you meant the People's Republic of California."

"I did."

"And that was always just a joke."

"It's not a joke. That's it's name."

"Seriously? Since when?"

"Since those people heard it straight from the mouth of some Chinese tough guy named Adder when he took their farm yesterday."

Green Ghost recoiled as if he'd been struck. "What did you say his name was?" he whispered.

"Adder."

"And he's twenty miles from here?"

"He was, but I don't know about now."

"Let's go." He scrambled out of the ditch and took off walking southwest at a brisk pace. "We're wasting time."

#

Chapter 17

The oldest and strongest emotion of mankind is fear, and the oldest and strongest kind of fear is fear of the unknown.
H.P. Lovecraft

North Central California
0031 hours, April 25

Jane had lived her entire life stalking the deserts, plains, and mountains of northwest North America. Sometimes her lifestyle had necessitated moving very fast for short sprints, but she'd never met anyone who could maintain such a relentless pace as Green Ghost. He always walked with long strides and a gait that made it seem like he was headed for some emergency. Even on horseback, he seemed to move as part of the horse, a horse he had only just met, in the way that long-time horses and their riders often coordinated their movements so perfectly they appeared to be one animal, and while they only moved at a slow trot, their speed never varied.

The only comment he made in the first hour was to ask for exact directions. After that, she tried several times to engage him in conversation, but avoided the subject of whoever Adder might be, since he'd had such a strong reaction to the name. The only response she got was a grunt when a breeze carried a familiar scent to her nostrils, the musky smell of a snake.

At length she couldn't take it any more. "Did you grow up riding horses?" she said sometime past midnight.

"No."

"You do it so good." He said nothing, so she changed her approach. "Who taught you to ride?"

"Nobody."

"Somebody had to."

"An instructor showed me how, then I did it."

"What about shooting? Who taught you how to shoot?"

"Nobody."

"Somebody had to."

"An instructor showed me how guns work, then I just did it."

After a few more attempts and failures, she gave up. "Who taught you to be such an asshole?"

Jane had reached the point where her eyes wouldn't stay open no matter how hard she tried. Even the throbbing ache in her foot had lost its edge. As sleep became harder and harder to fight off, she twice dozed and swayed in the saddle. Both times she jerked herself awake to see Green Ghost still slightly ahead and to her left, horse and rider plodding forward like a joined machine. She determined to stay awake until dawn, which wasn't too far off and would provide a strong reason for stopping.

The eastern sky showed the first traces of pink when Green Ghost spoke without preamble. "Adder was one of us," he said, as if they'd been conversing all night. "A Zombie, better than the best of the best. Then he sold us out."

It took her a second to realize he'd actually spoken the words and she hadn't dreamed them. She started to respond but a yawn overtook her. "You do what you want," she said. "But I've gotta get some sleep."

Green Ghost stood in his stirrups and scanned the land ahead. "Half mile up, there's some rocks. We'll stop there."

She saw the spot he meant. "Watch out for snakes."

"Yeah."

"So what's a Zombie? I've heard you mention it a few times, and I know you and Claw and Vapor are all Zombies, and this Adder, too, but I don't really know what that means."

He didn't respond right away. Even now, with the old world long gone along with its rules and loyalties, it felt strange talking openly about Task Force Zombie.

"I don't know how much you know about the world before the Collapse, so stop me if you already know some of this. Back then, most countries maintained extensive armed forces, but because of nuclear weapons nobody wanted to start a full-scale war."

"My father said something about those."

"Yeah, you didn't want to use nukes. They'd fuck up the planet along with your enemies. So wars got smaller and nastier, involving lower numbers of troops, but often with big consequences. So everybody developed what they called special operations teams, spec ops, the best troops they had. They gave them the best training and weapons and made them highly mobile. America had a lot of different such organizations. The Navy had the SEALs, which stands for Sea, Air, Land... the Army had Delta Force, the Marines had MARSOC, Marine Special Operations Command, and the Air Force had their Special Operations Command."

"That sounds like a lot."

"We needed every one of them and it still wasn't enough. Plus, you couldn't just go send your spec ops people anywhere you wanted, because if they entered a foreign country without permission that could trigger an all-out war. So a lot of countries had what were called black ops teams that operated outside of the usual force command."

"Is that what Zombies were, black ops?"

"Yes, but in a different way. We all had to give up our entire identities to join. That's why we all have code names instead of our real names. If we were captured on a mission, it couldn't be traced back to the United States. We didn't even know each other's real names... other than Vapor, I still don't. If Claw told me his real name, I'd still call him Claw. It's all I know him by. Originally there were fifteen of us assembled from all branches of service, and each of us had to give up our previous lives so nobody would know who we were or what unit we were part of."

"And Green Ghost is your code name."

While they spoke, their horses plodded right past the rock island where they'd planned to stop. Neither noticed or reined in their horse.

"Right. We also made sure that none of our procedures matched those of U.S. Special Forces units, in case our radio transmissions were overheard. Our uniforms and equipment came from countries all over the world."

"I must be missing something."

"Like what?"

"All this... what's the word... secrecy? Yes, secrecy... if they didn't know you were Americans, then why worry about things like your clothes?"

"We couldn't take any chances."

"I think I understand, but what's a zombie? What does the word mean?"

"It's like a science fiction monster, a dead person who walks around eating brains."

"Eww... those couldn't have been real."

For the first time in days, she saw a tiny smile outlined on his face in the waning moonlight. "No, they were pretend, like men from Mars or Bigfoot."

Jane wondered if he meant more by that remark than he'd said. Once she'd realized that some men wanted to kill her friends, the Hairy People, she'd stopped talking about them.

"To our friends, family, and the outside world we no longer existed, so we called ourselves zombies because we were dead men walking. But we couldn't even share that with people not on the team, so they only knew us as the Nameless."

"Okay," she said, not understanding but not wanting to pursue it, either. "And Adder was one of you?"

Green Ghost's hint of a smile disappeared. "He was one of the original fifteen. From day one, he resented me being in charge, but that didn't bother me. Being an alpha was almost part of the job description and some people deal with it better than others. Except in the teams, you absolutely cannot break trust with the people who've got your six. You can hate their guts all you want, but when it's time for business, all that shit's gotta stop. If you're number twelve out of a squad of twelve, then you prove you're ready for more responsibility by performance, not by undermining the chain of command..."

"Was any of that supposed to make sense? All I understood is that he doesn't like you."

"No, he didn't like me, which was fine because I couldn't stand him. But there was no denying his command presence, tactical skills, or qualities as a leader, and eventually he worked up to command Third Squad. Then, a little before the earthquake hit and the world fell apart, he took a team of eleven other Zombies into the country of Venezuela, down in Central America. The mission was to find the location of a dirty bomb that was being assembled, and before you ask, that was a kind of nuke, a nuclear weapon, a weapon of mass destruction that was intended for use against the American public. Three weeks later, Adder comes out of the jungle alone. He said all the others were killed in an ambush, but I, and a lot of others, didn't believe him. We think he sold the mission out for money. I had plans on finding out for sure, one way or the other, before the Collapse hit."

"So you think he helped murder your friends."

"Not just my friends, my subordinates, the people who entrusted their lives to my leadership. A dirty bomb like the one he'd been sent to find later went off in St. Paul, Minnesota, taking out five bridges over the Mississippi River and making them unusable. That was after the earthquake, when most of the bridges south of the Twin Cities had already been destroyed."

"That's awful. Who did it?"

He shrugged. "If they found out, I never heard it. The FBI thought it was an ISIS cell, but at that point, the country was under attack from numerous directions."

"And you think Adder caused all of that?"

"The bridges, yeah, I do."

"There's still one thing I don't understand. Why do *you* feel responsible if this was Adder's fault?"

"I'm the one who gave him command of Third Squad."

"Oh. Thank you for telling me all of this. Now I understand why you're so anxious to find him."

"Yeah."

"Some men tried to kill a friend of mine last year, so I think I know how you feel."

"What'd you do?"

She shrugged. "I got help from his mate... uh, wife, and together we killed them."

"Good. That's my kind of man."

Jane merely smiled, wondering if he'd still call him a man if they ever met.

As they headed southwest, the terrain changed from flat prairieland with mostly scrub trees for vegetation, to forested uplands with dense stands of mature pines. There was little undergrowth, which gave the entire region a park-like atmosphere. With the coming of sunrise, Jane led them to another small hill studded with trees and rocks jutting from the side of a mountain, which offered a defensible position with good sight lines in all directions, but better concealment for them between the boulders.

"I stayed here overnight once," she said. Fatigue drew out her words in a slower cadence than usual. "Let's make sure there are no rattlesnakes."

They got within twenty feet of the slope and tethered their horses to the low-hanging branch of a Ponderosa pine, with lots of other needle-filled branches within reach for them to eat. But when the horses snorted and pulled at their tethers, Jane froze and Green Ghost followed her lead. That was when both heard the characteristic buzz of a rattlesnake's warning. Jane waited to see if Green Ghost would check it out, but when he didn't move, she shook herself and climbed the humus-covered hill.

"Be careful," he said.

She didn't bother telling him that she'd learned to inspect the ground in front of every step she took from the first halting footstep she'd taken as a toddler. She moved with the confidence of a lifetime, since staying alive in the wilderness meant seeing dangers before they saw you. Once at the top, she found a long stick and began poking up under rocks. Then she stood, smiled, and waved him up.

Once there, Green Ghost poked his head around a large boulder and looked where she pointed. "Holy shit, there're two snakes and they're fighting."

Jane couldn't help but giggle. "The rattlesnake is fighting. The other one is hunting dinner."

"Huh?"

"The black and white one is a king snake. They're immune to rattlesnake venom and think of them like you and I would a thick slice of pig."

"A delicacy."

"A what?"

"Never mind, but even if the king snake's immune, doesn't the rattlesnake have fangs? It seems like getting stabbed with those would kill the king snake."

As if on cue, the rattlesnake struck. It all happened in less than half a second. The heavy triangular head shot forward, its mouth opened and twin fangs folded out, ready to inject venom. But the rattlesnake had made a fatal mistake. As fast as the pit viper was, the constrictor was faster. The rattlesnake's fangs plunged downward into nothing but air, leaving it overextended and vulnerable.

The king snake's head drew back to avoid getting bit, and then shot forward again to clamp its own jaws around the rattlesnake's mouth. In the next half second it looped its body around the first third of the venomous snake, the muscles in the zebra-striped body flexing visibly under its skin. The rattlesnake whipsawed and shook its rattle in fury, but with every movement the king snake tightened its grip.

Jane moved into the circular cleared space at the top of the hill between all of the rocks. Green Ghost watched her but didn't follow.

"It's safe now," she said. "We've even got entertainment."

#

Chapter 18

Into the unknown, take me by the hand,
Lead me to new vistas, lead me to strange lands.
Sergio Velazquez, from "Away and Away"

Willow Beach, Arizona
0544 hours, April 25

As dawn lit the desert in pinks and purples, the First Mechanized Infantry Regiment prepared to move out of its camp on a piece of level ground in rough country, near a place called Willow Beach, which overlooked the Colorado River south of Hoover Dam. The nature of the terrain would have made it hard for a large force of mounted cavalry to approach without being seen, a force such as the Rednecks, who seemed to infest the region. Colonel Young was not about to let his command be caught by surprise and attacked while bivouacked.

Angriff slept better in his tent, on a simple cot with his sleeping bag, than he had in months. He was in the field again, and while he enjoyed the comforts of home as much as anybody, he never quite felt as comfortable there as he did during operations. If he'd believed in reincarnation, as Patton did, he would have believed himself to be a nomadic warrior for some forgotten tribe that built no cities and never stayed long in one place.

When the operation began, he'd declined Colonel Young's offer of an orderly, but the addition of a headstrong nine-week-old puppy changed his mind. The unlucky choice was Corporal Tananda Isbukeke, universally called Kiki. As he stretched in the chilly morning air, Angriff couldn't help chuckling at the sight of the tall NCO trying to walk over the broken ground carrying a cup of coffee and a squirming puppy. Angriff reached for the coffee, but Kona half jumped, half fell into his hands instead.

"I think she's bonded with you, sir." Isbukeke had fashioned a crude collar and leash out of rope, the end of which he offered to Angriff. "You want the keys, General?"

Within minutes, Angriff wound up fifty yards away from the main camp, holding Kona's leash in a death grip as she barked at a coiled rattlesnake hiding under a rock. The serpent had been asleep when Kona nipped at it. Combined with sluggishness from the night's cold temperatures, the snake's strike at her nose missed by three inches, after which Angriff physically yanked her backward and prayed the rope's knot didn't unravel.

Hearing the commotion, Isbukeke came at the run. "General, Colonel Young sends his regards and asks that you join him in the headquarters tent."

Angriff handed him the leash. "Don't let her hurt that snake."

Isbukeke followed where Angriff was pointing. From his reaction, it was obvious he hated snakes. "I won't, sir. I can guarantee we won't get close to it."

The tent flap was pinned open, but Angriff ducked anyway out of habit. Young and his staff stood around a small table with a paper map spread on it.

"Old school," Angriff said. "I like it."

"It's a tourist map, General. One of the men found it back at Ma Kelly's. It's the best we can do."

"Don't apologize, Colonel. Whatever works, works."

Young outlined his proposed movements. Major Wincommer's 7th Cavalry Regiment would screen both flanks and stay within radio range to prevent any ambushes on the way to the Colorado River gorge. The 2nd Mech would take Highway 93 to and over the Colorado River below Hoover Dam. To Angriff's question, he replied that yes, the engineers had given the go-ahead as long as no more than two vehicles were on the bridge at any one time.

One company from First Battalion would veer from the main column east of the river and make for Hoover Dam itself, pausing at the Hoover Dam Lookout for any signs of trouble. If everything appeared safe, it would probe the Dam to investigate the current status of its electricity-making potential and any staff that might be on hand, in particular the mysterious Lulu.

Meanwhile, the bulk of the regiment would move through Las Vegas and pause at Nellis Air Force Base to assess whether or not to send patrols into the city itself. It was assumed the company at Hoover Dam would join the main body rapidly and then be left at Nellis when the regiment pulled out headed to Creech.

"Any new intel on Vegas?" Angriff asked.

"Nothing definite, but patrols got as close as ten klicks and definitely saw lights among the outlying buildings."

"No indication of origin?"

Young shook his head. "Permission to get underway, General?"

"This is your show, Colonel. I'm just along for the ride."

#

Chapter 19

I am who I am. I can't pretend to be someone who makes
$25,000 a year.
Gwyneth Paltrow

Malibu, California
0826 hours, April 25

Károly Rosos leaned on the third-floor balcony's wrought iron railing and deeply inhaled the salt air. He had always loved this time of the morning in California, when the rising sun turned the waters of the Pacific Ocean black to dark gray, then a succession of shades of blue and finally the turquoise he'd swum in most of his youth. Building clouds on the western horizon promised rain later that day, but for that brief period, he felt like he was ten years old again.

"Did you know there's no such thing as a sea gull?" he said, watching several birds skim over the breakers near the beach. "There are gulls, but none are *sea* gulls."

"Were you listening to me?" Adder said. The big man stood behind him and Rosos could feel his glare. Adder was necessary to his father's plan, but that didn't mean he had to like him. There was an indefinable menace about the man, some sense that if pushed too far Adder might forget his own best interests and go berserk.

"Yes, I was listening. You're a real buzzkill," Rosos said.

"I didn't come here to stare at the ocean or talk about birds, this isn't my childhood home, and I didn't come to California to fuck around. I told your father I'd do what I could to assess the Chinese military potential and then make suggestions, which is what I'm trying to do right now."

With an exaggerated sigh, the youngest Rosos turned away from the ocean and waved his hand. "Assess away."

"I've only been here two days, but I can already tell you that whatever combat potential Zhang's people may have had before the Americans kicked their ass is gone. The survivors of the original armored corps that landed here forty years ago are all in their sixties and seventies now, and the best of those died during that battle last year. The ones who are left don't want any part of dying for their Generalissimo."

Rosos yawned and picked up a mug from the wrought iron table to one side of the balcony. He closed his eyes and sipped hot, fresh coffee. "This alone made coming to Los Angeles worth the trip."

"Yeah, the coffee's good. So fuckin' what? Zhang has asked me to be his military advisor. You got any objection?"

"On the contrary, that's perfect."

"I thought so."

"You should really try the coffee."

"I already took some. Look, I'm heading back up north for a few days. Zhang's trying to spread his footprint into new areas and I wanna go back up there and supervise."

"You were just there."

"Yeah, I made an example of a couple of farms on how to press-gang recruits and scare the shit out of the farmers, so they'll be afraid to withhold their harvest from Zhang's people. But I want to go back and do some more. Two farms aren't enough to teach his people how to instill fear. They're mostly young recruits and I want to assess them in person. Then I'm going on a quick tour of their remaining mechanized units, which are mostly south of Sacramento. They lost a whole armored brigade last year trying to move into Arizona."

"Is that what Zhang alluded to at dinner the other night? The big battle over in Arizona?"

"Everybody's pretty tight-lipped about it, but here's what I've pieced together. They had some kind of partner in Arizona who they traded with, gas for slaves. It was called the Republic of Arizona, but it sounds to me like it wasn't much of anything. Zhang apparently felt the same way and saw no reason they couldn't have both the slaves and the gas. He sent out scouts to find a way for heavy AFVs to get there, and they found a bridge intact over the Colorado River that would hold main battle tanks. He wasn't sure how strong the Republic of Arizona was, so he sent an entire armored division manned by the original crews who invaded California."

"They were all still alive after four decades?"

"I'm tellin' ya what I heard, Károly. I'm sure they'd had to replace some of them. They loaded some of the fuel trucks with troops to unload once they got inside the town."

"Like the Trojan horse."

"I guess. So they got close to their objective, a town named Prescott, and out of nowhere American helicopter gunships bring hell down on them. The survivors swore they had American markings, and then they ran into a column of... get this... Abrams tanks. They get the shit shot out of 'em and hightail it for home, leaving fifty tanks burning on the field."

"American helicopters... sounds like our friend General Angriff was busy. But that all matches what Colonel Mwangi said."

"Couldn't be anybody else. If Mwangi has the dates right, this battle would have had to be right after they came out of Long Sleep. The Chinese might be old, but if they were sent to invade America, then at some point they were considered badasses. Old or not, to get your ass kicked by a unit just coming out of Long Sleep only adds up to one thing — Angriff."

Rosos sipped his coffee and made a face. It had gotten cold. He drank it anyway. "We knew he was the man in charge and we knew Steeple picked him for his battlefield prowess. I fail to see the reason for your surprise."

"It's not surprise, it's admiration. And concern."

"Oh? About what?"

"Haven't you been listening? Angriff's gonna be tough to beat."

"You misunderstand. We don't want to beat him. We want to control him. Failing that, we want to kill him."

"That's easier said than done. I can't imagine anybody controlling him."

"For the time being, that's not our concern, so let's quit this pointless debate. Your job now is to expand our new ally's combat power, to put in an effective training regimen and turn them back into an effective fighting force while using younger people to do it. I'm going to ask Zhang to make you his top military advisor."

"Already done."

"Excellent! I applaud your initiative."

"Unless you've got something else, I'm off to put the fear of God into some more locals up in the mountains."

"God? That sounds odd, coming from you."

"It's just an expression, Károly."

The top of Bravo Company, First Battalion, First Mechanized Infantry Regiment Commander Captain Bernita De Lorenzi's helmet came up to Angriff's shoulder, but as she stood with binoculars raised staring toward Hoover Dam, he might as well not have been there. Viewing everything below her from the lookout position atop the ridge east of the dam, she scanned from left to right and back again, slowly. Using his own binoculars, Angriff had already decided there were no immediate threats to a forward movement, but waited for her to conclude the same thing. As time dragged past the two minute mark, however, he began to chaff.

Until she stopped scanning, fixed on one spot, and adjusted the binoculars. "Sergeant O'Toole!" When her senior NCO came up, she handed him the binoculars. "Tell me what you see."

Angriff put his binoculars back up to his eyes and tried to find what she had seen, but he saw nothing... nothing... noth–... was that it? What was it? When it moved, he realized.

"That's a very small woman," O'Toole said. "I think."

De Lorenzi nodded. "Good, that verifies my observation." She seemed to only then notice Angriff. "Do you agree, General?"

"I'm betting that's Lulu."

#

Chapter 20

This morning I came, I saw, and I was conquered, as everyone would be who sees for the first time this great feat of mankind...
President Franklin Roosevelt on seeing Hoover Dam in 1935

Hoover Dam, Arizona side
0903 hours, April 25

Lake Mead lapped far up on Hoover Dam, nearly cresting the basin holding back its water. The road snaked downward from the lookout, past desolate parking lots with once-black asphalt bleached light blue-gray by decades of sunlight, until it finally crossed the top of the dam. Two Stryker APCs filled with troops crawled toward the eastern edge. Once there, two eight-man squads exited the vehicles and fanned out in case of attack, while their platoon commander approached within shouting distance of the tiny, bent old woman holding a broom and blocking the roadway.

Standing beside his Humvee five hundred yards back, Angriff thought the extreme caution being shown by Captain De Lorenzi was unnecessary, but said nothing. It wasn't his place to intrude on how she handled her company in a tactical situation, although even from that distance he could see the woman posed no threat. Sure, it *could* be an elaborate trap, and others *could* be waiting in ambush, maybe, but he highly doubted it.

Captain De Lorenzi spoke into a handheld radio and waved the column ahead. Then she walked back to him. "We're good to go, General."

"Thank you, Captain. I'd like to speak to that woman, if I could."

"Absolutely, sir."

Flanked by two soldiers, Angriff approached the gnomish figure of an elderly black woman bent nearly double, as if she carried a great stone on her back. Bright white hair ran from her forehead to the base of her skull in an afro Mohawk, tinged at the ends with pink. The rest of her skull was shaved to the skin. She clenched a pipe in her teeth and held a broom, with which she swept dust off the roadway.

"You bringin' a lotta metal for one old lady," she said without looking up. "Fancy stuff, too. Guessin' I must be mighty scary."

"You scare me," Angriff said.

A gust of wind howled over the dam, drowning out the *scritch scritch* of broom straws on concrete. "Doubt anything scares a big fella like you."

"Lulu does," he said. "She always has."

The old woman raised her head and stared at him through half-inch-thick eyeglasses that made her eyes look as big as oranges. Her saw her nostrils dilate, as if she sniffed his scent on the wind.

"Who dat Lulu?" Her voice was as much screech as cackle.

"You are."

"Why you t'ink I'm this Lulu?"

"Because we've met before, Dr. Repperton."

"Don't know no doctor named Zipperdoll."

But Angriff grinned. "Oh, I think you do, Louise. You gave me a tour of the dam a long, long time ago, when you were just starting to work here."

The woman twisted her head, moved the glasses down to the bridge of her nose and appeared to inspect him with her peripheral vision. Then she looked away, lost in thought, and her posture straightened a bit. When she turned around, she waggled her finger at him. "I know who you look like," she said. The cackle was gone, along with the bad grammar, and now she sounded like an aged but well-educated woman.

"But that was the better part of sixty years ago and you look the same, so you can't be the man I'm thinking of."

"Unless that man is General Nick Angriff."

Against Captain De Lorenzi's urgent advice, Angriff and Major Iskold followed Lulu, aka Dr. Louise Repperton, down an endless series of stairs deep into the bowels of Hoover Dam. The first thing she asked the general was how he'd remembered her.

"I might have lived a sheltered life, but before I met you, I'd never met a Doctor of Hydroelectric Engineering with a blue Mohawk."

"It stopped being blue a long time ago, but I'm lucky that it's still thick enough to have the Mohawk."

She'd asked how it was that Angriff hadn't aged in sixty years and he put her off until they had met with her *family*, the other people who lived there. Strangely enough, she accepted, as though meeting people who hadn't aged was an everyday occurrence. Lighting in the stairwell came partly from an ingenious series of mirrors mounted in such a way as to reflect sunlight down the shaft of the stairs. When they became too dim, LEDs took over. They weren't bright, but Angriff was surprised they worked at all.

What stunned Angriff most was how easily she moved down the long rows of steps. Although tiny and frail in appearance — she had to be nearing ninety — nothing about her suggested she was that old.

She noticed him studying her and laughed. "Clean living," she said, knowing his thoughts without asking. "Not by choice, just necessity."

"Before we get down there, let me ask you something. You didn't seem concerned about a column of armored vehicles pulling up to your doorstep. Mind telling me why? Did you know we were Americans?"

"I didn't know who you were."

"Then why just stand there sweeping? Why not hide and see if we were friendly?"

"That road you came in on?"

"What about it?"

127

"There's a few thousand pounds of high explosives lining each side, and it's in strategic places up on that ridge overlooking the dam. We had somebody watching the whole time with their finger on the firing switch. If I'd gone down, you'd have gone up."

"What if you'd had a heart attack?"

She paused at the next landing, turned, and shrugged. "Bad luck for you."

"Is she serious?" Iskold whispered from behind him.

"I'd like to think not. By the way, Lulu, Dave Weiner said to tell you hello."

"I used to babysit him when he was in diapers. Those were days when we tried to keep electricity flowing to some of the outlying communities. My second husband, Rory, he did most of the line work. I'd go along to help sometimes, but usually wound up doing things like babysitting while the dads went and helped Rory with the heavy work."

"Wouldn't that be sexist?"

"After the world ends, you stop worrying about stuff like that, and people do whatever it is they do best. Nobody cares who kills dinner and who cooks it, as long as everybody eats. In case you haven't noticed, I'm not exactly built for hard physical labor. Not now, not fifty years ago."

The place they met in had once been a communal dining room and was still used for that, and for the occasional community meeting. Forty-seven people stood, sat, or lay around the room, ranging in age from an infant to a man older than Lulu. Old as she was, and bent as she was, Lulu still managed to climb onto a low table and wave her hands for quiet.

"Our guests are Major Alexis... Iskold?" She turned to the young brunette woman, who nodded. "Major Alexis Iskold. I've never met her before, but this man here, General Nicholas Angriff, I gave him a tour of this place the year I started here. That was 2014 or maybe early 2015. As I recall, you had a lot more entourage on that day, Nick."

There were smatterings of nervous laughter, but the people did the math and then inspected Angriff more closely. He didn't look like more than sixty years had passed.

"How he got to be here without aging a day, now that's a trick I want to hear about. But I promised I'd tell him about us first." Once she'd finished introducing the room full of people to Angriff and Major Iskold, she explained this was the core of those who kept the turbines running and the dam in the best repair they could. "We've run out of a lot of maintenance items and replacement parts," she said.

"We might be able to help with that."

A man in the audience spoke up. "Now you've got our attention!" Everyone laughed.

"Who is *we*?" said another.

"We'll get there, Julie," Repperton said. "But our story first." She turned to their visitors. "It's a long one," Lulu said. "You two might want to pull up a chair."

"Let me tell it," said the man who'd spoken up before. "I want you to get the whole story, not the part Lulu leaves out 'cause she's humble."

The man identified himself only as Docker. Although he was well past sixty, his voice had a deep and melodious texture over a heavy Southern accent, much like that of Shelby Foote, who Angriff remembered from a documentary about the Civil War. At its core, the story was the same as Creech's. When the Collapse began, people initially flocked to the big cities, where central authority seemed most likely to feed and shelter them. But when the food began to run out, so did the people.

The first sign of societal disintegration was the hyperinflation. When the Chinese stopped buying U.S. Treasury Bonds and sold off the debt they held at bargain prices, the dollar collapsed. Civil services such as the police, firefighters, and postal employees gradually quit going to work when a week's salary couldn't purchase a loaf of bread.

In Las Vegas, the casinos closed in the third week of May, about five weeks after the New Madrid fault let go. With no tourists, they had no reason to stay open. Unemployed workers with no way to feed their families then went hunting for the necessities of life, and with no police to stop them, the streets became a shooting gallery. Some teamed up with friends and neighbors to increase their firepower. The owner of a pawn shop that became famous because of a reality TV show tried to stop a looter from stealing an 18th century French Charleville musket, and took three rounds to the head for his troubles.

By the end of the year, Las Vegas had lost 90% of its population. Those still alive coalesced around various gangs that had the organization, numbers, and weapons to survive the early violence. Over the decades, things settled down so that four gangs divided up the territory. Trade began with outside entities. The cartel that took over the Mexican government traded them coffee, tobacco, tequila, fruits, and vegetables, as well as a laundry list of other things. In return they got guns, locally produced gunpowder, cooking utensils scrounged from the ruins, and various tools. The arrangement worked because Las Vegas had reverted to what it had been throughout most of history, a dusty spot in the middle of the desert with no resources and nothing to offer a conqueror.

Meanwhile, the staff at Hoover Dam that once numbered in the thousands fell to under one hundred, mostly engineers and technical people with no place else to go. Nobody knew how they would survive, although protein would never be a problem with Lake Mead so near at hand. Eventually a large force moved out from Las Vegas to overrun the dam and thereby control the most precious commodity left in the world, energy. Hoover Dam's turbines were still online.

Technicians and engineers weren't fighters. With hundreds of armed men on their doorstep, they saw no alternative to surrendering and begging for mercy. After all, without them, who would keep the electricity flowing? But one voice convinced the rest of them that it would be better to destroy the dam and die than to live on as slaves... the voice of Louise Repperton.

Angriff thought that even in her early thirties, Repperton must have been a formidable presence, despite being less than five feet tall and weighing no more than 80 pounds. She had grabbed a broom and placed herself in the road leading to the western side of the dam. A few brave engineers went with her, although they stood well in back.

The mob consisted of lean, hard men and women carrying every kind of weapon imaginable, from hatchets to automatic weapons. They eyed Repperton like a snake in a nest of newborn mice. Standing alone, she gave no hint of being bothered by them. Instead, she swept the road.

"I wish you could have seen her," Docker said with obvious awe. "David against a few hundred Goliaths, with the flagpole and Winged Figures of the Republic at her back. They tried to threaten her, but she laughed at them. They demanded she turn the dam over to them or they'd shoot her, and she laughed again. The whole road was planted with explosives and if they killed her, the others would blow them all to hell, she said, including the dam itself. I don't think they believed her, but who could be certain? She sure acted crazy. Besides, she told 'em, they didn't want the dam, they wanted the *power* the dam produced. Did they know how to run the machines?

"No, they said, so she worked it out where instead of them worrying about forcing the staff to keep running the dam to give them power, why didn't they just barter for it? There was plenty to go around and nobody had to get blown up. So that's what happened. For the next forty years, they brought us things like food, tobacco, tequila, coffee, and other stuff like that, and in return we kept the current flowing and one power line to Vegas in repair. That only ended a few years ago. It seems like the gangs have all killed each other off to the point where none of them need much power any more."

"Could we be that lucky?" Angriff said. A few people chuckled but most still looked at him like he was a dead man who'd risen from his own coffin.

"That's our story, General," Repperton said. "Now let's hear yours."

"I don't know if I can top y'all's, Lulu, but here goes. Way back in 1996, a scientist approached the American government with a technique for freezing a human being and then bringing them back to life later."

"You mean cryogenics?" This time a woman in the back spoke out.

"So you've heard of it?" Many people nodded. During the nine years between when he'd gone into Long Sleep and the Collapse had brought down the nation, much had happened in the way of technology for cryogenics. "Okay, that helps. So the plan was to—"

He stopped when the corporal in charge of their escort turned away and pressed his right hand against his ear, obviously listening to someone speaking through the transducer in his left ear. Then he wheeled and stalked to Iskold, whispering in her ear. Once he'd finished, she stepped forward to Angriff, leaning forward to speak into his ear.

"Sir, the regiment has made contact with a hostile force on the outskirts of Las Vegas."

He turned to her and spoke in a stage whisper. "Engaged?"

"Affirmative."

"Tell the corporal to inform Captain De Lorenzi we're coming up and to be ready to pull out immediately."

When he informed his audience that an emergency forced him to leave, there were howls of protest for him to finish the story first. Already half-turned away, he stopped and spoke over his shoulder. "This is the five second version," he said. "Twelve thousand volunteers went into cryogenic sleep and now we're back to rebuild the country."

#

Chapter 21

Break the skin of civilization and you find the ape, roaring and red-handed.
Robert E. Howard

North Dakota
0949 hours, April 25

"You're asking me to change everything we've been planning for decades on a whim."

Amunet Mwangi blinked several times to hide her consternation. Even though Györgi was the older of the Rosos brothers, and by far the nicer of the two, at times like this she wished she was dealing with Károly. He was the faster thinker and utterly ruthless.

"That's not what I'm doing, George, and you know it. I'm asking you to take advantage of a limited opportunity to accomplish everything we want on a greatly escalated schedule. We may never get a better chance for Overtime to fall into our laps than right now!"

Unlike Károly's slim figure and natural charm, Györgi Rosos was built like their father, tall and stout, and had a clumsiness about him that made it seem like he always said or did the wrong thing. To Mwangi's eye, he had the look of a dog that had had all the spirit beaten out it.

"I don't see how that differs from my original statement. My father put a plan in place and now you want me to toss that plan aside and make up one of my own."

STANDING BEFORE HELL'S GATE

"Károly flew to California and that wasn't part of the plan!"

"My father made that decision."

"Then let's ask him."

"He's unavailable."

She closed her eyes and paused to calm herself. "George, sometimes you have to take a chance."

"I'll tell you what, Colonel. I'll think about it."

North Central California
0951 hours, April 25

Long before the last of the rattlesnake slipped into the king snake's gullet, Green Ghost was asleep. Jane had agreed to take the first watch despite her own sleepiness, because a lifetime spent alone had given her the ability to semi-sleep, to rest while keeping her eyes open. It wasn't the same as sleep, but it helped. She spent the two hours eating and watching the king snake finish its breakfast before slithering away to sleep off such a huge meal. Every fifteen minutes or so, she made a circuit of the little hilltop, which was about twenty feet across, to make sure no threat approached them.

Two hours later, she awoke Green Ghost, as agreed. She laid down but couldn't sleep and sat back up. After chewing some jerked deer strips washed down with water, and despite the wan starlight, he picked up his M-4 and began to clean it.

"Why are you doing that?" she said. "You haven't shot it."

"It's a habit I picked up in Afghanistan. We called the dust there *moon dust* because it was like powder that got into everything and could cause your weapon to malfunction. The dust in this country is almost as bad as it was there. You never know when you'll need your weapon, or when a jam might cost you your life."

"Have you been to the moon?"

It took him a moment to realize that was a serious question. "No, that's just another expression."

"Oh... tell me about your rifle. What's all this extra stuff on it?"

"Everybody in the teams set their personal weapon up as they saw fit. Trial and error taught me how I liked mine set up, and I was lucky enough to smuggle it with me when I went cold—"

"I don't understand that, either, going cold. Is that the Long Sleep?"

"Which question do you want answered, the rifle or about going cold?"

"The rifle."

He propped the gun between his legs. "It's a standard M-4, with defense rails along the top and bottom. This allows me to attach any accessories I might need."

"I don't know that word. Is it another expression?"

"Accessories?"

"Yeah."

"Umm... no, it means extra things that help the gun work better, like this flashlight which I attached to its side. This one has a switch on top that lets me turn it on with my left hand, or switch from white light to infrared. Over here is an ergonomic grip that allows me to pull it in tighter when firing."

"Erg?"

"Ergonomic. Never mind, it's a grip that makes it easier for me personally to shoot the gun. I brought two sights, but this one's a red dot sight, meaning it puts a red dot where I'm aiming the gun."

"I saw one of those when I was a girl," she said, shaking her finger. "When I was a girl, someone my dad knew showed it to me. He only turned it on for a few seconds because batteries had become scarce by then, but I remember thinking how amazing that was."

"It's a big help, that's for sure. I tend to be rough on guns, so I put on a bigger bolt release. SEALs called it a ping-pong paddle."

"You lost me again... were those the Air Force people?"

"No, Navy. Look here, see how much bigger it is than a standard bolt? It makes it easier for me to load new magazines. I also upgraded to a larger charging handle, so that if I'm wearing gloves, there's less chance of my finger slipping off the handle."

"So bigger is better for you?"

He paused and stared at her for a full ten seconds, then continued as if he hadn't heard her. "This butt stock I added feels really good against my cheek and has storage for extra batteries, which I'm glad for now, because I have no idea when I might be able to recharge what I brought with me. Uh, oh, yeah, it also retracts like this for easier carrying."

He showed her how it worked. "If you look here at my rear sight, I really couldn't find one I liked, so I cut down the one on the carrying handle. That way, if something happened to my optics, my scope, I'd still have a front and rear sight. I can adjust my sling by moving this front ring forward or backward, because the rear attachment point is fixed. As to the sling itself, it took me about three years of service to finally decide which one I preferred. This one is thin and light, but very strong, and is easy to tighten in case I'm carrying it and need it close against my body. Let's see, is there anything else? I don't think so."

"You talk about that rifle like it's your lover."

"I've been in too many fights where the difference between life and death came down to a fraction of an inch or of a second. More times than I can count, things like changing a magazine half a second faster than the other guy put him underground and me standing on his grave."

Jane stood and dusted the seat of her pants. *I never knew a man could be so hard to flirt with,* she thought. *I wonder if he even likes women...*

#

Chapter 22

The challenge of the unknown future is so much more exciting
than the stories of the accomplished past.
Simon Sinek

Hoover Dam
1250 hours, April 25

As Hoover Dam had neared completion in 1936, a Norwegian immigrant named Oskar J.W. Hansen won a competition to design and install a sculpture on the dam's western approach. The result was the largest cast bronze figures up to that time, twin figures seated on jet-black rock whose wings point to Heaven, with a 147-foot flagpole between them.

Driving straight over the dam, Angriff turned in his seat to get a better look at Hansen's breathtaking creation. "Make a note, Major. Find the largest flag we've got and have a detail run it up that flagpole. And if it doesn't look big enough, see if we can manufacture something bigger."

The road rejoined Highway 93 and they sped west, knowing that the road should be in good repair. Boulder City was the first sizeable town they drove through, and the first abandoned place Angriff had seen. On both sides of the Great Basin Highway, as Highway 93 was called at that point, stood derelict fast food restaurants, a grocery with a caved-in roof, and parking lots with rusted cars stripped of anything salvageable. "It's like driving through a cemetery," he said.

Iskold hesitated before answering. "It's hard to believe that America is really gone."

"Yeah." His voice sounded far away. "Until you see this, then it's all too real."

With ruins flashing by on both sides, the company column passed a casino partially collapsed on one end, and then turned onto Interstate 11. Countless single family houses flanked both sides of the interstate. The lead Stryker made it into Henderson, approaching the intersection with Interstate 215, before seeing stopped vehicles ahead. The fuel tankers were at the rear and Angriff was gratified to see that Colonel Young had surrounded them with APCs and at least a company of infantry to ensure their safety. Moreover, the laager stood on solid ground, not an overpass that could be destroyed.

Angriff found Colonel Young standing next to the M1130 Stryker command vehicle with his staff. The M2 50-caliber machine gun on top rotated, looking for targets, as did the weapons systems on all the other vehicles.

"What've you got, Colonel?" he said.

"Our scouts cleared that intersection up ahead and waved the engineers forward to check it out for structural integrity. As they began to unload, unknown enemy forces opened fire from both sides of the road. Caught in a crossfire, they withdrew half a klick to assess the situation and call in reinforcements."

"Then what's that shooting I hear?"

"We don't know. Major Strootman has a theory that we got caught in the middle of an existing conflict between two opposing forces, each of whom thought we were allies of the other."

"That actually lines up with what I learned at Ma Kelly's and Hoover Dam. Las Vegas has gangs that have been fighting each other for control ever since the Collapse. Hard to believe they're still at it."

"Fifty years is a long time."

"Casualties?"

"Two, neither serious."

"Good."

"I've sent two dismounted companies to clear both sides of the highway, each supported by their own APCs and a platoon of Strykers. Once fire is lifted from our route of march, we'll move out to Nellis, set up a defensive perimeter, and assess the situation."

"Good work, Colonel."

Despite wearing sunglasses, Angriff squinted as sunlight reflected off the metal trucks and APCs like blinding lasers. Although it was still early in spring, the mid-afternoon sun left him sweating and licking his lips. The twin Desert Eagles hung heavy in their shoulder straps and what Angriff wanted more than anything else was to lead the infantry through the side streets beyond the interstate. He couldn't, and he knew it. He was the commanding general and, while he'd gone running off on a rescue mission as a three-star in Africa, even then it had been reckless and irresponsible in the eyes of the U.S. Army. Now, all he could do was stand in the rear and encourage his subordinates.

The shooting had become intermittent, until suddenly from the northeast side of the road there erupted automatic weapons fire, including the unmistakable woodpecker hammering of a 50-caliber machine gun followed by three rounds from the 30mm cannon of a Stryker Dragoon. Whoever was on the receiving end of that fusillade wouldn't be sticking around for more, unless they were already dead. A few more rifle shots followed, then silence. Before long, both companies sent reports back to Young over the radio, while Angriff listened in via his own headset.

"Charlie One, go for sitrep," Colonel Young said.

"Enemy dispersed and fleeing east. I intend to pursue half a klick and set up defensive perimeter to prevent renewed attacks as column passes by on the interstate. Following that, I intend to withdraw and follow the regiment as rear guard."

"Casualties"

"Negative on friendlies, two enemy dead. They're... they're kids. They can't be more than thirteen or fourteen."

Both Young and Angriff noticed the hitch in the woman's voice. "Charlie One, please maintain radio protocol."

At the mild rebuke, the voice steadied and grew stronger. "Enemy dead appear to be juveniles. Both have complex tattoos on arms and torsos. Will send photos following this message. Both are female, neither wearing shirts or shoes. Weapons appear to be civilian shotguns."

"Roger, Charlie One, Forest Green Out. Delta One, this is Forest Green, go for Delta One."

Only Delta One didn't respond, Delta Two did. The Delta Company commander had taken a high-caliber round through his left shoulder and was being worked on by the medics, but could the colonel send a full medical team right away? Delta Company had suffered no other casualties and counted three enemy dead. Like Charlie Company, there were no enemy wounded. Unlike Charlie, the enemy dead all appeared to be adults wearing pants, shoes, and shirts, firing semi-automatic rifles modified to full automatic. They were also heavily tattooed, with all of the wording in Spanish.

Once finished with the report, Young instructed Delta Two to also set up a perimeter long enough to ensure the convoy moved safely past the point of contact, and then to pull out their company.

"Three wounded in a minor firefight," Young said to Angriff. "Damn."

"Your people did a fine job out there today, Bob," Angriff said as he toasted the foot of his first cigar of the day. Somehow, in the twilight of a cooling April afternoon, it tasted better than it ever did in the confines of the Crystal Palace. The regiment deployed on the old runways, where they had clear fields of fire in all directions.

"Thank you, sir."

"We're alone. Call me Nick." With hostile forces potentially in the area, four guards had accompanied them, but they stood well out of listening range.

"Thank you, Nick."

"That's better."

"Have you seen the photos of those kids we killed today?"

"I have. That's depressing stuff. Girls with guns but no shoes or clothes, and neither one of them looked like they'd eaten for a while."

"They definitely needed some groceries."

"There's probably a lot more of that out there. But the other three haven't missed *any* meals."

"Whoever they were, they're definitely from two different groups warring with each other, probably over food."

Angriff nodded. There didn't seem to be anything else to say.

West of the runways, the hardened bunkers and parking aprons that once housed squadrons of F-15s, F-16s, F-22s, and F-35s stood empty, except for a few skeletal wrecks. Records for the battle against the Chinese invasion of California were virtually nonexistent in Overtime's databases, but it stood to reason that any Air Force units still fighting would have staged through Nellis and Creech. Some buildings showed signs of recent occupation, although most were in serious disrepair.

He nodded west. "I bought a book from the base exchange once. It was right over there. I think I was a lieutenant dead-heading home on leave, but that was a long time ago. You ever come through here?"

"I was in Vegas once with some friends and we lost most of our money on the strip, so we pooled what was left for a cab and came over here to the O-club to drink cheap. Those were good times."

"They were indeed." From where they stood, there was no sign of the strip, the fantasy land where architectural excess had stood in mute testimony to the glorification of chance. Instead, on the horizon in every direction stood mountains, like the walls of a giant fortress, while nearer at hand were the ubiquitous fast-food and coffee shops that characterized every 21st century American city. "We lost so much, Bob. How many billions of man-hours did it take to build the USA? How many untold trillions of dollars, how much blood was spilled defending it? And in the end it all fell apart... We were Rome. Some people tried to warn us, but just like the Romans, we didn't listen."

"I've used that very analogy myself, Nick."

"Yeah..." Angriff drew on the cigar until the ash blew off in a swirl of orange and gray. The regiment's encampment was three hundred yards down the runway. From where they stood on the empty asphalt, the only sound came from the hissing of a desert wind as it sprayed them with pebbles and dust.

Neither man spoke for the next minute. Instead, both officers were lost in thought until footsteps alerted them to someone coming their way — Majors Strootman and Iskold.

"Per your orders, Colonel, the updated operations plan is ready," Strootman said. Being the XO for the regiment, he had responsibility for all tactical planning involving its forces. Iskold was there to frame those tactical maneuvers into the mission objective as it pertained to the brigade as a whole, in this case delivering the food, fuel, and medical supplies to Sierra.

At Young's nod, he laid out the plans. One company had already been left behind to guard Hoover Dam and the bridge over the Colorado River, with orders to request a civilian engineer team with heavy equipment to do some repairs on the Mike O'Callahan-Pat Tillman Memorial Bridge. Two more companies would stay in the Las Vegas area, one to guard the airfield and simultaneously search for any salvageable military materials, while the other would secure the main interstate roadway through the city. In addition, in case there was further enemy contact, a platoon of M1129 Stryker mortar carriers, equipped with 120mm mortars, would be on hand for fire support.

Three companies would be left at Creech, along with the other two M1129 platoons from 1st Battalion. These would act as a reserve that could reinforce the companies to north or south quickly. The allotted tanker trucks would also be left at Creech.

The remainder of the regiment would push on into central and northern Nevada. Hawthorne Army Depot would be the next place to put one of 1st Battalion's two remaining companies, both to guard it and to take inventory. Reports from the scrapers who'd brought word of the critical situation at Sierra had also mentioned that Rednecks had overrun Hawthorne, and it was time to take it back. No forces would be left at Carson City unless conditions warranted it. The remainder of the regiment would skirt Reno and not enter the city proper, and would leave one company behind to secure the route. That left seven companies to push on to Sierra as escort for the remaining logistics vehicles.

"I'll look over the details before we pull out," Young said. "But on the surface, it sounds fine. General?"

"I agree. Good job, Major Strootman, Major Iskold."
Angriff stepped downwind and drew on the cigar so the
smoke wouldn't blow toward the others, then it occurred to
him that he hadn't offered one to Colonel Young. Reaching
under his jacket into the inside pocket, he withdrew one and
held it out. "I'm sorry, Bob, that was thoughtless of me.
Would like to join me in a—"

"Down!" The soldier deployed twenty yards to their left
was half-turned toward them while on one knee, and was
waving at them to get down. Something stuck out of the front
of his body armor — an arrow.

An Eagle filled Angriff 's hand without conscious thought
and he was on one knee in firing position before the others
even registered the situation. With his left hand, he jerked
Iskold down, too. "Draw your weapon, Major!"

"I don't have one!" she said.

His eyes narrowed into a stern frown. It was the same
look he'd given Cynthia when she took the family car without
permission and crumpled the front bumper against a street-
light. Young and Strootman had followed his lead, gotten
low, and drawn their pistols. All eight of them, the four
guards and the four officers, swept their weapons back and
forth looking for targets.

Scrub trees and creosote bushes pushed up through
cracks in the runway and provided cover for the bowman.
"Whoever shot that can't be more than fifty yards out."

"Contact on the left!"

Four rifles and three pistols swung in that direction and
fixed on a lone figure standing no more than forty yards from
where Angriff knelt. Shirtless, it was a young boy in his early
teens, holding a bow with an arrow already nocked and ready
to release. He was yelling something and slowly walking their
way.

The situation was really Colonel Young's to control, but
he would likely order his men to kill their attacker. In less
than a second, Angriff knew the boy would die and he hated
the very idea of that happening. "Hold your fire!" he yelled.
The boy immediately shifted aim to him and fired. Angriff
moved with the reflexes that had saved him countless times,
and the arrow whizzed past his ear, exactly where his forehead had been a second earlier.

The boy drew and nocked a third arrow with the smooth precision of long practice, but seemed confused who to target.

Angriff tried again. "Put the bow down, son! Nobody wants to hurt you!"

"Fuck off!" Again he fired at Angriff, not as close as last time, and Angriff knew the emotions he could hear in the boy's voice had thrown off his aim. But he'd gotten within twenty yards of the first soldier and it was reckless to let him simply keep firing. Eventually he'd score a severe hit on somebody, so despite the nauseous twisting of his stomach at having to give the order, he didn't flinch from doing it.

"Bring him down!" There was no caveat about shooting to wound. That was only in movies; in real life that got people killed. But that didn't mean the men themselves wanted to blow away some pimple-faced kid who should have been in junior high school. Within a second of each other, the guards all fired at once, and without prior agreement they all shot at the right shoulder. Two rounds barely nicked the skin and one went completely under the armpit. Only the fourth round scored a clean hit.

In the reverse of what might seem like logic, the closer such a high-velocity round was to its target, the worse the wound it produced. As the range increased, with the standard M-16 round, the fragmentation of the bullet after impact went down as terminal velocity decreased.

At that range, the 5.56-millimeter round, traveling at 3,110 feet per second, should have blown out half of the boy's shoulder. As it was, it struck with terrible effect and left an exit wound the size of a nickel, although on a grown man it would have been much worse. But the boy was thin to the point of emaciation. His musculature wasn't as developed as a man's would be and so offered less resistance. Moreover, an M-16 bullet only began breaking apart after penetrating four or five inches of tissue, depending on the density. His shoulder wasn't thick enough and the existing tissue was softer than might be expected, so the bullet passed through without disintegrating.

Regardless, it did the trick.

The boy spun to his right and fell backward, dropping the bow. Lying on his back, he writhed and stamped his feet against the runway in agony. Angriff's first impulse was to run to the boy and begin first aid, but he resisted. Unlike Nipple the year before, during the Battle of the Highway, Colonel Young's men would probably not push him out of the way if they were better suited to treat the boy, and however well-intentioned he might have been, Angriff wasn't the right man to keep the boy alive. So he forced himself to stay back and let the others work. The first soldier reached the boy's side within seconds.

But the boy didn't want help. Instead, he clawed at the face of the soldier kneeling beside him, still screaming, and when Angriff drew close enough he could understand the boy's words.

"You killed Mina... I'm gonna kill you... you killed Mina..."

As he scratched and lunged at the Americans, blood poured from his shoulder. The other infantrymen knelt and held him down, and the first man pulled a bandage from his own first aid kit and pressed it against the wound. Still, unless he quit squirming before the medical team got there, nothing they did would matter.

The person who saved his life was Major Iskold. Angriff thought of her as quietly efficient although not assertive, but with the boy's blood spreading across the concrete, she knelt on the boy's left side. Using her left hand, she combed tangled brown hair away from his forehead and whispered a soft *ssshhh*. His wide eyes fixed on hers and she didn't look away.

"We're not here to hurt you. Now lie still so we can stop the bleeding."

His face had grown pale and his skin clammy. Even standing eight feet away, Angriff could see the signs of shock setting in. But her words and soothing tone had an instant effect. The boy stopped wiggling and stared at her like she was his mother.

Slowly, Iskold held out her right hand, palm up. "Morphine."

When, seconds later, her hand remained empty, she stroked the boy's cheek before looking up with a beatific smile. "That's an order." Her tone might have been inviting them to eat a slice of sponge cake, but the underlying menace was clear to all. Within seconds, two battlefield injectors appeared in her palm. She set one of them on the narrow, panting chest and injected the other one into his right upper arm.

The drug rapidly took effect. After the boy calmed, Iskold's hands moved with the sureness of a surgeon. First she told the man applying direct pressure on his Israeli bandage to keep it up, then, as gently as she could, she requested a second bandage and slid it under the exit wound. She then ordered the soldier applying pressure to increase it enough so that the shoulder pressed flat against the underlying bandage. After checking the patient's breathing again, shallow and rapid, and then extremity capillary reactions, sluggish, Iskold was thinking about how to move the boy to the regimental medical team when running footsteps alerted them all that the medics were on scene.

After briefing them, she stood back up and rejoined the officers. Blood covered her hands and forearms. A long strand of brown hair had escaped the bun at the back of her neck and fell over her face until she moved it. Dark armpits showed where sweat stained her shirt.

"Nice work, Major," Angriff said. One lifted eyebrow was his way of displaying a changed opinion of his heretofore quiet and reserved officer.

"Thank you, General. Permission to accompany the boy?"

"Granted." She turned to leave but he stopped her. "One thing, Major. If you get a chance, find out why he tried to commit suicide and if we should expect any more attacks."

"Roger that."

#

Chapter 23

With a kiss, let us set out for an unknown world.
Alfred de Musset

Overtime Prime 2nd Level Mess Hall
1314 hours, April 25

Nikki put her tray down across the table from Morgan and slid into the chair. Her sister — it was still hard to think of Morgan as her sister — had half a salad left, which was odd; Morgan was an omnivore, but with strong carnivorous leanings. And unlike her usual cup of coffee, she had a glass of milk.

Milk?

"What's with the healthy routine?" Nikki said.

Morgan didn't answer her question directly. "You look rode hard and put away wet."

Nikki tried to keep a straight face but couldn't. A grin cracked the façade. "Rode hard for damned sure."

Instead of a bawdy response, however, Morgan reached over and patted her hand. The smooth skin of her flawless cheeks sagged. "I'm very happy for you, Nikki. I really am."

"Joe's gonna be fine, Morgan. You'll see. They're both gonna come walking out of that desert any minute now, and then you can give him all kinds of hell for scaring you like this."

"I won't give him hell."

Nikki didn't explain that she'd been kidding about that. She also had a strange intuition that something else was bothering her sister, strange because she'd never felt empathy for people before very recently and wasn't sure how you dealt with that kind of thing. "So... I'm not very good at this big sister stuff, but is there something else bothering you?"

Morgan turned to pay attention to several mechanics from her battalion who came into the mess hall, seemingly fascinated with them. "You're going to be an aunt."

<hr />

Operation Comeback
1449 hours

Corporal Duglach knocked on General Schiller's door and stuck his head in after being answered. "That Glide woman wants to talk to you, sir."

Schiller's chin rested in his left hand as he leaned on the desktop, reading a sheaf of papers. Without speaking or taking his eyes off the reports, he used his right hand to wave permission for her to enter. He saw her come in with his peripheral vision but didn't look her way until he'd finished reading the memorandum on the top of the paper pile.

Schiller was punctilious about military decorum and so didn't know to react to Glide. She wore a tight black T-shirt that allowed every feature of her upper body to show through in outline. Not just her breasts, which is where most men's eyes went, but also the taut shoulder and abdominal muscles that showed her top physical condition. Old style Israeli camouflage uniform pants and boots completed her uniform, with a British SA80A2 rifle slung over her left shoulder and a Jericho 941 chambered in .45 ACP in a holster under her right armpit. A Kabar Marine knife hung from her belt.

"Yes?" he said. Like most men, he found her incredibly attractive, but unlike most men his disinterested façade never slipped. Over the years, he'd been compared to an automaton, or a robot. Little did those people know how far from the truth that really was.

"I think trouble is coming," she said. He was still having trouble getting used to her thick Israeli accent. "There is great resentment in many people who remain loyal to General Steeple. They believe it is he who should be in charge, not you and not General Angriff."

That got his full attention. "Oh? Is there open talk of mutiny?"

"Kanir'e shelo," she said in Hebrew, and then switched back to English. "Probably not, at least not yet. Frosty and I have made ourselves well known and conversations end when we are seen. But such talk is not far under the surface."

"Thank you for informing me of these developments... err, Glide."

"Do you have your personal weapon, General?"

"It's right here in my desk."

"Since I am in charge of Security here, I must ask you to wear it at all times. What type of weapon is it?"

"A Beretta M9."

"That's a good weapon. If you feel you need more, please let me know."

"If I feel that I need more than that, we are both in a lot of trouble."

Glide stared at him for a few seconds before pivoting and leaving. Schiller picked up the papers to read from where he'd left off, but found it hard to concentrate. After trying for a few minutes, he opened the bottom right drawer and placed his Beretta on the desk top. It had been at least a month since he'd cleaned it, and though he hadn't fired it since then, Schiller believed that all machines and tools needed maintenance whether they'd been used or not. He released the magazine and then ejected the round from its chamber. "Corporal Duglach, please bring me a pistol cleaning kit."

He also needed to find the practice range.

#

CHAPTER 24

Ceasar forgave his enemies,
Rather than cut them down;
They repaid his generosity
By planting him in the ground.
Oscar O'Connor, from 'Forgiveness can be fatal.'

Astride old New Mexico Highway 4, two miles south of Jemez
Pueblo
1524 hours, April 25

Johnny Rainwater passed the out-of-breath rider a cup of water and waited for him to drink it before pressing for details. The boy, Jimmy Two Trees, was young, it was true, and prone to exaggeration. Rainwater had known that when he'd included Jimmy in the patrols, but the teenager was an excellent rider with an outstanding horse, and in the face of the threat moving toward them, he needed every resource he could find. Besides, exaggeration was one thing and sheer terror another, and Jimmy Two Trees was terrified.

"Feeling better?" he said when Jimmy passed him the empty cup. He then dipped it into the water bucket and gave some water to the horse.

"I'm sorry, Johnny."

"Don't be sorry, just tell me what you saw."

"They're in Albuquerque, thousands and thousands of 'em. Got horses and cars and trucks and guns and anything you can think of."

"Were they on the move?"

"Huh-uh. Lots of men riding off everywhere, but it looked like most of 'em were camped."

"Good, Jimmy, good. This is very helpful. Did you see Tokar? I sent her down there, too."

"No," Jimmy said, shaking his head so hard that sweat droplets sprayed off the ends of his long black hair. "I'd have known her if I saw her."

"All right, Jimmy, you've done good. You get on back home and get Mottle bedded down and fed, then get yourself something to eat."

As the boy rode off to the north, Rainwater climbed a boulder beside the highway and cupped his right hand to shade his eyes. It was pointless; he couldn't see Albuquerque from the mountaintops on either side of the valley that led to Jemez Springs. He did it anyway, hoping for some hint as to how long he had to get ready before the hordes of hell were upon him.

The free community of Shangri-La sprawled in the small valleys and mountains surrounding Jemez Springs, the miraculous warm water pools that bubbled up from deep underground. Pre-Collapse archaeology had dated the first human settlements in the area to 2,500 B.C., the time of the building of the Great Pyramids in Egypt. Migrants through the area had built large numbers of pueblos, multi-story adobe houses, which eventually ran to a housing potential of 30,000 or more. When the Collapse had destroyed the United States, an experienced survivalist and off-grid homesteader named Winston Ballinger, who'd been familiar with the Jemez Springs area, had gone there and established a last outpost of American democracy.

Over the years, Shangri-La had attracted a large number of survivors who pledged to obey the only rule for admittance to the community: loyalty to the letter and spirit of the Constitution and Bill of Rights of the United States. With no enemies who could invade the well-defended valleys, the settlement had grown and prospered over the decades, until Johnny Rainwater had more than 3,000 people for whom he was responsible.

Hundreds of them had already gathered at the Roman-style amphitheater cut from the living rock of a mountain on the western side of the valley through which old New Mexico Highway 4 ran. Near the pools of hot water that gave Jemez Springs its name, the inhabitants called it *the True*, which was a bastardization of *teatru*, the Latin word for theater which Ballinger had originally named it. After years of fighting for proper pronunciation, he'd finally given up. The True it was and would forever be.

The cut-stone stage doubled as a speaker's dais for group meetings, trials, elections, and the like. Much like the Clam Shell at Operation Overtime, rows of stone bench seats marched up the eastern face of the mountain, with room for at least five hundred people. Another two hundred could stand at ground level below the stage.

Rainwater greeted everyone who entered but kept his demeanor serious. As much as he personally wanted to get into the field and eject the Sevens from their lands, being the leader meant that he had to consider all possibilities for the people he led, including whether they should defend Shangri-La at all. He knew how they'd answer that question, of course. They'd spent decades readying for this very moment and felt confident in their defenses. But this time, the Sevens had come in much greater strength than anyone had ever anticipated they could.

Ten others joined Rainwater on the rostrum, the elected representatives of the ten tribes, tribes being used in the ancient Roman sense of the word. The citizens were equally and arbitrarily divided ten ways to elect one man or woman to represent them in debates and in the enacting of laws. If it came to a tie, it was up to Rainwater, as the elected president, to break it.

When citizens filled most of the seats and the angle of the sun suggested there were less than three hours of daylight left, Rainwater nodded to a large woman standing below the rostrum. She lifted a dented bugle and blew three shrill blasts. The chatter of the crowd died off.

Rainwater lifted his arms to quiet the few people still talking. "Friends, time is short, so listen to me. The day we have prepared for has come. The Sevens have a large army at Albuquerque and we must decide what to do, whether to stay and defend our homes, or flee and wait for them to leave. I have already sent the Ready Guard south to warn us of imminent attack, and to block all roads and passes leading to Shangri-La, so we have a brief time to discuss what to do in the face of this crisis. What say you?"

In the raucous manner of their typical debates, people shouted over each other for a full minute, getting out their energy before lapsing into a moderated discussion. Rainwater listened closely to the yells. His personal instinct was to fight. The people of Shangri-La had spent five decades and countless man-hours constructing clever defenses for their special sanctuary. Simply abandoning it without a fight seemed unconscionable... and yet Johnny Rainwater, the president, knew that standing and fighting could lead to the massacre of his entire people.

The debate went back and forth for more than an hour before Rainwater decided the time had come to vote. "Any questions before the decision is cast?"

One person stood, but when she did the entire gathering quieted. Reddish-brown skin stretched over her small, bony framework, like animal hide dried too long in the sun. Rainwater waited for the final murmurs to end before addressing her.

"'Máá ba'litso," he said, using her native tongue, Jacarilla Apache. It meant *Mother Wolf*, a sign of the universal respect she held within Shangri-La. "I would hear your words on this subject."

No one knew exactly how old Mother Wolf was. Some said eighty, some said a hundred, and some said even older than a hundred, but everyone agreed she'd been past her youth when the Collapse had come. Regardless, her back was as ramrod straight as if she were twenty, and her brown eyes darted this way and that, missing nothing. She rarely spoke. When she did, mothers hushed their children so as not to miss her soft words.

"Peace is not possible with enemies at your door," she said. "Unless you are prepared to give up the sun."

Then she sat down again.

Discussion was over. Rainwater knew it and so did everyone else in attendance. So powerful were the old woman's words that he felt the vote might be unanimous. The way it worked was that the ten tribes would tally their own votes and then pass the result on to their elected representative on the stage, quaintly named Tribunes by Ballinger when he'd set up the refuge, very much like the old voting system of the Roman Republic except without a Senate.

As Rainwater had suspected, it was unanimous: the people of Shangri-La would fight for their homes and either win or die.

#

CHAPTER 25

But not all men seek rest and peace; some are born with the spirit of the storm in their blood.
Robert E. Howard

Northern California
1749 hours, April 25

They left an hour before sunset.

"Bring me up to date," Green Ghost said. "What did those people tell you?"

"I wondered if you'd ever ask. I thought maybe you were just following me."

Again he gave her the look she'd come to expect, deadpan expression followed by blinking. Only this time he said something. "Let's save the repartee for after the mission, okay?"

She wasn't sure what *repartee* meant, but it sounded promising. "Okay. Those people said they had a homestead near a place called Cascade Creek. Their family had lived there since before the Collapse. What did they call it? Living off the grid? Does that make sense?"

"Yeah, it meant living without electricity or cell phones or anything like that... some people called them survivalists and made fun of them."

"I guess they found out who was right. Anyway, three couples lived there. The younger couple had seven children and the two couples you saw had four more who were grown, three boys and a girl. Everything worked well because they'd been there so long. They even had a family cemetery under a big tree. When the Chinese came, most of them moved farther north, but the Chinese mostly stayed around Los Angeles and to the south, until San Francisco asked the Chinese to come in and run their city."

"Wait, they *wanted* the Chinese to run San Francisco?"

"Sure... everybody knows that."

"Go on."

"They never moved too far inland, but kept close to the coast. A few years ago, they started sending scouts into the mountains and forests of the north, and of course you know what happened when they went after Sierra. Five days ago... no, wait, six days ago, the Chinese showed up at their homestead without warning. A convoy of trucks carried soldiers who told them they no longer owned the homestead, that it now belonged to the People's Republic of California—"

"That still sounds like somebody's making it up."

"And then this big man showed up wearing a uniform. He said his name was Adder and anybody who didn't like being part of the PRC had fifteen minutes to leave. They couldn't take any animals except one horse for each wagon, nor could they take any food. The only weapons they were allowed were the homemade ones. Everybody was determined to get out, but then Adder laughed and said the younger adults had to stay and work for the Chinese. When the older couples heard this, they changed their mind and wanted to stay, too, except now Adder wouldn't let them. He said they'd have to take their chance out in the mountains. They begged me to help the ones left behind and I said I'd go see what I could do. Then I sent them on to Lake Tahoe. I've got a friend there who will take them in."

"Damn. How far is it to Cascade Creek?"

"I don't know exactly. We could make better time during the day, but I don't know how far north Chinese patrols might have come."

"We kicked their ass pretty bad last week."

"How will they react to that?"

"I wish I knew."

#

156

Chapter 26

Only the impossible has any real charm; the possible has been vulgarized by happening too often.
Clark Ashton Smith

Nellis Air Force Base, Las Vegas, Nevada
2128 hours, April 25

Angriff lay on his bunk, reading. Twilight had darkened into full night and the only light in the tent came from his tablet, which he held a foot from his face with his right hand. The glow of the device's e-reader mode cast shadows over his rugged features and, in his mind's eye, he imagined that he made a frightening noir pastiche, like some grotesque villain in a story about the Shadow. He tucked his left hand under the back of his head.

He'd been devouring the book for the better part of an hour, a rare chance to relax and forget the world, and *Voices of the Dead* by John Babb was exactly the kind of thing he loved, well-researched historical fiction. It was set in Memphis, Tennessee, during the yellow fever epidemic of 1878, and since the twins had been born and raised in Memphis, he'd been trying to learn more about the city. He tried not to think about its ultimate fate.

Beside his outside tent flap hung a small square of wood for visitors to knock on. After two loud knocks his orderly, Kiki, put his head in. "Sorry to disturb you, General."

"It's fine, Kiki. Is it Kona?"

"No, sir, somebody found an old shoe with lots of holes and she's been chewing that for the last half hour."

"I had a German shepherd once before, right after Mrs. Angriff and I got married, named Mack. He was a big boy, ate the linoleum floor in our kitchen... sorry, what's going on?"

"Major Iskold would like to speak with you, sir."

"Gimme a minute to put my pants on."

He clicked on the battle lamp next to his bunk. In addition to his ACU pants, he put the shirt on over his T-shirt and pulled on his boots, including socks, and tied them. Although not a marionette like Steeple, Angriff figured if you were going to wear part of your uniform, you might as well wear the whole thing.

"Send her in, Kiki."

Even in the dim lighting, he could see the dark blotches where blood stained her uniform, and the deep lines in her face. He'd always thought of her as young, but now he realized she was older than he'd first thought. "You look tired, Alexis."

"I am, sir, and after this I'm headed for my sleeping bag, but I wanted to update you on the boy."

Angriff nodded, then nodded again, before realizing she probably couldn't see him well enough to see the gesture. "Go ahead."

"His name is Nera. He's part of what I gather are the remnants of a family or tribe here in Las Vegas. From what I could gather, all of the adults are dead and other tribes, gangs, families, it's hard to tell exactly what the power structures are... all of the adults are either dead or badly injured. His tribe are called Zentinis."

"Why does that name sound familiar?"

"It did to me, too, so I pulled it up from the command computer. Giovanni Zentini was a West Coast Mafia boss who rose to power in the twenty-teens, and there were rumors he was involved in the drug trade in Nevada."

"So the kid is the grandson of a Mafia boss?"

"No idea, sir. He drifted in and out of consciousness. I got the impression there's at least three other families or tribes out there, but the only one he named he called simply the Russians."

"Do we know why he was shooting arrows at us?"

She looked down. "His sister was one of the girls with the shotguns. He blames us for killing her."

"Did we?"

"It's hard to tell without an autopsy. I think the kids had invaded Russian territory looking for food or weapons when they were discovered and chased back to their own part of the city, which includes Nellis. The Zentinis are expecting a Russian attack and don't have the weapons to fight them off any more."

"Thus the bow and arrows?"

"Maybe, but I got the impression that Nera prefers a bow."

"Huh. Makes you wonder if maybe he knows something we don't. Anything else?"

"That's it."

"Let's hope those Russians don't pick tonight. It's been a long day and I could use the sleep."

———

Near Cascade Creek, California
0415 hours, April 26

Another bright night gave all the illumination needed to crawl close to their objective. From where he crouched in the tree line, Green Ghost could see the entire compound spread out before him, six structures, two of which appeared to be barns and another was clearly the chicken coop. A goat wandered around the buildings, while he could see cows on the far side of the cleared space, some two hundred yards away.

He only saw one guard, seated at the entrance to what appeared to be the main house. Because the guard was leaning back against the wall, Green Ghost thought he was asleep and a quick look through his scope verified it. But he hadn't brought the silencer for his M-4 with him when he'd parachuted into Sierra, and shooting the guard would wake up everyone else.

Leaning close to Jane's ear, he cupped hands to keep his whisper from traveling and being overheard. "The prisoners should be in the big house. I think the guards are in the other one, to our left. I'll take out the guard, then we both go in and I'll clear the house. Do you understand?"

She nodded.

The guard was about thirty yards away from their position. Green Ghost held his personal sidearm, a Sig Sauer 1911 which he'd also brought with him from the old days, in his left hand, and drew the Marine Ka-Bar fighting knife from its sheath with his right. Without NVGs, he inspected the ground by moon and starlight, looking for holes, rocks, or sticks that might cause sound. Then he carefully moved out in a crouch, stopping every five feet or so to make sure he hadn't missed any obstacles.

With only ten feet left, he re-holstered the pistol and covered the last ten feet in one surge. The guard was sleeping and never felt Ghost's hand cover his mouth, or the tip of the knife slice through the left side of his neck and sever both the jugular vein and carotid artery. The man struggled as blood poured from the wound, but only for a few seconds, then he slumped to the ground. Green Ghost noticed that he was young and appeared to be Latino. He knew in his mind the term 'Chinese' had become a nationality and not a race, but only then did it sink in.

After wiping his knife blade on the dying man's uniform, he re-sheathed it and brought his rifle to the ready at his shoulder, switching on the IR sight as he did so. Waving Jane forward, he waited for her to join him and then pushed open the door to the house. The rusty hinges squealed, but Green Ghost had been taught long before that one long noise indicated confidence opening the door, like the person opening it belonged inside, whereas hesitation trying to minimize the squeal meant an effort at stealth and probably an enemy.

He let Jane enter first while he covered the door to the other building, the one where he suspected the guards were sleeping. As he knelt in the doorway, Green Ghost heard muffled voices behind him, then shuffling and rustling. Despite the chill of the early morning air, he felt sweat trickling down his temples and the back of his neck. Like most special ops veterans, he had a built-in stopwatch in his brain that kept accurate track of the passing of time. Eventually another guard would exit the building he believed they were in, and he wanted as much distance between those people and his as possible. But it was only after three minutes had dragged by that he started to actually worry. Then he felt a light tap on his shoulder.

"Ready," Jane whispered.

He nodded and stepped aside, the muzzle of his M-4 never leaving the doorway. Behind him, six distinct footstep patterns preceded a blur of people exiting the house and turning left to sprint toward the trees. One person, it sounded like a man, stumbled and cursed, but no other guards came to investigate. Then in his peripheral vision, he saw the outline of Junker Jane on his left. He felt her lips brush his ear and it felt like an electric current ran through his body.

"When I get to the trees, I'll cover you."

"Go!" he said in a hush, as much to stop the distraction of her being so near as anything else.

She made it safely to the edge, and he could barely make out the outline of her kneeling and pointing her rifle. He knew he should leave immediately, but there was one more thing he had to do first. It was distinctly irresponsible and he knew it, but the impulse was too much to fight. Drawing his knife again, he dipped the tip in the dead guard's congealing blood and, using it like ink with a quill pen, wrote something beside the doorway. The whole time he expected to feel the burn of a bullet sizzling into his back. Once finished, he again put rifle to his shoulder and backed out in the *ready* position.

"What was that all about?" Jane said.

"I'll tell you later. Let's get out of here."

#

CHAPTER 27

The true nature of evil is it is so very casual.
James St. James

Malibu, California
0631 hours, April 26

Károly Rosos yawned and let the incoming tide lap at his toes. Deep blue tinged with purple still blurred the western horizon, but as much as he hated getting up this early, it beat the hell out of North Dakota. The clear water washed sand off his toes, reminding him of the days of his childhood before he'd become old enough to worry about his father's operations.

"Mr. Rosos!" He turned. The teenage boy assigned to see to his needs bounded toward him across the beach, holding the satellite phone. What was the kid's name? He couldn't remember and then forget about it; his name didn't matter.

"This had better be important," Rosos said, even though he knew it had to be. Only two people could call him on the sat. phone, his father and his brother. Neither would do so without urgent cause.

Trembling, the boy handed him the phone and stood waiting for further orders. When Rosos scowled at him, the boy ran back inside. Rosos laughed, rose, and let waves lap over his toes. "Károly here," he said into the phone.

"Is Adder with you?"

"Good morning, brother. How nice of you to call."

"Cut the shit. This is important."

"I assumed that when you called me."

"Angriff is gone."

Rosos had been walking in the surf, but that brought him to a stop. "What exactly does that mean?"

"Angriff has left Overtime to inspect some air force base, which gives us a narrow window to get Steeple back into power there."

"I need details, Györgi. Take a breath and tell me everything."

As succinctly as he was able, Györgi outlined the situation for his brother, and the plan he and Mwangi had hurriedly come up with. Karoly and Adder would load the Gulfstream with as many Chinese troops as they could and immediately fly to the repaired airfield outside Prescott, Arizona. Once there, they would be met by someone named McComb, who would smuggle them into Overtime, at which time they would join General Steeple and effect a coup.

"What about Fleming?"

"Apparently he's in northern California. That battle week before last? He was there."

"Fascinating... it's a bold plan, brother, not like you at all."

"Fuck off, Karoly. We've already lost three days." He didn't say that part of that delay was his fault. "Just do it."

"I think it's an excellent plan, but I'm going to make one change. There's no reason for me to go. I'm no soldier, and it leaves one more space for someone who is."

"Afraid you might wrinkle your pants?"

"That's always a concern," Rosos said. "When do we expect Angriff back?"

"Nobody knows, so you need to hurry."

"Right... but Adder just left for some place up north. I'll have to get him back before we can do anything. But you know, this could work. I'm proud of you, brother."

"Like I said, fuck off."

"Now that I think about it, I'll go second. It never hurts to personally manage affairs."

"How's California?"

"Cold and wet. Might as well be in North Dakota."

"Fuck off."

#

CHAPTER 28

*We write our names in the sand; then the waves roll in and
wash them away.*
Augustus Caesar

1 mile west of Sanders, AZ
0852 hours, April 26

Far to the east of Angriff's column, a second line of vehicles idled on old Interstate 40 beside a sign that tilted to the left. Rusty holes in the green face showed where bullets had ripped through the metal at some time in the past, but the letters could still be read: SANDERS, with an arrow pointing right.

Standing in the turret of his LAV-25, with the visor of his Integrated Helmet Protection System flipped up, Captain Martin Sully scanned a pair of silos half a mile away. The IHPS had been the last generation of helmets designed for the army and drastically increased protection for the head, but Overtime didn't have many. As a reward for their suicidal stand the year before, Dog Company had received a full complement from the limited supply available.

Scaffolding surrounded both silos. A road passing over Interstate 40, with another green sign that pointed to an off-ramp and read ST. JOHNS, had collapsed, partly blocking the highway. Sully saw no signs of life.

The line of vehicles which comprised Dog Company, First Marine Recon Battalion, First Marines, better known as Task

Force Kicker, stood parked behind him on both shoulders of Interstate 40. To the south stretched empty desert, while to the north a second line of armored fighting vehicles marched into the distance like paving stones.

All of the AFVs were shut down to save fuel, which also shut down the heaters. Sully never showed emotion or discomfort, he considered it bad leadership, but even through his helmet he could hear the grumbling from his crew. Temps the night before dipped into the low thirties and in April the days didn't warm up until later in the morning. Chill lingered in the metal shell and they hadn't driven far enough to warm it up. But Sully wasn't going to be rushed into reconnoitering an unknown urban environment because of some minor nuisance, even such a small town as Sanders had once been.

Finally, having given the point time to trip any ambushes or locate any IEDs, he flipped down the microphone. "Crank 'em up, Dog Company. We're a long way from anywhere, so stay alert. Don't crowd the MARSOCs but stay close enough for immediate support. First Platoon, take the lead" Flipping a switch took him off the company's comm. network and into the LAV's intercom. "Stiggers, I want to go in after Second Platoon. Keep your eyes open."

Two Marine reconnaissance companies represented a tremendous amount of firepower, but it didn't take long before Sully realized that Sanders was a ghost town. The Marines cleared every building looking for signs of recent life. They found a few old fires and a lot of snakes, but nothing more. Only on the far northern fringe did the Marines discover signs of recent human activity, in the form of horses' hoofprints, at least a dozen and probably more. The best guess was that they were several days old.

Sully parked on a low ridge on the east side of town and watched the two companies work. Scouts had gone ahead to check out the Querino Canyon bridge.

Noon was still an hour and a half away when the commander of First Platoon, Lt. Onni Hakala, pulled up next to him and got out of his Humvee. "The tracks lead off to the northwest, Captain. No sign of who made them."

"Nothing to indicate Rednecks?"

"No. Could be anybody."

165

STANDING BEFORE HELL'S GATE

Sully nodded. "And the town?"

"It's dead, Captain. Nobody's lived here for a long time."

"Makes you wonder, doesn't it?"

"I don't follow."

"Where'd they all go? From the looks of it, at least a couple of hundred people lived here. What happened to them? Did the Sevens come through here? Some other bandits? Some kind of plague?"

"Plague? Now you're making me nervous, Marty."

"Sorry, Onni, I didn't mean to. I was just thinking out loud. Well, forget that, we're moving east and don't need to worry about lines of supply right now. I'm going to give both companies forty-five minutes' rest and then we're outta here."

"You think that Idaho Jack guy was dealing straight on where we can find Shangri-La?"

"I don't know. I'd like to think so, but that's not our mission. We're out here to collect data on the oil pumping and refining facilities, and now it's time to move east. If we find Shangri-La, that's gravy."

\#

CHAPTER 29

They who dream by day are cognizant of many things which escape those who dream only by night.
Edgar Allan Poe

Creech Air Force Base
1531 hours, April 26

Turning off the highway and driving through the front gate of Creech Air Force Base, the difference between the grounds there and the ruins they'd driven through for the past three hundred miles struck Angriff as dramatic. It wasn't the vegetation, which was overgrown with only sparse grass left in former lawns and opportunistic shrubs and cacti growing in its place, nor the condition of the roads where potholes and cracks made drivers pay attention. To him it was buildings, where some of the roofs showed signs of repair and doors hung straight in their doorways, and most of the glass remained in the windows.

When his Humvee rounded a corner and entered the tarmac, he saw two lines of people standing at attention in front of three Comanches. Vehicles from the previous column that had brought the paratroops were scattered around the vast space of the hangars and runway.

General Kando was easily recognized in the front rank by his worn and mismatched Air Force uniform, and the gray hair rimming his dark face. Angriff's Humvee stopped near the man and he stepped out and shook hands, blinking as dirt got into his eyes. Building clouds in the west spawned wind gusts that blew sand and dirt across the concrete, which prompted Angriff to suggest moving the welcomes inside.

Moving past the parked Comanches as their crews stood to attention, he stopped beside *Tank Girl.* For a few seconds, he stared at the big helicopter, then walked over to say hello to the two lieutenants standing beside her. As he approached, they held their salutes and became even more rigid.

Returning their salute, he put out his hand. "At ease, Lieutenant... Wang?"

"Yes, sir. And this is my co-pilot, Lieutenant Pra Sakoya."

"Take good care of this Comanche, Lieutenant. It's a vital asset."

"We will, General and — I believe I speak for Lieutenant Sakoya — we really hope Captain Randall and Lieutenant Carlos are found soon, alive and well."

"We all do, Lieutenant, but thank you." He saluted and rejoined Kando.

Once Angriff was out of earshot, Sakoya elbowed Wang. "You are such a damned liar."

"What did you want me to say? Hey, General, your son-in-law was overrated and the squadron's better off with me flying his bird?"

"At least that would have been honest."

"Yeah, and we'd have been shoveling horse shit for the mounted regiment."

"Don't include me in your vendettas, Ted. I happen to like Joe and Bunny."

"Carlos is okay, but Randall? He's an arrogant prick."

Sakoya shook her head and walked off. "You should know."

Angriff followed Kando through the door and immediately saw a first sergeant in a dirty uniform standing at attention.

"At ease, Top," he said, and stopped. "What's your name?"

"Wardlaw, sir. Permission to ask the general a question?"

"Granted."

"The man Green Ghost... is he really a colonel?"

The question took Angriff aback. "Why do you ask?"

"If he is, sir, then I owe him an apology. If he's not, then I need to report someone for impersonating an officer."

"I see. To answer your question, yes, Top, he's a full colonel. He's also our S-5, in charge of security for the entire brigade. Will there be anything else, Sergeant?"

"No, sir."

"Then carry on."

Angriff resumed walking, but had to crack half a smile when behind him he heard someone say, "I told you so. You owe me twenty bucks if we ever use money again."

He'd taken five steps when another sergeant stood to attention, one he recognized. The name on her uniform read *Rossi*. "At ease, Sergeant Rossi. Aren't you Captain Randall's crew chief?"

"Yes, General—"

"You and your people did amazing work getting that C-5 operational in such a short period of time. Because of your knowledge and efforts, the brigade won a great victory, instead of suffering a catastrophic defeat. There's a citation in this for you and your crew."

"Thank you, sir, but..."

"Ask me, Rossi. You don't strike me as somebody who's afraid of officers."

"Uh... yes, sir. I mean, no, sir. I mean—"

He held up a hand. "It was my poor attempt at humor, but if I had to guess, you want to know if I've heard anything about Captain Randall."

"That's correct, General, the captain and Lieutenant Carlos."

"Of course." When she said Carlos' name, Rossi leaned forward an inch and her eyes widened almost imperceptibly. Few people would have noticed, but Angriff did, and knew what it meant. "Lieutenant Carlos is special to you?"

"I... I..."

"It's all right, Sergeant. In the old Army, fraternization between officers and enlisted was forbidden, but that was then and this is now. You're not in trouble."

She swallowed hard and nodded. "He is, General. Special to me, I mean."

"I wish I had good news to share with you, but no, we've haven't heard anything. But now that we've brought fuel, the helicopters can be used to search the desert."

"A plane that big can't be too hard to find."

"May I ask your first name, Rossi?"

"Frances, General."

"That's a nice name. Let me caution you against giving up, Frances. In my experience, you can't make assumptions about these kinds of things. There's always something going on that you can't see and don't know about."

"Do you really believe that?"

He let it go that she questioned his honesty. "I do. Never give up hope, Frances. Say a prayer if that's your way, and let's see what happens."

As he walked away, she called after him. "General?"

"Yes?"

"Sergeant Moro was lead on the repair of the C-5, sir."

"Moro... thank you, Frances, you're a credit to your country."

1620 hours, April 26

The short nights had begun taking their toll and Angriff wanted nothing more than to lie down and sleep, but instead he let Kando show him around two of the hangars, the flightline, and some of the buildings before the sun set. He'd sent Major Iskold out by herself to gather information that might be hidden or glossed over for his benefit. As they walked together, accompanied by six men detailed by Colonel Young as escorts, Kando filled him in on how Creech came to still be occupied by him and his people.

Finally, with mosquitoes out in full force and the sun getting low, Kando said, "Let me show you my headquarters, General Angriff."

Show me a chair, he thought. Age had begun to show hints of the future in his aching calves and burning feet, although walking for hours on concrete might do that to anyone. Regardless, he wanted nothing more than to rest for a few minutes.

"There's still a lot to show you, but that can wait until tomorrow."

"I hate to ruin your plans, General Kando, but we pull out at dawn. We're leaving behind a powerful force, but the main body of the regiment is heading north at first light."

"Oh." Kando stopped and touched his arm. It wasn't a gesture Angriff welcomed from another man, but he only gritted his teeth and said nothing. "I'm sorry to hear that. I wanted you to see our library. We're really proud of it."

"Your... library? You mean like a book library?"

"That's right. I hated to see all those books go to waste, so whenever we happened to find any I brought them here."

"A library... I'll be damned. General Kando," and here he put his hand on the man's shoulder, "I'd very much like to see that right now, if we could."

~~~

Creech Air Force Base Library

"Oh... my..." Angriff said, staring from the doorway into the room filled with books. Every shelf was crammed with them. Stacks on the floor leaned this way and that, and some had toppled. He couldn't help gawking. "General Kando, if you had done nothing else but rescue these precious artifacts, you would have achieved something admirable."

"I like to read." The portly Kando swept dust off the sleeves of his threadbare uniform coat.

Angriff noticed. "Relax... Jamal? Is that right? Take the coat off, for pity's sake. The day's been warm enough already."

"Thank you, but I'm fine, General Angriff."

"Call me Nick. How long did it take to collect all of these?"

"I don't know, a long time."

Angriff picked up a few books and shuffled through them. He held up a paperback with three figures on the cover aiming futuristic weapons. "This looks interesting."

Kando squinted at the title and author. *Integration*, by Jonathan Brazee. "I've read that one. It's really good. The author was a retired Marine colonel. I wouldn't have taken you for a science fiction fan."

"Sci-fi, fantasy, and military history are all I read as a kid. My dad didn't like the fiction stuff, but since I also read history, he left me alone. You don't have any Four Horsemen Universe books, do you?"

"I don't think so. Who wrote it?"

"It was dreamed up by two guys named Chris Kennedy and Mark Wandrey. I read the first ones right before... well, right before I joined Operation Overtime. Great books, lots of fun. Anyway, if you run up on any of those, let me know, okay?"

"I certainly will."

He held up the paperback. "Mind if I take this on the road with me? I'll bring it back."

"Mind? Well... no, General, I don't mind. Take what you want. If you like science fiction, there's another one around here called *Jurassic Jail* I really liked. "

"Thanks, I appreciate it. Let's see if we can find it. And call me Nick, damn it. "

#

Chapter 30

*This I must fight against: any idea, religion, or government
which limits or destroys the individual.*
John Steinbeck

Port of Long Beach, California
1709 hours, April 26

Trade winds whipped Károly Rosos' light auburn hair as
he stood with folded arms, staring west over San Pedro Bay.
Generalissimo Zhang Wei stood on his left and Adder on his
right. Two steps forward, and he'd fall off the concrete quay
into the water. Less than a mile at his back, the SS *Queen
Mary* listed hard to port at its permanent berth.

Neither of his companions was happy about the meeting,
Adder because he'd driven north and then immediately been
dragged back south, and Zhang because he didn't like working so late in the afternoon.

Thousands upon thousands of rust-streaked containers
lined every available foot of space through the port. Rosos
stood between four cranes mounted on tracks that allowed
them to slide back and forth to unload ships, or would have
if they still functioned. Forklifts stood where they'd been
abandoned. What the port lacked was life. Once upon a time,
it had hosted hundreds of major cargo ships daily. Tens of
thousands of people had worked there, not just dock workers
but managers, customs officials, and salesmen. Now there
were only rats.

Sunken ships choked the port and bay. In particular, a fleet of military transports lay in the main channel, with masts and superstructures jutting above the waterline. A quarter mile offshore, Rosos saw clouds of marine birds circling the conning tower of a Chinese destroyer.

"That is the *Yinchuan*," Zhang said in Mandarin. "She went down when the Americans attacked during the course of our landings. We didn't think they had any ships left that were operational, but they did. It was a long and terrible fight; many died on both sides. Eventually the remaining Americans sailed north and never bothered us again. Across the harbor is the hulk of the *Kunlun Shan*. That is the ship I came in."

Rosos turned and looked down at his shorter ally. Zhang wore sunglasses, so he couldn't read the Chinese commander's eyes, which annoyed him. It took him a minute to form the Chinese words in his head. "With all due respect, Generalissimo, forty-year-old battles are not my reason for being here," Rosos said. "I came to help you expand your territory and sharpen your combat forces, but unless you formally appoint Adder here as your top military consultant, neither of those is possible."

"This confuses me, Károly. I have already given him complete freedom to inspect anything he wishes, and even to instruct some of the newer army members on the finer points of their duties. I am told that his work in the north was a great example for our men there on how to interact with new citizens of our great republic."

"That is not enough, my friend. Adder knows your enemy; he was one of them. You must give him the freedom to remake your forces so the next time you meet the Americans, you can defeat them."

Zhang rubbed his neck, stroking it up and down, which Rosos recognized as a stalling tactic. He knew then that the next thing the Chinese leader said would be a lie.

"Nothing would make me happier than allowing Adder to train my army," he said. "But I'm afraid my ranking officers would take offense, and they have great influence with the men. Many of them also have important positions in running the government. I do not believe they would look favorably upon my appointing an American as my head of training."

"May I be blunt without incurring your anger?"

The folds of loose skin on Zhang's face lifted when he smiled. "Friends cannot anger friends, except by design."

"Then I would have to ask how these officers feel about being soundly defeated twice by the same enemy?"

The smile faded. "It is not the ideal outcome."

"Yet they wish to continue doing the same thing while expecting a different outcome?"

Behind them, the approaching sound of a car's engine let them know someone was coming, which indicated importance. For the Chinese, fuel wasn't the restricting issue in using motor vehicles, since the oil wells in Los Angeles still pumped oil and two refineries still processed it into gasoline. For them, the problem was finding cars or trucks whose electrical systems hadn't been destroyed by the EMPs detonated in LA during the Collapse.

"The men whose power you wish to usurp have accumulated that power over four decades, and none of them have shown the least inclination to voluntarily give it up. *I* wish to expand our influence while we yet may, but with very few exceptions, *they* do not see the point in doing so. I am the one whose reputation suffered damage as a result of our setbacks, whereas their power increased. As of now, I cannot risk officially naming Adder as my chief consultant. I am sorry. I have given him all of the influence that I can."

"Then will they follow him into battle?"

Even behind the sunglasses, Rosos could see Zhang squinting at the question. "Why?"

"Here's why." In a few sentences, he outlined the plan to support Steeple in taking command of Operation Overtime, and the time frame it would require.

"That only gives us one day to prepare."

"We only need two dozen reliable men to begin with, and six dozen more to follow. That's not many compared to the potential gain."

"I shall have to ask my advisors, but I agree. It sounds like a fortune of war."

Rosos didn't have time to reply before a dented Chevy Suburban, circa 2024, stopped in a squeal of worn-out brakes. An officer emerged from the passenger seat and directed two younger men, neither of whom was Asian, in lift-

STANDING BEFORE HELL'S GATE

ing something out of the SUV's hatch. As they leaned it against the Suburban, the officer strode toward the general-issimo.

"My apologies for the interruption, sir," he said in Chinese.

"Mr. Rosos, allow me to introduce Captain Hu Yanlin. As you can see, Captain Yanlin was born after the People's Republic of California was founded. Captain, this our esteemed ally, Mr. Károly Rosos. I believe you know Colonel Adder already. Now that formalities are dealt with, I hope your reason for being here is important, Captain."

"I believe it is, sir. There is something I need to show you, by the car."

Rosos and Zhang followed the captain, but Adder didn't speak Chinese and turned to look out to sea, thoroughly bored with what appeared to be a bunch of nonsense. But the captain paused and Rosos saw him whisper in Zhang's ear.

The Generalissimo nodded and called out to the big American in perfect English. "Adder, I am told this concerns you."

The loud *shit* Rosos heard from Adder didn't come as a surprise.

Once they were all by the Suburban, Zhang crouched to get a better look at the flat, jagged object braced there. Made of gray wood, it measured two feet by three feet.

"This was found over a man whose throat was cut as he guarded some prisoners. Whoever did it came and went like the wind."

Zhang nodded and looked up at Adder. "He says a dead guard was found with this, and the prisoners he was guarding were gone. None of the other guards heard anything." He turned back to the wooden fragment. "There's something written here," he said, leaning in close, then moving so his shadow didn't block the words. A moment later, he turned to Adder. "This appears to be for you."

"Me?" Adder crouched beside him and squinted. The words had been scratched into the surface and some sort of brownish liquid used to highlight them. Wetting his finger, he touched the 'ink' and tasted it. "It's blood."

In one of those tricks of light, Rosos could read the words better from his standing position than either Zhang or Adder could kneeling in front of them. "Adder," he read aloud, "I'm coming for you. Green Ghost."

———∿∿∿———

1829 hours

Károly Rosos shoved the front doors of his family's home in Malibu open so hard that the inside doorknob smashed a hole in the wall of the foyer. Adder followed him inside and closed the door behind him. The Suburban pulled down the circular driveway after dropping them off.

"That was fucking embarrassing!" Unlike his father and brother, the youngest Rosos was tall and lean. Not as tall as Adder, but close. Long fingers better suited for playing the piano balled into fists as he raged down the entry hall into the living room of the empty old mansion. "I spent all afternoon kissing that greasy Chinaman's ass, only to have it blow up in my face! Now who the fuck is this Green Ghost character? It sounds like something out of a comic book."

Adder's wide shoulders straightened. His muscled chest expanded and his eyes became slits. A slight twitch in his left nostril should have been the sign to Rosos to shut up, but he was too enraged to see it. "Green Ghost was commander of Task Force Zombie, one of the Nameless. He cheated me out of the command that should have been mine, but he's still the most dangerous man I've ever met. If he's here, some of the others will be, too."

"Do I look like I give two shits about that? You're worried about one man while I'm worried about a whole country! You embarrassed me today and you'd better not do it again, you idiot!"

The narrowed eyes widened. When Adder spoke, it was through clenched teeth. "What did you say?"

Adder's tone triggered a primordial warning signal in Rosos' brain, an ingrained instinct that told him he'd made a huge mistake. "I didn't mean that."

The one-time commander of Task Force Zombie's Third Squad took a step forward. Rosos matched him by taking a step back.

STANDING BEFORE HELL'S GATE

"Never mistake me for one of your stooges, Károly. Green Ghost may be the most dangerous man that *I've* ever met, but I'm that man for you. Don't push me. It's a big, empty country out there, and I know how to survive in it, but I don't leave my enemies alive behind me. You take care of that fuckhead Zhang and I'll take care of my old commander."

"Sure," Rosos said, hands up in a placating gesture. "Whatever you say, Adder."

"He was a dickhead and an asshole who took what should have been mine, but he was still a Zombie. We were the best soldiers in the whole fucking world... one of us was worth a thousand of those red riders of yours, or these useless Chinese. Don't ever forget it. I'm leaving now."

"Where are you going?"

"I wanna see this place Green Ghost showed up to, see if I can track him."

"Why bother doing that when you can make him come to you?"

"What do you mean?"

"Go to Overtime and help Steeple take it back now, while Angriff is gone. Then this Ghost person won't have any choice except to come back, will he?"

"And I'll be waiting..."

"And you'll be waiting."

"You're a weasel, Károly, but you're a smart weasel. Let's get this shit show on the road."

Operation Comeback
0018 hours, April 27

General Schiller leaned back and rubbed his face. His eyes wouldn't focus any more and he knew that tomorrow would be a long, dreary day of sleep-deprived exhaustion, but he *had* to figure out the discrepancies in the inventory. It was the missing Stingers at Prime all over again, and he couldn't relax until he'd solved it. It was just in his nature. And this time it wasn't one or two cases of Stingers, it was ten.

They weren't missing, either. At least, not according to the paperwork, but this was the kind of thing he was known for. His specialty was digging through the paperwork of transfers and rearrangements designed to confuse an auditor by making it nearly impossible to track down missing items. After doing it for so many years, Schiller had developed a sixth sense of spotting suspicious transactions on otherwise routine-looking invoices and manifests. And now he knew, as sure as he was sitting there all alone past midnight, that ten cases of Stingers had vanished at some time in Operation Comeback's history.

The clock on his monitor read 2:21 AM when he found it. An invoice on an outgoing truck filled with leftover parts from construction of the heli-pad listed ten cases of *single person launch systems,* which could only be the missing Stingers. It was dated 12 March 2012. The only notation was a hand-written word that appeared to say *Steyer.* In a different hand beside that, this time in red ink, not black, was a scribble that read *per SoS.*

#

Chapter 31

Use every moment wisely, to perceive your inner refulgence, or
'twill be gone and nevermore within your reach.
Marcus Aurelius

Painted Desert north of Winslow, Arizona
0701 hours, April 27

As was their wont, they'd been in the saddle since before sunup. For the first four days of what they called their 'vacation', the *clop-clop* of the horses' hooves seemed like an old friend to Dennis Tompkins' little group of survivors. During their fifty years of wandering through devastated North America, they'd driven vehicles whenever they could, but more often than not the only mode of transport available had been equine. Nor had they been in a hurry to get anywhere; they all seemed to sense this was probably their last trip together and wanted to savor it for as long as they could. On day five, however, all six of them began to remember the biggest problem with long journeys on horseback.

"I cain't feel m' legs, Skip," John Thibodeaux said. "Tell me again why we ain't drivin'."

"There's two reasons, John," Dennis Tompkins replied. The burning in his lower back reminded him of the constant pain he'd been in during the long years in the wilderness. "First, I said this was more fun, and second, I'm an idiot."

Passing through a narrow valley, they rode single file. Sheer walls of rock rose close on either side. Riding first,

Paul Hausser chuckled and called back over his shoulder, "You're not an idiot, Skip. You just got old."

The usually taciturn Derek Tandy, bringing up the rear, almost had to shout to be heard. "Anybody who grew old during the last fifty years can't be an idiot."

"Asides," Thibodeaux said. "If we was in a Humvee, we couldn't be in this pass right now. I think riding horses was the right call, me."

Second in the column, Tompkins twisted in the saddle. The motion felt good to the stiff muscles in his back. "You were just complaining about *not* taking Humvees, John."

"That was a long time ago."

"It was thirty seconds!" yelled Tandy from behind.

"An' that's a long time," Thibodeaux replied.

They emerged from the pass facing the gently rolling dunes of the Sonoran Desert as it led north. The colors of spring carpeted the ground in pinks, blues, green, yellows, and every shade of red. They avoided the ruins of Holbrook and crossed Interstate 40, headed toward the Little Colorado River. Lunch was a leisurely affair of MREs eaten in a boulder field after ensuring that no rattlesnakes were using the area for a nest. But old habits die hard, and they took turns at guard duty. After fifty years, they couldn't relax without that ritual.

It paid off.

Monty Wilson had gained fifteen pounds since the previous summer, so his sagging face appeared less gaunt than it had. He wasn't a tall man and always scrambled to the highest available point when it was his turn to stand watch. Only Tompkins noticed him shield his eyes with his hand, and then bring the binoculars up to his face.

"See something, Monty?" he called.

"Riders, coming' this way."

"How many?"

"It's hard to tell; they're kicking up a lot of dust. More than a few, about two miles away. Maybe twenty, maybe more."

By now they were all on their feet, their food forgotten except for Thibodeaux, who held the edge of the MRE's plastic dish up to his mouth and scooped chicken, noodles, and vegetables it. With both cheeks filled like a cartoon chipmunk, he picked up his M-16, pushed in a magazine, and chambered a round.

"Are they wearin' red scarves?"

"Not that I can see, Skipper... but there's somethin' wrapped around their heads. It looks like... I can't make it out... it looks maybe like writing."

"Writing?"

"Yes, cursive writing... oh, shit!"

But Tompkins had already guessed what it was. "It's Arabic, isn't it?"

"Too far to tell for sure, but that's what it looks like."

"Have they seen us?"

"I don't think so. Looks like they're cantering but not galloping."

"But they're headed this way? No chance to lay down the horses and let 'em pass?"

"I don't think that'll work this time, Skipper."

"Dang it. Lemme know if that changes."

Nobody panicked. Instead they all turned to Tompkins. He'd been their leader for fifty years and they were all still alive because he'd made the right decision in countless situations like this one. Nor did he make a hasty choice. He mentally estimated they had eight to ten minutes before the riders would be on them, and it would take them less than thirty seconds to mount up. Turning in a full circle gave him time to look for better defensive territory. Two miles to the north he saw their chance, a ridgeline with what appeared to be a cave high on its face.

"All right, boys, there's our place to hole up," he said, pointing. "Let's ride like hell."

#

Chapter 32

*Some people wonder all their lives if they've made a differ-
ence. The Marines don't have that problem.*
Ronald Reagan

Eastern Arizona
1015 hours, April 27

Lara Snowtiger leaned on the sunny side of a Humvee,
munching on the high protein crackers developed from
pumpkin, sunflower seeds, and the limited grains available
to the Republic of Arizona. They tasted like cardboard but
were surprisingly satisfying when you were hungry. The Marines had adapted to eating them by dipping them in whatever liquid was available, preferably a packet of beef or chicken
broth powder in their MREs, mixed with water. Unfortunately, all she could find was some orange drink powder.

"It still sounds crazy, Lara," Zo Piccaldi said. As usual
during downtimes, he lay anywhere in the shade with his
boonie hat covering his face, trying to doze. In this case, it
was in the vehicle's back seat.

"If you could get inside here," she said, pointing at her
chest, "you'd know what I mean."

"If I could get in there, I'd be in Heaven."

Enough women had given him the *drop dead* expression
that he knew what it looked like. Snowtiger's version of that
look matched every other one he'd ever seen; he assumed it
was instinct.

"Do you ever think about anything else?"

"No, never."

"You need estrogen shots."

"I like my toxic manliness."

"Toxic, yes, but I'm not sure about the manliness part. What I'm saying is that if you could hear and sense what I hear and sense, you'd believe me. My sister is out there somewhere."

"Alive?"

"I think so. That's what it feels like."

"Whatever you say. Who am I to argue with a Medoh?" *Medal of Honor.*

"Bite me," she said, and stalked off.

"Just gimme the chance," he said to her back.

"Do you want me to hit you with a sexual harassment writeup?"

"You can hit me with whatever you want."

"How about a brick?"

"Oooo, talk dirty to me."

A Humvee sped their way, boiling a dust cloud in its wake. Both snipers stopped to await its arrival, but Snowtiger couldn't resist getting in the last word.

"When flying pigs swim in barbeque sauce."

The Humvee stopped in the center of the laagered vehicles of First Platoon. Without a word, the scattered Marines gathered around their commander, Lieutenant Hakala, known to them affectionately as *Loot Hack.* Hakala had been executive officer to Lieutenant Embekwe when the latter died in the so-called Battle of Last Stand Hill. The men and women of his platoon knew that when the shit hit the fan, he'd be standing right beside them.

"Listen up, jarheads. It's time to earn your pay."

"Yut!"

"We're moving east toward Gallup, New Mexico. That's about 45 miles east of here…" A low hum in the crowd made him pause. "What the fuck is going on back there?"

"Sorry, Loot," somebody called out. "L.C. Esserton is from Gallup."

"No shit? Esserton, when we're ten klicks from the objective, put on a headset. I may have questions. The rest of you, sitful!" He pronounced it *sitfoo,* Marine slang for *shut the fuck up.* "First Platoon is point, as usual. We stick to the interstate unless there's a sinkhole. The rest of Dog follows us and is split on both flanks. Piccaldi and Snowtiger on my six. Any questions?" Nobody raised their hand. "Oscar Mike in five."

#

CHAPTER 33

Let me tear my eyes out,
Lest I see her shade...
Murder defendant in a Roman trial on why he killed his wife,
circa 80 BC

Truckee, California
1126 hours, April 27

Green Ghost leaned over the railing of the overpass of California Highway 89 over Interstate 80. Once upon a time, the roadway beneath them had hummed with thousands of cars either heading west to Sacramento or east to Reno, but the reek of burning oil and rubber had long since been replaced by the sweet smell of pines, and while once the honks of angry drivers and roaring engines would have made it hard for him and Jane to talk without shouting, now the only background noise came from the rushing waters of the Truckee River.

"So this is Truckee," he said. "Doesn't look like much."

"What does?" Jane said, hands propped on the steel rail beside him. "I've scraped this place more times than I can count."

"Find anything good?"

"A lot of ammo. I must've pulled fifty thousand rifle rounds out of this place, mostly thirty caliber."

"Hunting rifles."

She nodded.

"Good to know. Where is it now?"

"At my place." She giggled, but not loud enough for him to hear. "I scraped the hand pump in my house here, too. Want me to show it to you?"

He turned to her, considering the question, but then realized she'd been flirting and blushed. Setting his jaw, he turned to face the other way. Then his body stiffened.

"Don't be like that," she said, trying to stop laughing. "I—"

He grabbed her arm and pulled her down. Using his head, he indicated a line of trees one hundred yards to their right. "Somebody down there," he said.

Jane's demeanor instantly changed. Crouching behind the concrete pillar into which the rails were mounted, both scanned the tree line.

"You sure it wasn't a bear?" she said.

"Do bears have red hair?"

"What color red?" There was an undercurrent of concern to her question.

"I guess more orange than red."

"Bright orange? Big all the way around?"

He cut his eyes to her. "Yeah... friend of yours?"

"I think it's Kody." She cupped a hand to one side of her mouth and yelled. "Kody, is that you? It's Jane!"

Green Ghost felt a strange sensation in his stomach, which he realized was jealousy. Who the hell was Kody? He wanted to ask but that wasn't his way, so he gritted his teeth so he didn't blurt out the question.

Which he did anyway, and then cursed himself.

"Boyfriend?" Jane said. "Why do you care?" Before he could answer, she went on. "Her name is Kodiak Kate, so no, she's not my boyfriend. Or girlfriend, either."

He looked at the sky, trying to think of how to respond, but was saved by a response from Kodiak Kate.

"Jane! You bow-legged whore, where the flaming fuck are you?"

"She's a friend?" he said.

Jane giggled again, and he assumed it was at his discomfort. "Kate has to be experienced to be understood."

They stood and Jane led her horse to the far end of the overpass, but Green Ghost couldn't bring himself to follow immediately. He'd only survived the last fifteen years by constant wariness, so instead he kept his rifle at the ready, just in case. And when he saw what pushed through some underbrush, he almost opened fire out of sheer reflex.

The figure stood at least seven feet tall and he guessed its weight at more than 300 pounds. Bright orange hair ringed a face with skin the color of dark chocolate. Kody's shoulders would have earned her an invitation to the NFL combine, while a hunting rifle looked like a toy in her fist.

"Girl!" She wrapped arms clad in animal-skin sleeves around Jane, who seemed to disappear in her grasp. Was this the Bigfoot Jane had alluded to? If so, he might have to change his opinion on their existence.

During introductions, Kody winked at Jane and said loud enough for him to hear, "He's cute... is he yours?"

The woman stood a foot taller than him and outweighed him by at least a hundred pounds, so when Jane answered, "Not yet," he instinctively backed up two paces. Both women laughed and walked down the highway toward the town, leaving him to wonder what had just happened.

They turned right at a traffic circle, where rusted signs identified the street as Donner Pass Road. Fifty yards away, and hidden behind a line of scrub pines fronting another stand of mature Ponderosa pines, a driveway curved back out of sight. Green Ghost recognized brick shrubbery planters lining it on both sides. After a short distance, the driveway branched off to either side and circled around a stand of trees. Behind the greenery was a large building with a partially caved-in ceiling and a sign that read TRUCKEE DONNER RECREATION AND PARKS DEPARTMENT COMMUNITY CENTER. Green Ghost followed Kody's massive backside down the cracked driveway, but stopped by a huge pile of scat. It wasn't bear or deer and appeared to be canine, but if it was, that was one big-ass dog.

"Kody!" he called. When she turned, he pointed at it. "Coyote?"

She came back a step, took two seconds to study it, and shook her head. "Wolf. They get big around here."

"A wolf left that?"

Kody's eyes fairly sparkled at his shock. "Probably not the pack leader, either. They can top 200 pounds." She pulled up a leather sleeve to expose long scars on her left forearm. "Got that about ten years ago. A bitch went for my throat and I got my arm up just in time. While she was chewing on me, I got out a .357 Magnum and stuck it down her mouth. Now I wear her when it's cold. So trust me when I tell you, by the time you hear them it's too late."

He picked up the smell of smoke well outside the building, but it wasn't the acrid smoke of a house fire or a forest fire; it reminded him of cooking meat. His mouth watered at the thought of fresh venison or sheep. They tied the horses so they could graze a large patch of grass as well as low-hanging pine boughs. Green Ghost took the water buckets and Kody showed him to a nearby stream that emptied into the river. While he filled up the buckets, Jane took off the saddles and gear. Once he'd lugged the water back so the horses could drink, they headed for the double doors where Kody had disappeared.

Inside the building, they found Kody's camp in a hallway where the roof hadn't fallen in, although from the way it sagged Green Ghost thought that might happen any minute. Nevertheless, the cinderblock walls and solid steel security doors at either end of the hall made a secure location; they wouldn't have to worry about sleeping that night.

Smoke poured out of a large metal box with a door in the front, escaping through a cracked window high in one wall that kept the corridor from filling up and asphyxiating them. He looked for clues as to what kind of animal Kody had in the smoker but saw none.

"Boar," she said, anticipating him. "Plural. They're all over the place. And lucky for you that's the second batch. You like pork, soldier boy?"

"I'm from Memphis," he said, before remembering that he wasn't supposed to reveal details about his life. Except... except that world no longer existed. Nobody cared who he was in the here and now, or where he came from.

"Is that supposed to mean something?" Kody said, looking at Jane, who shrugged.

"Memphis is... Memphis *was* known for its pork barbeque. Ribs, pulled pork, shoulder, there was even a festival on the banks of the Mississippi River every year. Everybody ate it."

Kody pulled out a package lined with, of all things, aluminum foil, and filled with strips of smoked pork that looked like bacon. She passed them out and when he tasted it, he realized it *was* bacon. Rarely had anything tasted so good.

The room warmed quickly under the spring sun. With a full stomach, he began to relax and felt sleepy. Meanwhile, Kody had stripped off everything but pants and shirt of soft deer hide. That was when he realized that, despite her immense size, Kody had no fat on her body, only heavy, well-defined muscles under her dark skin. Despite being as large as the rest of her, Kody's breasts were high on her chest. Where the orange hair came from, he couldn't even guess.

Sitting with her back against a metal desk with no legs, Kody pointed at Green Ghost like a customer selecting a lobster in a seafood restaurant. "Where did you find this tasty piece?" she asked Jane.

For the next five minutes, he listened as Jane filled her in on him, the battle at Sierra, the parachute drop, and what he'd told her about Overtime. The room grew warmer and they all began to sweat. As Jane finished her story, Kody reached up, fiddled with her hair, and then removed a huge orange wig, revealing a scalp covered with the barest hint of stubble. It didn't bother Jane but Green Ghost's eyes widened.

Kody shook the wig. "Keeps me from getting shot," she said. "This far south, there's other scrapers and hunters out there, and I know I look like a bear, so..."

"Like an orange hunting vest," he said.

"Yeah, 'cept I can't find one that fits. So you're a soldier boy from the past, is that what Jane told me?"

"Something like that."

Instead of immediately questioning him, or being suspicious, Kody rubbed her chin. "Huh... that's weird. Do you know them navy boys up in Alaska?"

Green Ghost sat up straight, leaning forward and suddenly tense. "Navy boys?"

#

CHAPTER 34

Who'd a thunk it?
Mortimer Snerd

Painted Desert, Arizona
1202 hours, April 27

The chill night air gave way to the warming of day earlier and earlier as spring moved toward summer. Three hundred feet above the desert floor, Sara Snowtiger had greeted the new sun as she did on warm days, totally nude and sitting cross-legged on the ledge in front of her cave. The isolation of the place allowed her to put aside her innate modesty and enjoy the wind on her body and the sun on her bronzed skin. As the daylight grew, she moved back into the cave far enough to escape the sun's harsh intensity.

With eyes closed, she let her mind wander the lands below. She felt a kinship with living things that others couldn't understand, or didn't believe. For example, she truly believed that somewhere out there her lost twin sister walked the land in physical form of some sort. There was no denying the energy she felt. She also knew that Sevens had returned to Central Arizona. The evil of their intentions couldn't be hidden from someone like her... with a start, she felt them now, and they were close and getting closer.

Still naked, she stood and shaded her eyes. Far-sight was something she couldn't explain to anyone who didn't have it, but with it she saw a small group of horsemen galloping her way, perhaps a mile distant. And right behind them rode a much larger group, and Sara knew those were Sevens. What was worse, all of them were headed right for the isolated peak where she lived.

What to do? She possessed no weapons and wouldn't have known how to use them even if they were present. That was not who she was. After slipping on her robe, she did the only thing she knew to do; she tried to sense who that first group of horsemen might be.

On hands and knees, she pressed her forehead to the dusty rock ledge. Eyes closed, she tried to sense the people coming, who they were and what their intentions might be. She acted on both instinct and intuition, as she had always done. With a sudden jump to her feet, she dragged the heavy rope ladder over to the edge and dropped it, as she'd done so many times for Govind.

Six men pulled up at the base of the escarpment and dismounted, their weapons at the ready. The Sevens were about half a mile away when one of the first group rode away, leading the other horses by their reins. The five remaining men started the long climb up the mountainside. They hurried, obviously knowing, as she did, that if they were caught still climbing when the Sevens got within range, they would die. But it still seemed to take forever.

Why were they going so slow? Their pursuers, who she instinctively felt had evil intent, drew close. It was only when the first man passed the halfway point that she realized they weren't young, but in fact were her age. All had white hair, if they had hair at all. That meant they had all lived through the Collapse, just as she had. The first man's long face was lean as he peered up at her, and a half-grown beard stood out snowy white against skin the color of burgundy leather, further reddened by the effort of climbing.

Snowtiger stared down at them until strong hands pulled her out of the line of fire. It was the first man who'd come up, the tallest of them. Then he arched his back to make it easier to breathe.

"Excuse me, ma'am, but you coulda got shot," he said. Leaning forward, hands on knees, he gulped a few breaths and then unslung his rifle. "You may want to... step into the cave... before... before..." He stopped and squinted at her. "Snowtiger?"

She took two steps backward until she felt the cliff wall. "How do you know me?" All of her senses were on alert, yet she felt no ill intent coming from the man.

"I was at your award ceremony with everybody else... but you look different, older. Your hair's partly gray... what are you doing here?"

"Skip!" yelled a voice behind him. "They's about to start shootin'!"

The big man helped a second, smaller man up onto the ledge and then he took aim at the Sevens, cracking off two shots. The small one helped the others up and soon all five were on the ledge. Someone pulled up the rope ladder. They all took carefully aimed shots at the twenty or so riders milling about below, and knocked three out of the saddle. They stopped firing when the Sevens rode out of rifle range, pausing about a quarter mile away. Within minutes, the Sevens were setting up camp for the night.

Retreating within the cave, the men sprawled and panted, letting the ambient coolness dry up their sweat. Each man had a canteen and drank from it. Satisfied everyone was all right, the big man walked over to Sara. She stood near the entrance, wearing a defiant expression that promised if they tried to rape her she'd go over the cliff and die rather than submit. In her heart, however, she felt no intuition of danger from them.

Once again the man who seemed to be in charge studied her face. He scratched his jaw and then shook his head. "You're her, but you're not her. What's going on, Lara?"

"Lara? Why did you call me that?"

"Ain't that your name?"

"No, my name is Sara."

"I'll be damned... you sure enough look just like her."

"Did you know this Lara? Who are you?"

"*Did* I know her? Not until recently. My name's Dennis Tompkins. I'm a general in the U.S. Army, although I admit I don't look much like one. I *do* know your sister. She's a sniper in our Marine battalion, won the Medal of Honor last year. Saved all of our butts."

"Wh-what?"

"I don't understand this."

"She's still alive?"

"Yes, ma'am. She almost died last year, but the doctors said a miracle saved her. She's somewhere in New Mexico right now, I think. You look enough like her to be her mother, or maybe even a twin, although..."

"I'm older than her."

"So you are related?"

Sara slumped to the ground, staring at nothing, the way Tompkins had seen men look after too many days in battle. The original name for that condition had been shell shock.

When Sara Snowtiger spoke again, it was in a soft voice that was hard to hear over the wind. "She's my twin sister."

Tompkins lay flat on the shelf of rock in front of the cave, staring at the two campfires half a mile away in the desert night.

"This has got a familiar feel to it," Thibodeaux said, lying next to him.

"You thinking about that night when we rescued those women?"

"I am for a fact. All them Sevens was down below, waitin' for dawn, just like tonight. I didn't like that much, me."

"We'd all be dead if it wasn't for you, John. Hell, if it wasn't for you, the whole Operation Overtime might still be in Long Sleep."

"You keep on sayin' that, Skip, an' I appreciate it an' all, but you cain't say that for a fact."

"Oh, I think it's safe to say it as a fact. But I did learn a lesson that night and I'm fixin' to do the same thing I did then. General Angriff made me bring a radio in case we ran into trouble and I think this qualifies."

"I reckon it does. I'll fetch it for ya."

Overtime Prime
1208 hours

Morgan Randall opened the door to her parents' quarters, letting in her sister Nikki and Nikki's boyfriend, Joe Ootoi. They stopped just inside.

Nikki spoke in an urgent whisper. "Is there news about Joe?"

"I'm glad I caught you before you left," Morgan said. "It's not about Joe... I'm sorry to mess up your hike... Mom and Cindy are both really sick. I wanted to call Dad, but Mom won't let me. I thought maybe you could talk to her."

"Me? This really isn't my thing, Morgan, and besides, while I love Mom, she's not really my mother, she's yours. What makes you think she might listen to me?"

"Just try, okay? If she refuses, we're not worse off than we are now. She's in the bedroom. Cindy's in there with her."

Morgan made tea while she and Ootoi waited for Nikki to return, which she did in less than ten minutes.

"What did she say?" Morgan said.

"She said, and I'm quoting, 'Tell Morgan I am fine and for her to stop polishing the same tableware.' I have no idea what that means."

"It means to quit beating a dead horse," Ootoi interjected as both women turned to him in surprise.

"Is that right?" Nikki asked.

"Yes, it is. How did you know that, Toy?"

"My mom came from Savannah, Georgia. She used to say it all the time."

Nikki leaned in close to her sister and dropped her voice. "Have you told her about... you know?"

"No, not while she's sick."

"If you wait too long, you won't need to tell her."

#

Chapter 35

Pay no attention to what he do, pay attention to what he say,
He's your voice to almighty god, obey him come what may.
Children's rhyme of the Caliphate of the Seven Prayers of the
New Prophet

Western New Mexico
1357 hours, April 27

Mohammad Qadim's heart pounded when Captain al-Naadi reined in atop a ridge and used his binoculars to scout the path ahead. It happened every time they stopped, as his fear of being discovered led to panic and became ever harder to keep off his face. So far his companions had written it off to his youth, but he lived in constant fear. Mere unbelievers were tortured in horrible ways, and he could only imagine how they would treat a spy.

Less than a mile north of the hilltop ran the roadbed of the old Interstate 40, while fifteen miles east was Gallup, where the captain hoped to spend the night. The other nine riders used the break to drink water and mop sweat from their faces.

"The horses need rest, Captain," one of the men behind Qadim said.

The captain looked at him, as if he'd said it. "The horses can rest when we get to Gallup!"

His men shared dubious looks. Care of their mounts had never been the captain's top priority, but without horses they were dead. The desert didn't forgive mistakes such as that.

He spoke loud enough for them all to hear. "The prayers of the New Prophet have led us to this spot and he will not abandon us now, if we but remain his good and faithful servants. The horses will be fine. There is what we've been searching for." He pointed at the cracked and weed-choked pavement. "That road connects the western ocean with the eastern lands. With the army of the Emir moving toward the city once called Albuquerque, our mission was to scout on their western side all the way to that road, which the Americans named Interstate 40. We have accomplished that directive and now we turn to the east. We next are required to investigate a town called Gallup. From now on, we are tasked with searching for any clues as to the location of the enemy stronghold known as Shangri-La. The mission of the Emir's army is to seize Albuquerque and destroy Shangri-La, so that we may avenge the loss of so many brothers last year. It's been a hard road and you've done well. Let us now finish our task and—"

"Dust!" one of the men screamed, pointing to the west.

Qadim's heart leaped at the fear it was the rest of the Sevens; the more people to watch him, the greater the chance of him being discovered. Somehow, he had to get away and warn Shangri-La of what was heading their way, but if surrounded by an army, that would be impossible.

Al-Naadi took out his binoculars and focused on the large dust cloud moving straight for his location. The westering sun poured into the lenses, so he couldn't distinguish details. Twice he turned his head because of the sunlight. "Can anyone see?" he said. "The sun has blinded me."

Qadim squinted. Spots danced in his eyes. All he knew for sure was that many vehicles were racing across the desert and down the interstate.

"Pull over!" Snowtiger screamed at the Humvee driver. "Now, now! Hurry!"

"Lara, what's—"

"Pull over!"

The driver swerved onto the shoulder and skidded to a stop beside a twisted section of guard rail. The rest of the company kept rolling by, but Snowtiger stood through the gap in the roof and scanned to the east with her regulation binoculars. She'd lost the 25X100MM Astronomical ones during the battle the previous year, and despite several days searching, she hadn't found them. Now she concentrated on what she knew she'd seen — the flash of sunlight off glass.

"What the fuck are you doing, Lara?" Piccaldi said. "Loot Hack's gonna have our ass."

"Can I please drive on, Gunny?" the driver said to Piccaldi.

"No, you cannot!" Snowtiger answered. "Zo, hand me my rifle."

"Your rifle? If you aren't hunting venison for dinner, we're fucked. We're supposed to be on his six."

"Give me the damned rifle!" she said.

Piccaldi recoiled and, in shock, did what she asked. He'd never heard her curse before. The high cheekbones that lent her usually stoic expression an ethereal beauty also made her frown appear more severe.

Snowtiger and Piccaldi had the only two M40A7 rifles in the entire brigade. The biggest difference with the older versions of the same bolt-action sniper rifle was the folding stock and ability to attach more accessories. Both had been offered the prizes after their defense of Last Stand Hill. They'd also been given two of the M110 semi-automatic rifles, but after using them in combat, neither sniper liked it much.

She locked the stock in place but didn't chamber a round. Instead, sighting through the scope, finger off the trigger, she searched for the source of the mysterious light. The hilltop she scanned had old homes and boulders and a few trees, so it was painstaking work, but work she'd been trained to do.

"Lara, we're gonna be dead-assed last if you don't hurry up."

She ignored Piccaldi and kept looking. Could it have been something natural? Some desert phenomena? Had she dozed off and imagined it, or... there! Between two large boulders... what was that? Men on horseback!

"Trenchard!" she said to the PFC riding shotgun. "Get Loot Hack on the radio, now!"

"What is it?" Piccaldi.

"Sevens."

—⁓—

"Enemies," Captain al-Naadi said.

Even without binoculars, Mohammad Qadim could see they were trapped. Vehicles extended a mile on either side of the highway, so if they tried riding back the way they'd come the enemy would see them. Nor could they use the road ahead because the enemy was already on it. All they could do was hunker down in a ravine and hope the enemy passed by without seeing them, men or horses.

—⁓—

"Snowtiger spotted Sevens on top of that ridge on our right, Captain," Lieutenant Hakala said into his mike. As he spoke, he swept the high ground with his binoculars, although bouncing along the broken asphalt made it nearly impossible to focus. "We're going to pass it on our right flank and I think we have to take the potential threat seriously."

"If Snowtiger says she saw it, we have to assume that she did," came Captain Sully's reply. "Deploy accordingly. See if there's a road leading up from the interstate and assume the enemy has RPGs and heavy weapons. I'm ordering the elements of Echo on that flank to envelope the ridgeline from the south."

"Roger that."

Hakala's LAV stopped half a mile from the ridge and his platoon did the same behind him.

"First Platoon, listen up. Reliable observation puts Sevens on that hill on our right. First squad, stay on the highway and flank the hill on its left, then see if there's a road leading to the crest. Take it slow and assume there's IEDs. Second Squad, support them in echelon. Third Squad, approach the hill from the desert and look for ways up while providing on-call fire support. Snowtiger, you and Piccaldi deploy at your discretion to cover the operation. Questions?"

"Loot," one of the LAV commanders said, "I see what looks like houses up there. What are the ROEs?"

"Try to identify your targets before firing, but do *not*, I repeat, do *not* hesitate if it puts you in danger. We assume all targets are valid unless otherwise identified. Any other questions? Move out."

Overtime Prime
1413 hours

Having something at stake was so much worse than being hopeless, Steeple thought. Before McComb's unexpected visit, he'd been dreaming about scenarios in which he might get out of his cell, things he'd say and arguments he'd make at his court-martial, fantasies that would never come true but were nevertheless highly gratifying. Then, out of nowhere, he had been given that most corrosive of emotions... hope. With a chance to not only get out but to gain the power he'd been denied, Steeple found the moments dragging by, so that when McComb again opened his door, he almost tackled the man.

"Well, is there any progress? What has been done? What is taking so long?"

"We have to be careful, General."

"Four days have passed. Angriff will be back if we do not act soon."

"Everything's fine! I just spoke to Colonel Mwangi for the second time and it's all set. Tomorrow night at 0200 hours, a Gulfstream G-650 will set down at the Prescott airport—"

"Has the runway been checked?"

"Yes, General, it has been totally repaired and restored. Now, it has to be done in the middle of the night to draw as little attention as possible. I'll be there with my two most trusted associates. We'll light oil fires to mark the runway..."

"Who's coming?"

McComb held up a hand. "I'm taking a truck from the construction motor pool. Once they're on the ground, they'll park the aircraft in a hangar there... it doesn't have a roof, but it doesn't need one for our purposes. I'll load the men on the plane into the truck. I'm told there will be close to two dozen."

"Are they mercs?"

"No... Chinese."

"Wait... Chinese? You're bringing Chinese troops into Overtime?"

"We don't have a choice, General. There's a lot of moving parts in this and they're all we can get on such short notice. They're led by an American spec ops guy named Adder."

Despite his legendary self-control, Steeple blanched. He'd been an NSA advisor during the Venezuela debacle. "Adder? From... from Task Force Zombie? *That* Adder?"

"Unless there's two. Now excuse me sir, but let me finish. We don't have much time..."

#

CHAPTER 36

It is better to trip with the feet than with the tongue.
Zeno of Citium

Eastern Arizona
1616 hours, April 27

Snowtiger and Piccaldi set up on a small rise close to the interstate. Both were going through their preparatory routines, beginning with inspecting their weapons and ammo, when Piccaldi spoke up. "If it turns out there really are Sevens up there, I'm never gonna hear the end of it, am I?"

She pulled back the rifle bolt and looked down the barrel from the chamber. Her natural expression was blank and a little sad, as if she kept terrible secrets she could never reveal. Piccaldi's breath quickened every time she looked at him that way. Despite her deadly prowess, he felt a compulsion to shield her and protect her. This time, when she looked at him, a small, sad smile joined that expression.

"No," she said. "You're not."

The crevice held four of them and their horses. The others were further back from the interstate in a bigger ravine. Qadim could see nothing beyond the sky above and the walls of the earthen gash where they'd hidden. Each rider spoke to his horse to calm it and to keep it from nickering.

"Courage, men," whispered Captain al-Naadi. "We have a good chance they will pass by and not see us. Have faith in your prophet."

Qadim was closest to the road, which ran from the old interstate over the hilltop and down the other side. A gentle slope led out of their crevasse to the backyard of a ruined house, which blocked their view of the road, but also blocked them from being spotted by someone on the road. The captain had been right; there was a good chance they'd never be seen.

Qadim desperately wondered who they were. To the rest of the riders, they could only be enemies, but Qadim was already among his enemies, so there was a good chance these were friends. They'd all seen the white stars painted on the vehicles. Qadim hadn't been with them the year before, but he'd heard all about the devils who'd slaughtered the faithful and their damned machines decorated with the white star.

Unbidden, a plan came to mind, one that might not get him killed. He'd been looking for an opportunity to break away from Captain al-Naadi's little band of scouts and this might be his last chance. But when he thought about his chances for survival, it was the word *might* that worried him. He could see at least three ways he could die in the next few minutes, including breaking his neck by falling off his horse. His mind had almost convinced him not to take the risk when he dug his heels into the horse's flanks.

Lieutenant Hakala's LAV was fourth in line ascending the hill when the lead vehicle, Dog One-One-One, squawked on the tactical radio. *Dog One-One-One* meant Dog Company, First Platoon, First Squad, First Vehicle.

"Lone horseman heading my way, no apparent weapons, hands in the air. Distance fifty yards. What are my orders?"

"Take no chances. Tell them to stop. If they approach within twenty yards, open fire. If you see a weapon or they reach for anything, open fire. *Do not take any risks*!"

"Rider is down. I repeat, rider is down."

"Did you shoot, Dog One-Eleven?"

"Negative. The rider fell off his horse."

———~~~———

Qadim rolled across the dirt, sending up clouds of dust. He couldn't feel his right shoulder, but pain shot down his neck into the small of his back. His right hip ached.

He'd fallen sixty or seventy feet short of the road. A huge vehicle with four giant wheels on each side stopped and its turret gun pointed straight at him. Four men wearing helmets and carrying rifles ran toward him from somewhere down the hill. They rolled him over and he screamed as feeling returned to his shoulder in the form of searing pain. Somebody used a device that made a *zipping* noise to bind his hands behind his back.

Face down, with his mouth full of dirt, he tried to speak. A rough hand rolled him over and he saw himself reflected in the visor of the man's helmet. "Friend," he said, spitting dirt and hoping these people weren't allies of the Sevens. "Friend... Shangri-La."

———~~~———

Three of the four MARSOCs knelt with rifles aimed in different directions, including both sides of the caved-in house from behind which the rider and his horse had appeared. The LAVs had turrets sweeping for targets.

Lieutenant Hakala approached the prisoner with M-16 held in the crook of his arm. "What have we got, Sergeant?"

The man wore loose pastel clothing, like all the Sevens did. He'd been helped into a sitting position and given water. As Hakala watched, he rolled his right shoulder as though it hurt.

"Says he's a friend, Loot, and something about Shangri-La. We found this in his saddlebag." The man held out a flare gun with an inscription etched into the underside of the barrel: *To Idaho Jack, a true friend of Shangri-La! From Mohammad Qadim.*

"What is this?" Hakala asked the prisoner. "A war souvenir?"

The man shook his head. He appeared sleepy and grimaced every few seconds. "I gave that to Idaho Jack and couldn't let the Sevens find it."

"If you gave it to this Idaho Jack person, then why do you have it?"

"I'm Mohammad Qadim."

"That didn't answer my question."

"It's a long story... a *very* long story. If you're going to kill me, then do it. But if you're not, I need to warn Shangri-La before it's too late."

"Warn them about what?"

"The army that's heading their way."

———

From behind the house, horses nickered and Qadim heard hoofbeats. He reached up and grabbed the arm of the man kneeling over him. The man — the name on his shirt read HAKALA — raised a balled fist while the man standing beside him stuck a rifle barrel in Qadim's face, but the frantic look in his eyes made them pause.

"Sevens are coming!" he said, knowing that if the Sevens got hold of him he was a dead man.

The man Hakala blinked and stared into his eyes for two seconds. "Sevens!" he screamed. "Incoming! Let 'em have it!"

Five riders galloped into view from behind the wrecked house. They rode single file and each sprayed fire from a small sub-machine gun, while the kneeling Marines returned fire with their M-16s.

The firefight was over in less than five seconds. Two LAV-25s had been in position to shoot and the 25mm chain guns ripped horses and men into bloody chunks, but not before two sub-machine gun rounds hit the man standing over Qadim. A second Marine, one of those kneeling, rolled in the dirt with a shoulder wound. At the head of the column, more gunfire erupted, but ceased within seconds.

Corpsmen were treating the wounded within twenty seconds while the other Marines checked the Sevens they'd shot up. As usually happened when a chain gun got into the fight, they were all dead. One horse had to be put out of its misery.

Hakala helped Qadim to sit up. "Thanks," he said. Qadim nodded. "Maybe you *are* legit."

"We have to warn Shangri-La," Qadim said.

"I said maybe."

"You've got to believe me! We're running out of time."

"Does Shangri-La have a radio?"

"No."

"I'm going to radio for orders, then we'll see what happens."

"But you've got to—"

"You heard me! Sergeant, remove the prisoner to a safe location. If he gives you any promises or just won't shut up, gag him. Then get me Captain Sully on the horn."

———

Painted Desert, Arizona
1647 hours

Govind heard the distant cry of a prairie falcon as it circled high overhead. Somehow he found the bird comforting, for he'd always considered falcons part of the spirit of the land, as if the desert had manifested into animal shape. But the falcon could only observe; it couldn't intervene in the affairs of men, which at the moment were all that concerned him.

From his position high up on a ridge east of Snowtiger's cave, he'd seen the men scrambling up the rock face, but couldn't intercede because of the Sevens right behind them. The thought of strange men attacking his tribe's beloved Seer, in her own language their *Oboyo*, drove him mad. He loved her as he'd never loved anyone except his cherished wife, but not in the same way, in a way he couldn't explain.

Then he saw the men were old and knew they came from Overtime. That meant they were all in danger. By himself he could do nothing, and while he might round up enough of the tribe to intervene, it would take too long. But that afternoon he'd seen great dust clouds down near Holbrook, the kind made by machines and not horses or men. The day's sunlight was draining away toward night, but having no other recourse, he climbed back down the ridge, mounted his horse, and galloped south. The risks of a night ride were high. The risks of waiting for dawn were unacceptable.

#

Chapter 37

Some snakes prefer to eat their prey alive.
Cagliari the Unfeeling

Malibu, California
1658 hours, April 27

It wasn't a beach chair, but Rosos didn't care. For some reason, he couldn't get enough of staring at the ocean, particularly late in the afternoon as the sun began to set. In the sand beside him was a glass filled with fresh orange juice and honest-to-goodness rum. Even without ice or grenadine, it tasted good.

Shouts from the house let him know Adder had returned and didn't sound happy, so he finished his drink. The volatile head of security tended to do crazy things, including throwing a perfectly good drink into the ocean. No reason to take that chance.

He didn't turn around to gauge Adder's progress; he didn't have to. Heavy footfalls crunching through the sand pinpointed his progress as well as watching him would have.

"We're as ready as we'll ever be." Adder planted himself in front of Rosos' chair, bent over, and then gesticulated wildly, waving his arms as he raged. For his part, Rosos just let Adder vent, since he was always angry about something. "I finally got to Bumfuck Nowhere to the training camp, where they beat these worthless Chinese into some sort of combat troops, and then I find out that even the DIs are use-less. This whole army is a clusterfuck!"

"Did you select the men to accompany you to Overtime?"

"I got bodies. I'm not sure they're men."

"But enough?"

"Yeah."

Rosos smiled. "Excellent. Would you care for a drink?"

"What a stupid fucking question. Of course I do."

1548 hours, April 27

Piccaldi and Snowtiger were attached to First Platoon and arrived on top of the hill after the shooting was over. Except for one young, scared prisoner, the rest of the Sevens were dead. Two Marines had started a small fire while two others gathered wood. Most of the rest were involved either in checking the dead for intel or digging a pit to bury them. The two snipers had no assigned duties, so as the lowering sun cast lengthening shadows, they sat on the sunny side of the Humvee to take advantage of the day's last warmth. Nights that time of year frequently dipped near freezing.

"You're waiting for me to say it, aren't you?" Piccaldi said.

"Yes, I am," Snowtiger replied, although she had no idea what he meant and wasn't waiting for him to say anything. However, she did have one faint *hope* of what he might say.

"Yeah, I figured... okay, here it is... that was a damned good pickup this afternoon."

That wasn't it. "Thanks."

"I mean it. One little flash, and you're the only one who saw it out of two whole companies. I mean, *damn,* girl! Maybe you do have some kind of Indian hocus-pocus goin' on."

"I've told you before..." She stopped and her eyes opened wide. Her mouth hung open from her unfinished sentence.

"Lara, are you okay? What—"

"Ssshhh!" She held up her hand for him to be quiet. Piccaldi's concerned face hung at the edge of her vision, but she ignored him.

A voice spoke to her inside her head.

When it finished, without questioning whether it'd been a hallucination or real, she got to her feet and ran to find Captain Sully. Piccaldi was right behind her.

———

Captain Sully stood on a large boulder, scanning as much of the surrounding territory as he could see. First Platoon had cleared the rest of the hill and no other dangers appeared imminent. He allowed himself to blow out one breath of relief before stepping down to see to his command's dispositions. As his boots hit the dusty desert floor, he saw Snowtiger bouncing on the balls of her feet and running straight for him.

She drew herself up and gave a sloppy salute, followed a second later by Piccaldi.

"What's the matter?" he said. In the brief time since Overtime had gone operational, he'd learned to trust Snowtiger's insights.

Panting, she gasped out the words by twos and threes. "The prisoner... he's not a Seven... he's on... our side... you've gotta listen... to him."

"Do you recognize him?" Sully said with obvious skepticism.

"No, Cap, never seen him before."

"Then how do you know I should believe him?"

"I just do, sir."

"That's no answer, Sergeant."

"If I told the captain how I know it, he wouldn't believe me and I'd be declared unfit for duty."

"That's all the more reason to tell me how you know it."

"Please, Captain..."

Snowtiger was a stone cold killer. Hearing a pleading tone in her voice made Sully uneasy. Twice now she'd kept his command from being surprised in the field, so she'd earned a lot of credibility. Moreover, she'd won the Medal of Honor. He looked from her to Piccaldi. "What do you know about this?"

"Nothing, Cap. We were talking, then she got this weird, blank look. I could've sworn I saw her lips movin', like she was talking to somebody. For what's it worth, I'd believe her, sir."

"Give it to me straight, Snowtiger. Who told you about this prisoner?"

Instead of hesitating or biting her lip, she looked straight into Sully's eyes. "My sister, Captain."

———

Operation Comeback
1919 hours, April 27

Lt. Colonel Astrid Naidoo held her uniform cap as the Bell UH-1Y Venom utility helicopter increased rotors to take-off speed, which sent blasts of air across the heli-pad. Scurrying through the swirls of dust while lugging her duffle bag, she stopped, closed her eyes to keep particles from getting in them, and waited for the rotor wash to die down. Once moving again, she saw someone waiting for her beside a small concrete building housing the elevator, a blond woman in unfamiliar pants and shirt, holding an M-16 at the ready. As Naidoo trotted toward her, the woman opened a door into the building and followed her inside.

"My name's Frosty," the woman said once the door had closed behind them. There was a coldness to her tone that made Naidoo wonder if that was how she'd gotten her name. "You could be in danger."

"It's a pleasure to meet you, Frosty." She extended her hand.

But the Zombie didn't shake it. "Maybe you didn't hear me, Colonel, but you might be a target. Did you bring a sidearm?"

"No. I didn't think I'd need one." She also didn't have one.

Frosty clucked in disgust. "Here." She passed over a standard issue Beretta M9 and two spare magazines wrapped in an M12 holster. "I tried to find you a Sig Sauer XM18 but couldn't find one, but that's a helluva good gun if you've never shot one."

"I shot one in Iraq," Naidoo said, without adding it had been only during the once-a-year required qualification at the base shooting range. Her expertise had always been administrative and not combat.

Frosty seemed to sense the unspoken truth behind Naidoo's brief answer, though. "Maybe you and General Schiller can practice together," she said. They stepped into the elevator. Frosty punched a floor number and pointed at the pistol. "You might want to put that on."

"What kind of danger could I be in here?"

"More than you think. There're a lot of people in here who're loyal to General Steeple, and they are royally pissed that he got locked up."

"To the point of hurting me?"

"To the point of hurting all of us. They view the people from Overtime as some sort of enemy. Also, we apparently abducted some sleepers from here and took them back to Prime. And one last thing is that a Zombie got killed who'd been part of their security team, a really talented sniper named Scope. She and I roomed together I don't how many times. Add all of that up and we're sittin' in a pile of shit."

Naidoo turned to the younger woman, aghast. "You do not use that kind of language around a superior officer. Do you understand me?"

Frosty rolled her eyes. "Lady, I'm a Zombie. We ain't got no superior officers. We've just got Green Ghost."

———

General Schiller looked up at the knock on his door. Before he could say *come in*, Frosty entered without being told, followed by Lt. Colonel Naidoo. Taking advantage of the open door, Corporal Duglach slid into the office, too.

Schiller put down a pen and crossed his arms. "Colonel Naidoo, I'm very glad to see you. Frosty and Corporal Duglach, I do not remember telling you to enter my office."

"You didn't," Frosty said. "Glide told me to update you on the security situation. You wanna hear it or not?"

The tips of Schiller's ears turned red. Having been described by more than one fellow officer as the hardest-ass stickler for military protocol who ever lived, he found it very difficult to accept the casual manners of his two Zombies. With a force of will, he kept himself from shouting. "Yes, please give me the information. But first, Corporal Duglach, what do you need?"

"General, you haven't eaten since breakfast. Let me bring you some dinner."

"I'm fine, Corporal."

"Sir—"

"I appreciate it, but I'm not hungry."

Then something happened that had never happened during his entire military career — a subordinate called him out.

"Did you ever think she might be hungry?" Frosty said, pointing with her rifle at Naidoo.

He gaped at the wiry blonde woman, who merely stared back.

"I'm fine," Naidoo said. "I had a big lunch."

Schiller ignored her. His voice remained even but his flushed cheeks and noisy inhalations were all that was needed to show his rage. "I don't know who you think you're talking to that way, but I could have you court-martialed for insubordination and half a dozen other charges, and maybe I will."

"Two things wrong with that," Frosty said. "First, I'm not in the Army, or the Marines, or any other branch of service. You can't order me around because I'm not in your chain of command. And second, if you want me arrested, who's going to do it, me? You've only got two security people on this base you can count on, General, me and Glide. Now let's all eat something so we can get on with our meeting and the colonel can find a bunk."

"I'm the commanding general of this base," he said, his voice rising only slightly but carrying even more menace. "While you are on this base, you will do as I order, or you can get out. You will show me the respect due to my rank, or you can get out. I don't care if I have to defend myself all by myself, but I will not be disrespected by you or anyone else."

Frosty cocked her head, letting her short bangs dangle to one side. A lopsided grin took the place of the scowl she'd worn only seconds earlier. Pointing at General Schiller, she began to nod. "Now *that's* a man I can fight to keep safe. Well said... sir."

Schiller blinked several times and let his breathing slow before he spoke again. "Corporal, please bring dinner for everybody. We'll be eating in here."

Duglach left and the two women pulled chairs closer to Schiller's desk.

Without preamble, Frosty launched into what she had to say. "This base's security battalion was hand-picked by General Steeple, but it wasn't because they were bad-asses. Most of them are walking around with their dicks in their hands..."

"That is *not* language I want to hear in a report!" Although his voice had shrillness when he raised it, there was surprising power, too. Before Frosty could say anything he added something else. "It's not professional."

Her rebuttal froze on her lips; instead she laughed. "You got me there, General. I'm nothin' if not a pro. All right, see if this is better... most of the security people were picked because of their extreme loyalty to General Steeple personally. You've should have their personnel files, but from what I hear, he intervened in a lot of their careers to help them advance. This whole operation looks like it was set up as his personal little kingdom. That includes Overtime, and now that he's been arrested there's open talk of how to bust him out of his cell. Right now their anger is focused at you, General, because you're his replacement here at Comeback. So far there hasn't been a catalyst for their anger, but that could change. Glide is out right now keeping an eye on them."

Schiller listened, his face tight in concentration. "First, thank you for your efforts in collecting this information. I know it must be difficult to acquire."

"Without hurting anybody, yeah, it's tough. We're not allowed to hurt anybody, right?"

Schiller couldn't imagine how the slender woman could hurt a well-trained soldier. At five feet, seven inches tall, she wasn't short, and from the way she moved, her toned musculature was obvious, but still, she couldn't weigh more than 135 pounds, at most. And yet he never doubted the casual danger she alluded to possessing.

"Second," he went on, "I'd like you to identify any individuals who might remain loyal to the chain of command."

"Meaning *you*?"

"Yes."

"We can do that. But General, for your own good, don't go anywhere without your personal weapon and if it comes down to it, don't hesitate to use it. Same goes for you, Colonel."

"Thank you, Frosty. I'll keep that in mind. Is there anything else?" When nobody said anything, Schiller relaxed his scowl. "Very well, then... is anyone hungry?"

\#

CHAPTER 38

Ask not the Elves for advice, because they will tell you both no and yes.
J.R.R. Tolkien

North of Beaty, Nevada on Highway 95
1921 hours, April 27

Bumping along the highway leading north from Creech, Angriff was surprised at how good the reception was with Colonel Kordibowski back at Prime. Sitting beside him, Major Iskold waited to take notes or write up orders, although the failing light made her squint at the notepad in her lap.

"The two Marine recon companies ran into a patrol of Sevens west of Gallup, New Mexico," Colonel Kordibowski said. "One of them claims to be from Shangri-La and we believe him. He says it's located in a valley north of Albuquerque."

"Not Colorado?" asked Angriff.

"Not according to this guy. He even had some sort of evidence to back him up, but on the other hand he's a Muslim. Do we trust him or not?"

Twenty seconds went by before Angriff spoke again. "Didn't that Idaho Jack guy gives us directions?"

"He said it was somewhere northeast or east of Gallup. When I asked him how far it was, he said it took him six days to get there, but had no idea in kilometers or miles. According to this man, it's about 200 miles to the east, in a mountainous region near the San Antonio and Jemez Hot Springs."

"Where's that?"

"North of Albuquerque."

"And they believe him?"

"Yes, sir, they do."

"What about you?"

"I do not have a satisfactory response for that, General. I can see both sides. However, and I think this is the deciding factor, I am not the officer on the spot."

"Come on, Rip, don't hand me that crap. You're the S-2. It's your job to answer such questions."

"Very well then, sir. Keeping in mind this is pure speculation, I do believe him and then again I do not. Since he is a Muslim, I have to think he could be a plant, although the Sevens are not true Muslims, so perhaps I am equating the two in error."

"That's not speculation, that's the educated guess of an experienced intelligence officer I trust implicitly. The fact that he's a Muslim matters to me only because we are at war with a Caliphate that claims to be Islamic, and that makes this man a potential security risk. But it remains to be seen whether his information is valid or not, and if it is then we owe him a debt of gratitude. It's a complicated business... so in the end I'm giving the decision to the officer on the spot, as you suggested."

"That would be Captain Sully."

"He's a good man... hang on a minute, Rip." Covering the microphone, Angriff turned to Iskold. "Aren't we sending two tanker trucks to meet the Marines in the vicinity of Albuquerque, escorted by 2nd Army Recon Battalion? Have they left yet?"

Iskold shook her head.

"Let's also set up FOB in eastern Arizona, with a protected landing area for our helicopters, plus a supply and fuel dump. Then ascertain the status of the armored battalion elements currently at Prime, in case they're needed to support the Marines."

"That would create a lot of wear and tear, sir."

"I know. I won't order it unless it's an emergency. This is where not having rail flatcars inhibits our projection of force."

He turned back to the radio mike. "Tell Sully it's his call, Rip, and I'll back him up on whatever decision he makes."

———

2055 hours
Hawthorne, Nevada

Thirteen hours in a Humvee with only three ten-minute rest and refueling breaks left Angriff's lower back feeling like several knives had been inserted into his spine. Tight neck muscles caused spasms that ran down his right shoulder blade and left him closing his eyes against the pain. As he opened the door and stepped into the last of the twilight near an elaborate brick sign that read HAWTHORNE ARMY DEPOT, WORLD'S LARGEST AMMO DEPOT, he was nearly overwhelmed with *déjà vu*. A visit in early 2012 flooded his mind with memories of pyramidal bunkers lined up like some giant cemetery of forgotten Egyptian pharaohs.

The scraper Jingle Bob and his companion, the socially awkward young man named Nuff, had both said they'd seen Rednecks pillaging the base a few weeks earlier. Bob was missing along with Randall and Carlos, but he'd met Nuff the night before, as well as the man named Joshua Dalton. They'd told him all about the Rednecks at Hawthorne, and Dalton had related the horrific story about the massacre of a father and three boys, plus the gang rape of the mother. Angriff believed their story. For that reason, Colonel Young had decided not to take any chances on moving into the depot itself until morning. That allowed patrols to clear the space before the regiment itself moved in, while maintaining a strong defensive position outside the main gate. They all hoped the Rednecks would be stupid enough to engage them.

But from all appearances, Hawthorne the town had been hastily evacuated. A large fire pit right outside the gate still had glowing embers, so there seemed little chance of the riders coming back until they'd left. After a brief conference with Young and his staff, they ate dinner and Angriff turned in. Tired as he was, he looked forward to starting the book he'd gotten at Creech, *Integration*. Few things took his mind off immediate worries like a good sci-fi story.

#

CHAPTER 39

Good cheer is no hindrance to a good life.
Aristippus

Sierra Army Depot
1959 hours, April 27

Norm Fleming felt himself falling sideways and woke in a panic. When he jerked himself upright, the bolt of pain through his chest pushed a low "ahhhh..." from his lungs. He tilted back in the rusty office chair and took several shallow breaths until the ache faded. Only then did he realize somebody stood in the doorway of his makeshift office.

"How do you do that?" he said.

"Do what?" answered Green Ghost.

"Appear like that, out of nowhere. It's not natural."

"I've been here for a few minutes, but you were asleep."

"Weren't you due back three days ago?"

"Four."

"Have it your way. Weren't you due back four days ago?"

"Long story."

"Fortunately I wasn't worried. Where's Jane?"

"She went home. Lights out early tonight."

"I've been up late every night worrying," Fleming said. "I needed a nap."

"I thought you weren't worried."

"I don't know how I never noticed the similarities between you and your father."

Since it wasn't a question, Green Ghost had no response. "I've got intel."

"Of course you do."

"The Chinese have named their government the People's Republic of California."

Fleming couldn't help laughing, and it hurt. "I never expected that from you."

"It's not a joke."

"Oh, come on, you can't be serious."

"I don't make this stuff up. There's something else."

"It can't top that."

"Adder is with them."

Fleming's good-natured grin faded into his more familiar stone face. "Do you mean *our* Adder?"

"I doubt there're two of them."

"Assuming it's the same man—"

"It is."

"Why would a Zombie squad leader be in league with the Chinese? For that matter, how did he get here? Meaning sixty years later?"

"It's sixty for you and Saint. For some of us, it's only fifty-one years. A lot happened in those nine years. Adder took all of Third Squad with him into the Venezuelan jungle and came out as the sole survivor. No one could ever prove anything, but we had intel that he'd been paid off."

"Paid off by whom?"

"We never found out. But it seems like a safe bet that whoever it was also had access to CHILSS."

"We've already had plenty of traitors, so I suppose one more won't make any difference."

"Yeah... and one more thing."

"Good grief, something else?"

"There might still be a U.S. Navy."

#

CHAPTER 40

It is difficult to free fools from the chains they revere.
Voltaire

0149 hours. April 28
Prescott Regional Airport

Norris McComb glanced at the illuminated hands on his old-style wristwatch for the fifth time in the last two minutes. The Gulfstream could show up any time now and they really needed to get the flame pots lit, but the damned Marine sentry from Prescott wouldn't leave. He'd tried everything he could think of to get the man to dope off, just this once, but he wouldn't do it. *Damned jarhead*, he thought.

"Son, there's no reason for you to be out here tonight," he said, trying yet again. "It's getting chilly, you should get on to bed... we'll keep an eye on things. Hell, we're gonna be here anyway."

"I appreciate that, Mr. McComb, but like I told you before, I was given this duty and I'm going to carry it out. Those are my orders."

"How old are you, son?"

"What does that have to do with it?"

"Nothing, just curious, that's all." Even in the moonlight, McComb could see tension in face of the young Marine. He also saw firmness and irritation, and decided to try the last idea he had. "You said your name was Rothena?"

"Yes, sir, PFC Dantarius Rothena."

"All right, Private Rothena—"

"PFC Rothena, Mr. McComb." There was an edge to the young man's voice.

McComb held up his hand, and thanked God the moon-light was so bright that the Marine could see it. "I am very sorry, PFC Rothena. As you can see, I'm not a military man. I'm an engineer and a construction foreman. But I do have a high security clearance, which is why I'm standing here right now. Do you have a high security clearance, PFC Rothena?"

"I don't know what you're getting at... *sir.*"

"Did your commanding officer not tell you anything about what's going to happen here tonight?"

Despite Rothena's dark features McComb could see that confused the man.

"What's going to happen?"

"Weren't you told anything?"

"Just to guard the airfield in case any Rednecks were around."

"Damn!" McComb paced in a circle and rubbed his chin. He checked his watch again: 0155 hours. "Why does every-thing get fucked up? Okay, here's the deal, Rothena. In about five minutes, an airplane is going to land at this field carrying some very high level VIPs, people you shouldn't even know exist, and you can't breathe a word of it to anybody, got that? Not... one... word. If you do, you'll be brought up on charges."

"An airplane?" Rothena said.

"Didn't I just say that, *PFC?* Yes, a small jet, and before that happens we've got to light oil pots so the pilot can see the runway. Now, you've cost us so much time that you're going to have to help."

"But—"

"What *but?* When General Angriff chews my ass for not having those pots lit, do you really want me to tell him it's because some tight-assed PFC got in the way? Well, do you?"

As they spoke, McComb heard the third man on the field, a welder named Nalfon, running toward them. Puffing and heaving, he came to a stop and began waving his arms. "What are you doing, Norris? We've gotta get this done."

"PFC Rothena here has refused to vacate the field as General Angriff ordered—"

"You never said the general ordered it!"

"—and delayed lighting the pots," he continued, ignoring the suddenly frantic Marine. "But to make up for it, he's now gonna help us get the pots lit, right?"

"I..."

"*Right?*"

Rothena hesitated another few seconds, and then nodded once.

McComb held out a hand to Nalfon and wiggled his fingers. "Gimme your box of matches." He pressed the cardboard square into Rothena's right hand and held up his index finger the way a parent does to make a point. "There's two pots halfway down and two more at the other end of the field, and you're gonna need to run, got it? You can use five matches to light those four pots, no more. Give me your rifle."

He held out his left hand but Rothena pulled it back. "I will not surrender my weapon."

"Listen, dumbass, you're gonna have to sprint and you can do it faster without that gun."

"A Marine does not surrender his weapon unless ordered to do so."

"Fine, keep it, but if that plane gets here—" As if that was a cue, they all heard a distant, high-pitched whine.

"Go!" McComb yelled.

Ten minutes later Rothena was back, breathing heavily but not panting. The Gulfstream displayed no running lights, so they only caught occasional glimpses of the white aircraft as it lined up for landing.

"I've never seen an airplane flying before," Rothena said, sounding much younger than twenty as wonder filled his voice. "I know there used to be lots of them..."

"Yes, there did," McComb said, patting him on the back. The foreman wore a pistol in a holster around his shoulder, as all construction workers did in an area infested with rattlesnakes. He realized now that he might have to use it on Rothena and hoped it didn't come to that; he'd never killed anybody before.

PFC Rothena bounced on his heels with excitement. The Gulfstream touched down and bounced a few times before taxiing to the old terminal where McComb, Nalfon, and Rothena stood waiting for them. Once the pilot engaged the parking brake, McComb excused himself and went to await the stairs folding down. The instant they touched down, he disappeared into the fuselage and came back accompanied by a very large man in a nondescript but unfamiliar uniform.

In the darkness, Rothena couldn't be sure if that was General Angriff or not. He'd seen the general a few times from afar, and knew he was not small, but this man appeared much bigger. Whoever he was, he made a direct line for Rothena, eating up the distance in long strides. He wore a boonie hat that, even at close range, cast shadows over his face. Since he wore no insignia and Rothena was unable to see the details of his face, Rothena didn't know how to react. Taking no chances, he came to attention and saluted; the man acted like an officer, so saluting was to cover his ass.

"Private First Class Rothena?" the man said.

"Yes, sir," he said, holding the salute.

"You're a good Marine, Rothena," he said. "Your country is proud of you."

Rothena didn't smile outwardly, but his chest inflated the slightest bit before a long knife slid between his ribs and into his heart.

#

CHAPTER 41

I never ask a man what his business is, for it never interests
me. What I ask about are his thoughts and dreams.
H.P. Lovecraft

Overtime Prime, Middle Western Gate
0354 hours, April 28

Although the airport was only a few miles from the center of town, nobody came to investigate the first landing in more than fifty years. Prescott slept right through it. Adder deployed a dozen of the Chinese in a semi-circle around the truck as the rest dug a shallow pit and buried Rothena a hundred yards out in the desert. Then they piled into the truck and headed north.

They used the smaller middle western gate instead of the larger southwestern one, which was the one Angriff's convoy had used. It took an extra half-hour's driving time, but that gate led into the lesser-used Motor Bay B instead of the busy Motor Bay D. It made for less chance of being challenged by an officer with the rule book up his ass.

In the rear of the large truck, Adder and the 23 Chinese soldiers had all changed into American uniforms supplied by McComb. Most already carried some version of the M-16, a few had civilian AR-15s, but three who didn't were given the American weapon. The idea wasn't to pass close inspection, merely to avoid unwanted attention inside the base. But time was of the essence. Reveille was 0600 hours and by then they had to have General Steeple in his headquarters, ready to broadcast the message that he was assuming command.

Nalfon drove while McComb rode shotgun.

The guard waved them through without even requiring them to stop. After all, McComb came and went all the time, and so did Nalfon. Their arrivals and departures were part of the everyday functioning of the base.

As expected, the construction motor pool was silent. The first men wouldn't be showing up for another hour or so. The mornings still took a while to heat up, so there was no reason to be at an outdoor jobsite before dawn, like there would be June through September.

McComb watched the Chinese troops jump out of the truck with surprise; in American uniforms they all looked very... *American.* Three were of Asian heritage, five were black, four appeared either Latino or maybe Indian, and the rest were white. That was when he realized the term Chinese now meant something other than merely a racial identity.

But American soldiers they weren't. Adder did his best to keep them organized and quiet, but for most of them it appeared to be more of a party than a covert op. They laughed and talked loud and moved as if it was a holiday, until Adder grabbed his own M-16 and leveled it at them.

"If you fuckers don't shut the fuck up, I'll blow your heads off and do this by myself."

The Chinese were all young. Wide-eyed, McComb could tell from their stares they believed Adder would actually cut them down where they stood, and doubted they'd ever been yelled at like that. Immediately their entire demeanor changed and they all fell into line.

After aligning them two by two for the trip through the corridors of Prime itself, McComb stood at the front to lead the way, with Nalfon bringing up the rear. Adder caught up to McComb and shook his head. "Worthless pieces of shit. Let's go."

Their route led through a dizzying series of hallways and corridors, but they saw no one. McComb explained the rooms were mostly for storage or specialized workshops unlikely to have traffic so early in the day. The most remote service elevator was in the far northwestern corner of the base, which they took to the level of Steeple's cell. After stalking through a long hallway, they rounded a corner and came to a place where the walls abruptly changed from the finished poly-foam used in much of the base to bare stone. Likewise the ceiling went from sound-absorbing tiles to granite. Only the floor had been leveled and finished with sealed concrete.

At the far end were double doors with a lone sentry on duty. McComb recognized his fellow RSVS comrade and waved, but instead of opening the door, the man held up a hand in the universal signal for *halt* and put a finger to his lips.

"We've got a problem," the sentry said in a low voice. "Major Noshimura is here tending to one of the prisoners."

"She's not a doctor!" McComb said.

"She's a shrink, but she went to med school. She's been treating prisoners for the past few months to practice doing medicine again. I guess we need more doctors. Anyway, what're we gonna do?"

McComb rubbed his lips. "What about the uniforms?"

"Yeah, yeah, I delivered them half an hour ago and got Colonel Claringdon up to speed. He's all in, but what about Noshimura?"

"We don't have a problem," Adder said, pushing past the sentry and through the door beyond. "She does."

"Do *not* kill her!" McComb said while running to catch up the Adder. All of the Chinese followed them, as they'd been instructed to stay out of sight.

"That'll be up to her," the huge man replied.

"This isn't some enemy base and we need all the doctors we can get. Don't hurt her."

"Whatever. This place smells like mold and farts."

Ahead they saw a short, stocky woman standing in a puddle of light from the overhead LEDs, talking to someone through a door.

"That Noshimura?" Adder said.

"Yes. Remember your promise."

Adder quickened his pace and she turned at the thumping of boots. Instinctively she recoiled as he approached. Six feet from her, he unsheathed the Marine combat knife and flashed it at her throat, stopping inches away. Her mouth opened but he put a finger up to her lips.

"Ssshhh," he said. "I'm not here to hurt you, but you have to be quiet. Can you do that?"

She nodded and he edged the blade away from her skin so she didn't inadvertently cut herself. "Good girl. Now stay right here with some of these fine gentlemen, and in a minute I'll come back and let you know what to do next, 'kay?"

This time she swallowed before nodding.

"General Steeple, in the flesh."

The door opened and a very large man entered. He stood at least six feet three inches tall and 250 pounds, and Steeple doubted any of it was fat. The black T-shirt he wore seemed stretched to its limit above the standard issue ACU pants and decidedly non-regulation black boots. A knife hung in a sheath under his right armpit and a pistol under his left. But it was the scarred face that gave away his identity; Steeple recognized the face from the Venezuela affair.

Steeple stood before a three-foot high mirror that he'd been given when someone had brought his newly cleaned uniform. Propped on the small table, it leaned against the wall as he turned this way and that, tugging at loose folds to eliminate any wrinkles. Under no circumstances would he betray the revulsion he instantly felt for this brutal narcissist. "Adder, I presume."

"Yeah."

Feigning interest in his collar, Steeple delayed turning for five more seconds, then extended his hand. "It's my pleasure."

Adder looked at the general's proffered hand like it was covered in anthrax. "Yeah."

Wearing his best Congressional smile, the one reserved for powerful politicians and which looked like he'd just drawn a royal flush but which in fact had no pleasure in it whatsoever, Steeple withdrew his hand and ran it one last time through his hair. "Shall we go?"

#

Chapter 42

*Usually the first problems solved by the new paradigm are
those that couldn't be solved by the old paradigm.*
Joel A. Barker

Overtime Prime
0502 hours, April 28

McComb stood right outside his cell door and Steeple
beamed on seeing him. Clapping him on the forearm, he met
the foreman's eyes and held them. "Well done, Norris, well
done. You'll be richly rewarded for your work today."

"Thank you, sir," McComb stammered. It was the first
time he'd felt the palpable aura of charisma that surrounded
Steeple. It was the first inkling he'd had of how the man had
stayed at the center of power for so long.

When they passed Major Noshimura, she didn't know
whether to salute or not and finally decided she should. Then
she was hustled into Steeple's cell for safekeeping.

"That's why this will be successful," he said to McComb.
"The good major was surprised to see me free, and had a
choice in how to react. Confronted with the reality of me being here, in this place, in a vacuum of power and backed up
by armed men, she acknowledged my superior rank with a
salute. Now she's committed."

"What happens when General Angriff shows up?"

"That depends on the circumstances." Steeple was genuinely surprised when Colonel Claringdon stepped out of a cell
on their right and joined the procession. "Major Claringdon?

What are you doing here?" Steeple said, until noticing the birds on his collar. "Excuse me, *Colonel* Claringdon. To what do I owe this unexpected pleasure?"

"The colonel was arrested right after you were, General," McComb explained. "He tried to kill Angriff and his whole staff."

Steeple stopped and turned to Claringdon. He took a moment before speaking. "While I appreciate your support, Colonel, I trust that isn't some new hobby of yours? Killing generals, I mean."

Claringdon smiled. "Only if they aren't you, sir."

Although Overtime was an enormous military base, the sight of two dozen armed soldiers marching down the corridors was highly unusual. Fortunately for Steeple and his bodyguards, they encountered few base personnel at such an early hour, and only two of the ones they did see gave them more than a cursory glance. Those two snapped to attention at the sight of a five star general, and both times Steeple gave McComb a look that meant *see?* After the second, he raised his nose from ninety degrees to one hundred.

Every bit of this felt right to Steeple, like a Roman emperor surrounded by Praetorian Guardsmen making his way down the Palatine hill to the Forum, from where he would run the empire. He'd spent much of the past two days planning what to do and say once he'd assumed power, but there had still been idle moments when he'd compared himself to the greatest Roman Emperor of them all, Augustus. He could be ruthless if anyone crossed him, but much preferred ruling with a light touch.

Instead of taking elevators that would have limited their exposure, however, Steeple insisted they take the main elevators that opened near the Clam Shell. When the doors opened, a private looking down at a tablet went to get on, looked up, and came to rigid attention. Steeple waved him out of the way and said, "Move aside, private," in a quiet voice.

Adder posted men on each side of the hallway in both directions at intervals of 100 feet, then 75, then 50 feet from the large entrance doors to the headquarters. Two more flanked the bank of four elevators and another two stood to either side of the headquarters doors. He posted two on the top level of the Clam Shell, two at the ramp leading to the Crystal Palace, and the final three on the platform surrounding the commander's office.

Once he'd given his men their assignments, he pointed at Steeple. "It's show time."

05280 hours

The doctors had told him it would be best if he stayed in bed a few more days, but when push came to shove, Colonel Friedenthall signed off on Schiller's return to duty in the Crystal Palace, provided he not engage in any more gunplay for a while. Schiller also agreed to take a sling, although he never agreed to actually wear it, and it remained on his nightstand, right where he'd left it.

It being his first day back, he wanted to get to work early and see what needed doing. His shoulder ached and he moved his right arm in slow, careful motions, but it was his thigh that bothered him most. It was stiff and hurt like hell, and the doctors said it would take weeks to truly heal and even that depended on him doing the exercises they gave him to keep it limber.

Getting shot hurt.

Down in the Clam Shell, the night shift monitored various systems in puddles of light from their personal lamps. Without the hum of the day, everything seemed preternaturally quiet.

Corporal Diaz had the day off after covering for him all the days since the fight for the Crystal Palace, and had left a detailed list of everything Schiller needed to know. He'd been told that Colonel Saw got to work earlier than General Angriff did, usually being in the office by seven, and that he drank his coffee black and wanted a cup as soon as he arrived.

The platform surrounding the Crystal Palace was made of mesh metal to save weight, the same material as the ramp connecting it to the ground floor. Only the actual commander's office had a solid floor. Schiller was on the far side of the platform, checking the coffee station to make sure it was ordered the way he liked it, when he felt the characteristic vibration of people coming up the ramp. Had Colonel Saw shown up early?

Keeping his right leg stiff, he limped around the Crystal Palace to where the ramp met the platform, and froze. A young soldier in uniform aimed an M-16 at him as people came up the ramp behind him, but Schiller couldn't tear his gaze away from the muzzle of the gun. He held his hands palm out. "I'm unarmed," he said, wishing his hands weren't trembling. Part of that was the pain in his shoulder.

"Who have we here?" said an officer behind the man.

"Colonel Claringdon?" Schiller said.

Hands behind his back, Claringdon stepped closer to Schiller, inspecting him like a slave trader at an auction. His voice was nearly a hiss. "You're going to be very sorry for opposing me."

But before he could continue, a loud, authoritative voice cut in, enunciating each word like it came straight from God. "There will be none of that!"

Schiller tilted to his right to see around Claringdon and tried to keep a straight face when he saw General Steeple at the top of the ramp. Although he wasn't a large man, Steeple's face had purpled with rage and Schiller felt something strange, a feeling that, if he were forced to describe it, could only be compared to power. It didn't feel electric, exactly; it felt... tangible.

Claringdon visibly cringed.

"There is no time for that sort of thing, Colonel, no time at all. Whatever happened in the past is now forgotten and forgiven. Do I make myself clear?"

"Yes, sir." Claringdon's lips pressed tight against his teeth.

"I mean it, Colonel. I will not condone or forgive personal vendettas. Period. As for you, Sergeant..." Steeple paused and moved closer to inspect Schiller's chevrons. Then he nodded at Schiller once. "Sergeant Major, I'd like to speak with you in my office."

"Now, General?" Schiller said.

"Yes, now."

232

Schiller didn't know who the soldiers were or why their uniforms didn't have any insignia, or how Claringdon had gotten out of the guardhouse, or for that matter what Steeple was doing strolling into headquarters in full regalia. He only knew that he had to keep calm. *Find out what he wants, John*, he said to himself. *Whatever it is, go along for now.*

—⁓—

Steeple paused on the office threshold and thought, *How often have I dreamed of this moment?* He stepped through, took two steps, stopped, sniffed, and then snarled. "Damn that man!"

Claringdon stepped up behind him. "The cigar smoke?"

"Yes, the damned cigar smoke! It smells like a bar in here."

"Not any bar I've ever been in."

Steeple turned to see Adder push past Claringdon into the office.

"Maybe a pussy-ass officer's bar, but a really good bar stinks of beer and piss and sweaty sex, and usually blood. That's when you know you're gonna have a good time."

Steeple eyed him and crossed his arms. After a moment, he walked behind the desk and sat down. The chair would have to be adjusted, but that could wait. Folding his hands on the desk, he looked up at Adder. "Don't ever contradict me again."

There was something about the way he said it that made even Adder pause. "I don't work for you," he finally said.

"Not yet. Would you like to?"

Adder laughed and sat down, although he hadn't been invited to. "I guess that depends on the job."

"I want you to be my S-5."

"What is that?"

Steeple tried to remember everything he knew about Adder. They'd never met before, but he'd nearly memorized the personnel files of every member of Task Force Zombie. Clearly, though, he needed this man on his side for the time being, since he commanded the only troops who might be willing to fight on Steeple's orders. "Head of Security."

"Do you mean like your bodyguard? Or, like, security chief for this whole underground shithole?"

"The whole thing. And everywhere outside of Overtime, too."

"Do I have to rejoin the Army?"

"Only as a technicality, but of course you'll need a rank commiserate with your duties. Colonel should about do it."

"You're gonna make *me* a colonel?"

"If you accept the position..." Steeple spread his hands. "Why not?"

"Me, a colonel." With hands clasped on top of his head, Adder craned his neck while laughing. He pointed at Claringdon. "Do I get to order him around?"

"In matters of security... yes. When it comes to protecting Operation Overtime, you're top of the food chain, reporting directly to me."

"Fuckin' A. Where do I sign?"

Schiller didn't have to wait long until the big guy named Adder motioned him into the office. Colonel Claringdon stared at him with slit eyes.

But General Steeple wore a noncommittal smile and leaned forward with hands clasped on the desk. Then Steeple's eyes flicked behind Schiller, where he could almost feel Claringdon's glare burning into his back. "Colonel, please give us a moment."

Schiller heard the scuffing as Claringdon got up. "General—"

Eyes fixed on Steeple, Schiller saw him hold up one hand in a *stop* gesture. Then the office door closed, leaving the big man named Adder as the only other occupant of the room.

"Sergeant Major of the Army... congratulations, Schiller, I'm sure you earned it."

Steeple waited, but Schiller remained silent. As an officer under arrest, Steeple did not hold any authority over him, although that distinction seemed to have been rendered moot. Steeple waited him out and after a few seconds Schiller decided that pissing him off this early wasn't worth it. "Thank you, General."

"I am not sure that you are aware of it, but I personally had to sign off on your inclusion in this unit because of the false burial it necessitated at Arlington. Despite your case not including the need for a burial plot, the one for your brother required calling in a few favors. For you the paperwork was daunting, even for inurnment in the Columbarium. I authorized this because of your indicated skills at organization and teamwork. In short, you were worth it."

Schiller simply stared without speaking. What was it General Tompkins liked to say? *You can butter my butt, but don't call me a biscuit.*

"I'm telling you this so you know how much I value your talents. You ran General Angriff's headquarters for him, correct?"

"Yes."

"And you like him personally." It wasn't a question.

"He's my commanding officer. Whether I like him or not isn't important."

"So you could serve a new commanding officer just as well?"

Schiller recognized the trap but could see no way out. "I would serve any legally appointed C.O. just as well."

"Legally appointed... I am not going to argue legalities with you, Sergeant, as I suspect it would be pointless. As of this morning, I have taken command of Operation Overtime. I intend for General Angriff to fill the role he was originally selected for, namely that of commander of combat forces and my executive officer. What I need to know from you is, can you serve the same role for me as you did for him?"

And there it was, the stark choice he'd been hoping he wouldn't have to make. Everything had happened too quickly for him to have time to think. Serving Steeple felt like a betrayal of General Angriff... hell, it *was* a betrayal of General Angriff. And yet by remaining at the center of power, he would be in a good place to help in whatever might be coming.

"I can, General Steeple. I will." Even as he spoke the words, though, they tasted bitter, like the coppery flavor of blood.

"Be certain, Schiller. There is no going back from this. If you say no there will be no repercussions, but if you say yes now you cannot change your mind later. Regardless of what happens, or any orders I give with which you might disagree, it will be your sworn duty to carry them out to the best of your ability. Do you still say yes?"

"Yes... sir. What about Colonel Claringdon?"

Steeple's face changed into yet another smile, this one that of a generous benefactor. "Leave Colonel Claringdon to me. Now, find out where General Angriff is at this exact moment, please."

"I can already tell you that, General. He's with First Mechanized Infantry Regiment on the way to Sierra Depot with a relief column."

"And who is the regimental commander?"

"Colonel Young, sir, Robert W."

"Young, of course. Please get him on the phone for me."

Operation Comeback
0605 hours

Astrid Naidoo found a bleary-eyed General Schiller already at his desk. Her two previous bosses, Lt. Colonel Ashley Wisnewski-Smith and Colonel Charlie Kinokawa, had arrived at work no earlier than 0800 hours and sometimes later. Schiller, on the other hand, got there just after 0500. He never said she had to be there that early, too, Naidoo just assumed it, but today she'd slept right through the wakeup alarm.

"I'm sorry to be late, General. It won't happen again."

Schiller waved at her to indicate it didn't matter. He looked much the worse for wear. Besides the color of his eyes, his face had gone slack and his clothes were rumpled. She wondered if he'd even slept the night before.

"General, would you like some coffee?" she said.

"I found it," he said in a cracked voice. "I found what happened to the missing Stingers."

"That's wonderful, sir!"

"Benghazi. You remember Benghazi?"

"Do you mean the attack on our embassy there, back in 2011?"

"2012, September 11, 2012. Do you remember that?"

"I remember the attack, not the details. What do the Stingers have to do with that?"

"It's why we didn't send in air support. The terrorists had those Stingers and somebody in our government knew about it."

#

CHAPTER 43

Politicians are not born; they are excreted.
Marcus Tullius Cicero

Overtime Prime
0639 hours, April 28

Colonel Khin Saw got off the elevator and started walking toward the Clam Shell while looking down. Only when a man in a uniform with no insignia pointed a rifle at him did he stop and see the sentries in the headquarters.

"Either you move that," he said, pointing to the gun, "or I'll shove it up your ass."

The man ignored him. "Who are you?" he said.

"Who am *I*? I'm your commanding officer."

A second guard in similar attire strolled over from the other side of the entrance, laughing. "Not any more."

Finally a third man came forward and ordered the other two back into their positions. "Come with me," he said.

"What in the flying hell is going on around here?" The veins on his neck stretched like ropes under purpling skin.

"Follow me and you'll find out."

Seething, Colonel Saw stalked after him. At the entrance to the Crystal Palace, *his* office, however temporarily, the man stopped him, ducked inside, and then stepped aside. Only then was Saw allowed to pass through the door.

He stepped into the office like the hero in a comic-book movie stepping through a doorway into another dimension.

Buzz-cut hair did nothing to soften the angles of his square head, or the hardness of his slit eyes. Saw was a combat commander and looked every inch of it, despite his current assignment as the S-1.

Steeple waved him in, rose, and met him halfway across the room. As they shook hands, Steeple put his left hand over Saw's right. Saw's wide body and massive shoulders strained his uniform coat as he stared into Steeple's eyes. He did not stand at attention, as he would when formally and officially reporting to a superior officer. Steeple understood what it meant. As always, his irritation hid behind a friendly smile.

"Why are you sitting behind my desk, Tom?" Colonel Saw said in a decidedly non-friendly way. "And what the fuck is going on around here?"

"Please sit down, Khin. Relax. Despite what you might have heard, I don't bite." He grinned and his voice had the same friendly tone he'd used with Nick Angriff on that little airplane in Switzerland. It was a practiced persona so ingrained he never had to think about adopting it any more. "I am damned glad to see you, Khin."

"Do I need to repeat my question, General?"

"Old friends like us do not need formalities in private, so for God's sake, call me Tom."

In the far corner of the Crystal Palace was a sliver of shadow where the blast doors on the mountain ended and morning light couldn't come through. The colonel started because he hadn't noticed the large man tucked away over there.

"And let me introduce our new S-5... Colonel Khin Saw, meet Colonel Adder."

Saw stood and extended his hand without taking his eyes off of Steeple. Adder stepped over and shook it. "My pleasure," Saw said. "So I ask again... what's going on, Tom?"

"Sit, sit." Steeple moved back behind the desk and resumed his usual position, with hands folded on the top. Saw remained standing. "I know this came as quite a shock to you."

"I don't know what this is, but yeah, it's a shock."

"Let me explain, Khin. Hear me out."

"Answer my question. What the fuck is going on here."

"I will, I promise, but *please* sit down. There." He indicated the chair facing the desk. With nostrils flaring, the colonel sat ramrod straight in the chair facing Steeple, which wasn't easy because it had a curved back. Steeple waited for a response but Saw said nothing. Since no question had been asked, no response wasn't required, and his silence told Steeple that the stocky, muscular officer was not an ally. Yet Saw's approval of his taking command would go a long way toward mollifying the rank and file.

As he steepled his fingers, the irony wasn't lost on the general, and with elbows propped on the polished wooden surface of the desk, he tapped his index fingers against his lower lip.

Saw's eyes had been fixed on the American flag hanging behind the desk but now shifted to Steeple's face. His expression remained devoid of emotion, except for his eyes, which were just a little too wide. It was a tell. No officer in the U.S. Army, then or now, ever read facial clues better than Steeple. He knew Saw represented opposition.

"Get to it," Saw said.

"The short version is that I have taken command of Operations Overtime and Comeback."

"By who's authority?"

"By the authority of the United States Army, which named me as commander effective the moment that I entered Long Sleep."

"The Army? The same one I belong to?"

Steeple didn't like sarcasm when it was directed at him, and insubordination would ordinarily have gotten Saw thrown into the stockade without any discussion, but he needed the colonel on his side, so he held his tongue and kept the smile on his face. It wasn't easy. "Yes, Khin, that Army."

"Is that who those people outside are? Because they sure as hell don't look like American soldiers."

"Them... no, they're not. They're... allies."

"What does that means?"

"You know, Colonel, I have great respect for you, but either you drop the attitude or we're going to have a problem."

Saw had unconsciously been leaning forward. At that he straightened. "I'm the acting commander of this base and you're a disgraced officer awaiting trial for treason. If any-body *should* have an attitude, it's me. And I'm on the verge of calling the MPs and having them jerk you out of my chair."

"You do approve, do you not?"

Saw had no option except to respond, "I'm not qualified to rule on such legalities, General Steeple."

Steeple's sigh was well practiced and sounded wistful. "Let me turn my cards face up, Chain. I removed Nick Angriff be-cause he was never intended to be the commander of the combined Operations Overtime and Comeback. His place in the chain of command was second, right behind me. I hand-picked him to be my Chief of Staff, second in command and military advisor. We both know Nick is the finest battle com-mander America has produced since Norman Schwarzkopf, maybe even better. His ability to win battles when others could not is uncanny. But as great of a warrior as he is, one thing he is not is an administrator. That's where I come in.

"Overtime was built by *me*, not Nick Angriff, *me*. It was designed for him to use the powerful military force that I per-sonally recruited and equipped from day one to overcome any opposition we might face once awakened. My job started once a territory had been pacified, in restoring infrastruc-ture, government, services, and security. Every inch of this place owes its existence to me. I fought tooth and nail for every dollar that went into getting it built, and believe you me, it took a lot of dollars.

"Are you familiar with the flak towers in Berlin, Ham-burg, and Vienna?"

"What?"

"The flak towers, during World War Two. Built by the Germans to combat the American strategic bombing cam-paign."

"I'm vaguely aware of them, but no details. And I don't understand the relevance."

"Hear me out, Khin. We worked together long enough at the Pentagon for you to know that I do nothing without a good reason."

"Good is subjective."

Steeple ignored the comment. "The flak towers were huge fortresses so thick with steel and concrete as to be almost indestructible. After the war, efforts to destroy the ones in

Vienna failed, and as far as I know they are still there today. Each tower had gondolas with 20 and 37 millimeter cannon on them. On top were not just the ubiquitous 88 millimeter gun we have all heard of, but its big brother, the 128 millimeter heavy flak gun. Their firepower was extraordinary.

"But as massive and heavily armed and protected as they were, those flak towers were only the fighting part of the fortress. As strong as they were, without being told when and where to shoot, they were ineffective. That was the role of a second tower near each of the gun towers, where the command and control were housed. That's where the radars were, the communications center, and, most important, the commander of the whole tower complex.

"When I started this project back in 1996, that's how I envisioned it being constructed — that was my vision. Operation Overtime would be the gun tower, the combat arm of the renewed United States armed forces, while Operation Comeback would be the command and control part. Except General Angriff apparently didn't understand the whole picture, and that may have been my fault. Regardless, I'm here now, and I intend to do what I do best: manage. You're a combat commander who happened to be good at his job while at the Pentagon, but can you imagine Nick Angriff in the Personnel Department, or Procurements? That's an actual question, Khin, it's not rhetorical."

"I imagine he'd do the best he could."

"I do not doubt it for one second. Nick is a fine soldier who would perform his assigned task to the best of his ability, but what a waste! Putting Nick Angriff behind a desk would be like trying to convert a tiger into a vegetarian. He needs to be in the field, at the head of his troops. Likewise, putting me into a combat role would be foolhardy. It is not what I do well.

"Let me be clear about this... I personally admire, respect, and like Nick Angriff. He is an amazing man. Unfortunately, Nick's precipitous decisions have made our situation much worse than it had to be."

"What?"

There it is! Steeple thought. "There were alternatives to fighting the Republic of Arizona, ways that could have reformed the existing government and acquired it as an ally instead of an enemy. Americans killed Americans, and that wasn't necessary. That would have left the entire brigade to deal with the army of the Caliphate when it showed up, the ones you've nicknamed Sevens. Angriff could have destroyed its combat capabilities in one fell swoop but now, mark my words, we'll have to deal with that army again in the future. And now I understand there are riders wearing red scarves moving into the region?"

Saw sat quiet.

"That was a question, Colonel."

"Which you don't have a right to ask me."

"It's just a question."

"Yes, there are horsemen we call Rednecks coming into the area, although we don't know where they're from."

"Would it surprise you to know that I do know where they come from?"

That hit home as Saw leaned slightly forward. "Do you, General?"

"Yes, I do. Contrary to what you may have been told, I am the only five-star general appointed by Congress since Omar Bradley died in 1981. That rank had been retired until it was given to me, and I didn't receive such a high honor by being a fool. So yes, I know precisely where those riders come from, I know why they're here, and I know how to counteract them. I also know more about this so-called Caliphate of the New Prophet than you might imagine. I bleed Army green just like you do, but I do the dirty work men of action like Nick Angriff don't want or need to worry about. It's not what they're good at, and if we're going to rebuild this country we have got to have both."

"Are you implying that if you regain command of Operations Comeback and Overtime—"

The word *regain* didn't go unnoticed.

"—that you are going to restore General Angriff to his command?"

"I'm not implying it. I'm *saying* it, Khin. I have ordered him detained but not arrested, and treated with all of the courtesy due to a lieutenant general in the U.S. Army, because Nick Angriff will again command Operation Overtime just as he always has, from this office, and the only difference will be that I have his back, and yours, once an area is liberated. I will also negotiate ceasefires and treaties with those of our enemies who are willing to listen."

"What does that mean?"

"It means that twelve thousand people cannot conquer an entire continent. We are going to have to make decisions we might not like in pursuit of the greater good, and before you argue that point, remember, America took more than two hundred years to grow to the point it was at during the Collapse. We can't rebuild that in a year or two, or a decade, or maybe even a century. All we can do is make a good start and train the next generation. I hope that makes sense to you."

Saw's nod was reluctant, but it was there.

"Good. Together we can put this country back on the map. Can I count on your support, Khin?"

"I'm not sure I have much choice."

"It's not like that."

"I think it's exactly like that... but I suppose you can count me in, General."

"Guesses don't help us move forward. Either you're in or you're out."

"Yes, you can count on me."

"You're in?"

"I'm in."

"You're sure about this?"

"I'm sure."

"I appreciate you not opposing me," Steeple said. "You could have, but I'd like to believe that you understand the legitimacy of my taking over command from General Angriff."

"I don't know if I do or not, but it seems to be a *fait accompli* at the moment. So yes, I'm willing to serve under you again."

"Excellent!" Steeple rose and extended his hand.

Colonel Saw hesitated, then stood and took it. "So what exactly do you want from me, Tom?"

Steeple feigned surprise at the question. "I want your support. I want you to be my S-3."

"Operations? That's Norm Fleming's job."

"I think General Fleming would be more effective as the S-1. You would, of course, be elevated to 0-7 and work closely with me. Is it a deal?"

"Can I think about it?"

"No, I need to know right now. Just say yes, Khin, and let's get down to work. We have a lot to do."

"All right. I'll do it."

Steeple grinned like a boy with his first girlfriend, but behind the well-rehearsed façade he studied Colonel Saw's face and read signs of doubt.

"Can I ask you one thing?"

"Absolutely, Khin."

"People are going to be hurt by this, a lot of people. It may be for the greater good, but does it bother you?"

"It is the curse of great men to step over corpses," Steeple said.

Colonel Saw's expression didn't change. "You have quite a way with words."

"Not really, just a good memory."

"Oh? Who said it, then?"

"Heinrich Himmler."

"The Reichsführer SS?"

"Just because he was a mass murderer doesn't make it any less true."

#

Chapter 44

It is easier to forgive an enemy than to forgive a friend.
William Blake

Hawthorne Army Depot, Nevada
0731 hours, April 28

"General, wake up, sir."

Feeling a light touch on his shoulder, Angriff rolled over in his cot and tried to open his eyes. It wasn't as easy as it used to be. Once upon a time, being awakened in the middle of the night would have meant springing from bed and reaching for a weapon. Now when he tried to speak, he yawned instead. "Major Strootman? What is it?"

"Sir, Colonel Young requested that you join him in the headquarters tent."

"Are we under attack?"

"No, sir."

Angriff nodded and swung his legs out of his sleeping bag. When in the field, he'd always slept in his pants and undershirt, but the desert air turned cold at night so he pulled on his well-worn multicam winter weight coat. It was only when he stood up that he noticed the guard at his door. "What's he doing here?"

"The colonel will explain, General."

Angriff could only see one explanation for having an armed sentry standing at the entrance to his tent — more assassins. When two more armed men fell in on either side during the walk to the regiment's headquarters, it convinced him that was it. He wished he'd strapped on his pistols.

"Am I in danger?" he said upon entering the tent and seeing Colonel Young waiting for him. His mind registered that only he and Young occupied the large space, and that Major Strootman and the guards stopped outside and closed the entrance flap.

"What?" Young's face scrunched in confusion. "No, sir!"

"So it's not assassins?"

"Beg your pardon, General?"

"The guard on my tent, the escort over here... if I'm not in danger, then what's going on, Bob?"

"Sir, I... I'm not sure how to tell you this."

"The only way to tell it is to tell it."

"That doesn't make it easier, General. I just received a phone call from Prime—"

"Has something happened to my wife, or one of my daughters?"

"What? Oh, no, sir, nothing like that, it's... sir, General Steeple has taken command at Overtime and ordered you detained."

———

Angriff's eyes narrowed and his fists clenched involuntarily. It all made sense now, the guards, the escort... he was under house arrest. Despite his rising anger, however, he kept his voice under control. "How do you know this to be true? Did you talk to Steeple yourself?"

"I did, General. He said to make clear that you are not under arrest, but neither can you be allowed to leave my custody. You are to be treated with the utmost courtesy and respect due to a man of your rank."

"My *rank*? By Congress acting in joint session under emergency conditions, and signed by the president, I'm the highest ranking officer in the United States armed forces. I can't be removed from command of Overtime unless I'm deemed incompetent, in which case Lieutenant General Fleming takes over."

"Sir, please understand my position."

"Your position is quite clear, Colonel. I am your commanding officer and General Steeple is a traitor who apparently has illegally tried to seize command of the Seventh Cavalry. Therefore your position is to follow my orders to help in ejecting Steeple from that post and bringing him before a court-martial to answer for his crimes."

Young held out his hands in a pleading gesture. "General Angriff, sir, I have limited fuel, supplies, and military assets. Resupply is now at the pleasure of General Steeple. Moreover, trying to retake Overtime would likely involve shooting at other elements of the Seventh Cavalry, including air assets, of which I have none."

"You're taking his side in this?"

"I have no other choice, General. My regiment is my first responsibility."

"In that case, I relieve you of your command, Colonel."

Dipping his head, Young slowly shook it. "You no longer have that authority, sir." He looked up and Angriff could see the tears welling in his eyes. "I am so very sorry to have to do this. There's no officer I respect more than you, General."

"Apparently there is," Angriff said, his molars clenched tight.

#

Chapter 45

It is a man's own mind, not his enemy or foe, that lures him to evil ways.
Buddha

Overtime Prime
0756 hours, April 28

Steeple could only shake his head in bemusement when he realized that nobody had known it was possible to sound-proof the office's conference room. He returned from his phone call to Colonel Young and could see in Saw's face that despite his pronouncement of loyalty, doubts remained. With the smooth reflexes of a trained politician, however, he didn't allow his face to reflect his skepticism. Chain Saw could always be gotten rid of later, if it came to that.

Meanwhile, he pumped him for as much information as he could get.

"...so as I said, the construction people have some of the wells near the Verde River nearly functional. We should have oil flowing again very soon."

"Excellent!" he said.

Silent until now, Adder interrupted the colonel's report without apology or warning. "If Green Ghost is away, who did he leave in charge of security?"

Saw narrowed his eyes and Steeple read in them that he didn't like the hulking man.

"A man named Wingnut. I think two or three of that group are also still here, including that strange blonde woman."

Adder leaned forward at the waist. "Blonde woman?"

"Yes... Nipple, that's her name."

Steeple turned, curious about Adder's reaction toward his former teammates in Task Force Zombie.

The man's lean cheeks and small eyes folded into slits as a strange smile, half snarl, half laugh, crossed his lips. "Where are they?"

⁓

Sergeant Major Schiller knocked, entered, and handed Steeple the morning's reports, including a routine copy of an order given last night by General Angriff for two Apache gunships and half a platoon of riflemen to fly northeast and intervene in some contact between Dennis Tompkins and a band of Sevens. Steeple read the order twice, and immediately called Schiller on the intercom. "Schiller, get me the aircraft dispatcher, now!"

Once seated behind the desk, he started the checklist of things he still needed to do, prioritizing those actions necessary to prevent a counter-coup. But first, he spent a few minutes adjusting the chair to fit his smaller frame. Then he rearranged the desktop's few neutral items to his liking and had started riffling through the middle desk drawer when a phone call interrupted him. He knew it was going to take some time to get Overtime exactly the way he wanted it.

"Dispatch? This is General Steeple, your new commanding officer. I want you to cancel a scheduled mission..."

With any luck, this Tompkins man would die and he'd have one less headache to worry about. But why did that name sound so familiar?

⁓

0913 hours, April 28
Sara Snowtiger's Cave, Painted Desert, Arizona

Sometime past midnight, Dennis Tompkins finally fell asleep inside the cave, near the mouth. Someone had placed a blanket over him and he assumed that was Sara

Snowtiger, since their gear had been left tied to the horses. Monty Wilson had put the horses up the previous afternoon, but Derek Tandy scrambled down in the pre-dawn darkness to make sure they were okay. Being the youngest often meant him doing things like that, even though *young* was a relative term; Tandy was 74.

Tompkins discovered this after the fact, when John Thibodeaux shook him awake with news of a radio call from Prime. The sun was well up by then, which surprised him; Tompkins usually woke at dawn when they were in the field. Wiping sleep from his eyes, Tompkins tried to blink away blurred vision with no success. The chill of night left him tired and stiff. Not daring to stand up until his eyes could focus, he scooted past the cave's entrance so the rock didn't interfere with reception, but low enough that a sniper didn't pick him off.

"Tompkins here," he croaked. Thibodeaux heard it and handed him a canteen, from which he took three long pulls.

"Is this Major Dennis Tompkins?"

"This is *General* Tompkins."

There was a pause. "The purpose of this call is to inform you that your request for air and ground support has been denied. General Steeple also orders you to return to Overtime as soon as practicable."

"What?"

But the only response was static.

———

Stunned, Tompkins leaned against the cool rock wall inside the cave, near the dwindling fire. He wasn't conscious of anything until Sara Snowtiger crouched beside him and touched his cheek. "You've had bad news?" she said in a gentle tone.

Their eyes met. "Apparently so... something's happened to a dear friend of mine, 'cept I don't know what."

"This is your friend the great warrior?"

"Yes." Tompkins' surprise at her insight made him forget his plight for a second. "How did you know?"

She smiled. He wasn't sure he'd ever seen anything so beautiful. Her caramel skin had lines around the eyes and corners of the mouth, and strands of purest white hung beside those of night black, but none of that mattered. He'd never felt anything like it before.

"I sometimes see things," she said, turning away and touching her cheek.

"Like hallucinations, or visions?"

"I put no labels on them, but others have called them visions."

"What do you think they are?"

"I think I see possibilities."

"Can you see what'll possibly happen to him? Or to us?"

"Perhaps." Once again she reached out as if to brush her fingers against his cheek, but then stopped. Her eyes widened in panic. "Get your friends inside. Hurry!"

Before Tompkins could move, they heard a grunt followed by the distant *crack* of a rifle. John Thibodeaux began screaming. "Skip! Skip! They done hit Monty!"

Tompkins pushed to his feet and ran onto the ledge, where Hausser, Zuckerman, and Thibodeaux lay on their stomachs.

"Git down, Skip!" Thibodeaux and Hausser reached up and jerked him down seconds before a series of bullets spattered the cliff face behind him.

"Where's Monty?"

"He's gone."

"Gone where?"

The three men exchanged glances and he could tell none of them wanted to speak up.

"John? Where's Monty?"

"He's on the ground, Skip. We was layin' here talkin' an' I guess he forgot where he was. He stood up, then got this funny look on his face, and I heard the shot. He fell over 'fore I could catch him... he didn't suffer none, Skip, they hit him in the temple." Thibodeaux tapped the side of his head.

"Monty's dead?"

"I gotta tell ya it's true, Skip." Tears like summer raindrops fell from Thibodeaux's rheumy Cajun eyes. "Them devils, they finally got 'im."

Tompkins lay there a moment, stunned. He'd always been an even-tempered man even when fast action was called for, but now he felt rage boiling within his mind.

Monty had been there with him from the start and for fifty years they'd wandered the ruins of America together. They'd survived everything, only to have Monty die *after* they'd all been saved, and it was his fault. If he'd never agreed to leave Overtime, they'd never have gone without him, and Monty would still be alive.

Pushing to his feet, Tompkins ignored a few incoming rounds that buzzed past his head and stalked into the cave, retrieving his personal M-16. Snowtiger waited inside and reached out a hand to him, but he walked past her and grabbed the rifle. With the expertise of long practice, he pushed the Geissele High Speed Selector to the automatic position. From his peripheral vision, he saw her face twisted in sorrow. Ignoring her and shouldering the weapon, he walked back out onto the ledge.

Likewise he ignored the pleas and hands of his friends, who begged him to take cover. Dennis Tompkins rarely got angry, but when he did, it consumed him. Bullets ricocheted around him and sprayed him with rock splinters. Aiming carefully, he emptied the magazine at the little blob of white-robed men far out in the desert. Even as he fired, he knew they were out of range. Finally, after the magazine ran dry, he walked back into the cave, slid down with his back against the wall, and burst into tears.

Tompkins wouldn't open his eyes. The image of Monty's wide face and irresistible grin splitting his chestnut-colored face filled his mind. Monty had been the one he'd counted on doing what he needed without having to ask, whether it be cooking food, gathering firewood, or systematically scouring the ruins of a building for useable items. He'd always been there and Tompkins never had to worry about him. And now he was gone, and Tompkins worried that if he opened his eyes, he would never again be able to visualize his dead friend's face.

Despite their own pain, Thibodeaux, Hausser, and Zuck-erman all tried to comfort him, but Tompkins only shook his head and motioned to be left alone. Then he felt a hand on the back of his own left hand, and from it spread a feeling of peace that eased his tensed muscles like a drug flowing up his arm. When it reached his mind, Monty's face seemed to fade as if he were merely walking away for a little while. He opened his eyes to see the slight form of Sara Snowtiger sitting beside him.

"Be at peace, Dennis Tompkins. Your friend's *shilup* dwells now in the wide green lands set aside by *Chitokaka* for good men such as he, and his *shilombish* will follow you all of your days."

Tompkins had never felt the emotions that flooded through him now. He didn't even know what to call them, except that he felt a sudden yearning never to leave this strange woman he'd only just met. Over his long life, he'd heard people say that when they met their soul mate is was like they'd known each other all their lives... now he knew what they meant.

"I don't understand your words," he said in a low voice. With obvious shyness, he placed his right hand on top of hers. "But they make me feel better."

"Only Monty's physical body has died. Part of your friend lives on in the glorious place prepared for him by the Creator, and part is still with you and always will be."

"He's still got my back?"

Her smile widened. The crow's feet at the corners of her eyes loaned her face an empathetic look that somehow made him feel like he never wanted to leave her side.

"Yes," she said.

The cave tunnel disappeared into blackness. Tompkins stared into the void for several minutes. "Why do they do it?"

"Why do the Sevens hurt people?"

It surprised him that she'd understood his question. "Yeah, why are they like the way they are? I don't get it and never have."

At that her smile faded and her eyes seemed to focus on something Tompkins couldn't see. "I can only answer you in my own way. Nalusa Chito is the great deceiver, the soul eater who turns men to evil if they have thoughts of ill intent. Most of the Sevens believe they follow a prophet from their god, but that is false. He is instead a servant of Nalusa Chito, and by worshipping this deceitful man they have allowed evil into their hearts. Do not feel sympathy for such men, General Tompkins, Nalusa Chito cannot force himself on you. You must ask him to enter your soul. They asked for their guilt."

"Please call me Dennis."

Snowtiger's blush was hidden by her dark skin. "All right." When he simply stared at her, she smiled. "My family's lore says that my great-great-great-grandmother Nara Snowtiger confronted Nalusa Chito himself once, on the banks of the Mississippi River."

"I'll bet there's a story there."

"One of our tribe lost his family on the Trail of Tears—"

"I thought that was the Cherokee."

"Yes, but years before Cherokee were ejected from Georgia and Tennessee, my people were forced off their lands in Mississippi and made to march to Oklahoma. Many died along the way, including this man's wife and daughter. His name was Nita Tohbi, and his wife was my great-great-great-grandmother's sister. Their loss drove him mad. He vowed vengeance on the men he blamed for his family's deaths, and in his despair the Great Deceiver came to him, whispering that only revenge would let him be at peace. It was a lie, of course, but he embraced Nalusa Chito, who wanted only to eat his soul. On the night that the steamboat *Sultana* exploded, my grandmother confronted the Soul Eater and saved the man's *shilup* from being devoured."

"The *Sultana*? Your great-great... grandmother was there when the *Sultana* sank?"

"Yes." He could think of nothing to say to that, and so they were quiet for several long minutes. The other three men scooted to the cave mouth to give them as much space as possible. Finally Tompkins said, "Can I hug you?"

Snowtiger's expression betrayed surprise at her answer. "I would like that."

\#

Chapter 46

Welcome to my Nightmare.
Alice Cooper

Operation Overtime
0936 hours, April 28

"Hey, Yuri!" Nikki Bauer yelled through the doorway of the small room used for weapons maintenance. An M-16 rested in her hands with the charging handle open. "I thought you said you lubed these weapons... what did you use, an eyedropper? You know that wet and dirty is a lot better than dry and clean... Yuri, you out there?"

"So you like to be lubed up, huh?"

The voice was deep, with a distinct New England accent. In the second before she turned to see who had spoken, Nikki's brain registered it as familiar, unfriendly, and dangerous.

He stood with arms crossed and legs splayed apart in a fighter's stance. The man's wide shoulders and immense bulk blocked the doorway. Adrenaline flooded her body as her heart kicked into fifth gear. Memories flooded her consciousness and she knew that despite his size, he was very fast. Not as fast as her, but fast enough in this confined space.

"Adder..." she whispered.

"Well, well, well, what do we have here... if it's not the psychotic brat," he said. "Where are the rest of your playmates?"

She hesitated. "My brother's bringing them all down here... they oughta be here any minute."

Adder cocked his head to the left. She could see his eyes roaming over her body before locking into hers. "You didn't used to be such a bad liar, or able to hold your temper... you were crazy. It's the only thing I ever liked about you..." He pointed right at her. "You've changed."

"Like hell I have," she said, but cringed at her own words; they came out weak and whiny. She spoke louder, hoping that would make up for the lack of power behind her voice. "My brother is due back any minute and you'd better be gone when he gets here."

Adder only shook his head. "I'm disappointed. I was looking forward to fucking your brains out while you tried to stop me, but shit, girl, you're not worth the trouble now. Whatever happened to you broke you. You're just a normal skank now."

"Nick's gonna kick your ass!"

"Nick's under arrest, so he's not gonna do any ass-kicking for a while, and your worthless piece of shit brother is up in Northern California, so now it's just you and me. Good thing for you I don't rape helpless women."

"Just ones that fight back? What a man you are."

He grinned. "You're starting to change my mind about you."

"Try it and you won't have a head left," said a voice from behind.

"Hello, Wingnut," Adder responded without turning around. He didn't even seem startled. "Put the gun down. I heard you coming at least thirty seconds ago. You never were the quiet type."

"Turn around slow." Wingnut rarely spoke and Nikki jumped at the sound of his voice. "I'd love to shoot you, but I won't unless you make me."

"That's not gonna happen, but here's what *is*... I'm the new S-5 for the Seventh Cavalry, which makes me your commanding officer. I know you've got a rifle aimed at my head, but I haven't seen it yet, which means I can't prosecute you for it. Lower it now and everything's copa."

"I don't think so. We answer to Green Ghost."

"That worthless piece of shit has a shoot-on-sight order on his head. You won't be seeing his ass around here again in this life."

As he'd spoken, Nikki's fists had balled. She took a step forward, but when she spoke, it sounded more like a petulant teenager than the deadly, borderline psychotic Nipple. "You take that back, asshole!"

Adder frowned. "That's just pathetic."

"I'll show you pathetic. I should whip your ass!"

"I wish to hell you'd try."

Nikki's face turned red and she blinked several times. Her brain choreographed the moves to her attack exactly as they always had. She threw herself forward into a tuck and roll designed to come up inside of Adder's reach for a two-fingered thrust at his Adam's apple, but when she moved it felt like her limbs had bricks strapped to them. Compared to all of her previous fights, the world moved in slow motion. Instead of a potentially fatal blow to his throat, Nikki came out of the roll with the heel of Adder's hand slamming into her forehead. Like a speeding car hitting a brick wall, she recoiled backward, stunned into semi-consciousness.

Adder had always been the biggest of all the Zombies, but his speed took people by surprise. As he stopped Nikki and drove her backward, Wingnut aimed a vicious kick at the base of his spine. It should have been a crippling blow, except Adder anticipated exactly that move and twisted out of the way. Wingnut's foot slid past his stomach and he grabbed the ankle with both hands. Shoving up and back, he sent Wingnut hopping backward on his left leg until he tripped over a case of ammo and fell hard to the stone floor.

Adder followed and raised his foot over Wingnut's head. "Want some more?"

Then he stiffened and stepped back. Nikki had come to enough to see him raise his hand and touch his ear, the characteristic sign of someone listening to an ear mike.

"On my way," he said, apparently into an unseen microphone. Then he turned to them. "Looks like you two dipshits got off light today. The next time we meet, show more respect to your new commander. If you decide to join us and obey my orders, I'll forget all this. I can use you. I never had anything against you guys, only Ghost."#

Chapter 47

And so at last the bitter road ends
And we stand before Hell's Gate;
The Devil awaits us just inside,
We should not make him wait.
Sergio Velazquez, from "Impatient Satan"

Overtime Prime
1022 hours, April 28

Nervous officers filled the conference room. They'd all passed the strange men bearing rifles on their way to the hastily called meeting of the commander's staff, and endured the men's insolent glares. Now two more such men were stationed at either end of the narrow room. Khin Saw stood in front of his chair at the close end of the table, the commanding officer's chair, and nodded as each department head entered and found their seat.

The seat to his left stayed empty. That was the seat for the S-1, Operations, which is where he sat when the commanding officer was on hand.

"Thank you all for coming on such short notice," he said, still standing. "I know you have a lot of work to do, but this meeting comes at a critical point in the history of Operation Overtime. First, to allay any fears that General Angriff may have been injured or even killed, he is in good health. The purpose for this meeting is otherwise.

"I think we can all agree that Operations Overtime and Comeback are unique in the annals of human history. Even dreaming up something on this scale is beyond the ability of most people, and from their very beginning, Operations Overtime and Comeback were designed as a single overall mission. The purpose of that mission was to protect the unique American experience against any potentiality. When we all agreed to undergo Long Sleep and joined in this mission, we also accepted the chain of command that was put in place by the founder of these extraordinary operations.

"That chain of command was interrupted when General Angriff was illegally raised to the rank of General of the Army. I say illegally because the order, which I have personally observed, was voted on by a Congress that cannot be verified to have been elected according to the Constitution, and signed by a president that existing records do not even acknowledge to have lived."

Sitting to Colonel Saw's right, Rip Kordibowski raised a finger to indicate he wanted to ask a question. It was rude under the customary rules of a briefing by the commanding officer, and Saw ignored him.

"Many of our brothers and sisters in arms at Operation Comeback strongly believe that General Angriff has usurped the command that rightly belongs to another. Our situation demands unity of purpose, which we currently do not have. Therefore, after careful consideration as the acting commander of Operation Overtime, I have decided to restore the chain of command as it was originally intended to be. Ladies and gentlemen, I give you the father and commanding officer of Operations Overtime and Comeback, General of the Army Thomas Francis Steeple."

———

Steeple had presided over countless meetings in his long career and rarely felt nervous about them. Only when in the presence of superiors did his stomach churn with anxiety, and for all of his time as Chief of the General Staff and, later, as the Assistant to the President for National Security Affairs, that number had been exactly one; the president, the only person who could fire him. So the queasy feeling as he entered the conference room was new.

Adder went first. The intended intimidation of his hulking presence and scarred face couldn't be missed, nor could its message; Tom Steeple had powerful allies. Adder took the third seat on the left, the empty place where Green Ghost usually sat. Next to enter was the newly reinstated Colonel Claringdon, who sat in the seat reserved for the S-1, Personnel, where Khin Saw usually sat. Saw, meanwhile, waited until Steeple entered, then saluted to indicate he was reporting for duty and as a sign of subservience. He then slid down to the S-3 slot, prompting the others at the table to exchange glances; that was Norm Fleming's place.

The rest of the table was lined with his appointees, hand-selected for their personal loyalty to him. It wasn't like Steeple to have such a show of force in a meeting. He'd often said, *"Those who have to portray their power have less than they believe."* Few people ever held more actual power than Tom Steeple had as the long-time Chairman of the Joint Chiefs of Staff and he had always downplayed that power, but not this time. This time they all needed to see his power.

"Good morning," he said, trying to keep his voice even. As he spoke, his gaze swept around the table, meeting the eyes of every attendee before moving on, and a feeling of warm welcome gave strength to his voice. With the exception of Colonel Kordibowski, Steeple thought of these as his people, not his friends, exactly, more like his followers.

"Forgive me if I seem emotional, but this is a day I was unsure would ever come. This day, this *moment*, is the culmination of my professional life's work. And now that it's come, it seems surreal... but enough of that. Colonel Saw, as acting commander of Operation Overtime, has turned over command to me, but as the dutiful officer that he is, he only did do so after I proved to him that the position is rightfully mine."

With that, he smiled down on the colonel like a beneficent pope greeting a child in Vatican Square. Colonel Saw, on the other hand, squirmed in his seat.

Kordibowski wasn't so shy and interrupted without raising his hand. "Were the charges against you dismissed by General Angriff?"

For those familiar with Steeples' moods and facial tics, the broadened grin indicated rage, as did the slightly widened eyes. The placating tone of his answer warned of dangerous consequences to the questioner. "The charges had no validity in the first place; therefore their dismissal proved unnecessary."

But Kordibowski pressed on regardless of what might happen to him. "Who released you from the stockade?"

"That's not important, Colonel."

"Maybe not to you—"

"Please await me in your quarters, Colonel. I'll be there as soon as the meeting ends."

With a finger, he beckoned Adder out of his seat. When Adder bent close, he whispered, "Take him to the stockade and put him in my old cell. Let's see if that shuts him up. Use whatever force is necessary."

The former squad commander for Task Force Zombie replied, his voice louder than Steeple would have liked. "Finally some fun."

He stood behind Kordibowski's seat and motioned one of the guards to join him.

The Intelligence officer glanced over each shoulder and rose. "Nothing but yes men, eh, General?"

"There are ladies present, too, Colonel," Steeple replied with a small bow of his head. He resumed once Kordibowski had left the room. "As I was saying, we've lost nearly a year now. Mistakes have been made, lives lost, and potential allies turned into enemies. But that's going to change and that change starts right this minute. From now on, we negotiate first and shoot only as a last resort. Within three years, I want a functioning country again, even if it's not precisely what we would like it to be. America must rise from the ashes."

That brought a round of applause. Steeple studied every person at the table as they clapped, noting who clapped enthusiastically and who was going through the motions. Colonel Saw disappointed him with a polite but listless clap.

"I will meet with each of you in private to discuss your current status and both short- and long-range plans. Any questions you may ask then. For now, it's time to get back to work."

———ᨆ———

Operation Comeback
1032 hours, April 28

The file was one of thousands General Schiller had scrolled through on his computer monitor as he investigated the missing Stingers. Now that he had solved that mystery, he could go on to other things. The particular file he was reading wasn't flagged and there seemed no special significance to it, but his particular talent was in recognizing important anomalies. The file's name read HAPTIX 7.2.2. When he opened the file, the title at the top read *Hand Proprioception and Touch Interfaces, External*; the supplier's name read DARPA.

The tips of his ears warmed and turned red, one of the only physical reactions William Schiller had to excitement. It made him shy around women and a terrible poker player. When something involved the Defense Advanced Research Projects Agency, it promised to be ground-breaking technology, and Comeback had more than its share of such surprises. When he looked at its physical location within the complex, he didn't recognize the designation — GOATS.

The file showed a pair of items that appeared more like medieval gauntlets than gloves, with operating instructions, a key for the meaning of the numbered arrows pointing toward points on the devices, and how to adjust them to a particular hand. Along with them went something called a *Smart Decal.*

"Corporal Duglach," he said into the intercom receiver, "please come here."

When Duglach entered the commander's office, worry twisted his face, but Schiller stared at the monitor and didn't look up. "Sir?"

"Do we have something called GOATS here?"

The question clearly surprised Duglach. "Yes, General, we do."

"Is that an acronym or do we have animals in a holding pen somewhere?"

"It's part of the compound. I've only seen it from down the hall, sir, but I think it stands for *General Officer Access Top Secret.*"

"And where is this section?"

⁓

Rio Rancho, New Mexico
1214 hours, April 28

Lying prone on the narrow table, head facing down through a hole in the wood with edges lined in soft leather, Abdul-Qudoos Fadil el Mofty moaned as the woman's fingers dug deep into the tight muscles of his neck. Her name was Joan and she was an infidel, but he didn't give two shits if she worshipped Satan himself. It was irrelevant when stacked up against her magic elbows. Joan knew where all of the trigger points were in his muscles and used the perfect amount of pressure to release them. Her training had taken years and he didn't give a rat's ass whether she converted to his brother's cult or not. As long as she filled him with endorphins and kept her mouth shut, Joan was safe.

He'd fallen asleep beneath her ministrations when he felt a tap on his shoulder. Without opening his eyes, he rolled over so Joan could work on his legs, torso, and shoulders. And his hands, too, particularly the thumbs, where arthritis left both so painful that sometimes he couldn't pick up a mug of coffee.

But it wasn't Joan who spoke to him. It was his nephew, Sati Bashara. "Forgive the intrusion, Uncle."

El Mofty opened his right eye and scowled. "What?" he said, the single word conveying his irritation at having his moment of tranquility interrupted.

Sati bowed his head. "General Muhdin would see you, Uncle. Riders have returned. We have news."

The Emir wanted to scream. He was sick to death of being the Emir. Not the perks, just the work. Instead, he closed his eyes and rubbed them. It felt so good. "Tell Muhdin I will join him in a moment."

"You do not wish to see him now?"

"No, I do *not* wish to see him now!" he exploded. Trying to be unobtrusive in the corner, Joan shrank back even more. Sati's disapproving glance at her wasn't lost on the Emir, but

WILLIAM ALAN WEBB

for the moment he allowed his anger to vent. "Tell him I will join him shortly."

Sati bowed and walked out backward. When he was gone, the Emir reverted to being Larry Armstrong for a moment. "C'mere, baby," he said, and Joan slid over to the table.

———

The home el Mofty had made into his headquarters sprawled atop a rocky hill overlooking an old golf course. Huge picture windows allowed light in from all four directions and by some miracle, most of the glass remained intact. Much of the furniture also remained usable, as the house's position and limited access made looting it difficult. Other than the usual squirrels and mice, the only thing of note that his men had cleared before he occupied the house was a nest of Western diamondback rattlesnakes that hadn't scattered yet after the winter hibernation. The men had offered him some of the snake meat but he'd declined, telling them since they had killed the snakes, they deserved the meat. The truth was he preferred eating his shoe to eating a reptile.

Emerging from the back bedroom, he found Muhdin, Bashara, and several of his advisors standing around the picture window looking down on the 18th green. On the table behind them, a metal box overflowed with golf balls, many of them showing no damage from use. The first thing el Mofty had done on entering Albuquerque was order his men to scavenge anything of use, with golf balls being a high priority. Several sets of clubs also lay on the floor in golf bags.

They turned as he pulled out a chair and sat. "What was so important that I had to be interrupted?"

As if on cue, the men all turned to Muhdin.

"Many of our scouting parties have come back, Excellency, and bring news of our enemies."

"Well?"

Muhdin cleared his throat. "In the west, one group encountered Americans and drove them into a cave, where they are trapped. While attacking this cave, they were attacked in turn by Apaches, but they drove them off. A second group has now joined our men."

265

"This was in the west."

"Yes, the farthest group in the west."

"Go on."

"Another western group, which was supposed to be up in the Gallup area, hasn't been heard from for several days. It could just be a radio problem—"

"They are very good radios," chimed in Ibrahim Yaleen, one of el Mofty's least favorite people. He was the Minister of Production for the Caliphate, however, and procurement of equipment came under his responsibility. "Most likely one of your horsemen dropped it."

"My horsemen know the value of a radio, Senior Minister!"

"Apparently not, General, otherwise—"

"Enough!" cried el Mofty. "If I wished to hear bickering, I could have brought my wives! Continue with your report, Hussein."

Both men bowed in apology. "The center groups have encountered men of the so-called Shangri-La to the northwest, north, and northeast of our current position. The eastern groups report nothing more than scattered settlements."

"There is no sign of the Americans?"

"No, Excellency, except the small number in the west. But the failure of one group to report I believe to be cause for concern. At least for caution."

"It worries me as well, Muhdin, but my brother, our beloved Prophet, already chaffs at our inaction. He wants proof that the expense of pouring so many of the Caliphate's resources into this army was worth it. If I now have to tell him that we have found no reason to delay our move against the infidels other than one reconnaissance group of cavalry going silent, he will be very angry. He will begin to question the leadership of this army. I do not think any of us wants that."

"No, Excellency, of course not."

"You are prepared to put your attack plan into action?"

"Of course, whenever you give the word."

"Consider the word given, then. Send your outriders to the west and east to seal them in their valley, after which we will attack with the main force."

"Do you still intend to use the infidels as human shields?"

"Of course. What else would we do with them?"

"May I ask, O Blessed One, if you still intend for the woman Tracy Gollins to participate in our actions?" interjected Yaleen.

El Mofty's voice dropped into a hoarse stage whisper so low they all had to strain to hear him. "Have I not made myself clear on this matter, Senior Minister? Or do you challenge my decision?"

"I would never challenge you, Excellency," Yaleen said with less of an apologetic tone than El Mofty wanted to hear. "I merely wished to verify your decision."

"If you ever question me again, Yaleen, it will mean your head. Tracy Gollins is leading one of the regiments and there is nothing more to be said on the matter. She is more of a warrior than most men in my army, and is more ruthless than any of you here. Women *are* meant to be seen and not heard, it is true, but when you question me, you question the will of Allah. Is that what you are doing, questioning Allah?"

"Never, O Blessed One."

"Good. Let us speak no more of this."

Once his visitors had left, including his nephew, the Emir sank into a chair wearing a dark scowl. A servant came in to see if he required anything.

"Send word to General Gollins that I wish to see her."

1521 hours

El Mofty lay on his bed with the drapes closed, trying to nap in the stifling heat of the late New Mexico spring afternoon. With an arm shielding his eyes, he heard the door open and one of his servants start to speak, only to be cut off by an all-too-familiar female voice.

"I'm here. What do you want?"

Moving his arm, el Mofty saw the guard standing in the doorway, wearing his anxiety on his face. "Leave us," he said, and the guard quickly scooted backward and closed the door.

"Where's the poison dwarf?" the woman named Tracy Gollins said.

El Mofty sat up and swung his feet over the side of the bed. The mattress was very old, yet still remarkably comfortable. He hated having to get up from it. "You know he's back in Houston with my brother. Besides, that's no way to speak about your father's most senior advisor."

"What do you want, *Your Majesty*?"

El Mofty squinted. "One of these days, you're going to slip up and say that in front of the wrong people. They already want to know why you're even allowed to come along on this expedition, much less lead men into battle."

"Is that why I'm here? You dragged me away from my regiment to tell me the boys don't like me? Like that's news..."

"It's dangerous for you to have your command and you know it. Just because I'm your father doesn't mean anything since we can't tell them that, and even if we could, that wouldn't make any difference. They'd still expect you to wear black and spit out babies."

"And whose fault is that?"

"That's not the point. We've been over all of this a dozen times... I want you to get battle experience and earn their respect, not piss them off more than they already are."

"What did I do?"

"Look, some of these people are whack jobs, okay? Just be careful. And beat them all into Shangri-La so I can point to that success as proof of your talent for command."

"Can I go now?"

"Win and win fast, right?"

"Yeah, yeah."

#

CHAPTER 48

A very little key will open a very heavy door.
Charles Dickens

Groom Lake Air Force Facility
1540 hours, April 28

Standing atop a cantilevered ladder, Joe Randall ran the tip of his index finger along the platter-sized connector on the XF-77's upper fuselage, feeling the smooth metal for imperfections and finding none. Shaped like an upturned funnel, it differed little from refueling connectors on other aircraft.

Although neither man considered himself an airplane pilot, both he and Carlos had experience flying fixed wings and both had been instantly fascinated by the XF-77. The enormous size of the experimental orbital fighter, in particular, made it seem more like a new bomber than a fighter. Since it hadn't flown in over four decades, Major Cole allowed them to examine it all they wanted. Randall suspected that his magnanimity had more to do with keeping them from bitching about leaving than learning more about the plane, but Randall didn't care why he allowed it as long as he did.

Carlos had removed an access panel midway up on the nose, where two molded gun ports on each side confused him. Obviously they were there for cannon, but what the hell did a modern fighter need with guns? The framework for the mounting of a gun made even less sense, since the area would only have allowed a moderate ammunition supply.

"I wonder who decided to put cannons on this thing," he called up to Randall. "I mean, a gun in space?"

Leaning over the ladder's rail, he called the answer down. "You heard the man. Homing rounds. Like the Exacto rounds we've been using since wake-up."

"Sure, that makes sense. You don't need to chew 'em up. One or two hits might compromise the enemy's heat shielding. I just wonder which came first, the idea for the cannon or the homing rounds. Either way, whoever designed this wasn't a dumbass."

"An aircraft designer with a brain? Who knew?" Climbing down the ladder, Randall once again walked under the plane's belly, which was far enough off the ground that he could walk upright. Once again he ran his hand along the composite surface, as if the tactile sensation could provide understanding. "How was this thing supposed to achieve orbit? From what I remember, achievement of a stable orbit using single-stage engines wasn't even close to being a real thing."

"The fuel problem, right?" Carlos called, still inspecting the interior structure of the gun mount.

"More or less. I'm no expert, but I understand the basics. Single-stage to orbital flight is damned near impossible, because the delta-v gives it full-weight-vehicle to empty-weight-mass ratios that are beyond current science's ability to overcome. *Current* meaning pre-Collapse."

"Maybe they solved it right before everything went to shit?"

"Maybe..."

"A lot can happen in ten years."

"Yeah..."

"Randall? Carlos?" The voice of Major Cole echoed in the huge hangar.

"Back here," Randall yelled. "At the XF-77."

"I don't know why you're being nice to that guy," Carlos said before Cole got within hearing range.

"If I've missed a viable option, please tell me."

"Taking him hostage?"

"If I thought it'd work, I'd do it in a heartbeat." He nodded with his chin to indicate Cole was getting close. They both shut up.

Cole noticed. "You must've been talking about me," the major said when he stood before them.

"Don't flatter yourself," Carlos said.

Cole ignored him and looked up at the belly of the orbital fighter. "I wish I could have seen it fly."

Randall folded his arms, not letting himself be distracted from what he really wanted to know. "Did you send it?"

"I said I would, and we did. Ten times over a three-hour period."

"And?"

"Nothing. Whoever Judge Gomorrah is, he didn't answer."

"We want out of here, Major."

"I'm not stopping you."

"But you're not helping us, either."

"You two want to leave, go ahead. I'll even give you all the water you can carry."

"But you won't help."

"No, I won't. I don't *want* you to leave. Anybody else, and I'd order them shot to keep them here. I'm only makin' an exception because you flew that C-5 in here. But I was ordered to lock this place down right before you two showed up out of nowhere, so what I ought to do is lock you two up until I know what's what. However, if you want to face that desert on foot, be my guest. If we ever find your bodies, I promise to give you a proper burial."

"You've got two operational F-22 Raptors, Major," Carlos said. "Do a recon, see if we're not telling the truth."

"You want me to use my only serviceable aircraft to do what? Overfly Creech? I already know Kando and his people live there, they've tried to join forces with us before, but I can't do that since they aren't authorized."

Randall could see Cole was getting angry again and nodded, as if he understood. "All right, I get it, Major. Sir."

Cole wasn't done, though. "There's something fundamental you two are missing here. For close to fifty years, the only purpose most of us have had is keeping this place safe for the U.S. government. That may sound stupid to you... hell, it sounds stupid to me when I say it out loud, but what you don't understand is that it's all we've got. It's our sole purpose in life. Most of us were raised here, on this base, and we don't have skills to go survive in the desert beyond. But men can't just exist; we need a purpose, a reason to keep going. Discipline is critical, because it would be all too easy to just sit around and do nothing. Maintaining the security of this base gives our lives meaning."

Cole quieted and waited for a response. Randall said nothing. The dark redness of the major's face warned against it and even Carlos kept silent.

After a moment Cole turned to leave. "Dinner is on soon, and then I'm posting the duty schedule."

"Hey, Major," Randall called.

"*What?*"

"Not about us, about the XF-77."

Cole's body visibly relaxed when he realized it wasn't further confrontation. "What about it?"

"Do you know how they planned to get this thing to orbit? Did they discover some new power plant or fuel that allowed for single-stage operations?"

"Not that I know of. It was simpler than that. The aircraft takes off as usual, climbs to a high altitude, and then refuels for the boost into orbit. My father could have explained it better. I never learned all that higher math."

Randall wondered why he hadn't thought of that.

1657 hours
Hawthorne Army Depot, Nevada

Nick Angriff sat on the cot, elbows on knees, wondering what the hell to do. In the back of his mind he knew there was only one thing he could do... nothing. If Colonel Young wasn't going to obey his orders, and he didn't have his Eagles, then there wasn't a whole lot that he could do. Even if he got away from his immediate captors, there was nowhere to go. He couldn't risk going back to Creech and there was nowhere else within hundreds of miles.

How had Steeple gotten free? More to the point, how had he taken command of Overtime? Angriff knew how pointless wondering about that was at the moment, but when a man of action couldn't take any action, there wasn't much more to do except think.

The tent flap opened and Young's executive officer, Major Strootman, stepped into the darkness inside. "Good morning, General. I hope you slept well."

"Wolves don't do well in captivity, Major, and neither do I."

"Yes, sir. I'm very sorry about all this, General."

"Colonel Young is making a serious mistake. You know that, right?"

"Sir, Colonel Young thought you might need to use the latrine. He asked me to escort you."

Angriff tilted his head. "I have a latrine out back." He pointed to the closed flap opposite the main entrance.

"That one's not available, sir."

"No?" Squinting in suspicion, he realized the major was implying something unspoken. Hesitating only a second, he got up from the cot. When Angriff rose, his knees popped and he felt the familiar stiffness in his back. "How thoughtful of the colonel."

"If you'll follow me, sir."

Angriff shielded his eyes from the morning sunshine. The guard at the tent started to follow, but Strootman stopped him. "That won't be necessary, Private. The general is to be accorded all courtesy due his rank." Pointing, Strootman let Angriff get in front.

"Not bringing a guard, Major? Aren't you afraid I'll over-power you and escape?" Angriff looked back when he said it.

Strootman ignored the remark and pointed. "It's straight ahead, sir, out there by that Humvee."

"That's a helluva long way for a latrine. I can barely see it."

Once out of earshot of the camp, Strootman spoke in a low voice, as if still afraid that someone might hear. "Your pistols are on the passenger's seat, General. There's a pack with food and water, a blanket, and a few other essentials. There are eight containers of gas in the back seats."

The left corner of Angriff's mouth turned up in a half-smile. "I'll be damned. Tell Colonel Young I said thanks... but what about you? General Steeple will undoubtedly consider this a court-martial offense."

"General Steeple said to treat you with all respect due to your rank. The colonel interpreted that to mean he shouldn't send an armed guard every time you need to use the latrine, so he sent his executive officer as an escort, an executive officer who happens to be fifty pounds lighter than you and was overwhelmed when you took my gun, which you dropped once you had gotten away."

"So I'm going to assault a fellow officer?"

"No offense, sir, but would you rather be a prisoner?"

Angriff had to laugh at that. "I guess not."

"Once we're a mile out, you can drop me off to walk back. That should buy you at least an hour."

"Do you smoke, Major?"

"Not really, sir... maybe an occasional cigar."

"I'm going to get Overtime back, Strootman, and when I do, you and me are gonna smoke a fine cigar together. That's going to be an order."

"I look forward to it. I'd go east if I were you, General. There's nothing out there except desert, but if you go far enough you might find Crystal Springs."

"What's there?"

Strootman shrugged. "No idea, but the maps show some old towns out that way. I'm really not familiar with the Nevada desert. I'm from Philadelphia."

"Anything else?"

"I think Area 51's out there somewhere."

"Yeah," Angriff said, his eyes shifting back and forth as he thought about it. "Area 51... I think you're right."

———— ᨒ ————

Dust swirled away in a light breeze as Angriff stopped the Humvee.

"End of the line, Major."

Strootman opened the passenger door but paused before climbing out. "I'm really sorry this happened, General, and I know Colonel Young is, too. I want you to know that he considered telling General Steeple to shove it up his ass and putting the regiment at your disposal..."

Angriff handed him back the Beretta M9 pistol. "But he couldn't do that because all of his logistic support is back at Prime."

"Yes, sir, that's about the size of it."

"Tell the colonel that the time's going to come when I overturn all of General Steeple's orders, and all I ask is that he follow mine. If he does that, we won't have a problem."

"Sir? One final question?"

"Sure."

"How did all this happen?"

Instead of a quick answer, Angriff looked into the distance and thought about it. "The collapse of any civilization brings forth scavengers looking to feast on the corpses. My mistake was thinking you can reason with a buzzard. Take care of Kona for me."

#

CHAPTER 49

I'd fight the devil to save your soul.
Anonymous woman on daytime TV, circa 2019

Operation Comeback
1724 hours, April 28

At the direct request of Glide, instead of using the small office formerly occupied by Colonel Mwangi right outside the C.O.'s, Astrid Naidoo used a table to set up a workstation in General Schiller's oversized office. This allowed the two Zombies to sleep in that room, close to Schiller. For his part, outwardly the commanding general declared the alleged threat to his personal safety to be overblown. Inwardly, however, it shook him to his core. Operation Overtime had already suffered multiple mutinies and now it appeared Operation Comeback might suffer the same fate.

"General?" Naidoo said. "Is something wrong?"

"Mmm... I'm sorry, Colonel, please continue."

"As I said, sir, progress on the A-10s has been slowed by multiple causes. Probably the most significant factor is the confusion that followed General Steeple's arrest and Colonel Mwangi's disappearance. There was no officer to drive the project forward, and no prioritization until just a few days ago. Most of the technical personnel needed to assemble them were still in Long Sleep until yesterday, so it's going to take a little while until they are acclimated and ready to work."

"I know the disorientation associated with waking up, but we need to push those people on an accelerated schedule."

"A further hamper is the number of technicians available. There's less than two dozen people qualified to do the work, and that's not even an ideal number to assemble one aircraft at a time, much less ten. You would think that someone as meticulous as General Steeple would have seen the necessity for having more technicians."

"I feel certain he did see the need, but private companies snatched up Air Force trained aviation technicians and paid them very well. Turning their back on such a good life and going into Long Sleep for some unknown and ill-defined future, centered primarily on appeals to patriotism, was likely very difficult to sell. So in answer to our lack of technicians, put out a notice for volunteers to assist with the less-technical work involved, and for anyone who might be interested in training to become such a technician in the future."

She typed a note into the tablet on her makeshift desk. "Would it be acceptable to allow the senior master sergeant to oversee the recruitment process?"

"I would rather have an officer in charge."

"There are no Air Force officers among the technicians, sir."

"What about the pilots?"

"Some, but we've left them in Long Sleep until needed."

Schiller nodded while thinking. "Promote the senior master sergeant to first lieutenant and let him run it, but with regular reports to you."

"It's a female, sir, Shannon Hartmann."

Schiller's first instinct was to ask whether she was up to it, but he refrained. His time in the Army dated from an era when women in the service were unusual and they rarely had much command responsibility. Over the years, he'd seen first-hand evidence of how antiquated that notion had become. "Good. Keep me apprised of progress on those aircraft. General Angriff made it clear that getting them operational is the number one priority for this command. What about runways?"

"Have you not seen the underground aircraft complex, General?"

"I only arrived here a few days before you, Colonel. So no, I have not toured the entire facility."

"I've never seen anything like it, sir—"

Schiller interrupted and blurted out something he'd thought but never intended to say. "When we are alone, please call me Bill."

"Yes, sir... I mean, all right, Bill. Please call me Astrid. The... ummm... oh, yes, the facility is amazing. There's a complete five-thousand-foot long underground runway, with separate revetments for the maintenance of more than one hundred aircraft. By this I assume the air component was intended to be much larger. Blast doors at either end open in an upward curve so launches be made directly from underground."

"Much like some aircraft carriers."

"I didn't know that."

"Yes, the Russians and the British had some like that. Please go on."

"Well, apparently that is a risky way to take off, so there are also two elevators to take planes up to ground level. Maybe the most ingenious part is a steel-reinforced concrete runway aboveground that was designed to allow the desert to reclaim it until it's needed. To make it operational will require a week or so of bulldozing, and we have the machines available for that, and manpower."

"That is truly incredible."

"What's remarkable is that the entire aircraft complex is only accessible by one tunnel that connects it to Comeback. It's a very wide tunnel, but still there's just the one. And at the end are blast doors resistant to anything up to a direct hit from a nuclear weapon."

"That truly sounds fascinating Astrid. I believe you are correct, I will make seeing the airfield complex a priority."

———— ~~~ ————

Somewhere in the Great Basin Desert, Nevada
2008 hours, April 28

Full darkness had yet to fall, but Nick Angriff couldn't wait any longer. The day's heat radiated upward from the desert floor even as the ambient temperatures began their nightly plummet. He'd spent the day hunkered down in a ruined building made of concrete blocks and wood. A sun-faded sign read *Coyote Hole.* He guessed it had once been a mining camp. On the other side of that mountain was a valley with what appeared to be the abandoned town of Dyer, just inside Nevada along the old border with California, southeast of where he'd started near Hawthorne.

He intended to turn due east now, to circumvent the area once known as Area 51 to the north. General Kando had mentioned that facility still had a garrison and there was no way of predicting their reactions if he showed up there. Besides, he'd calculated his fuel and water supply and figured there was enough to get him somewhere near the Colorado River. How he'd cross that obstacle was something he'd worry about when the time came. All he knew for certain was his destination — Overtime Prime. What happened once he got there depended on how fast he could strangle Tom Steeple.

Caution ingrained from decades of living in a combat zone sent him behind a broken building to relieve himself before heading out for the night's driving. By unthinking reflex, he wore his Desert Eagles in their shoulder straps.

He had finished and was adjusting his clothes when voices came from the other side of the building, near the Humvee. Sinking into a crouch, he drew a pistol in one huge hand and stopped breathing to listen. The voices were loud and indiscreet, seeming to come from only two men. They argued over his gear, about who got what, and neither one seemed concerned that it all might belong to somebody else. With great care, he picked his way through the building's debris to where both men stood twenty feet away, pawing through his stuff.

"I'd appreciate you boys not doing that," he said. Both men whirled. One started bringing a rifle to bear. "Don't do it!" Angriff said. "I don't want to kill you but I will. I've got a burning madness to hurt somebody, but it's you and there's nothing here worth dying for. Now, you boys leave your guns here and get on down there, at the base of the hill. I'll leave and you can come get your guns back. Nobody needs to get hurt."

"You might not have noticed," replied the shorter of the two men, "but it's dark out here and there's two of us. I can't even tell if that's a real gun or not, so it's you who needs to hightail it outa here, not us. You shoot one of us and the other one will sure as hell shoot you back. You go in peace and we'll leave you be."

"Just let me get my things and I'll be on my way."

"Naw, can't do that. We found this stuff abandoned and it's ours now. You be happy we let you live."

The wind shifted and Angriff was hit full in the face with their smell. Sour body odor made his eyes water, even blown on a breeze. He knew he didn't smell like roses, but those boys took stink to a different level. "Not gonna happen. I've gotta get going, so I'm telling you one last time, get away from the car."

"Looks like we got us a problem."

"I don't understand," Angriff said. "I've got a powerful handgun pointed right at you, and at this distance I can't miss. Both of you will be dead before you know you're going to die. You can't survive. So why do it? Just step away and you'll be the same as you were twenty minutes ago. I don't want to kill you."

For a moment, Angriff thought they might do it. The one on the left, the taller one, took a half shuffle-step sideways, but then stopped when his partner didn't follow.

"I wish I could do that," the shorter man said. "But out here you can't do it and survive."

"Dying's not surviving."

Without warning, the man reached for his rifle, followed by his buddy. Despite the darkness, Angriff only had to fire twice to put both men down. With the Humvee at their backs, he'd hoped the bullets wouldn't be through-and-throughs. Both were. The man on the left had moved far enough so the fifty-caliber round that blew a softball-sized hole in his back only spewed blood and bone over the hood, while the bullet itself spun harmlessly into the desert. But the other man was slammed into the Humvee's side and crumpled to the ground, while the round shattered the rear window and sprayed the interior with his blood.

"Damn!"

He stood a moment, breathing hard. Without him realizing it, rage had boiled up within him, a burning anger at Tom Steeple that shooting the two men had done nothing to assuage. Angriff had killed many men during his years in combat and always felt empty afterward, regardless of how much bravado he showed, and so it was now. *Why couldn't they just leave?*

He felt the pulse at their necks and both men were dead, which spared him the choice of whether to put them out of their misery or not. But if he didn't clean all the blood out of Humvee, he'd be swarmed with feeding flies. Using a small flashlight Strootman had put in the vehicle, he first found the casings for his bullets so he could reload them, and then tore strips off the dead men's clothes. At sunup, he would stop and clean up the blood as best he could. In the meantime, he tossed their guns into the passenger's seat and headed east.

#

CHAPTER 50

In this world the unseen has power.
Apache proverb

2243 hours, April 28
2 miles east of Gallup, New Mexico

"Cap? Captain Sully?"

Sully rolled over in his foxhole and looked up at the man standing at the edge. The day's operations had left him with an aching back, while partial dehydration gave him a grade-A headache. "What?" he said in a hoarse voice.

"Sorry to wake you, Cap. We've got visitors."

Sully pushed the button on his watch to illuminate the numbers. "Who is it?"

"It's that Indian again, the same one as last year. Right before the battle, remember?"

"I'm coming."

He needed to pee but held it. The temperature had dropped as it always did during desert nights and he wanted nothing more than to crawl under his blanket again, but the company came first.

A clouded moon left the land dark under wan starlight. With reports of any enemy force in the area, no campfires or lights were allowed, so all Sully saw of the Indians were black silhouettes. They numbered five, with the tallest standing in front of the others.

"Govind, isn't it?" he said, extending his hand.

"Yes," came the response. "And you are Captain Sully."

"That's right. So... may I offer you something?"

"No, thank you. I would speak with Lara Snowtiger, but first I come again with a warning. You heeded my words once and I hope you do so again. The men behind me are friends of my people. Two are Jemez Pueblos and two are Mescalero Apache. One is my cousin. I trust their words."

"Is this about the army of Sevens coming up from the south?"

"You know of them?"

"We encountered a scout group of horsemen west of Gallup," Sully said, standing with arms crossed and eyes shifting side to side as his brain worked to think of his situation while maintaining the conversation. "One of them claimed to be from Shangri-La who joined the Caliphate as a spy, and he told us of this army. He said they'd sent other out other groups, too."

"Other groups? Did he say where?"

"No."

"Is he near? May I speak with him?"

"I thought you wanted Snowtiger."

"I would speak with this man first."

Sully half-turned his head but kept his eyes on Govind. "Sergeant Meyer, please bring the prisoner up here."

No one spoke for several seconds, then Govind said, "Your man is injured?"

"You mean Meyer, because he limps? That's from last year's battle. He was severely wounded and only returned to service a few weeks ago."

"He must be a true warrior to be out here with you, so soon after his return."

"He's a Marine," Sully said, as the only explanation needed.

While they waited for Mohammad Qadim to be brought forward, Govind changed the subject. "The Choctaw is still under your command, isn't she?"

"Yes, Sergeant Snowtiger is here. You're a regular man of mystery, aren't you? Why do you want to see Snowtiger?"

"I mean no insult, Captain, but the message is only for her ears."

"Not in a Marine unit in a combat zone, it's not."

283

"Then I shall leave it up to her whether she wishes to hear it."

Scraping boot steps alerted them to Sergeant Meyer's return with Qadim. Sully introduced the Indians and stepped back to listen.

"You are from Shangri-La?"

"That's right," Qadim said.

"I am Govind, chief of the Coyotero Apache."

"I know. I've seen you there."

"Who is the chief of Shangri-La?"

"It doesn't have a chief, but Johnny Rainwater runs things now that Steve Higdon died. You know, the same Johnny Rainwater that's your nephew. Abigail Deak leads the Pueblos."

"Steve is dead? If this is true, then I'm sorry. He was a fine man. And yes, Johnny is my sister's son, but you could have heard that from others. What do you do at Shangri-La?"

"I tend the animals and help with the greenhouses."

"The pigs as well?"

"Yes. As I'm sure you know, the few Muslims there help with the pigs if we must. We consider them unclean, but Shangri-La means everyone must pitch in to do everything. They took us in when no one else would. Thank Allah we are rarely expected to deal with the pigs."

Govind shifted his attention to Sully for a moment. "He is truthful." Then, to Qadim again, "Why did you ride with the Sevens?"

"The Caliphate's patrols started showing up near Santa Fe and Steve, he was still alive then, thought we should try to find out what was going on. If they were moving our way, we needed to know. As a Muslim, I volunteered. I trained on riding a horse for two months before I rode south. During that time Steve died and Johnny took over. The Caliphate gave me a hard time at first, but they need trained riders to go in front of an army and see what was out there.

"They suffered a defeat last year that left many of them dead. I was told Americans defeated them, but that had no real meaning to me as we hadn't heard of any Americans. As far as I know, Shangri-La still hasn't. The Sevens learned from last year's fighting and didn't want to be surprised again. I was in one of ten patrol groups scouting ahead. The army stopped about sixty miles south to await our reports."

Sully thought of a question and interrupted. "Where did the rest of these scout groups go?"

Qadim was only a dark shadow, so when he shrugged, Sully couldn't read his body language. "I don't know. Some to the west of us, some to the east."

"To the west? How far to the west?" A slight note of fear crept into Govind's voice.

"I don't know."

"What's the matter?" Sully said to Govind.

"May I speak with Lara Snowtiger now?"

"How did you know her first name?"

Govind was quiet for a long while, but Sully knew better than to say anything else. If he waited the Apache chief out, he would eventually answer, and it would be the truth. "We have met several times before. But I also know her sister."

Govind, Sully, and Snowtiger separated themselves from the group by moving fifty yards into the desert. Sully used a flashlight to avoid stepping on a rattlesnake.

"Do you remember this man, Sergeant?" Sully said.

"Aye, Cap. We met again when I was at FOB Junkyard."

"Yes, but I hope the circumstances of our meeting today brings you happier tidings. I bear a message for you."

"From my sister." It wasn't a question.

"Do you also have the Sight?"

"No, but of late she's been in my dreams. Is her spirit in danger?"

"Why do you say that?"

"She comes to me when I sleep and I see fear in her face. I was asleep when you called for me, but I dreamed that I saw her high up on a mountain, standing in front of something dark. A cave, perhaps, and a tall man stood with her. He looked familiar, as if I should know who he is."

"Was this man Indian?"

"No, he was white, but with dark skin as if he'd spent many years in the sun... wait, now I know who it was! The face I saw was General Tompkins'."

"Tompkins? A major by that name has roamed these lands for many years. I hear that he is a good man."

"That's him! Why did I dream of those two together? And I also saw... horse riders. They were at the bottom of a cliff."

Those words galvanized the Indian chief. "Never say that you have not the Sight... but now I must go."

Snowtiger reached out and grabbed his arm. "What is going on?"

"It is not my place to say."

Snowtiger's normally polite speech crumbled in the face of her fear. "Like hell it's not! I'm not letting go until you tell me what going on!"

Sully decided to intercede. "She's a Marine, Govind. You'd better do what she says. She's tougher than anybody I've ever met, including you."

Govind inhaled so deeply Sully heard it, and then exhaled with a snort. "I'm betraying a trust by doing this. Your sister is alive, Lara. And based on what you have told me, she is in great danger."

"Alive? Her spirit lives, right?"

The Apache chief slowly swung his head from side to side. "No, she is alive."

"You mean, like... *alive* alive?"

"She yet walks this Earth, yes, in her physical body. She is a seeress. In the language of your people an *Ohoyo*, and we Apache have protected her for many, many years. But your dream was her reaching out for aid, and now I must ride throughout the night if she is under attack by Sevens."

"Oh, my God! Why didn't you say this right away? We've got to go help her... I mean, I request permission to accompany Govind to aid my sister, Captain."

Sully had no illusions about whether he could legally detach her from the mission; he couldn't. But if anybody had earned the right to pursue a private matter, it was her. And there *was* a slight justification. "Sergeant Snowtiger, I need you to go with this man and investigate whether General Tompkins, third in command of the Seventh Cavalry, is in danger. Take a radio."

"Thank you, sir. May I also take Gunny Piccaldi?"

If you're in for a penny, you might as well be in for a pound. "Take him and the Humvee. Draw extra fuel. But I need you back by dawn the day after tomorrow. And remember the governing ROEs. You may not fire on the Sevens unless they fire on you first."

"Thank you, Captain."

"Rah."

———※———

As they loaded up the Humvee, Govind brought his horse close to give Piccaldi directions in case they became separated. Snowtiger dumped some equipment in the back seat and when she went to retrieve more, Piccaldi saw Govind's eyes following her.

"Are you married?" he asked to the back of the Apache's head.

Govind immediately turned back to him. "Is that important?"

Piccaldi smiled. "Just being friendly."

Govind's eyes narrowed. "No, I am not married."

"Oh. Too bad."

"Why?"

The big gunnery sergeant clapped him on the arm. "It's just an expression."

#

Chapter 51

It was the Marines who taught me how to act. After that, pretending to be rough wasn't so hard.
Lee Marvin

Painted Desert, Arizona
0302 hours, April 29

Lying on the dune, Piccaldi flipped on the IR sight for his rifle. He'd grown used to the sounds of the desert at night and no longer jumped every time a small creature dislodged a pebble, or a cactus pygmy owl sang, or the wind rattled a bush. But while he consciously heard nothing unusual, his brain picked out a faint scrape that was out of place and flashed a warning to his body. He tensed, sensing nothing specific, only danger. Through the infrared sight, a mere twenty yards out from their position, a man moved their way in a crouch.

He nudged Govind, who slept beside him. The man who led those referred to by others as the Ghosts of the Desert woke as he slept, without making a sound. The overcast night blocked most starlight, but when Piccaldi pointed to the approaching man, Govind saw him.

Looking over the rim of the little hill using only his eyes to see, he touched Piccaldi's arm and leaned close to whisper. "It is my brother Gosheven."

Seconds later the second Apache slid beside his brother without making a sound. Piccaldi gently shook Snowtiger awake, realizing for the first time that, while safe in camp or back at base she snored when sleeping, out in the desert she never did.

Once they all huddled close, Gosheven filled them in on what he'd seen. "I count twenty-one riders and twenty-five horses. They have guards aiming at Ohoyo's cave. None face in other directions."

"Keeping their fire high tells us they fear the *Honágháahnii* more than men," said Govind.

"The hona-what?" Piccaldi said.

"One Who Walks Around Clan," Govind answered. "It is a word the Apache gave the Navajo. It means the mountain lion."

"Why can't you just say that?"

Govind didn't move, and Piccaldi couldn't make out details of his face in the dark night, but his voice sounded confused. "The Apache call it *Ndotlkah*, if that is what you mean," Govind said.

Snowtiger slapped his arm. "Ignore him, Govind," she said, careful to keep her voice low. "Their camp is vulnerable. What is your plan? Are the others here to help us attack the camp?"

"Others?" Piccaldi said. "What others?"

"Six of my people are in the desert two hundred yards to our left."

"How did I miss that?"

"Sshh!" Snowtiger said. "Keep your voice down. Govind?"

"I wish to drive them west, where five more warriors await them. They are surrounded but do not know it. If we attack their camp, we are likely to suffer heavy casualties, but if we can drive them out then we might kill them in the open. When we start shooting, my people to the south will, too. I am hoping the men with Ohoyo will realize what is happening and also take them under fire. This should drive them in the only direction from which no one is shooting at them, to the west. Then we move in on their rear and side as my warriors to the west open fire."

"What if they don't pull out?" Piccaldi said.

"Then we will devise a new plan."

"Can we wait that long? For all we know, they have wounded up there at the cave."

Once again Govind's expression lay hidden in shadow, but his voice left no doubt that the Apache chief was not used to having his authority questioned. "Since you take issue with mine, then I trust you have a better plan?"

"I don't take issue with it," Piccaldi said. "But you're depending on the enemy to do as you need them to do. I'm more direct."

"The Apache take orders from Govind, not from Sergeant Piccaldi."

"All right, let's try it your way first."

As Piccaldi lay back on the hillside, Govind couldn't help whispering and getting the final word. "The big man I understand being as quiet as a buffalo, but you should know better, Lara."

Her first impulse was to defend Piccaldi, but she had to first stifle a giggle. Then, before answering, she thought about it long enough to realize Govind was right. As snipers, they both knew better than to make so much noise... *she* certainly knew better. So why had Piccaldi argued with the Apache? Something was bothering him.

Regardless, they all focused on the task at hand. Gosheven slipped back into the darkness to relay the plan to the other Apaches. The night stayed quiet except for a chorus of cicadas.

"When do we open fire?" Piccaldi whispered as he turned the IR scope back on and centered the reticule on the head of a green figure leaning forward on a dune about fifty yards away.

"Wait for the signal."

"What's the signal?"

"The bark of a bobcat."

"Don't they meow?"

"What?"

"Never mind."

Snowtiger found her own target and adjusted her scope during the brief conversation. She took her eye off the scope only long enough to stare at Piccaldi's outline. Why was he being more of an ass than normal?

It was time to shoot. Something in Piccaldi's mind clicked into place, and he forgot Snowtiger and Govind and once again became the killer he'd been trained to be.

The Sevens had pitched camp in a bowl-shaped depression surrounded on three sides by low dunes, leaving only the lookout on the north side, facing the cave, visible. It was sloppy security but Piccaldi wasn't complaining. The man showed up bright green in his IR scope.

"Target acquired," Piccaldi said in a voice lower than a whisper.

Nevertheless, Snowtiger heard it and replied. "Negative acquisition. I'm tee-double-oh." *Target of opportunity.* After Piccaldi fired, she would shoot the next target to appear while he chambered another round and sought a new target. Both went into automatic mode, with heartbeats and breathing slowing and fingers barely touching their triggers.

The faint bark went unnoticed by Piccaldi amid the background of desert sounds, but not by Govind.

"That was the signal," he whispered.

The crosshairs centered one inch in front of the man's ear, where the upper and lower jaws met. Head shots had a higher risk profile than body shots, but his only other choices were the man's right shoulder and neck. The neck was an even more difficult shot and the shoulder wouldn't kill him, so the head it was.

Gently he squeezed the trigger like he might brush the lips of a lover with a first kiss. The rifle's report sounded to his ears like that lover moaning in orgasmic ecstasy and its recoil like the culmination of their love making.

The reality was different. A 7.62 x 51mm NATO round traveling at more than 2,500 feet per second struck exactly at the joint of the man's two jaws, drove through bone and brain while it also partially splintered, and exited by smashing through bone again while leaving an exit wound the size of a baseball. The force of the impact knocked him sideways to his left, so Piccaldi didn't see the top of his head fly off and roll down the dune.

Experienced warriors would have suppressed the reflex to look up and would have gone to ground at the sound of the gunshot. The man named Qadim had said they'd trained all winter to be better soldiers, but training was no substitute for experience. So when a face appeared over the crest of the dune facing east, toward her, Snowtiger wasted no time in putting a round into his forehead. Then the Apaches opened up.

0320 hours
Sara Snowtiger's Cave

"Skip, Skip!"

Dennis Tompkins woke and sat upright at the report of the first gunshot, and hadn't needed Thibodeaux to alert him. Fifty years surviving in the desert had left even his aging reflexes sharper than those of most men half his age. At the cave's mouth, he dropped to all fours and crawled to the lip of the ledge beside Thibodeaux. The rest of his men lay spread out with rifles at the ready. By now a fusillade of gunfire echoed in the dark desert night.

"Any idea what's going on?"

"Near as I can tell, they's three groups got them Sevens boxed in."

"No sign of who they are?"

Thibodeaux shook his head and picked up the binoculars.

"It is Govind," Sara Snowtiger said. She stood beside him. Terrified for her safety, he grabbed her arm and pulled her down to her knees. Snowtiger stared at his hand and then met his eyes. Embarrassed, he let go.

"I'm sorry, Sara. You scared me."

"It is well," she said. Was there a slightly confused tone in her voice? "You did it to protect me, and I am unhurt. I did not mind your touch."

For nearly a minute they stared into the shadows of each other's face.

"Skip, I likes romance as much as the next fella, me, but right now we got's a problem."

It took several seconds for Thibodeaux's words to sink in. Tompkins' brain felt sluggish. Feelings washed over him that he'd forgotten, a sensation of longing unlike anything he could remember. "What, John? What did you say?"

"Quit moonin' over the girl like a damned teenager, Skip. What're we gonna do 'bout this shootin'?"

Tompkins tried to act mad, but his men had known him way too long to believe that. Fortunately they couldn't see his face very well. "Can anybody pick out a clear target?"

"I get a glimpse when they fire," Hausser said.

"We don't have ammo to waste. If we can't get a good look at 'em, we can't shoot. We've gotta wait for dawn. The Apaches should have been here soon after that, but now we're on our own."

"Is Govind coming here?" Snowtiger asked.

"Not those Apaches, Sara. I'm talking about the helicopter gunships. Remember, I told you they weren't coming any more?"

"Oh." She stopped a minute and closed her eyes. "It is just as well. Govind is already here." Without another word, she crawled back into the cave.

"She's a fine lookin' woman, Skip, but 'scuse me for sayin', she kinda gives me the creeps."

Tompkins couldn't help watching her crawl away. "Yeah... me, too."

Thibodeaux glanced at Tompkins, then Snowtiger, and then back at Tompkins. "I don't t'ink it's the same kinda creeps."

———

After three minutes the firing died down to an occasional shot. Snowtiger and Piccaldi each nailed two Sevens apiece, after which no targets presented themselves.

"Are you seeing anything?" Govind asked.

"Nada," Piccaldi said. "Lara?"

"Nothing. They've gone to ground."

"Why are they not firing from the cave?" Govind asked. "I know the men are still up there."

"I'm guessing they don't have that much ammo. It's unlikely they can pick out targets in the dark from that far away."

"Yet if we wait for daylight, we give up our advantage in the night." Govind went quiet for a moment. "What is this plan you had in mind?"

Piccaldi pushed up into a crouch and walked toward the Humvee, which they'd left behind a low hill two hundred yards to the east. "Tell your people to wait for my diversion, then do that ghost of the desert thing you do and wipe those fuckers out."

"Zo!" Snowtiger hissed.

He kept walking.

"I'm going with you!"

That stopped him. "No, you're not, Lara. Stay here. Kill."

"I outrank you."

"Yes First Sergeant, you do. And I'm more expendable. Trust me, I'll be back."

After a moment's hesitation, she answered, "You'd better be."

But he hadn't gone more than ten more paces before Govind called him back.

"What?" he said, squatting next to the Apache; from somewhere Govind's brother Gosheven had materialized.

"We have a new problem."

Gosheven took over. "More Sevens are coming up from the south, another group of twenty or more riders. They will be here soon."

"Damn."

"We are now outnumbered and cannot fight them in the open desert. Come with us to our village. You will be safe there."

Before Piccaldi could speak, Snowtiger answered. "I am going to my sister."

"You will be trapped with her," Govind said. "I cannot guarantee that my people can help you. We are few in number now."

"I do not care. I am going to Sara. You go with them, Zo. Take the Humvee, but first take me to the base of the mountain so I can climb to her."

"I'm not doing that and neither are you. It's a fool's play."

Snowtiger's voice took on a steely tone he'd never heard before. "I am going to my sister."

He responded in kind. "No, you're not! You're going with Govind!"

She stalked off toward the Humvee, not caring that she was standing. "Like fuck I am."

That shocked both men silent. Only when she was out of sight did Govind say anything. "I did not expect to hear such language from Sara's sister."

But Piccaldi had to smile. "Why not? She's a Marine, ain't she?"

\#

CHAPTER 52

In the land is found the ancient wisdom of life.
Native American proverb

Painted Desert, Arizona
0349 hours, April 29

Piccaldi followed her into the darkness, but only Gosheven went with them, since he knew how to drive and could hide the Humvee after they unloaded at the cave. Govind stayed behind to organize cover for them.

Driving with the lights off, Piccaldi risked hitting a deep hole rather than creeping at a safe speed. The distance was only about half a mile from where they'd parked the Humvee, but it was impossible to know how much time they had. A trick of the land hid them from the Sevens most of the way.

Snowtiger held on tight as they bounced from gopher hole to antelope squirrel hole to bigger depressions, like badger dens. Piccaldi couldn't see Gosheven, sitting in the back seat, although he heard him grunt whenever the Humvee bottomed out. They pulled up to the bottom of the cliff and got out quickly. A distant shot came from somewhere, but just one.

Piccaldi cupped hands around his mouth and tilted his head back as far as he could. "We're coming up!" he yelled, and then helped Gosheven and Snowtiger unload their gear. "Where's the rope ladder?"

"It isn't here," Gosheven said. "They must have pulled it up."

"Throw the ladder! Throw the ladder!"

The voice shouting from above sounded thin. "Who are you?"

"We're Marines, damn it! Hurry up!"

Two more shots rang out closer, followed by two more and then another three.

"C'mon, c'mon," Piccaldi said, tapping his foot.

"Take the Humvee," Snowtiger said to Gosheven.

Even in the dark, Piccaldi recognized the actions of her unslinging her rifle, turning on her sight, and preparing to shoot. "No, Lara," he said. "You go first. I'll cover you."

"Negative. I'm lighter and faster than you are. If one of us has to go up under fire, it should be me."

"No way I'm gonna let you do that."

"Quit arguing with me. That's an order."

"I—"

"An order!"

Gosheven wasted no time pulling away at less than half the speed Piccaldi had driven.

"C'mon..."

Thunk, thwip, thunk, thwip... falling down the cliff face, an intricate and heavily-knotted rope construction bounced and unraveled until stopping four feet above the desert floor. It wasn't a rope ladder as much as it was a pulley system, with a wide and sturdy plank at the bottom like the seat of a swing. The wooden board was fire-hardened oak, and while it showed extensive wear from hitting the rock over and over, stainless steel strips nailed to each side and cross-braced across the bottom kept it intact.

A second item dropped down beside it, lowered slowly and not thrown from above. This was a large pulley about two feet across that appeared to have come from an industrial site. A large hook held a looped coil of steel cable and it only took Piccaldi a few seconds to realize there had to be an anchor somewhere nearby. He found it soon enough several feet to the left, and the cable slid perfectly over a granite point near the base of the cliff. He began piling equipment onto the plank, securing it with leather straps and buckles attached to the board, and tugged hard to indicate to those above to pull it up. Just as he turned to get his rifle and rejoin Snowtiger, something hissed nearby, struck the cliff, and splattered with a loud *chit.*

"Fuck me!" he said as something tiny struck his jaw.

"Not tonight, big boy," she answered. Two seconds later, she fired one round. There came no screams to indicate a hit and Piccaldi knew there wouldn't be any. He simply assumed the target died a millisecond after she pulled the trigger.

Once he'd gotten his own rifle and turned the scope on, they both saw and heard a small knot of horsemen heading their way.

Ten seconds later Govind reined up, no more than a dark shadow against the overcast night sky. "I will gather my people and we will come back for you, but it will be after nightfall tomorrow. You must hold out until then. The cave is deep; you should all be safe there." Two of the Apache riders near the back of the group squeezed off solitary shots. Govind paused and Piccaldi sensed a shift in his position atop the horse, but it was impossible to tell what he did as the nervous animal stepped and snorted in its eagerness to get the hell out of the shooting zone. In his mind's eye, however, he thought the man was staring at Snowtiger. "I will not abandon you."

"I never thought you would," she answered, without removing her eye from her scope.

With that the Apache rode off, followed seconds later by the plank being lowered again.

"Lara..."

"Go!"

Still hesitating, he started to blurt out what he'd been trying to say for weeks when a bullet passed two feet to his right and ricocheted. That was all the encouragement he needed. Sitting on the board, he pulled on one of the ropes and shouldered his rifle. He'd never before tried a shot while being hoisted 300 feet in the air, but if one of the Sevens gave him the least target to aim at, there would be a first time.

———

It seemed hours before the ledge came in sight and hands reached out, grabbing his arms and pulling him to safety, although in reality it was about four minutes. Despite the number of people pulling the rope, they were all aged and he weighed more than 180 pounds. The trickiest part was unbuckling without losing his balance.

Once he was on solid ground, they all got down on hands and knees and pushed the board back over the ledge. He took over the job of lowering it. Even up that high, it was too dark to make out facial details, but the panting and wheezing of the other men told him all he needed to know.

A thin smell of smoke came from within the cave. As he let out lengths of rope, Piccaldi realized it was carried outside by a draught from inside the mountain. Hauling so much wood using the pulley system took nothing short of incredible dedication. If Snowtiger's sister really lived up there, she had to be even more amazing than Lara herself.

He felt the plank touch bottom and weight pulled the ropes taut. Then Snowtiger tugged to be hauled up.

"All right, boys, she's on."

Without a word, the six old men grabbed the rope with him and began pulling. It required standing up, exposing themselves to anybody who could see them from below, and when shots echoed off the cliff, several of them nearly let go. But nothing hit close enough to hurt anybody even with flying splinters, such as had happened to Piccaldi earlier, nor for Snowtiger to expose her own position by returning fire.

A chill breeze dried sweat on his cheeks and turned his damp collar cold. Heat built up under his armpits and he could feel wetness running down his back and stomach, but when more firing erupted, he redoubled his efforts. Some of the shots came closer as the Sevens got the range, but fortunately for them all, him helping to pull, combined with Snowtiger's lesser weight, got her to the ledge in less than two minutes. He pulled her off the plank and pushed her prone, then fell beside her to the right. The others also took cover.

"Welcome to our little slice of the world," Dennis Tompkins said from her left.

Both Snowtiger and Piccaldi half-rolled to salute. He returned it, although Piccaldi judged that more from sensing movement than seeing the actual gesture.

"What are you two doing here?" Tompkins said.

"We heard you were in trouble, General," Piccaldi answered.

"Did you now? Who told you, the Indian? What's his name?"

"Govind, General Tompkins," Snowtiger said. "He told us you were pinned down up here with... others."

"Others?" Tompkins voice seemed to carry a note of humor. "Or *other*?"

"Well..."

"She's in the cave, First Sergeant. She's waiting for you."

———

Lara Snowtiger didn't stand until inside the cave. The floor angled slightly downward about five feet from the mouth before flattening out again. It was just enough to put the interior out of line-of-sight from below, making it safe against almost anything save a heat-seeking missile.

The smooth floor had none of the pebbles or dust that would normally be found in a cave. Nor did the interior smell of mold or wet, despite water she could hear falling somewhere down the tunnel. Light flickering on the walls came from a fire down the passage, where a rock basin acted as a hearth.

In a small wooden chair near the fire, surrounded by stacks of books, sat a tall woman dressed in well-made animal hide pants and what looked like a white wool shirt. Her back was straight. Dark skin contrasted the clothing and black hair streaked with white fell past narrow shoulders in a braid. When she looked up, Snowtiger saw the sharp cheekbones and brown eyes she saw every day in her own face.

"Sara..."

Before the old woman could move, her young twin sister fell to her knees and clutched her like a frightened child does her mother. Tears flooded eyes that had coldly killed scores of men, and she pressed her cheek against her sister's.

———

Overtime Prime
0531 hours, April 29

"Is everybody clear?" Wingnut said to the other three people in the tiny room. Rather than use their normal quarters, which Adder had probably bugged, they'd found an empty ammunition ready room in the hangar complex. "No shooting today no matter what. Adder's gonna push your buttons, so act like a fuckin' pro and take it. He's got a big mouth, but they're just words. Any problems?"

"What if we get a clean shot at Steeple?" said One-Eye.

"If you get a shot today, it's a trap. Adder's not gonna let you kill his meal ticket. Without Steeple at the top, the whole thing falls apart, and I'm bettin' Adder knows it. So today we play nice and earn his trust. Everybody capiche? Razor, you're the new guy. You get it?"

"Fuck you, nut-for-brains, that joke's getting old. I was with the team for four years before we went cold and you know it. Pick on H.P. next time."

"Hollowpoint's been around longer than you, but all right. H.P. you down with this?"

The tall man nodded his long, narrow head, and not for the first or last time, Wingnut thought he should have called himself Horseface.

"What about Nipple?" One-Eye asked.

"Nipple's gone, man, and she ain't comin' back. Weirdest thing I ever saw, someone changing overnight like that. I never really bought that whole psycho thing before, but now... something's wrong. It's not natural for a person to totally change their identity. But forget her and concentrate on the mission."

"I still wish you let me kill Adder," One-Eye said with a faux snarl.

"If I actually thought you could do it, I'd let you."

#

Chapter 53

Get ye hence, stand to God's ramparts,
Take thy shield to ward off the darts
of the servants of foul Perdition;
Wield thy sword with all courage and skill,
Fell the foe and know it is God's will
that you obey of your own volition.
Unknown, found after the Siege of Vienna in 1529

Groom Lake Air Force Facility
0612 hours, April 29

By dawn, the concrete runways and tarmacs had radiated all of the previous day's heat away and absorbed cold during the long desert night. Randall stuck his hands between his thighs, took them out and blew on them, and stuck them between his legs again. His breath came in huffs that filled the air with icy vapor.

Carlos walked in a circle, his hands in the pockets of the old jacket they'd given him. "I'm freezing," he said.

Rifle in hand, Bondo stood in the shadows near the hangar door, grinning.

"You're lovin' this, aren't you?" Randall said.

He nodded. "Yeah, I am."

"I thought we'd at least get a decent breakfast."

"You did. Desert duty gets extra rations."

"I could still eat a dozen eggs," Carlos said. "And two pounds of bacon."

Randall rubbed his eyes some more. "I just want coffee."

Bondo shook his head in disgust. "No wonder the old world died."

The fourth member of their group pushed through the side door into the hangar, carrying a leather sack filled with gear and provisions. She was almost as big as Bondo, only with a worse disposition. They called her Roe.

"Where're your guns?" she said.

Randall shrugged and stuck his hands down the front of his pants, not giving a damn what it looked like.

"Do that on your own time," Roe said. "What about your rifles?"

"They're on the fuckin' flitters," Bondo said after a few seconds. "No thanks to these desert flowers. I put 'em there."

Randall made no obvious sign of excitement, but his mind started racing when he heard the word *flitter*. Those were the hovercraft they'd flown the other day, and if he and Bunny could get their hands on a couple of those...

"Let's go," Roe said. "It's a long trip."

"Mind telling us exactly where we're going?" Randall said as they walked. Out from the shadows of the hangar, they found a patch of early morning sunlight, and the temperature increased at least ten degrees. This was more like it!

"You've got EP1 today. It's about fifteen miles from here, about as far out as we post sentries. Today's the first of seven days on, three days off."

"We're going there for seven days?"

"Relax, Petunia, you get to come home at night."

"All right."

Bondo laughed and Roe joined him.

"Are we funny?"

"Just obvious," she said. "You're wondering if you'll be far enough out to take off, leave, try to get back to wherever you came from. Go ahead and try it. I hope you do."

They took four flitters, with Roe in front, Bondo in the rear, and the two semi-prisoners in between. With Randall and Carlos being less skilled at handling the nimble aircraft, it took half an hour to get there, not to mention their need to battle brilliant sunlight as the sun cleared the mountains to the east. As they skimmed low over the desert floor, and wildlife scurried for cover, Randall noted any terrain features he thought might come in handy later on.

EP1was an acronym meaning East Point 1, an important sounding name for a half-ruined concrete bunker on a small hill overlooking the main road leading in from the east. Inside the structure, a concrete platform allowed observers to see intruders coming many miles across the desert. But that was assuming the intruders were human and not reptilian, avian, or mammalian, which Randall was told hadn't happened for at least ten years. Otherwise their job was to enjoy the view.

Desolation stretched away in all directions.

And if they did see something suspicious?

"That thing there is called a crank phone," Bondo said, pointing at a homemade device that was half radio phone, half hand-crank ice-cream maker. "Turn that handle and it sends an electric charge down the line, which they'll pick up in the comm. room. Then you can talk to them."

"How clever is that? Is it a radio?" Randall wondered aloud.

"No radio. There's a cable all the way back to the comm. center. It was part of the original security setup."

"Awesome," he said, but couldn't completely hide his disappointment.

For once Bondo didn't pick up on the sarcasm. "Yeah, it is. The network is so extensive, you wouldn't believe it. They used to have cameras and pressure sensors everywhere out here, thousands of them, but that was a long time ago." For a short moment, his eyes wandered off to the left. "So, if you have a problem, let us know and we'll be here on the double quick."

"If a bunch of Rednecks show up, do we just pull out?"

"No, you can't." Roe had come into the bunker and held out her palm, where two identical rectangular metal items caught a ray from the rising sun and reflected on one wall in a pinpoint of yellow. Her other hand held a pistol that was not pointed at them, but wasn't pointed away, either. Randall understood both implications immediately.

"Relays?" he said, pointing to the odd devices in her hand.

Bondo nodded. "You're grounded until we come back." He then shifted his finger to the gun.

"I thought we were part of the happy family now. Trusted comrades."

"Trust, yes, but verify."

"So what do we do if bad guys show up?"

"Can't our hotshot pilot figure that out? Why do you think we gave you rifles?"

#

CHAPTER 54

*All the great things are simple, and many can be expressed in
a single word: freedom, justice, honor, duty, mercy, hope.*
Sir Winston S. Churchill

Shangri-La
0832 hours, April 29

From the first day he settled in the valley that become
the core of Shangri-La, Winston Ballinger had conceived of
the compound being a fortress for the protection not only of
its citizens, but of as much collected scientific knowledge of
the United States as possible. In the early years, when fuel
was still available and heavy equipment hadn't worn out yet,
under Ballinger's direction the land had been reformed with
an eye toward not just defense, but livability. For example,
the huge underground hothouse and solar ovens had required months of work, while under Ballinger's direction
they'd simultaneously created defensive valleys that chan-
neled would-be attackers into killing zones, and bunkers at
critical points with escape tunnels carved from the living
rock.

Subsequent leaders had continued the work. An extensive tunnel system honeycombed the ground under the desert. Forward firing pits, concealed by wooden hatches, had
crawl tunnels for the shooter to get out alive. Blast doors had
even been installed, heavy sheets of scrap metal that could
be swung into position behind someone evacuating the hole

and fastened down to absorb the blast of a hand grenade or other explosive device.

Other traps had been constructed, such as a trench with a thin wooden cover that could be covered with dust and which appeared to be solid ground, but would collapse under the weight of a man or horse. Sharpened spikes lined the bottom eight feet below, but an even nastier surprise had been planned for any attacker who fell in there. Rainwater ordered the plan put into action and dozens of people began gathering rattlesnakes from the area. Once captured, they were then thrown into the trench. Hundreds of smaller holes were also dug, with scrap metal embedded in the bottom that had been sharpened and smeared with animal feces, or with rattlesnakes ready to strike. These were covered with thin wooden lids designed to crack underfoot, then camouflaged with topsoil.

In another place, a rocky hillside beside the main highway leading into the compound, Highway 4, had been hollowed out and more than one thousand pounds of black powder poured into a specially protected chamber designed to both keep out moisture and funnel the blast outward. The ingredients for black power were abundant in that part of New Mexico, with the potassium nitrate being the hardest to get, but between the numerous caves and deposits southeast of Los Alamos, the supply was never a problem.

The forge and blacksmith shops turned out many of the guns the defenders were busy cleaning, primarily rifled muskets and some handguns. Modern weapons equipped the fittest and best trained of the militia. After so many years, most of them had been repaired multiple times and all of the ammunition used were reloads. Policing brass was mandatory. Hundreds of double-fired ceramic hand grenades had sat for years in rows in a cave near the springs, waiting to be filled with powder and fused. And now that day had come.

Rainwater personally oversaw the placing of the two homemade Gatling guns, built to fire nine millimeter rounds. They'd gotten the parts from Idaho Jack, the scraper who came around every now and then, who later dug up more than thirty thousand empty casings to go with them from an old shooting range somewhere. Operating them required four people, mostly to rotate cranking the firing mechanism.

The first thing he'd done after the meeting was send scouts out as far as Gallup in the west and to Santa Fe and Angel Fire in the east. If the Sevens meant to surround them, he needed to know. The very old and the very young he ordered to get ready to move north to San Antonio Mountain, which had been prepared over the years as a final refuge for just such an emergency.

Not until after midnight did he return to the simple pueblo that served as his home and fall fast asleep on a blanket four feet inside the door. He didn't bathe in the hot springs, or even check for scorpions, a precaution he'd learned when still a toddler. He simply grabbed a blanket and lay down. Sometimes exhaustion demanded immediate sleep.

Abigail Deak had only taken over as Governor of the Pueblo of Jemez two weeks earlier, and while the area comprising Shangri-La had traditionally been the homeland of her tribe, she immediately recognized Johnny Rainwater as leader of the community, with her as his second. Rumors of an invading army of Sevens were already in circulation and she considered him a much better warrior if it came to a fight. Her specialty was the agricultural side of things.

She'd spent the early morning preparing their food supply for the coming battle. The staple would be hard, twice-baked bread made from barley and wheat, various jerked meats that could be boiled to soften them, with the water then used to soak the bread. Under her direction, the food staff had spent the previous week drying various beans and legumes. Livestock was slaughtered, butchered, and washed for cooking, and the trimmed fat and marrow used as the basis for large vats of pemmican.

The potters fired new vessels for hauling food to men guarding the passes into Shangri-La, many of which would have challenged a brown mountain goat not to slip. An ingenious strap and buckle system, combined with a tight-fitted lid, allowed sentries on the highest peaks to eat hot food at least twice a day. The dried foods the men and women in the defensive positions held against the day of battle, when exposing yourself to bring food could be fatal.

Water had long since been supplied to the community through the original system that had supplied the Pueblo of Jemez, which had been expanded using salvaged pipes from abandoned settlements from as far away as Santa Fe. Hand- and water-powered pumps allowed distribution to even the farthest reach of Shangri-La, including many of the defensive positions. The underground facilities, including the hot-house, got their water from a gravity system using old garden hoses brought in by the scraper named Idaho Jack.

Anyone could bathe in the once-famous hot springs, as long as they didn't use soap and bathed nude. As might be expected, after dark the springs tended to be popular with young people. Early on Ballinger had tried to prohibit such behavior, but quickly realized that, short of posting round-the-clock guards, it was futile. The rules on soap still ap-plied, however, and the usual routine was to bathe first in cold water and then float in the hot water, much like the an-cient Romans.

By midday, Deak was satisfied she'd done everything possible to prepare, and went to find Johnny Rainwater. She found him on a towering slab of red rock that had made the area famous as a tourist destination in the years preceding the Collapse. From atop the outcropping, he could see down a long slope toward the flat ground north of Albuquerque.

He turned at the soft scrape of her double-soled mocca-sins on a stairway cut into the rock on its north side. "They're coming, Abby," he said.

"We've heard that for three days," Deak answered.

"That's what worries me. These Sevens aren't reckless. They seem to be held under tight control by someone."

"We've hurt them many times in the past, so maybe they are simply being cautious."

"Mmm... maybe. It's just a feeling, but I think this time is different. Are we ready in the homestead?"

"As ready as we'll ever be. The food is prepped and ready, and we had so much extra fat and bones that I had the cooks make it into pemmican."

"The bones?"

One side of her mouth curled up as she looked at him sideways. "The marrow, not the bones themselves."

"How should I know that? I just eat it, I don't make it."

"Well, you should. Everybody in Shangri-La should know how to cook basic foods."

"Let's argue that some other time, eh? How's everything else coming along?"

"Granny Guntree organized the oldest of the women to cut bandages from the clothing discards. Once cut, they're boiling them. Century Tom and the other men who either can't walk or can't hold a gun to shoot straight are behind the stone wall surrounding the Council house. They're the last line of defense."

"They'll be useless. All they'll manage is to get killed."

"What else are they gonna do, Johnny? They can't run away."

"Yeah." He turned back so she couldn't see his face in the afternoon sun's glare. "What motivates people like the Sevens, Abby? Why can't they live in peace? Life is hard enough without making war."

"How should I know? I don't understand it either. All I know is that if they're really coming this time, we need to be ready."

"I sent out riders looking for the Americans we heard about."

"Who did you send?" she said, knowing who he was going to say and dreading hearing it.

"You know who I sent."

"Not Billy Two Trees. Please tell me you didn't send Billy."

He nodded. "And Sally Makepeace and Ronald Hampton."

"They're just kids!"

Rainwater wasn't usually a stern man. Indeed, she'd opposed him as leader because in a crisis, she hadn't been sure he could take the situation seriously enough. But the expression she now saw on his square face frightened her with its intensity.

"In a fight for your life, there are no children. Everybody's a warrior."

"But we both know Billy hasn't got the sense God gave a rabbit."

"He's one of our best riders."

"He's fifteen!"

310

Rainwater stopped in mid-response as a young man scampered between two boulders and ran toward the rock where they stood. They were nearly fifty feet high and words tended to be swept away by winds racing through the narrow canyons.

Cupping hands around his mouth, the man shouted up at them. "They're on the move, Johnny!"

#

CHAPTER 55

The most glorious victory of all time!
Adolf Hitler, June 25, 1940, after the surrender of France

Overtime Prime
0619 hours, April 29

The first thing Tom Steeple did on the first morning he awoke as commander of Operation Overtime was to order everything cleared from Nick Angriff's office except for the furniture. He wanted a Spartan office in which to begin his tenure at the helm of the Seventh Cavalry, and he wanted it by precisely 0800 hours, by which time the work had better be finished so he could broadcast to the brigade.

Sergeant Major Schiller directed the activities, but most of the actual work was done by Corporal Diaz with help from a few technicians in the Clam Shell. Rather than carry everything down the long ramp to the ground floor, they piled it on the back side of the platform that encircled the Crystal Palace, near the coffee setup. Mostly it was files and papers and computer equipment, but there were a few personal photos and Angriff's most prized possession: his humidor. That Schiller directed Diaz to carry downstairs and hide in a closet.

Steeple still had only the uniform he'd worn when he'd arrived at Overtime and found himself under arrest, and at first no one even knew where it was stored. A frantic search two days before had turned it up in a little-used storeroom, crumpled and wrinkled, under his shoes. Fortunately McComb had had it cleaned and pressed before he was released from the stockade, but he was still angered at what he considered disrespect. Schiller also found him an ACU uniform to get by with, but Steeple ordered his personal uniform cleaned a second time and delivered to his quarters by 0530 that morning. The laundry took longer than expected and when it arrived at 0537, he chewed out the hapless private who'd brought it. Steeple never shied away from shooting the messenger. He believed it increased efficiency.

Steeple was not a man to make impulsive decisions, so when, while shaving, he decided to leave a small mustache on his upper lip, it surprised him more than those who saw it. Tilting his head this way and that when viewing it in the bathroom mirror, he thought it lent him a certain *joie de vivre* in the mold of Errol Flynn.

Four Chinese MPs accompanied him on the short walk from his quarters, right next to the Angriffs' apartment, to the elevators and up to the Clam Shell. All eyes turned to him and conversation stopped as he walked up the ramp to the Crystal Palace. He felt their animosity like a fog hanging over the headquarters, but it didn't worry him; Steeple was used to being hated. As long as they obeyed his orders, they could hate him all they wanted.

Once all of Angriff's things had been removed, Steeple felt calmer, more in control, and more ready for the busy and important day to come.

Operation Comeback
0724 hours, April 29

When Corporal Duglach put through a call from the commanding general at Overtime Prime, Major General Schiller expected the slightly hoarse and Virginia-accented voice of Nick Angriff. What he had not expected was the smooth but nasal Midwestern voice of Tom Steeple.

"Good morning, Colonel, how are you on such a fine morning? General Steeple here."

Schiller paused in confusion. "My current rank is major general, not colonel, and may I ask why you have been released from confinement? General Angriff must have had a good reason."

"I admit to being surprised, Bill. I would have thought someone from inside Prime would have alerted you to the new situation by now. Yesterday I took back the command that is legally mine, although I have no intention of bringing General Angriff up on charges. He was given a spurious document that misled him about the true nature of his position within my command. I still intend for him to be the commanding officer of Operation Overtime, and my second in command. And just as we originally planned, you will remain as the S-4, a job you are more qualified for than anyone else alive today."

"You did not answer my question."

"Did I not? What question was that?"

"How did you escape confinement?"

"I must tell you that I do not appreciate being interrogated by my staff, Bill. I will answer this one question for you, but never again treat me as anything except your commanding officer. I was released from my illegal imprisonment by some loyal patriots whose only desire was the good of the brigade moving forward."

As Steeple spoke, Schiller took the time to analyze his situation, which on the surface appeared to be serious. If Steeple had truly taken command of Overtime, then he commanded an overwhelming volume of firepower which the forces at Comeback couldn't possibly oppose. After all, Operation Overtime and the Seventh Cavalry was the combat arm of American forces, while Comeback was the administrative portion. Making things worse, Schiller knew he couldn't count on the loyalty of his own command, most of whom owed their position to General Steeple personally.

On the reverse side of the problem, his orders from General Angriff said that only he, Angriff, or his designated successor could remove Schiller, and Steeple was not in that line. As far as Schiller could tell, Steeple had illegally seized control, thereby invalidating any and all orders given by him. So it boiled down to whether Schiller would fight for the command he'd been given, defending it from an illicit coup.

"You have no authority whatsoever, General Steeple. You are under arrest awaiting a court-martial. I do not know what you have done with General Angriff, but your orders are invalid as far as I am concerned."

Steeple's voice changed in an instant, from the collegial tone of a friendly fellow officer to that of an angry serpent, complete with sibilance. It struck Schiller that Steeple must practiced that very change for it to be so perfectly pitched.

"It is a dangerous game you are playing, Colonel."

"I am not a colonel. I am a major general. I am also the commanding general of Operation Comeback until it pleases General Angriff or his legal successor to withdraw or make permanent those designations. Heretofore you will address me as such."

"I am very sorry you have made this decision, Bill. I genuinely liked you."

0746 hours

"Corporal Duglach, get Glide and Frosty up here on the double."

A minute or so later, Astrid Naidoo came in holding a squeezer of coffee, her eyes streaked with red. Even against her dark skin, the blue-black circles around her eyes were visible from across the room. "I'm sorry that I'm late, Bill."

Standing with arms folded, scowling in thought, he waved a hand to dismiss her concerns. "I just received a call from Tom Steeple. He has taken control of Overtime Prime."

"*What?*"

"It is true. He ordered me back to Prime to act as Brigade S-4."

"What'd you tell him?"

"I informed him that I would not be doing that unless ordered to do so by General Angriff."

She smiled at him.

"Is that amusing?" Schiller said in confusion.

"Yes, Bill, it is. In your own way, you told him to fuck off."

Overtime Prime
0800 hours, April 29

Adder leaned back on the couch, reading the Congressional proclamation that promoted Nick Angriff to general of the army. He flipped it over, then felt the paper and sniffed it. "Seems legit," he said at length. "Although it's impossible to know for sure. But I get where Schiller is coming from. If he believes this is real, then it puts Angriff in charge."

"That is not my concern," Tom Steeple said. "I reject any legitimacy from such a document out of hand. What I need to know is how such a thing got in here in the first place. If the timeline of events that we think we know hold, true, that paper was signed two years after the Collapse."

"Which makes no sense."

"Correct, which is why we are having this discussion. Unlike our friend Nick Angriff, I am not so sanguine about latent threats from within this organization. But whoever injected this spurious item into the situation needs to be ferreted out and their motives discerned. You have authorization to do whatever is necessary to accomplish this mission. Are we clear about what you are to do?"

"Very."

Steeple nodded. Seconds later, a knock at the door was followed by him calling out, "Enter!"

Sergeant Major Schiller stepped into the office and stood at attention. "Colonel Santorio says everything is set up and ready, General Steeple."

"Simultaneous broadcast to Overtime, Comeback, and all units in the field?"

"As you ordered, sir."

"Very well." The general looked back at Adder. "Are you ready?"

The big former Zombie stood and hefted his rifle. "Ready for anything." He stepped onto the platform and took up position atop the ramp, beside the four Chinese guards.

"Colonel Santorio will make the introduction from her post in the Comm. Center, then you push in on that big white button and you'll be patched in."

"Thank you, Sergeant Major. You wait outside."

Steeple pulled the microphone closer and cleared his throat. A squeezer of water sat near his left elbow and a mug of tea to his right. This was it, the moment his entire professional life had been building to, and for one of the few times he could recall, Steeple was nervous.

───♪───

"Hey, Toy, hand me those vise grips."

Joe Ootoi started to jump off the rear of *Joe's Junk* to fetch the requested tool, but stopped when Morgan Randall appeared from the door leading into the base interior. She'd heard the request from her mechanic inside her tank, found the vise grips among a table full of other greasy tools, and passed it up to Toy, who handed it down into the interior of the tank.

"What'd the doctor say?" Joe asked.

Randall shook her head. "He said I'm pregnant."

The sweaty face of the mechanic they'd nicknamed Oscar popped up from inside. "I told you that before anybody else. Does that make me a doctor, too?"

"Oscar, that makes you—"

The conversation stopped when a voice rang through the complex through the overhead loudspeakers. "Attention all ranks, this is Colonel Santorio. Stand by for the commanding officer."

Toy and Randall looked at each other. "Your dad's back already?"

She shrugged. "No idea."

The mike keyed on again, and it was still Santorio's voice. "General Thomas F. Steeple."

Randall's face whitened. Without knowing it, she bit the knuckle of her left index finger.

"Ladies and gentlemen of Operation Overtime, Operation Comeback, deployed members of the Seventh Cavalry Brigade, both civilians and military, and all of our esteemed countrymen wherever they may be, in accordance with long-standing plans made before the calamity which temporarily interrupted the proper governance of our beloved republic, known to us all as the Collapse, as of this day I have officially taken control of all United States military operations worldwide.

"I am forever indebted to General Nicholas T. Angriff and have nothing but the highest respect for this outstanding officer. General Angriff has done a remarkable job in my absence and your record in combat is in the finest tradition of the American armed forces. I assure you that under my command, risking your lives in furtherance of our mission will never be done without grave consideration. To that end, moving forward I hope to have more allies in our mission to rebuild the United States and fewer enemies. We have, therefore, opened negotiations with the Chinese government in place in California, to find mutual ground for the resolution of our differences. In furtherance of that goal, I have invited them to send representatives to our forces in the field, to Operation Comeback, and here, to Operation Overtime. If you encounter them, you are expected to show them the courtesy due to a potential valued ally.

"I demand and expect the same loyalty that you have so far given General Angriff as together we march confidently into the future, a future that will see the rebirth of a new and better United States of America. I know that I can count on all of you to help me fulfill this sacred task."

———

The mechanics' station was at the far end of Motor Bay B. As soon as the announcement ended, voices echoed through the vast chamber as people tried to make sense of what they'd just heard. Ootoi and Oscar exchanged the universal look for *what the hell?* Morgan Randall stood like a wax statue, barely breathing as she tried to register the words. Then she took off running for the elevators.

———

Nikki Bauer looked up from the couch where she sat with Janine and Cynthia Angriff as her sister Morgan almost ran into the room.

Hands on knees and panting, Morgan looked up. "I'm sure Daddy's all right, Mom," she said.

"Yes," her mother said with the smile she always wore in times of trouble. She was pale, with dark circles under her eyes. "I'm sure that he is. General Steeple was good enough to send word that he is in good health and still with his men, although being detained until his exact status can be worked out."

"What does that mean, Momma?" Cynthia said in a voice that sounded surprisingly young. At that moment, Nikki realized how much of an age gap existed between them. On impulse, she put her right arm around her youngest sister and hugged her.

It was all surreal to Nikki. Nipple wouldn't have sat there empathizing with and comforting others. Nipple would have sprung into action and probably shot her way into the Crystal Palace, either to die herself or kill Steeple, Adder, and their entire cabal. But Nipple wasn't there. Nikki was. She *was* angry. She could feel something she knew to be anger, but it was different from the rage she had lived with all of her life.

"It means he's a prisoner," Morgan said. The matter-of-fact tone of her voice left no room for argument.

"What do you think they will do with him now, Morgan?" Janine said. Sitting beside her, Nikki felt strength emanating from the woman she desperately wanted to mother her as she did her own children. The modulation of her voice gave the impression of implacable strength, but up close Nikki saw the slightest quaver in her chin.

"I don't think they'll hurt him, Momma. Dad's very popular with the troops and General Steeple has to know that. I suspect they'll bring him here and try to make a deal with him to serve under Steeple in some capacity."

The crow's feet around her eyes deepened as Janine smiled. "Thank you, sweetie. I believe everything will be just fine. Is there any word on Joseph?"

"No. He and his co-pilot just vanished. Searches have turned up nothing."

"I would not worry about him, either. I do not know your chosen man well, Morgan, but I do know you, and you would not choose someone who was unable to take care of himself. He will return, you mark my word."

"Thank you, Momma. You've never been wrong about things like that."

"And I'm not wrong now."

∼∼∼

In the hallway outside, Morgan waited for Nikki to leave. Two sentries flanked the next door down, the apartment that Steeple had appropriated for himself, and they wore plain khaki uniforms with no insignia or names. Both eyed her like she was a butter-basted T-bone steak hot off the grill, behavior which the Army found unacceptable and cause for discipline.

When Nikki stepped out, both men turned for a better look at both of them. "Who are those creeps?" Nikki said.

"I don't know. I've never seen them before, but that's where Steeple lives now."

"Oh..."

"Let's move down the hall."

The corridor curved and they stopped when out of eyesight from the guards. Both women knew that cameras still watched them, but that was different from enduring leers at close range. They kept their voices down anyway.

"What have you heard about all this?" Morgan asked.

"I was in the weapons room a little while ago when Steeple's new head of security showed up, gloating about how things were going to be different from now on. I knew this guy from TFZ. He was leader of Third Squad for a while. His name is Adder... he and Nick hate each other."

"Green Ghost Nick or Dad Nick?"

"Brother Nick, but I don't think Dad liked him much, either. He's a whole new level of asshole."

"This is bad, really bad. I wish Joe was here. Or Uncle Norm... General Fleming. They'd know what to do."

"So what *do* we do?"

"I can't think of anything we can do, except stay alert. Once Dad gets back, we can try and come up with a plan. But they'll be watching us, so be careful."

"All right."

"Are you gonna be okay?"

"I don't know. I think so, but... I don't know."

Morgan noticed that Nikki's whole demeanor had changed when she'd met Joe Ootoi. There was now a soft-

320

ness in her sister's face that hadn't been there before and just seemed out of place. The blue of her eyes was also paler somehow, as if they'd been backlit before and that light was now extinguished. Instinctively Morgan knew that Nipple would have sprung into action, reckless, violent action, but Nikki had no clue of what to do. For the first time, she found herself missing the psychopath a little bit.

#

CHAPTER 56

Neither a wise man nor a brave man lies down on the tracks of history to wait for the train of the future to run over him.
General Dwight D. Eisenhower

Operation Comeback
0919 hours, April 29

"Did the entire base hear that?"

"Yes, General, they did," Astrid Naidoo said. "The officer on watch in the communications room said he didn't realize he needed to clear an announcement from Prime before patching it into our system."

"Do you believe him?"

"I don't know, sir. He seemed sincere enough, but I don't know any of these people. He may have done it from loyalty to General Steeple. I don't think we could prove it, though."

"None of that matters now," Glide said. "This office is a mousetrap. If that long hallway leading here is blocked, we cannot escape. We must evacuate to a more defensible location."

"Does anyone have any suggestions?" Schiller said.

"What about the Air Force compound? It already holds a lot of the base's food supplies, it has its own water source, and nobody's coming through those blast doors if they're sealed."

"Kamuvan, maskima," answered Glide.

"English!" said Frosty.

"I am sorry. Yes, I agree, the Air Force complex is perfect. Frosty, escort the general and the colonel there, please. I am going to collect a few security battalion members that Frosty and I think will be loyal to you, Red Ears. We will meet you there, but do not lock the blast doors before we arrive, please."

"Did you call me Red Ears?" said Schiller, unsure that he'd heard correctly.

Glide answered in her matter-of-fact, never-less-than-serious way. "It is your code name."

Sierra Army Depot
0942 hours, April 29

Green Ghost pulled his coat over his eyes as an indication to whoever shook him to go away and leave him alone. It was more a reflex than a conscious action, since he was still more asleep than awake. But the intruder poked his shoulder and words filtered through to his brain.

"General Fleming wants to see you, sir."

"What time is it?"

"Zero-nine-forty-two."

Fuck. I hadn't meant to sleep that late. "Yeah, okay, I'm coming." A groan punctuated the last two words.

"He said to tell you it's urgent."

It's always urgent.

Rolling over on his back, Green Ghost rubbed his still closed eyes with the heels of his hands. He felt them watering against the rough skin of his palm. Blinking them open, he found that even the dim lighting of the old warehouse that acted as a barracks burned. He squinted but they watered more and blurred his vision. "Tell General Fleming I'm on the way."

His bed was a bare spot on the concrete floor of a building that had formerly been a machine shop, and his mattress was his field jacket. There had been a time, not too long before, when that had been enough to get a good night's sleep. But as he pushed to his feet, every muscle in his back and legs screamed in protest.

Fleming's headquarters were in a small building near the center of the camp, close to the makeshift chow hall and with the newly dug latrines in a strip of unpaved ground nearby. An obviously homemade well pump stood in a small shack outside the headquarters. Green Ghost paused there long enough to pump the handle and splash water on his face, sipping some from his cupped palm, before heading inside. At the sight of the massive black woman taking up most of the tattered metal couch in Fleming's office, he stopped in the doorway and blinked, wondering if he was still asleep.

Fleming stood behind his desk, his thick arms folded. Green Ghost recognized his smile as sarcastic, since he'd seen it many times before. The woman, however, didn't give any sign she'd seen him come in. Her eyes remained fixed on Fleming with a wide-eyed leer as if he was a sizzling, medium-rare T-bone steak. Even seated, Ghost could tell that, while Fleming himself stood six foot four inches, with a deep chest and weightlifter's arms, she dwarfed him.

"There you are," the general said with a tone that meant *what took you so long?* "Nick, this lady says she knows you."

"We've met, Socrates—"

"You said your name was Norm," she interrupted. When she smiled, Ghost saw a gap in her front teeth he hadn't noticed on the road back to Sierra. Little wrinkles sprayed from the corners of her eyes.

"It's a long story," Green Ghost said. She still didn't look at him. "What are you doing here, Kody?"

"I came with news, but stayed for the view."

"Jane's not here."

"So I heard. She will be."

"Why's that?"

For the first time she looked at him, and Ghost felt like an insect on a microscope slide. "Is he really married?" The question caught him so off-guard, he couldn't block an involuntary reaction. "That's what I thought!" She waggled a finger at Fleming. "You shouldn't lie to Kodiak Kate."

"Kody! Why is Jane coming back?"

"Hmmm... oh. Maybe she won't, but the Chinese are patrolling toward Lake Tahoe and she doesn't live too far south of there. Now that I think about it, she might just take to the woods... that's probably safer than coming here."

"The Chinese are moving into the Sierra Nevadas?"

"The what? Oh, the mountains. Sure, but not too many. Most are staying in the group that's coming this way."

"What?" Fleming said. The embarrassed man vanished and was replaced by the professional officer. "Why didn't you say that right away?"

"You're cute when you're mad."

"Get out of my office!"

"Who the fuck do you think you're talking to?" Kody said in a sudden rage. Her huge breasts bounced for a few seconds after she lurched to her feet. One hand strayed toward a large knife strapped to her thigh. Seeing that, Fleming reached into a desk drawer for his pistol.

Green Ghost stepped between them, arms outstretched in a *stop* motion, like a school crossing guard. "We need to hear her out," he said to Fleming. "And Kody, we're grateful you came to us, but if the Chinese are on the way, we need to get ready. How many are coming?"

Heaving in deep breaths, she pointed at Fleming and there was nothing flirty about it. "I don't know who you think you are, but I came here as a favor to Jane and Green Ghost here. Next time, I won't make that mistake."

"I'm sorry," Fleming said. "Can we start over?"

"I don't know how many Chinese are headed this way," she said, ignoring Fleming and turning her attention to Green Ghost. "They're strung out for miles. A lot, that's all I can tell you."

"Tanks? AFVs?"

"I don't know what an AFV is, but I saw a few tanks."

"How fast are they moving?"

"You mean when will they be here, don't you? Probably tomorrow afternoon, or maybe the next morning." She picked up a huge, wide-brimmed leather hat from the couch and headed for the door. Streaked with stains, the hat fit perfectly over the crown of bushy reddish-orange hair.

As she walked out the door, Fleming called out behind her. "Thank you!"

She paused, half turned, and then kept going. Green Ghost followed her. Even with his own long strides, he found it hard to keep up.

Tethered to the tree where he'd found Vapor and Jane after the last battle was the largest horse he'd ever seen that wasn't a Clydesdale. She picked up a folding metal container filled with water, dumped out what was left, and slid it into a pouch looped around the horse's neck that appeared to have been custom-crafted for that purpose. A black leather Western saddle creaked as she put a foot in the stirrup and pulled herself up. Along with a bedroll and two saddle bags, the butts of three rifle holster scabbards hung from the saddle.

"General Fleming's really a pretty nice guy," Green Ghost said. "I know he appreciates you coming here. You just took him by surprise is all."

"He called you Nick."

"Oh, yeah... it's another long story."

"Well, whatever you call yourself, you're a nice guy. I see why Jane has a crush on you."

He took a step back without realizing it. "She likes me?"

"Oh, man, she's right. You really are thick. Listen, don't you dare get killed in the fight that's coming, you hear me? Jane's good people and I don't want to see her get hurt again."

"Hang on, what do you mean 'hurt again'?"

"Like you said, it's a long story, and I've got a long ride before nightfall. I'm supposed to meet Liar Lem tomorrow with stuff his Navy boys want, and if I don't leave now I won't make it."

His mind was still processing the *Jane has a crush on you* remark when something in her last words set off an alarm and he called after her, "You still haven't told me about those Navy boys!"

Vapor lay propped on his elbows on a long metal work table, so he saw Green Ghost the instant he entered the warehouse that doubled as the hospital. Sited on the northern side of the administrative complex, it stayed cooler than any of the other buildings, although *cool* was relative.

"How ya feeling?" Green Ghost said.

"Getting shot in the leg is awesome. I highly recommend it."

"If you like it so much, I can shoot the other one."

"I'll bet you would, too. Where ya been?"

"Recon. Got back last night."

"Hey, is Jane still around? I haven't seen her for a while."

"You haven't seen me, either."

"You're not a hot blonde. You're an ugly dude."

"She wanted to bury her friends who got killed a few miles west of camp and I went along to help. While there, we came on some information that sent us south for a few days, where we ran into work of an old friend of ours."

"Yeah, who's that?"

"Adder."

"Our Adder?"

"I doubt there's two."

"Son of a bitch." Vapor looked away. "I hope you smoked him."

"He wasn't there in person, just his handiwork. But I left him a message."

"Written in blood?"

Green Ghost blinked in surprise. "Yeah, how'd you know?"

Vapor couldn't help laughing. "I didn't. I was fuckin' with you. So look, I'm glad you're back okay and all, but it can't be much past oh-seven hundred and you've never been an early morning guy unless you had to be. So why are you here?"

"More Chinese are coming and I need to know what's headed our way. I thought I'd see if you were tired of this place yet."

"The leg's pretty stiff. I'm not sure how far I can walk."

"And staying on a horse wouldn't be any easier... okay, stay here and help Socrates get ready, then. Any word on Claw?"

"I saw him yesterday. He was out of it, but the doc says he'll pull through as long as he doesn't get an infection."

"Lasting effects?"

Vapor shrugged. "Without all the doctor gizmos, they can't tell."

"All right. If he comes around, tell him I asked."

"Do me a favor?"

"Sure, what?"

"If you see Adder, cut off his nuts."

#

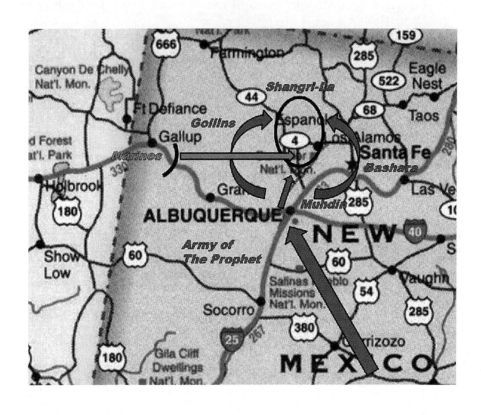

328

CHAPTER 57

*War loses a great deal of its romance after a soldier has seen
his first battle.*
Colonel John S. Mosby

Albuquerque, New Mexico
0952 hours, April 29

General Ahmednur Hussein Muhdin swatted at the flies
that wouldn't stop buzzing his face. For the fourth time, he
combed his beard in case food had become stuck there to at-
tract the damnable insects. He'd worn his brand new combat
uniform, the one he'd personally designed and had sewn
from the best cotton and wool in the entire Caliphate. The
medals and ribbons adorning his entire chest nearly to his
waist were all authentic, too. They'd been found at a U.S.
Navy warehouse in New Mecca, formerly Corpus Christi, and
Muhdin didn't care that they were all from a defunct navy or
that many were duplicates. The bright colors and shiny medals looked as impressive as they did on the Russian generals
he'd seen in a book, and that was all he cared about.

Impressive uniforms had one downside, however, and it
was a big one. They were hot, especially standing in the midday sun in the Chihuahuan Desert, on the cracked asphalt
of New Mexico Highway 550. Heat radiated upward from the
bleached-out roadway and Muhdin felt sweat running from
his armpits. Nevertheless, he understood the need to appear
sympathetic to the plight of his men, who had no choice except to stay put and bake. The Emir had made it quite clear,

repeatedly, that Muhdin must lead by example if he wanted to get the most out of his troops, and if he couldn't do that, then why was he a general in the Army of the Sword of the Prophet?

So Muhdin stood facing north, surrounded by his staff and officers of the unit stationed there on the northern fringe of Albuquerque. To the east were the distant Sandia Mountains and the Rio Grande River lay a few miles south. Lifting the binoculars to his face, Muhdin felt the hot metal even through his gloves and so held the eyepieces half an inch from his eyes. He couldn't see anything through them doing that, but it didn't matter; this was all for show. The only thing between them and the mountains to the north was empty desert. He turned this way and that as if examining the terrain; once he felt he'd done it long enough, Muhdin handed the binoculars to an aide and addressed the slight young officer in charge of the company camped in the area.

"Are your men eager, Devotee Mohammad?" Officers kept the standard ranks of most militaries, beginning with lieutenant, then captain, major, and so on. But the lower ranks began with aspirant, the lowest and equivalent to a private, then came adherent, acolyte, and finally devotee, which equaled a sergeant. The entire rank structure was new, having been installed during the intense training of the previous winter, and Muhdin was proud that he had suggested the names for the lower ranks.

"Yes, General, they can't wait to wipe out the infidels."

Muhdin waggled a finger. "If the infidels surrender, Devotee, you *will* accept it. Is that clear? Not only does the Caliphate needs laborers, but every man and woman must be given the opportunity to follow our beloved New Prophet. So it is written and so must it be done. Only after having one year to repent their sins and join us can retribution be justly administered."

"Yes, General." Devotee Mohammad's disappointment was obvious. "And must we respect the women, as well?"

Muhdin smiled and put a hand on the younger man's shoulder. His small size and thin beard likely meant women did not find him attractive.

"Once they convert, yes, they are then children of Allah. But until that time they are infidels, property to be... *used...*

in whatever way best aids the Caliphate. If that means relieving our brave soldiers of their stress, I can think of few ways better for them to aid us."

"The blessings of Allah upon our New Prophet!" Mohammad said.

"And all his servants," Muhdin answered.

South of Topaz Lake, Nevada
1117 hours

Major Dieter Strootman opened one of the M1130 command vehicle's rear doors and waved at the driver of the Humvee directly behind to pull over so he could relay a message to Colonel Young. It took several tries, but eventually the driver understood and pulled onto the shoulder of old Nevada Highway 395, leaving plenty of room for vehicles behind them to pass.

Everyone took the opportunity to stretch and relieve themselves behind a series of small hills close by in the desert.

Once they were standing away from the others, Young got off the first question. "Have they recaptured General Angriff?"

"No, sir, as far as I know there's been no sign of the general. We've been ordered to make camp soon to await liaison officers from the People's Liberation Army."

"We've *what?*"

Strootman held up his hands. "I'm just the messenger."

"Damn that man! So we're expected to be nice to the damned Chinese?"

"It would appear so."

Young sucked a deep breath and rubbed his lower lip. "All right, make camp north of Topaz Lake. I want this time used for vehicle maintenance and weapons cleaning. This dust gets in everything and if it comes to a fight, I want us ready."

"Begging your pardon, Colonel, but if we're on the same side as the Chinese, who's left to fight?"

"I don't even want to think about that, Dieter. Not for a second."

#

Chapter 58

Get off your butt and join the Marines!
John Wayne

Outside Gallup, New Mexico
1836 hours, April 29

Captain Sully tried to chew without tasting. He concentrated on the purples and oranges that the sun cast on some distant mountains, hoping he wouldn't think about what he was eating. The MRE packs weren't rat-fucked when the company got them, but he'd let the men have first choice over the officers, and then his subordinate officers before him. Naturally all that was left by the time it got to him were *vomelets*, veggie omelets, chicken fajitas, and Jambalaya with shrimp. Before the first time he'd tried any of those three, he'd thought he'd won the MRE lottery. The reality was far grimmer.

He sat in the dirt near his command LAV. Halfway through the alleged meal, he began swigging water after each bite so as to swallow without chewing. When he saw Sergeant Meyer crunching through the dirt toward him, Sully put the MRE down and hoped the ants would get it.

"What is it?" Sully said.

"Prime, sir. General Steeple wants to speak with the captain."

"General Steeple? Did you verify his earlier broadcast?"

"I did, sir. I contacted Echo Company and they heard it, too, so then I called a buddy of mine back at Prime. He said Steeple has taken over the entire operation and has opened negotiations with the Chinese, just like we heard."

"Thank you, Meyer." Sully pushed to his feet and brushed himself off. This was one call he was not looking forward to.

———

Only five minutes passed before Sully re-emerged from his command LAV. Eyebrows arched downward in a V and his jaw moved back and forth as he gritted his teeth.

"Bad news, Captain?" Meyer said.

"We are to hold our position and not fire unless fired upon. I have a call with the platoon leaders now, but... First Sergeant, I need you to oversee construction of defensive positions that will allow maximum flexibility for attack or retreat. Make sure the men understand our situation. We're to stay put right here even if there's a whole army out there."

"Did they give a reason?"

"Negative."

"We kicked the Seven's asses once, Captain. If we have to, we can do it again."

"It's not the Sevens I'm worried about."

#

CHAPTER 59

...even Satan disguises himself as an angel of light.
2 Corinthians 11:14

Prescott, Arizona Region Airport
1106 hours, April 29

The whine of the Gulfstream's jet engines died away as Károly Rosos stepped down the ladder onto the tarmac of the Prescott airport. Awaiting him nearby stood Adder with six heavily armed guards. At his heels came Amunet Mwangi, followed by six men in the uniform of the Rosos family and sixteen more wearing the fatigue uniforms of the Chinese, complete with insignia.

"Welcome to paradise," Adder said to Rosos.

The younger man turned in a slow circle, taking in his surroundings. Mountains could be seen in all directions, some closer and some more distant. Beyond the dilapidated airport was desert to the north and west, and the buildings of Prescott to the south and southwest. "I prefer Malibu. I can already feel my allergies kicking in."

"North Dakota's nice this time of year."

Rosos lifted an eyebrow, his version of a half smile. "Any problems?"

"Not yet, but I'm glad for the reinforcements. I'll feel even better when we get more Chinese troops in here."

"But nothing yet?"

"A lot of bitching, but everybody who might lead resistance is away. Angriff and Fleming you know about. Green Ghost is with Fleming, and something's happened to his psychopath sister... she's, shit, she's normal. She was never like that in the old days.

"Should we take her out just to be sure?"

"I will if I need to, but there's no reason to stir up the natives any more than we already have. I didn't know the Zombies were even here until Ghost left me that message, but it looks like all of First Squad came along for the ride, with a couple of exceptions. But no Second Squad... some of Third Squad is, though. Gomorrah's not here, or Judge, or Esther, or most of the others, but Claw is, although he's with Green Ghost up north."

Mwangi interrupted. "How did Claw get there? He was at Comeback."

"Fuck if I know. The point is, there're only a few at Prime, and none are likely to start trouble. There's some old guy that Angriff promoted to major general, but he's away, too. The only other two we needed to worry about are both neutralized. One's in a cell; the other signed on to serve under Steeple. That's Colonel Saw, the man Angriff gave the keys to when he left."

"By the way, Scope was also at Comeback," Mwangi said.

"Good, we can always use a first-class sniper."

"Not any more, you can't. She's dead."

"What happened?"

"She met a better sniper."

Rosos shot her an irritated look. "So this colonel, his name is Saw?" He headed for the lead Humvee and Adder matched him step for step, ignoring Mwangi, who fell in behind. Had either man bothered to look, they would have seen her face twisted in anger.

"Yeah, nickname's Chain Saw, but I don't think he likes being called that."

"He doesn't," Mwangi said from behind them. They ignored her.

Rosos noticed smoke rising from the far end of the runway and pointed. "What's that?"

"Somebody didn't want you to land safely."

"Oh?"

"Yeah. Got an RPG from somewhere and put himself right next to the runway. He wanted to hit you as you touched down."

"But we came in from the other direction."

"I guess he didn't understand wind currents when landing a plane."

"Lone wolf?"

"Far as we know. He was the only one we found."

"Dead, of course."

"Very."

"And the smoke?"

"Right after I took off the top of his head, he put the RPG round into the grass at his own feet. That's him you see burning."

"Glad he's downwind. I'm hungry and that might ruin my appetite. So what's the food like here?"

They all headed for a convoy of three trucks and two Humvees. Adder detailed four of the Chinese to supplement the guard already at the airport. Dozens of people from Prescott stood back from the road to get a glimpse of the airplane, as none of them had ever seen a fixed-wing aircraft in flight before. The Chinese had their rifles at the ready, just in case, but as Prescott faded into the rear, everyone relaxed.

Flashing by north of the road into Prescott, Rosos pointed toward the ruined mall on the outskirts of town. "In my entire life, I never went into a mall."

"No shit?"

Elbow propped on the window sill, Rosos stroked the short beard on either side of his lips like he would a cat. "That's what the little people were for. When we were younger, my brother and I wanted to stand in the protest lines with *Antikap,* you know how they did, faces covered and screaming insults at the police. We bought the whole capitalism is bad program. But Father wouldn't allow it. He explained that most of those people were professionals, and that they were well paid to make a lot of noise that looked good on the nightly news. That's not what people with power did; that's what you hired other people to do. It was that way with

Antikap, or buying groceries or a new pair of shoes. Never confuse the message with your true objective."

"I always liked your father. He knew what he wanted."

"He certainly does. Well, enough of that. Now I'm excited to see what my father's money bought," he said with sudden enthusiasm. They sped up in the open country, where ambush wasn't as likely. "I came along late in the game, but wasn't sure he'd spent it wisely."

Adder held up a cigar that Steeple had found in the Crystal Palace. "I used to smell these things when Saint smoked 'em and wished he'd offer me one, but he never did. Habana Monte Cristo Number Three. I'll never forget that."

"Just don't light that thing in here."

Adder cut his eyes toward Rosos and the younger man held up his hands.

"Please," he said.

Adder slid it into his breast pocket. "I don't smoke."

"Then why did you want Angriff to give you one?"

"You wouldn't understand, Károly."

On the approaches to the southwestern entrance, they passed the newly plowed and planted fields. Rosos watched people with sun-browned skin doing whatever it was such people did in their farm fields, and nodded to himself. Every society needed peasants to grow food and it pleased him to see this natural order of civilization taking hold again.

When the convoy pulled into Motor Bay D, the few technicians going about their work paid it little heed. Instead of unloading near the entrance, they kept going until reaching the bank of elevators at the northern end of the vast expanse. Once they stopped, the Chinese jumped out and formed a defensive ring, rifles at the ready.

When the first elevator door opened, a corporal staring down at a tablet stepped out without even noticing the group waiting to get in. Rough hands grabbed the woman and threw her up against a wall with a rifle barrel sticking into her back. She held her hands high and gasped out words. "Stop, stop, I'm an American!"

STANDING BEFORE HELL'S GATE

Adder shook his head and glanced over at Rosos. "I love his enthusiasm." Then, stalking toward the eager man, he pushed the gun away from the woman's back and clapped the man on his shoulder. Gently he turned the terrified woman around. No insignia marked her uniform. "What's your name?" he said in a neutral tone that still brooked no refusal.

"Torrehon. I'm a civilian engineer..."

"Sorry for the fright, Torrehon. Our new allies are a little trigger-happy. You might want to tell your friends."

She nodded, her eyes still wide. Adder bent down and picked up her tablet, handing it back. Torrehon walked away very fast.

"That'll get around quick," he said to Rosos as they got onto the elevator.

"Good."

For one of the rare times, Adder smiled. "Yeah, very good."

Initially, the faces Adder and his men passed showed curiosity before snapping to attention on sighting Colonel Mwangi. But then they recognized the odd uniforms of the guards flanking the dark-haired man in the middle. Their expressions darkened as reality dawned. One lieutenant holding a tablet recognized Chinese uniforms and went for his sidearm.

Adder saw it and stopped him by squeezing his forearm in a vise-like grip, fingertips digging into the man's nerves to deaden his fingers. "They're on our side," he said in a low growl.

Outraged, the lieutenant met Adder's eyes and both men recognized a fellow combat veteran. "They're Chinese. Let go of me!"

"They're... on... our... side!"

"They killed my best friend at Prescott."

"And no doubt we killed a lot of theirs. Let it go, Lieutenant."

"Who the hell are you? I'll have you court-martialed for assaulting an officer."

"Go ahead and report it to security. I'll give it top priority. See, I'm the new S-5." Adder let go and stuck a finger in the man's face. "I'm a colonel. I'm not busting you now because I'm not wearing insignia, but you've been warned. Next time, show me the proper respect or I'll break your balls."

Two guards had stayed back with him and sneered at the lieutenant before flanking Adder as he caught up with Rosos and Mwangi.

———

Despite the knowledge that Steeple awaited him, and the danger that came from being surrounded by armed people trained to kill as a career even though he was escorted by Chinese soldiers, Károly Rosos took his time walking down the hallways. Hands in his pockets, he strolled along as if he were shopping on the Champs Elysees, eyeing the merchandise and the passersby like a taxonomist studying unknown organisms. The tailored black suit, well-trimmed black beard and hair contrasted sharply with his pale skin to lend him a ghostly pallor.

"What are you doing?" Adder whispered in his left ear. "Let's get going."

But Rosos held up his left hand like the pope waving at cheering throngs in St. Peter's Square. "There's no rush," he said without deigning to look at Adder. "I'm inspecting my family's new home to see what needs to be changed."

"I can't guarantee your safety out here like this."

"You're very good at what you do, Adder, one of the best."

"*The* best."

"All right, *the* best at what you do. That makes my point even better. You'll keep me safe and these people will get used to the new order of things."

"This ain't *Antikap* we're dealing with, Károly. These people aren't baristas covering their faces and spitting on cops. They're all trained to kill."

"You know how to fight, but not how to lead. These people are trained to kill who and where they are told to kill... isn't that what you've always told me? They believe in the sanctity of their chain of command? That's what makes them weak."

Adder hated Rosos at that moment. Some part of him still loved the camaraderie he'd felt in the teams and he wanted to rip the man's head off. Instead he fell into step behind the arrogant asshole, where he could see any threats ahead or to the side, the most likely ambush directions; and, as much as he hated it, the further they walked into the base, the more it became clear that Rosos was right. With no one to rally around, the seething hatred in the faces of everyone they passed didn't boil over into violence.

He couldn't believe they'd rolled in so easily. What the fuck kind of warriors were these people, anyway? By now Rosos and his Chinese escort had been inside Overtime for more than twenty minutes. Where were the Zombies? Even if nobody else fought back, he'd assumed Wingnut wouldn't passively accept such an invasion. Most of all, he was disappointed in Nipple. He'd have killed her without a second thought, even if down deep he liked the psychopath, because she reminded him of him. But now she looked to be gone, and he hated that, too.

Then his sweeping gaze stopped on a knot of armed people up the hallway. Drawing his personal weapon, a Sig Sauer full-size P320-M17 chambered to 9mm with a 17-round magazine but without the Electro-Optic reflex sight attached, he held it in his right hand beside his leg. His left hand reached toward Rosos' left shoulder so he could throw him to the ground if shooting erupted.

Thirty feet down the hall were four faces he recognized, behind a knot of unfamiliar ones looking their way. He could only see their faces and shoulders, but that was enough. Wingnut he'd already seen earlier, but with him were One-Eye, Frosty, and Zeus, four of the original fifteen Zombies, and from the way they stood, he knew they all held rifles.

"Alert, left ahead," he called out. Rosos turned to him, as did all of the Chinese guards. The four Zombies stepped out into the middle of the hallway. Adder shoved Rosos to the ground and brought up the pistol with both hands, ready to fire.

But he didn't. The Zombies all stood casually with their weapons pointed up. Only when the Chinese saw Adder ready for combat did they turn around and see the Americans arrayed in front of them. Panicking, several almost dropped their weapons.

"Nobody shoot!" Adder called out.

"Hey, Adder, you want us to do you a favor and shoot these people?" One-Eye called out.

With his right knee in front of Rosos, Adder lined up his sights on One-Eye's chest. "What do you want, Wingnut?"

"You said you're our new commander."

"Yeah, so?"

"So command."

Adder stood, slowly, and while still holding the pistol in both hands, moved its barrel to point over the Zombies' heads. He didn't bother hiding his skepticism. "Just like that?"

"Just like that."

"Does he speak for all of you?"

The other three nodded, although One-Eye rolled his eyes while he did so.

"Take the point. Make sure we don't get jumped."

Rosos finally got to his feet. "You're trusting them?" he said in a low voice.

"Not even a little bit," Adder answered.

1203 hours

"Sorry to keep you boys waiting," Adder said as he joined Wingnut, One-Eye, Razor, and Zeus well down the hall from the Crystal Palace. His four former teammates wore scowls to express their displeasure at being treated like new recruits. "General Steeple was very pleased to hear that you've pledged to obey his orders. In fact, he was so happy that he decided to give you a crucial mission to accomplish."

"I ain't givin' him a blow job," said One-Eye. "I'll let you do that."

Adder threw back his head and laughed. "Aw, man, I do miss the camaraderie of the teams. Always kidding around. No, he is entrusting you with doing a lurp to Phoenix, where you are to penetrate the city and determine what went on there during the Collapse. You are then to radio your results here to Prime, but not to re-enter the base until given specific authorization to do so."

"Wasn't Phoenix wiped out by an infectious agent?" Wingnut said.

"Maybe. We don't know. That's the whole point. That's why we need you to do a recon. Check out a Humvee, draw whatever food and fuel you need, and go find out for us. It's what you were trained to do."

Instead of protesting, Wingnut help up two fingers. "Two Humvees, one equipped with a fitty." Slang for *fifty caliber machine gun.*

"What do you need with so much firepower?"

"I don't know. That's the whole reason we need it."

"Huh... all right, but don't start any wars. I mean it. If you encounter Sevens, don't engage without getting permission first."

"What if they shoot at us?"

"Permission first."

"Roger that," Wingnut said.

Once Adder had walked away, Razor grabbed Wingnut's arm. "I'm not about to let some Sevens shoot at me without firing back!"

"Of course not."

"But you just said..."

Wingnut pointed with his thumb at Adder's back. "To that asshole? I lied."

"That prick is going to be a major pain in my ass."

Alone in the Crystal Palace, at last, with Amunet Mwangi, Steeple turned the glass opaque and scratched his right ear canal with his left pinkie finger. The office smelled fresher after having the filters cleaned, although traces of Angriff's cigar smoke could still be smelt. Or maybe that was just his imagination.

"Try spending a winter with that family," she said. "I've met some arrogant people in my life, but none to compare with them. And I'm here to tell you they think they own this place."

"Overtime?"

"And Comeback."

"They contributed three billion dollars, that much is true, but compared to what all of this cost, that is a drop in the bucket."

"I'm on your side, Tom."

He smiled. "I was practicing."

#

Chapter 60

The woman shall be the helper of the man. Each has their own duties and these should never mix. Above all, a woman may never oppose a man.
From The Revelations of Nabi Husam Allah, *Chapter 2, Verses 1–3*

Rio Rancho, New Mexico
1248 hours, April 29

"I do not like that woman," Muhdin said in Arabic. Despite the Caliphate being made up almost entirely of North Americans and their descendants, the Armstrong brothers had mandated the teaching of Arabic in the *madaris.* Despite intense tutoring over many years, neither of them had ever mastered the language and only spoke enough to get by.

"You do not like any woman who serves in the Sword of the Prophet," el Mofty replied in English. With the two of them far enough from their aides to be unheard, the Emir relaxed around his best general enough to poke fun at him.

Characteristically, Muhdin missed the humor in his remark, since there were no other women in the army. "She leads men into battle. That is not a woman's place. It is an abomination!"

"Beware your words, Muhdin." The low baritone of the Emir's voice held the warning his words only hinted at.

"I am sorry, my lord, but we have been taught all of our lives that women were not meant to be warriors. Are we now saying that is wrong?"

El Mofty sighed, another exaggerated gesture he knew Muhdin would miss but which felt good in the moment. "Typically, no, they are not. And we are not saying that women should interact with men who are not their husbands or families. But Tracy Gollins is no ordinary woman. She is a beast from Hell, sent to us by Allah to be used as we see fit, and I choose to use her to kill our enemies, as I would any other beast."

"She is evil, my lord. There is nothing but hatred in her heart."

"You speak of evil as something to be avoided, and yet Satan exists at the whim of Allah, does he not? Does our beloved New Prophet not teach that evil in the hands of a righteous man is a weapon to serve Allah?"

Muhdin nodded.

"Therefore, evil has a purpose in this world. It is to be used by the righteous to expand the Caliphate to the unfortunates who have not yet heard the teachings of the one true faith. Once we have achieved our goal, Gollins will be disposed of as the trash that she is, but in the meantime it is my responsibility to use her in the best way to serve our beloved Prophet."

"Her aggression will yet endanger us, my lord."

"Yumkin," he said. *Maybe.* One of the Arabic words el Mofty felt comfortable using, after which he switched back to English. "But I *know* she will endanger the infidels."

"She does not fight out of allegiance to our beloved New Prophet. She fights because she likes it."

"Yes, she fights because she cannot help herself, and because she loves death. She fights for us because we give her the means to do so. Like an attack dog, she bites whoever her owner tells her to bite. The owner is only in danger if they neglect to feed the dog. I will not make that mistake."

El Mofty had backed Muhdin into a corner and both men knew it. The general couldn't argue further without impugning the judgment of the Emir, and that could be fatal.

"Your word is law, Blessed One."

"Good. The matter is settled then, so let us speak of it no more. Now, the time has come for you to move forward toward Shangri-La. According to the plan you drew up, I gave General Gollins the Mecca Regiment to flank the enemy from our left, their right, moving through the old town of Cuba down Highway 126 toward Jemez Springs. My nephew Sati has regiments Rasūl and Ayyub, and is attacking them through the city of Los Alamos and the Valles Cardera Preserve, down Highway 501. Both are strong enough on their own to break through to Shangri-La itself, so the enemy will have to divert great strength to stopping them. They should be in position now, which means it is time for you to drive north using Highway 4 through San Ysidro."

"Have you decided whether or not to give me the Life Guards?"

"For now, no."

"Neither regiment?"

"No. That still leaves you with 4,000 men, Muhdin, more than enough to destroy the enemy. And you have all of the human shields. But I intend to keep reserves this time. Rest assured that if you need them, you will receive them."

"Your word is law, Blessed One."

The general bowed, which was the equivalent of a salute in the Sword of the Prophet, and turned to leave.

"Muhdin."

Stopping, Muhdin turned back. "Yes, my lord?"

"Do not fail this time. There are no Americans here to stop you. Bring this place into the Caliphate."

The general swallowed, nodded, bowed, and left.

#

CHAPTER 61

I'm positive about the negative, but a little negative about the positive.
Curly Howard

Junker Jane's house near Dardanelle, California
1613 hours, April 29

The damaged shutter near Junker Jane's front door still hung from two of its three hinges, but the brute strength of the bear that had gouged the wood with its claws nearly took it all the way off. The next time, it would have ripped it away with the first swipe and been free to climb through the window and ravage her house and all of her stored food. Nor would simply replacing the damaged shutter with another like it solve the problem permanently, so she'd spent the morning searching the pile of scrap metal for a thick sheet of iron or steel that could seal the window for good. An old piece of cast iron did the trick, but she needed old Tenuhci's help, plus that of his son, to lift it into place while she attached the hinges. It took hours before they'd secured it and now she only needed to attach the locking bolt to the inside.

A pile of the largest nails she possessed dwindled as she hammered them into place both inside and out. As the afternoon waned, the light under her porch grew dim. She finished as the first mosquitoes emerged to search for blood. Dinner was going to be potluck stew the way pioneers did it, with family members throwing whatever they'd found during the day into the bubbling cauldron. Tenuhci had thrown two dressed squirrels into the mix and his son had brought a basket of spring porcini mushrooms, which despite trusting his eye she inspected anyway. Eating the wrong mushroom could be fatal. Simple corn tortillas grilled in a cast iron skillet used up last year's corn flour. A salad of miner's lettuce, clover, dandelions, pine nuts, and pine needle tips completed the meal.

One of the first things she'd scraped in her career was an old style whistling stainless steel teapot from the ruins of Carson City. Decades later, scorch marks blackened its bottom and dents rippled the metal sides, but it remained watertight and therefore ideal for boiling water for tea. Tenuhci mixed the ingredients to his own recipe, mostly herbs, aromatic leaves, berries, and flowers, all of which he dried and crushed together in a pestle. She sweetened it with honey and poured three cups, with hers being the familiar mug with *Union Bank of Fullerton* written on the side in gold script.

She had set the dining table with places for three, even using some of the real napkins she'd found at a casino buffet in Reno, and hummed while dishing out bowls of stew. For anyone else, she would have waited until her fellow diners arrived, but somehow Tenuhci, the old Miwok of the Southern Sierra tribe, always showed up within seconds of her placing food on the table. And right on time she heard footsteps on the wooden slats of her porch, but it wasn't Tenuhci. Instead it was his son, Tuketu, *Bear Making Dust.*

"Where's your father?" she said.

"He's watching. He sent me to get you."

Clarifying questions could wait; the tone in his voice told Jane that danger was close. The first order of business was choosing a rifle to take with her, but with only one clean, there really wasn't much choice. She limped over to the high table under the east-facing window, where her Winchester 70 Coyote Light lay in pieces after she'd cleaned and lubricated it. By sheer reflex she began screwing the firing pin assembly back into the bolt. As she spoke, she continued reassembling the gun, including the integrated base, and selected the best scope she owned to attach to it, a Nightforce Optics NXS 5.5-22x56 Tactical ZeroStop with MOAR reticle.

"Where is he?"

"North of Topaz Lake, overlooking the old highway."

"That's Highway 395, leading up from the south... that's the American relief column heading for Sierra! This is what I've been waiting for, Tuketu!" For a brief moment, she considered swapping out the scope for something easier to replace if something happened to it.

"They have stopped for the night and made camp."

"This is great. My friends at Sierra will be so happy..." Tuketu's broad, dark face scowled but he kept quiet. "What's the matter?"

"Should you go with your injured foot?"

"My foot is fine. That's not what's troubling you."

"There are many men and women in uniforms I do not recognize."

She described the standard American field uniform and he nodded. "Yes, that sounds like what I saw."

"Then what's wrong?"

"Two of the people wear Chinese uniforms."

"Oh." She decided not to change out scopes.

———

Jane followed Tuketu along narrow paths through rough country under the light of a waxing quarter moon. For those two, who'd grown up riding at all times of day or night, it was simply a watchful three-hour trip at moderate speed. No sense wearing the horses out by riding too fast when dawn wouldn't arrive for another eight hours.

She'd taken the time to spoon stew into a camping pot with clamps on each side. The tortillas she baked and threw into a leather pouch, while the tea filled two canteens. Tuketu promised to return bowls and cups to her home if she needed him to. Enemies would have heard her clanking along from miles away but so would predators, and neither cougars nor bears tended to hang around long in the face of loud metallic noises.

They arrived on a ledge overlooking the highway where Tenuhci stood atop a boulder watching the camp below.

"Get down!" she called up to him.

"It is dark, even with the moon. I am but a shadow among shadows to anyone who sees me."

"They can see in the dark!"

He turned, sure-footed despite the curve of the huge rock. "Is this true?"

"Yes! Get down from there."

Tuketu helped his father slide down the boulder. Full night had fallen by then and the shadows on the mountainside under the trees made for impenetrable darkness. Camped in the open on both sides of the highway, however, the Americans might as well have been lit by spotlights to the sensitive eyes of Tenuhci, who besides a flashlight had not seen an electric light since his childhood.

"How can they see in the dark?" he said. "They're not demons; they're men."

"They see you the same way a rattlesnake does, by the heat of your body. They have devices that allow them to do this. You said there are Chinese among them?"

"I said that two men are wearing Chinese uniforms."

"Can you show me which tent these men were in?"

"We will have to risk being seen by these snake devices you spoke of."

"It is a risk I must take."

The downward angle of the mountain allowed them to crawl through dense grass on a slope which eventually joined the desert below. Five hundred yards from a group of tents surrounding a large campfire, they halted and Jane took out her binoculars. It took a while to locate the men Tenuhci had referenced, but eventually she spotted them talking to another American, and between the moonlight and the firelight she got a good enough look to be certain — they were definitely Chinese.

Once back behind the boulder, Tenuhci asked her the question she couldn't answer. "What does it mean?"

"I don't know," she said. "But I know someone who will."

#

Chapter 62

Now underneath this drowsy tree I lie
And turn old dreams upon my lazy knees,
Till ghostly giants fill the summer sky
And phantom oars awake the sleeping seas.
Robert E. Howard, Dreaming on Downs

East of Gallup, New Mexico
0517 hours, April 30

Captain Sully heard the voice through a fog of sleep and thought it was part of a dream. "G'way," he mumbled, and rolled over in his sleeping bag. Semi-conscious, he heard a zipping sound, but his brain didn't translate it as the bag being opened from the outside.

"Captain? Captain Sully?"

"I'm awake." He didn't feel awake. Opening his eyes seemed like too much effort. "What is it, First Sergeant?"

"A rider from Shangri-La, Captain. They're requesting help."

"I'm coming."

Because he was still dressed from the previous day, including boots, the joints and torso of his uniform were wet from sweating during the night. Despite temperatures in the forties overnight, they all slept buttoned up to keep out snakes and scorpions, while their breath and body heat created a warm, wet environment inside the bag.

The chill of pre-dawn made him shiver, so he slipped on his jacket and followed First Sergeant Meyer to a Stryker with an open rear door. Seated on the bench inside, lit by red battle lamps, a young man of fifteen or so stared at him wide-eyed. Sully noted the homemade clothing, dirty white pants with leather knees, thighs, and trim. His shirt was a simple one-piece white cotton pullover.

"His name is Billy," Meyer said. "He's been riding for two days to get here from Shangri-La. He says there's an army of Sevens in Albuquerque and moving north, and he was sent out to scout their flank."

Sully nodded and stepped into the APC, taking a seat opposite the young man. "Billy?"

The boy looked up and gave a short nod. "Billy Two Trees."

"That's a cool name, Billy. What tribe are you part of?"

"Jicarilla Apache."

"Apache, good. Do you know Govind?"

"Yes, sir." Billy's face changed into an expression of pleasant surprise. "He's a chief, a great warrior. He doesn't know me, but I know him."

Sully returned the smile. "He *is* a great warrior, I just saw him the day before yesterday. Now what is this about an army of Sevens?"

Billy licked his lips, started to speak, then stopped to clear his throat.

"You want some water?"

"Yes, please."

Someone handed Sully a squeezer of water and he passed it over. Billy inspected it, unsure how to use the un-familiar device.

"See this little thing?" Sully reached over and flipped open the inch-long spout. "Put that near your mouth, not in it, then squeeze."

The boy did, squirting water into his nose first but then finding his mouth. He drank the squeezer dry and passed it back.

"More?"

"No."

"Good. Now, what about those Sevens?"

"What are Sevens?"

Sully glanced up at Meyer. "First Sergeant Meyer spoke of an invading army from the south, and I assumed they were the ones we call Sevens. Part of a Caliphate down in Texas."

"Oh, the Indaa." He pronounced it *in-dah-ah.* "Yeah, they're in Albuquerque now, thousands of them. Moving north toward Shangri-La. I spotted them first." Billy leaned back, obviously proud.

"Wow, that's pretty amazing, Billy. Thousands of them, huh?"

"At least."

"And they're moving north?"

"Well, not yet. But they will be."

"How far is Albuquerque from Shangri-La?"

"A hard day's ride."

"Do you know what a mile is?"

The teenager looked at him like he was a talking donkey. "Of course I do."

"Good, good. So how many miles do you think it is? Thirty?"

"More than that. Fifty at least."

"You can ride fifty miles in a day?"

"More. I got here in a day and two nights."

"You've got a good horse."

"He tells me the same thing."

Sully squinted. "Who does?"

"My horse."

"Oh... how far do you think it is from here to Shangri-La?"

"Depends on how you go. The big roads all go to Albuquerque first, then they turn north and you take Highway 4 to Jemez Springs. That's where most of us live, around there. That's a long way to get there... probably five days riding, maybe six."

"Is that what you did?"

"Heck, no. I went straight from there to here. Horses ain't got tires and don't need roads."

"Go on."

"You could go up through Crownpoint and Torreon, but that's not a lot shorter."

"What if we went the way you went?"

"These cars will do that?"

"We call them armored personnel carriers, and yes, they can do that. It's kind of what they're made for."

"Huh... you could take the old I-40 to Thoreau, then go cross country to San Ysidro and get on Highway 4. That takes you right into Shangri-La. Or maybe it would be shorter to pick up Highway 126 further north, if those things go faster on roads."

"Who all lives there?" He was losing Billy's attention. Sully knew it from the boy's fidgeting and looking around.

"Lives where?"

"Shangri-La. Who all lives there?"

"I don't know. The people."

"You hungry?"

"Yeah. I didn't get a chance to hunt."

"I'll have First Sergeant Meyer find you something to eat. How would that be?"

"Great!"

"Good... so while he's doing that, tell me who all lives at Shangri-La."

"Mostly the Jemez Pueblos, then there's my people, the Jicarilla—"

"Are you Pueblos also?"

Billy gave him the weird look again. "No, we're Apaches."

"Sorry, go on."

"There's others, but they don't have a tribe. Unless you count the Muslims as one."

"Muslims? How many are they?"

"I ain't counted 'em, but twenty or thirty, maybe."

"Do you know someone named Qadim?"

The boy jumped like he'd been stuck with a cattle prod. "Qadim? Yeah, sure, we're friends. Is he here? Is he okay?"

Meyer appeared at the open rear of the Stryker, holding an MRE. Sully stood and smiled down at the boy. "He's here and he's good. I'll send him in. Oh, one last thing. When you saw us, how did you know we were friends of yours?"

"The flag painted on your thing here... your armor something. That's how."

"The flag? You recognize that flag?"

"O' course. It's the same one that flies at Shangri-La."

"You fly the American flag?"

"We're Americans, ain't we?"

———

Sully stared at the lightening eastern sky until he saw First Sergeant Meyer leave the APC and return a minute later with Qadim. Seconds later, Meyer looked around, spotted him, and walked over.

"Officers' call in ten minutes," Sully said. "That includes Echo Company, but not our First Platoon. Get me Lt. Hakala, now. Then get me Captain Jones on a private call."

Five minutes later, Hakala walked briskly across the field from his LAV-25 to where his commander stood with arms folded, watching him. When the lieutenant got close enough, Sully made a follow-me gesture and walked into the desert about forty feet. Pre-dawn lit the ground enough so they didn't step in any holes.

"What's the state of readiness of your platoon, Onni?" he said without preamble.

"I could leave in five minutes if we had to, Captain."

"Fuel situation?"

"Topped off before we hunkered down last night."

"I now have two eyewitness reports of an enemy army to our east. I have orders to hold our position, but I need to know what's coming. As we know all too well, two companies aren't much against an entire army. So I need you to get out there and find out who they are, where they are, manpower and vehicle totals, and direction of movement. This is critical to my mission orders to hold here at Gallup."

Hakala squinted and Sully hoped he understood what he was being told.

"How far out do you want me to go?"

"Far enough that we get a good idea of what we're facing, say, head due east at maximum possible speed to the position called Shangri-La, guided by the two guides we've got."

"Two?"

"Another came in a few minutes ago, a young kid on horseback."

"You believe him?"

"I do. But look, do nothing to endanger your command. Take any measures necessary to ensure their safety."

"What do I do once I get there?"

"Await further orders."

In the growing light, Sully read concern on the lieutenant's face. They both knew this was skirting the line of disobeying a direct order, as General Steeple had made it clear they were to take no offensive action against the Sevens.

Sully wasn't going to let Hakala ask the question he could see the lieutenant was about to ask. "Go, Onni. Now. Let me worry about everything else."

Hakala came to attention and saluted. "Semper Fi, Marty."

Sully responded in kind, straightening his back as a show of respect for his loyal subordinate. "Do or die, Onni."

———

Meyer stuck his head out of the command LAV. "Captain Jones on the line, Cap."

Sully stepped next to the open ramp and took the handset, then walked a few paces into the desert. "April?"

"Good morning, Marty. What's up?"

He filled her in on the morning's events, including his decision to send a platoon to investigate the whereabouts of the Sevens' army. He left out the part about reconnoitering Shangri-La. The less she knew, the better for her.

"What are my orders?" she said when he finished.

"Hold in place, prepare for fight or flight. I'm not sure what we're facing yet."

"You want us to dig in?"

"Yes, as deep as you can while minimizing danger to your people and still maximizing your firepower. There won't be a stand-or-die order this time."

"We didn't see it coming last time."

"True, but if it happens again, I'm overriding it. That'll give you cover in case of a court-martial."

"Marty! You can't do that. It'll ruin your career. You could wind up in the stockade, or worse."

"Not worse, April. Nothing is worse than seeing your command die all around you for no purpose."

"What if there's a purpose to standing fast?"

He didn't answer. "Sully out."

#

CHAPTER 63

Do I look like someone who cares what God thinks?
Elizabeth Báthony

Near Cuba, New Mexico, west of Shangri-La
0619 hours, April 30

"Move, you worthless dogs!" said the woman who put a lie to the Caliphate's rules about women.

General Tracy Gollins stood atop one of the last working American military vehicles left in the Sword of the New Prophet, an M2A1 Bradley with the six firing ports for men inside to shoot from. The turreted 25mm M242 Bushmaster chain gun was still operable, but a low ammunition supply meant it had to be used judiciously. The vehicle still had the faded markings of the Texas Army National Guard.

Short and heavy set, with black hair flying loose in the breeze, she stood with legs braced wide apart as if daring any of her white-robed troops to challenge her. Early on there had been surly remarks and widespread resentment at being commanded by a woman. That had ended when she'd personally executed a ringleader who'd tried to murder her in her sleep, along with his family, mother, wife, and a two-year-old little girl with dark curls and big eyes. In front of her entire command, she'd shot each one of them in the back of the neck, killing the little girl last.

People had begged her to spare the child, and Gollins had said, all right, she'd spare her, if someone else volunteered to take her place. No one had. As General Muhdin and the Emir himself had looked on, she'd loaded a 9mm Glock and gone to work. From that day onward, her men no longer grumbled and they obeyed her orders without delay. She could feel their hatred, but she could not have cared less about that. As long as they did what she told them, nothing else mattered.

The long column of infantry had mostly passed through the relatively flat desert southeast of the Jemez Mountains and approached Highway 126. She'd driven them half the night and was ahead of schedule, only allowing four hours of rest instead of the usual eight. Two men had been lost by stepping into shallow holes, hidden by thin wooden covers, which had both contained rattlesnakes, and two more men who had done the same thing were bitten by the much-feared desert brown spider. One of them died almost immediately, a rare reaction, while the other man walked for nearly eight hours before having to drop out with worsening symptoms. When told of the losses, Gollins only said, "If the fools stepped in holes, they deserved what they got."

With the sun up but blocked from their position by the mountains to the east, she increased their pace. Her regiment of one thousand men, known as the Mecca Regiment, used Highway 550 to move north from Albuquerque. Instead of cutting across the desert south of the little town of Cuba, she moved through it. She'd hoped they might find some women or livestock to let the men vent their aggressions, but the place was long since abandoned. So she had her Bradley parked at the intersection with Highway 126 as it turned southeast toward the Jemez Mountains and let the men's anger focus on her. Rusted-out cars and trucks littered the shoulders and desert on both sides of the highway

As they trudged past her and turned onto the cracked pavement of Highway 126, a few gave her sidelong glances that betrayed their hatred for her. Others breathed heavily and licked dry lips, their gait deteriorating into more of a shuffle than a walk. Gollins didn't care. She had to release the pressure somehow before it boiled over into mutiny. Now, united in their hatred for her but unable to do anything about it, they would be refocused on killing their enemies, while ransacking this Shangri-La place would make up for any fatigue they felt now.

A slender young man named Yusuf took up position in front of her Bradley. He was the muezzin for Mecca Regiment, the man who called *adhan*, or the call to prayer. They'd already had Fajr before setting off for the day's march, and now it was time for Muntasaf Alsabah, one of the two additional *salat*, or prayer times, that followers of the New Prophet adhered to. The term meant *mid-morning* and preceded the midday prayers, or Dhuhr.

On the front of the Bradley, a small flat strip behind the glacis plate accommodated a hatch. Gollins knelt there so all the men could see her. One of the teachings of the New Prophet was that spiritual and military leaders could say prayers in place of their men if conditions demanded they do so, leaving it up to the leader as to whether they did. Yusuf's strong baritone echoed over the desert, cueing the men to begin silently reciting their litany of prayers while Gollins said hers out loud as they streamed east around her. She repeated the words so those around her could hear them clearly.

"Allah is the greatest. I acknowledge there is no deity but Allah. I acknowledge that Mohammad and Nabi Husam Allah are the prophets of god..." The entire sequence of prayers went on for nearly five minutes, after which she started over and repeated them twice more.

It was at the beginning of the third cycle when the blast wave from a massive explosion knocked her over at the same instant the noise roared in her ears.

Gollins rolled off the AFV and hit the ground hard, but that side of the Bradley was in the desert, which was marginally softer than the asphalt. She landed on her left hand and shoulder. The arm went numb. Rocks gouged through her heavy denim pants and shirt, tearing the tough fabric and lacerating hands, knees, and shins.

Men ran in all directions, some toward the blast area and others away from it. None stopped to help her get to her feet, not even her chief lieutenants. Instead, Gollins got to one knee and then used her thick legs to push herself upright. Sweat ran down her horse-shaped face into the folds of her drooping jowls.

Smoke boiled up from the blackened hulk of an old bread truck thirty yards ahead. Men, and pieces of men, lay scattered about like a butcher's trimmings in a blast ring around the twisted metal frame. More than a dozen men lay on the pavement without moving and at least that many more groaned and rolled in pain. Others of their uninjured comrades ran to their sides to administer first aid.

Gollins stumbled toward them, looking worse for wear herself. Dust formed a thick yellow paste as it mixed with sweat on her face and neck. Feeling had begun to return to her left arm, but she still couldn't move it, so it hung limp, as if broken. Likewise her left wrist had begun to swell.

"What happened?" she demanded of a man standing on the periphery of the blast area. "Did you see what happened?"

"I did, Lord General," said another. "He opened the side door of the truck and then it blew up."

"Who is *he*?"

"Him." The man pointed to a heap of mangled metal shards from the truck's door, blasted fifty feet into the desert on the opposite side of the road. Still attached to the handle were someone's hand and forearm.

"Get moving!" she yelled, walking among the milling men and kicking them. "Let the *atibabas* take care of the wounded. That's not your job!" *Atibaba* was a bastardization of the Arabic word for doctors, *al'atibba'*. "Get up and get moving!"

The bread truck smoldered at her back as Gollins stood outside the column of gray smoke coming from the ruined vehicle. Her left wrist throbbed and the hand had swollen badly enough that she doubted she could hold the AR-15 slung over her shoulder, so instead she drew the Colt Single Action Army 7.5 inch .357 Magnum from the holster on her hip. Once she'd drawn the huge handgun, she turned and used the heel of her left hand to push back the hammer. Pain raced up her arm from the injured hand, but Gollins kept her expression stern, and silently prayed she didn't actually have to shoot the gun. She was a terrible shot using two hands. With only one, she doubted she could hit a target ten feet in front of her.

But her men didn't know that.

#

CHAPTER 64

The Army of Northern Virginia was never defeated. It merely
wore itself out whipping the enemy.
General Jubal Early

EP1
1140 hours, April 30

Their second day in the old blockhouse was no better than the first and maybe worse. Now there was nothing left to discover in their immediate vicinity and therefore nothing to do all day, except stare at empty desert. A prairie falcon had circled high overhead when they'd arrived, but finally flew off to the east.

Randall flapped his shirt, got up, and scooted the rusty folding chair back out of the sunlight pouring through what had once been a floor-to-ceiling window of blast-proof glass, shards of which still littered the floor. Threads of titanium webbed the glass and he wondered what force had destroyed such a resistant material. "What are you doing?" he yelled to Carlos, who was outside.

"Trying to see where the wasps are coming from!"

They'd been chased several times by two-inch-long wasps with blue-black bodies and orange wings.

"What're you gonna do if you find the nest?"

"I don't know. Burn it?"

"Like hell... hey, come here a minute. I've got something to run by you."

"I hope it's a plan to get out of here," Carlos said as he came through the doorway. Powdered dust coated the old concrete floor, which he kicked into clouds that left them both sneezing and coughing. "And fuck the details. I don't care what it is; count me in. Two days in this oven's enough for me."

"Yesterday was enough, huh?"

"I don't know how they've done it all these years, but now I don't care. Just get me home."

"See what you think of this. When Cole explained those hoverthings... flitters... he said they only had twenty minutes of full power, right?"

"I think so, yeah. For the single-person ones."

"He also said top speed was around sixty, right?"

"Where are you going with this?"

"Hear me out. If top speed is sixty but you can only maintain that for twenty minutes, that's only a range of twenty miles without recharging."

He saw recognition dawn in Carlos' eyes. "But this post is a thirty-mile round trip to the base."

"Yeah, exactly. Now, granted we weren't doing anywhere near sixty mph." He pronounced each letter, *em pee aitch*, and not *miles per hour*. "But even at reduced speed, that's an increase of fifty percent in range, not to mention any side trips or detours along the way."

"The math doesn't add up."

"No. It doesn't. So where does that leave us?"

"Knowing they've lied to us and jury-rigged the battery gauges?"

"That's all I can think of. But we're only gonna get one shot at this. If it doesn't work, they'll never trust us again."

"They'll have to kill me to stop me, Joe. I mean it. I wanna see Frame."

"Just so you know."

"I do. So what's the plan?"

Near Fenton Lake State Park, New Mexico
1241 hours, April 30

As the Mecca Regiment followed Highway 126 east, the land slowly began to change from rolling desert with no trees and long sightlines, to higher hills and dense woods flanking the road. The advancing Sevens split into two columns, one on each side of the highway, and maintained their spacing so as not to present a bigger target.

Gollins followed in the Bradley. Her stated purpose was to guard the regiment's sole supply truck, a Chevrolet 6500XD with a rebuilt engine that bypassed the onboard computer and burned regular gasoline. Because of the Frankensteined main engine, a secondary wood-burning engine took up part of the cargo space. That left food and ammunition as the only supplies it hauled, and not enough of either one. The men might have known the truth, that she followed them so she could flee if things got too hot, but none of them were stupid enough to say it out loud while she was in earshot.

The head of the column was six miles past Cuba when two shots rang out. One man went down with a shattered ankle, while a second buckled when a heavy shell hit the left side of his throat. Gollins heard both shots, followed by a short fusillade of automatic weapons. Her heartbeat quickened and it was hard to keep the joy off her face. It was time to kill!

Then nothing happened for ten long minutes. She drummed her uninjured fingers on her thigh. Finally an out-of-breath soldier ran up to her to report. Gollins told the driver to move and she stood in his hatch while listening to what the messenger said. When the firing had started, the men had gone into battle formation, leveled suppressing fire on the hill where the shots came from, then advanced on the enemy position. They'd found the position from which they'd fired, but there had been no sign of the shooters; the infidels had vanished.

He stopped to gulp another breath when a dull explosion echoed down the highway.

"J–...Damn!" she said. She'd almost said *Jesus Christ,* but caught herself.

This time the bomb had been centered in the highway itself, using the webbed and cracked asphalt as camouflage.

363

The hole it left was nearly three feet deep, and Gollins stood beside the crater and listened as one of her explosive experts explained the bomb's construction. The infidels had used black powder packed into a large wooden box. Sharpened stones piled on top of the box had acted as shrapnel, and then the whole thing had been covered with asphalt. It had appeared no different than most of the road's surface.

But all of that was fairly straightforward as bombs went. The clever part was the fuse.

"It was some type of very sensitive impact fuse," he said. "They are simple to make if you know how, but unless they found pre-Collapse technology that still works, they had to make it."

"So if there was one..."

"There are likely more."

———

Johnny Rainwater watched as Junior and Hap, two of their seven elephants, pulled at one of the revered bur oaks growing near Highway 4. It was the only stand of the rare trees in Shangri-La and the acorns were a local delicacy, being very sweet. Killing it to block the highway had been debated for decades, in case there was ever such an invasion as was now happening. Ultimately it was left to the leader at the time to decide whether to pull it down or not. With tears welling in his eyes, Rainwater ordered it brought down.

Arms crossed and lost in thought, he didn't hear Abigail Deak ride up until she reined in her horse ten feet behind him.

"They're coming down 126," she said, still sitting in the saddle. "At least a thousand men. Shouldn't we send some reinforcements up there?"

He shook his head while still watching the elephants. "No. The main attack will come up Highway 4, just like we always thought it would. Don't be surprised if they also attack through Los Alamos. They're trying to weaken us here, in the south."

"That tree's not gonna stop them, Johnny."

"I know."

"It won't even slow them down."

"I know that, too."

"Then *why*?"

"You know what we've got waiting down the road. This will make them less careful."

"It's a trick? You tore down one of the ancestor trees as a trick?"

All he could do was nod.

Deak fought back tears. "I hope you're right."

"Yeah, me, too."

#

Chapter 65

Those are my principles, and if you don't like them... well, I have others.
Groucho Marx

San Ysidro, New Mexico
1307 hours, April 30

What was once the town of San Ysidro had never been more than a scattering of small homes, farms, barns, and utility buildings lining Highway 4 after it branched off from Highway 550, so it surprised General Muhdin to find signs of recent habitation there. In most settlements, the first thing to be repurposed was sheet metal, but in San Ysidro he saw lots of it, corrugated or otherwise. One of his men found an axe with a sharp blade and new handle, which would have been the first thing taken by scrapers, and in one outside hearth, the ashes still glowed orange from the last fire.

All of the people had fled and he felt sure they'd gone north to Shangri-La, taking with them all livestock and food. After a cursory inspection by his advance patrols, he forbade any looting on pain of death. Not that he cared even a little bit about respecting the people's property, but time was of the essence and any delay could mess up the timing of his three-pronged attack plan.

Speed was his friend. His army wouldn't encounter serious defenses until it moved north of the old town of Canon, where the hills flanking the road came right up to the shoulder, making ambushes easy. There he'd have to slow down and send out flankers to prevent that from happening. The closer he came to Jemez Springs, where Shangri-La itself was said to be, the stronger the resistance he expected.

The Emir had allowed him to use one of their last two working Abrams tanks, along with one of the four Bradleys that made the trip. Sati Bashara had two of the Bradleys and Gollins the other one. Muhdin also had 25 vehicles of various makes, from SUVs to pickup trucks, all with some version of a heavy automatic weapon mounted on top. One Chevy Tahoe, for example, had a square hole cut in the roof with a metal pole and brace supporting a 50-caliber machine gun salvaged from a disabled Humvee at the Texas National Guard Armory in San Angelo. Nearly a hundred cavalry flanked the Bradley where Muhdin stood in the commander's hatch.

As he stared at the crumbling ruins of an old store, the Bradley's radioman touched his leg. "Blessed general," the man said, his bearded face split in a smile, "General Gollins reports traps and heavy resistance in her sector."

Muhdin understood the man's pleasure, but couldn't let his face reflect his own satisfaction at his fellow general's difficulties. "I shall pray for the success of the men under her command, and for the souls of those who are lost."

The smile vanished from the radioman's face. "Yes, my general." Crackling from the radio speaker sent him back inside for half a minute before he reappeared. The smile was back. "General Bashara reports driving the enemy from Los Alamos in heavy fighting. Four enemy killed and five captured. He requests instructions on what to do with the prisoners."

Muhdin considered a moment. Bashara was the closest thing he had to a rival, and it didn't help that the young man was the Emir's nephew. Worse, he was competent and smart. But Muhdin was responsible for the overall attack plan, so he needed Bashara to be successful.

"Tell him it's his choice. If they refuse to join us, he may execute them or use them to shield his own men. But whatever he does, the attack must continue without pause."

Passing the last dilapidated structure in old San Ysidro, Muhdin felt a growing excitement as his plan began to unfold. The first hints of doubt didn't arise until they neared Jemez

Pueblo and he heard a distant shot, followed by a fusillade of gunfire. Then came a period of silence, followed by a single shot. There was only one radio available for those leading them down the highway, so he had to wait five minutes until a rider sped toward him from the front of the column.

"Blessed General," the man said, giving the official salute of a fist over his heart with head bowed, "the enemy ambushed us. A sniper shot Usama Mohammad from behind a tree. We returned fire and when no more shots came from the infidels, four men went to investigate." He hesitated, obviously not wanting to deliver bad news.

"Continue."

"Yes, my general. They found no sign of the enemy, but two men fell into a covered pit. Inside were sharpened wooden stakes. Ali died when a point went through his neck, but Khalil still lived. It was terrible to see, my general. He fell face forward and it drove through his chest and out his back, yet he still lived. He cried and begged us to help him. Our sergeant, Burhad al-din Rahal, saw that we could do nothing for him and sent him to Allah with a bullet in the back of his head. It was the merciful thing to do."

"I decide what is merciful!"

The man bowed his head.

"Tell Sergeant Rahal that I approve of his difficult decision. What happened to the first man who was shot?"

"Usama died, my general. The bullet struck his thigh and cut the artery. There was nothing we could do."

"Allah's will be done. Were the human shields in place?"

"Yes, my general. The infidel waited until they had passed."

"I see." Muhdin thought for a moment. "Who is in charge of your *sharika*?" *Company.* "Is it Captain Deak?" The man nodded. "Tell him to use the shields on both sides of the column, not only in front. Do you understand?"

"I do, my general."

"Go."

Muhdin scowled. One infidel rifleman fired one shot and killed three of his men, while delaying the column by more than fifteen minutes. He prayed that wasn't a harbinger of things to come.

#

Chapter 66

That we are blessed to take from unbelievers what we need is
a central pillar of our faith.
From *The Revelations of Nabi Husam Allah*, Chapter 3, Verse
5

Los Alamos, New Mexico
1328 hours, April 30

Rolling hills covered with pine trees flanked Highway 501 as Regiment Rasūl moved out of Los Alamos headed southwest, closely followed by Regiment Ayyub. Sati Bashara rode in a Bradley near the head of the column, with his best friend and chief lieutenant Haleem preceding him in a motorcycle sidecar. Wounds received the previous year had left Haleem partially crippled and dragging his right leg, but Bashara valued him enough to provide him with scarce transport.

The bodies of the prisoners captured in Los Alamos hung from a stand of trees near the road. Haleem had counseled that they be used as human shields and Bashara had preferred doing that, but his men had been too angry at their losses in taking Los Alamos. Between gunfire and carefully laid traps, he'd lost more than 100 men killed or wounded, including forty who took refuge in an old office building when they came under automatic weapons fire, only to have the entire building blow up around them. He'd tied the prisoners' hands behind their backs and allowed his men to kick and stone them to death, after which they had been hung by their ankles from tree branches near the roadside. That allowed others to vent their anger by spitting on the infidels or throwing things at the corpses. One became so damaged that its left leg split in two, leaving it hanging by the right ankle. The left foot slipped out of the ropes and fell to the ground, where it rolled downhill and stopped on the shoulder, attracting flies.

Rasūl Regiment was the youngest regiment in the Sword of the Prophet. Most of the men had not been part of the previous year's campaign into Arizona. They tended to be impulsive and impetuous in their eagerness to impress, so Bashara put them in the lead. The Ayyub Regiment, on the other hand, had only men who'd fought the summer before and were veterans. Anticipating traps and ambushes, he'd decided the best way to blood the Rasūl was to let them trigger a few fights and lose more men. The survivors would be the warriors he wanted, while the weak would be winnowed out like overripe fruit.

Wildlife had gone quiet. The only noises came from the sound made by thousands of feet shuffling on the asphalt, the low murmur of men talking as they marched, and the engines of the vehicles. Horses whinnied as Bashara kept his messengers close by on either flank.

Half an hour and another mile later, a volley of gunfire rippled from ahead, sharp, deep reports that sounded different from his men's mixture of AK-47s, M-16s, and hunting rifles. Seconds later, he heard his own men shooting back.

"Driver, go! Hurry!"

The Bradley lurched ahead, passing the motorcycle on the right and forcing soldiers onto the shoulders to avoid being run down. Men ran toward the sound of the guns and slowed him down as they were forced off the road. The cavalry and the other Bradley followed him. Shooting continued, but now he only heard the guns of his own men.

When the Bradley rolled up on the point of contact, Bashara spotted a line of bodies lying in the road. He counted nine, at least two of them rolling on the pavement in pain, but no medical helpers were in sight. At least fifty riflemen knelt in a roadside ditch, pouring fire into a line of trees at the crest of a fifty-foot-high ridge.

"Cease fire!" he yelled. "Cease fire! Cease fire!"

It took a dozen more tries, but eventually all of his men stopping shooting.

Crawling toward him in the ditch, so as not to expose himself to fire, came Captain Istvan Mateescu, commander of the lead company. "Get down, my general! It is not safe!"

"Stand like a man and come here!"

Mateescu hesitated, glancing over his shoulder at the ridge.

"Come here, qayid siriya!" *Company commander.*

Mateescu closed his eyes and stood up. When no shots rang out, he walked quickly to stand before Bashara and saluted with fist over heart and head bowed. "I am y-your servant, my general."

Bashara lowered his voice so only Mateescu could hear. "I should have you shot, you coward! Were you trained to have your men cower in the dirt when facing infidels?"

"No, my general."

"Then why are they?"

"I... I..."

"How were you trained to handle this situation?"

The company commander thought for a moment, and Bashara made a mental note to replace him at the first opportunity.

After what he felt was long enough, Bashara answered his own question. "You leave one third of your men in place to provide suppressing fire, then have the others attack up the slope using whatever cover is available. Is this not what you were taught to do?"

"It is, my general."

"Then why didn't you do it?"

"I felt casualties would be heavy."

"So? The man who dies at the command of our beloved New Prophet is with Allah before the first fly lands on his corpse, and isn't that what all of us strive for?"

"It is, my general."

"Then by sending them into the attack, if they are killed, are you not fulfilling the purpose of their lives?"

"Y-yes."

"Then why didn't you do it?"

371

Mateescu's head sank to his chest. "I was afraid, my general."

Behind Mateescu, Bashara saw all of his men riveted on their interaction. Even if they couldn't hear the words, their expressions showed they understood the content. More men watched from the road and the opposite ditch.

"Lead them now, Istvan. You can do it. Go up the hill and bid them follow. The infidels have obviously gone, but we must be certain. Do this thing yourself and show them your bravery."

Mateescu looked up with tears in his eyes. "Thank you, my general."

Bashara watched as Company Commander Mateescu rallied his men and led them up the rocky slope. As they went, he positioned men behind strategically placed trees and taught them to leapfrog upward, so that if someone opened fire on them, they could respond immediately. Within fifteen steps, Bashara could tell they all remembered the winter's training, and they began to look like a military unit.

Arms folded, he saw Mateescu go over the ridge top first, look around down the opposite slope, and then wave his rifle overhead as an all-clear sign. The Company Commander grinned and Bashara knew his pride had been restored. Mateescu took a step to the left, and a small explosion sent his body flying forward to roll down the slope toward the road.

His men hit the ground as shrapnel rained on them. Mateescu came to a stop against a large pine tree. The back of his robe was shredded and smoking, turning red with blood. The company *tibs*, short for *musaeid tibiyin* or medical helpers, ran to his side. After examining him, one of them looked at Bashara and shook his head.

"Where is the lieutenant?"

"I am here, my general." A young man with a wispy brown beard stood up and saluted.

"Mulazim Latif Gerges, am I correct?"

"You are."

"You are now Company Commander Latif Gerges. See to your men and move toward the infidels with all possible speed."

"As you command, my general!"

———···———

Smoke rose on the horizon, a tall column of black that hung in the still desert air. Even with binoculars, Johnny Rainwater couldn't see the burning building to his south, but he didn't need to see it to know what it was. Sevens always burned Christian churches and Jewish synagogues, and based on where the fire was along Highway 4, he knew it had to be Our Lady of Guadalupe Catholic Church.

He had anticipated that.

Now, if they would only fall for the trap...

#

Chapter 67

Once more unto the breach, dear friends, once more.
William Shakespeare

West of New Mexico Highway 4
1427 hours, April 30

The shadows of midafternoon stretched far down the slope in front of him as Platoon Sergeant Dajuan Wiseman lowered his binoculars. "That's a battalion at the least," he said, turning to face Alpha Section and Platoon Commander Hakala. "Hard to tell from here, but it could be a regiment."

"Yeah," Hakala replied. "Hell, it could be a division for all we know."

They stood on a ridge facing east, toward the settlement that Billy Two Trees and Qadim both identified as Jemez Pueblo. A knot of infantry hurried north in the distance down old New Mexico Highway 4, with the tail end of a much larger group disappearing behind a mountain.

"What do you want to do?" Wiseman said.

"Let me interject something, Loot," said Tosen Ecker, the vehicle commander of the other LAV-25 in Alpha Section. "I think we need to consider the operational status of the Destroyers." Marine nickname for the LAV-25.

"What does Whitworth say?"

"He thinks Alpha Two may have a worn bearing."

"Can that be fixed in the field?"

"Yes, but it's time-consuming."

"How much time?"

"Hard to say; it depends. With enough help, it could only be two hours, but it could also be two days."

From down the reverse slope, Billy Two Trees shouted up at them. "We're gonna be late for dinner!"

None of the Americans turned to him, but Wiseman commented, "He's got a point, Loot. We've got maybe four good hours of daylight left. Whatever we're gonna do, we need to do it."

Hakala nodded. After turning north off Interstate 40, they'd literally raced up Highway 371, then east on 57 and over side roads and open country, averaging nearly thirty miles an hour for six hours. The crews were tired and hungry, and the point about the mechanical state of their machines was a good one. Each LAV carried four Marine riflemen, and they needed to stretch their legs. Plus, and not least, since he needed to use the head, he knew everybody else did, too.

"Here's what we'll do," Hakala said. "Platoon Sergeant, establish a perimeter. Crews, see to your machines, refuel, check your filters, and make sure everything's good to go. Alert Whitworth to any issues. Have him check Bravo Two for that bearing. Hit head in shifts and have your men eat something when they can. I want a report on all Destroyers in half an hour."

"Qadim!" Hakala motioned the young man to meet him atop the ridge. He'd been speaking to Billy Two Trees, but trotted up the slope at Hakala's call.

"Tell him about dinner!" Billy yelled after him.

Once Qadim stood beside the lieutenant, the American officer said, "What's his issue?"

"I do not understand."

"Billy. Is he... right in the head?"

"I still do not understand. Billy is Billy."

"Never mind." Hakala pointed toward the distant road. "Help me understand what's going on over there."

Shading his eyes, Qadim focused where Hakala pointed. "We are too late."

STANDING BEFORE HELL'S GATE

"Are we? Is that Shangri-La?"

"No, that is Jemez Pueblo. The town is north of there."

"Town means Shangri-La?"

"Yes."

"Will they fight?"

"The people? Oh, yes, but we are few. There are many traps, though. I have personally helped dig many tunnels and pits. Some will have rattlesnakes in them, others sharpened stakes. One may even have a cougar, if they could catch one. There are many places where black powder has been buried. It is hoped this will discourage invaders."

"Black powder?"

"Yes. We make it ourselves. We also make our own weapons, mostly single-shot rifles. Automatic weapons are few, but those we make are very accurate, even if they are muzzle-loaders."

"You're armed with muzzle-loaders? Like a Civil War musket?"

"I know of the Civil War from our schools, but not much about their rifles, so I cannot say. We do have a few modern weapons. There are also three cannon made by the armorers. I think you call them mortars."

"Muskets against M-16s... but your people will fight? They won't surrender?"

"We will fight. And then we will die."

Overtime Prime
1513 hours

Sergeant Schiller glanced at the Chinese guard near his left elbow and knocked on the conference room door. Apparently the sullen man had orders to be his shadow, since he followed him everywhere, including into the bathroom. Schiller had shut that down quick; he wasn't about to piss while some enemy soldier stood next to him. He didn't know who had issued those orders, but he guessed it was Adder. The guard refused to leave until Schiller grabbed him by the balls, snatched his rifle out of his hands, and marched him to the exit. Only when he'd finished in the bathroom did he give the man back his gun.

"I will kill you for that," the man had snarled, still bent over to relieve the pain of his injured testicles.

"If the day comes when the likes of you can kill me, I'll deserve it."

The conference room door opened and Colonel Mwangi motioned him inside.

"Is that the deployment list?" Steeple asked. Besides he and Mwangi at the small table were Colonel Claringdon, Adder, and the newly arrived man identified as Károly Rosos.

"Yes, sir. The location of every Overtime component, civilian or military, its strength, current status, and mission."

"Thank you, Sergeant Major. That was quickly done. I appreciate it."

"Yes, sir." Schiller turned and began to leave, saw the guard standing in the doorway, then stopped and turned back around. "General Steeple, if I may?"

"What?" Steeple looked up from his copy of the list Schiller had brought. "What is it, Schiller?"

"Sir, I'm being hampered in the performance of my duties by having a guard constantly looking over my shoulder."

It was a risky thing to say. He didn't know General Steeple very well, and if Adder had issued the order for him to be closely watched, he wouldn't like Schiller speaking up about it, especially in front of others. But he didn't really want to stay in the Crystal Palace anyway; he wanted a transfer to the field and if that happened, he was fine with it. Serving Angriff had been honorable duty, while serving Steeple wasn't.

Steeple looked him over and then spoke to Adder. "Tell your people to leave this man alone."

Adder's eyes narrowed. The hate-filled glare he gave Schiller frightened most people, but not the sergeant major. He returned the expression without blinking. Nobody scared J.C. Schiller. Nobody. Then a vagrant thought made him smile. He was already buried at Arlington, wasn't he? And there were no cowards in that hallowed ground. His grin made Adder's face turn red.

"You, get out," Adder said to the Chinese soldier. The guard gave the back of Steeple's head a sullen look and walked away without a word. Schiller followed him a few seconds later.

———

Amunet Mwangi pointed to her copy of the deployment list. "I'm worried about the construction crews in area seven. Aren't there supposed to be Caliphate patrols in that area?"

"I agree. Until we can formalize relations with the Caliphate, we need to avoid potential incidents. Orders those people back to base ASAP."

"We've already got an incident, sir," Mwangi said.

"What?"

"The Dennis Tompkins party, trapped in the cave?"

"I'm not worried about a few old men, but why does that name ring a bell? Ever since I heard it, I can't shake the feeling that I know this man. Anybody?"

Colonel Claringdon spoke up. "We rescued him and his friends the first day of activation. They'd been wandering the country since the Collapse."

"They lived through all of that? Fifty years?"

"Yes. General Angriff said that fifty years of active service deserved two stars, so he promoted him to major general, if you can believe it. He said if it wasn't for Tompkins, he would never have been here."

"Tompkins, Tompkins... wait a minute. His first name is Dennis?"

"It is," Claringdon said.

"Well, I'll be damned. I remember him now. Tompkins performed an important service for me when he was still a lieutenant. He's part of the reason Angriff wound up in charge of Overtime."

Claringdon crossed his arms. "Therefore he is our enemy."

Steeple's disapproving glance differed from that of most powerful people. He wasn't an imposing man, so unlike someone such as Nick Angriff, his expression wasn't overtly menacing. Instead his eyes narrowed ever so slightly while his face relaxed into a featureless blank. Claringdon's smug smile showed that he didn't recognize Steeple's reaction for what it was, but the instant he heard Steeple's tone he knew that he'd miscalculated.

"General Angriff was given this command by *me*." Steeple's voice dropped to little more than a whisper. "He was personally selected for it by *me*, and it was *me* who went to great lengths to arrange the circumstances for him to agree. Do you disagree with my choice?"

"Err... I probably would have chosen someone different, sir."

"Which is one reason you did not do the choosing." Steeple's voice softened and returned to normal. After chastising Claringdon, he needed to restore the man's confidence. "No one knows better than me how difficult General Angriff can be, how intransigent, how old school. To this day, and despite everything he has witnessed, the man still believes in the sanctity of the original Constitution." When he smiled, it allowed Claringdon to do the same, which dissipated much of the tension.

"But despite sometimes being a royal pain in the ass, he was and remains the finest combat general we could have leading the Seventh Cavalry. I went to great lengths and sacrificed much to make that possible. Therefore he is critical to the success of this mission, and I firmly believe that he will come around to our way of thinking. If he is restored to command, then you may be assured that he has my full confidence." Pausing, he sipped water from the squeezer at his elbow. He wasn't thirsty, but it allowed for them to think his words through. "Does anyone have a question pertaining to this issue?"

"I got something to say," said Adder.

"Yes?"

"If you think you're gonna play Saint Nick like a piano, you're out of your fucking mind."

Colonel Claringdon's eyes widened, but he fixed on a joint of two stainless steel panels across the room and stared. Rosos smirked. Colonel Mwangi only raised an eyebrow, more curious to see how Steeple would react than fearful about that reaction.

"Thank you for your first-hand observation," he said after a brief pause. "We all know that you served under General Angriff. I would only submit to you that I... arranged the circumstances that put Saint Nick, as you so quaintly refer to him, here in the first place. I trust that I can once again make it clear where his best interests lie. Now, let's get these deployments ironed out—"

"If I may interject," Rosos said, "the Chinese were adamant they want liaison officers with all of your units. They indicated this was not negotiable."

Once again Steeple swallowed his anger. He'd dealt with the Rosos family for years and knew their rudeness and arrogance better than anyone. "Thank you, Károly. I see no problem with such an arrangement. In fact, since the First Mechanized Infantry Regiment will soon be in close proximity to Sierra, and you tell me that a Chinese force is headed for the same destination, then we should start there immediately. Amunet, can you see to arranging that?"

"I can do it easier," said Adder.

"Very well, Colonel, I'll leave the matter in your hands. Now, since we are speaking about Sierra, I see no useful alternative to our acquisition of this potentially critical source of weapons and munitions."

"What if General Fleming and the paratroopers resist?" Mwangi asked.

"I believe my previous statement covers that contingency. Moving on to the next item, I want all forces to immediately stand down from any actions or movements that might provoke combat with potential allies. This includes the two Marine companies north of Yuma, the infantry companies in Las Vegas, any air missions in support of Tompkins and his people, and especially the two Marine companies in New Mexico. They are to stand in place and do nothing that might bring them into conflict with forces of the Caliphate."

"Can they shoot back if attacked?" Mwangi asked.

"Not without specific permission from me."

"That could take time and cost lives."

"Fighting the Caliphate will cost a lot more lives. If we have to sacrifice a few people to have peace, it is a lamentable but justifiable price to pay. Now, tell me about this so-called Marine battalion in Prescott."

Claringdon cleared his throat. "Well, they were members of the so-called Army of the Republic of Arizona who passed the psych tests and made it through boot camp. Training was conducted by Major Strickland, who went on to become their commander."

"Strickland is a good man, but were you considered for the job?"

"Not that I know of."

"I realize that a commanding officer from a different branch of service would seem odd, but those men could just as easily have been an army battalion, could they not?"

"They could."

"So this was General Angriff playing favorites?"

"That's how I see it."

"Amunet, I want the word *Provisional* added to this unit's designation. Fitz... may I call you Fitz?" he said to Claringdon, who nodded assent. "I want you to go to Prescott and evaluate the readiness of this battalion. Tell Colonel Strickland he is to give you all cooperation. Now, as to Comeback, Colonel Schiller is currently in command there and he is a very loyal and competent officer. Are there any reasons not to leave him there? No? Is there anything else?"

"One thing," Adder said. "There's four Zombies still here at Overtime, not counting Green Ghost's psycho sister. I ordered them out on a lurp because I didn't feel safe having them around. If you'd rather I do something different, I will."

"Why not simply imprison them?" Mwangi asked.

"It's cool with me, but remember, they're four of the best special ops people who ever lived. Seems kind of a waste not to use 'em."

"That is in your house, Colonel," Steeple said. "They're under your command now. Do as you think best. The same holds true for any SEALs you might think are a danger."

"What about other special forces, such as MARSOCs?"

"Hmmm... thoughts?"

"I wouldn't remove them from Marine control," Mwangi said. "I can't imagine anything that would negatively affect their opinion of you as their commanding general more than permanently separating them from their parent regiment."

"That's exactly why it's a good idea," Adder said. "They're dangerous as hell and we need to keep tight control of them."

"The only people who can keep tight control of Marines are other Marines."

Steeple held up a hand. "I agree with Amunet on this point. If we encounter problems, then we can revisit the issue."

"Whatever you say, Preacher. You're the boss."

Steeple squinted. "I beg your pardon? Preacher?"

"That was your code name."

"I see. Well, you may call me General Steeple."

Adder shrugged. "Whatever you say, General Steeple."

#

CHAPTER 68

Battle is an orgy of disorder.
Lt. General George S. Patton, Jr.

Near Jemez Pueblo
1524 hours, April 30

Standing in the commander's hatch, General Ahmednur Hussein Muhdin stroked his beard as his command Bradley rumbled past the burning Catholic church. Less than a mile behind him, a small wooden Baptist church likewise belched fire. Both had showed signs of recent use.

The topography on either side of Highway 4 began to rise as they approached the Jemez Mountains. Three ambushes had already killed nine of his men, with no known losses among the infidels. The number by itself did not trouble him. With more than 6,000 men available, the loss of nine was trivial. The real problem was that his men had begun grumbling about ghosts and curses and traps. Not loud, and not in his presence.

Not yet.

Muhdin positioned himself closer to the front troops. With the rolling hills closing in on both sides of the road, and vegetation increasing, he ordered the infidels brought forward. The column halted while the hostages were dragged into position. Dirty, emaciated, and all with bleeding feet, the only ones who had survived the long march north from Texas were a hundred or so younger women and children, the youngest being six or seven. The old and the very young had died along the way and been thrown into hastily dug pits.

Earlier in the march, the children had cried and clung to their mothers, but now all of them were too exhausted to do more than shuffle one foot in front of the other. As they stumbled and trudged past his vehicle, Muhdin called out to one of their guards. "Hurry them up. If they cannot do it, they are of no use to us. Shoot them."

Ten seconds later, one woman who had fallen and twisted a knee fell with a bullet in her brain. The others jumped at the sudden noise. Adrenaline flooded their emaciated bodies and they picked up speed. The Sevens waited until they were fifty yards ahead of the column before following.

Muhdin spotted the danger before any of his men did. A clump of boulders sat atop a sheer hundred-foot-high ridge near the highway, precariously balanced in an unnatural way. From his position, he couldn't tell for sure, but the human shields appeared to have moved past the danger point, while his men... his men were directly under the rocks.

"Retreat!" he yelled. "Retreat! Get those men back from there!"

Men looked back at him, and it took a second for the warning to sink in. Then the word was shouted up the line to get back, retreat. The leading men turned at the shouts just as an explosion sent rocks raining down on the highway from the ridge. The boulders rocked, held in place for a long moment, and then rolled down toward the hundred or so men staring up at them from the highway.

There was no time to run backward, but on the far side of the highway was an unusually deep ditch. A few men tripped and several more were hit by flying debris, and the huge rolling boulders crushed all of those who fell to bloody paste. But most made it across the road to the ditch and crawled to the bottom. None of the boulders rolled that far and as the pebbles quit rolling and the dust settled, they appeared to be safe.

None of them heard the low hiss of the black match fuse burning its way across hundreds of feet of desert until it was too late. One man stood to run, and then hundreds of pounds of tightly packed black powder under the entire length of the ditch ignited and erupted in a huge explosion.

Sharpened rocks spewed out and cut down every man within thirty yards.

Muhdin could only watch in anger as tibs ran to help the injured. Once again he had fallen for the infidels' trap. Once again they had bled his army while getting away unscathed. And once the dust settled enough to see, he realized that his human shields were gone.

———

Abigail Deak heard the distant blast and hurried to find Johnny Rainwater. She ran him down farther to the south than she'd expected, standing atop a ridge with a clear view all the way to the Catholic church on Highway 4. Four armed men stood nearby.

Binoculars up to his eyes, Rainwater heard her coming. "I wish you could have seen that, Abigail."

"How did you know it was me?"

"I could tell by the sound your shoes made on the stone."

"Bullshit."

He laughed and lowered the binoculars. "I saw you coming. Here, take a look."

Focusing the binoculars, she stared for nearly a minute. "What's going on, Johnny? I mostly just see dust."

"You know that rock trap, with the ditch on the other side loaded with powder?"

"Yeah."

"They fell for it hook, line, and sinker. We probably nailed a hundred of them."

"That should put the fear of God into them."

"You would think so." He accepted the glasses back and took another look. A few seconds later he tensed.

She sensed something had gone wrong. "What is it?"

He didn't answer right away. "They're coming on without stopping. They aren't stopping!" Jumping to the ground, he began to run along a path between giant rocks toward the south. "Get everybody ready, Abby! They're coming!"

———

Muhdin's first instinct was to pull his men back and proceed even more cautiously up the highway to defeat any more traps or ambushes. After all, the previous year he'd thrown in attack after attack at the Americans and lost a third of his soldiers for no purpose. It wasn't the deaths that bothered him; it was wasting them by achieving nothing. Nor was it him who'd become angry after such temporary set-backs; it had been the Emir. Muhdin had been entrusted with command of the Sword of the Prophet and failed once already.

And here it was, happening all over again.

Not this time!

Sitting beside his LAV, Lieutenant Hakala felt guilty about eating his beef ravioli MRE. Although some people pre-ferred the chili and macaroni and others the meatballs in marinara, he'd never met anybody who didn't like the beef ravioli. And like any good field commander, he'd allowed all of his men to pick their meals first. The fact that they'd left him the beef ravioli damned near made him cry.

He'd downed the ravioli in six bites, followed by the crackers and jalapeno cheese spread. The orange drink pow-der — aka bug juice —he mixed in his mess kit cup and drained after the spread, which to his taste was hot. Most people skipped the toxic-orange, gluey paste, but Hakala liked it. He liked the concrete cookie, too, which was a very hard oatmeal cookie. Finally came a minty caffeine candy he knew from experience would kick away any after-lunch sleepiness.

He stood and turned his back to his driver. "Bug check." It was necessary to have other Marines check your back for scorpions or spiders after you'd been on the ground.

"You're good, Loot."

Hakala stiffened at a distant sound. The first explosion sounded like nothing more than the faint *pop* of a bursting balloon. Seconds later, the second one echoed much louder and deeper, like a heavy clap of thunder. He'd already start-ed up the reverse slope of the ridge when one of the men on the top called down to him.

"We got smoke, Lieutenant."

Loose gravel rolled away as he trudged up the fifty-foot slope and followed the sentry's finger. Two pillars of smoke rose from behind a mountain.

Qadim followed him up and knew right away what they were. "Those must be the churches near Canon."

"How do you know?"

"Sevens burn all Christian churches and Jewish synagogues."

"But how do you *know* that?"

"I have never seen a tornado, Lieutenant, but I do not need to see one to know they are real."

Frustrated by the non-answer, Hakala changed the subject. "What were those explosions?"

"I believe the Sevens triggered a trap. The first was meant to cause a rockslide and force anyone on the road below into a deep ditch. Unknown to them, large kegs of black powder were buried under the ditch. It means they are getting close to the main defenses. We need to help them!"

"Listen, I know you want to help your people, but there's an army out there of unknown strength and firepower between us and them. Probably thousands of men. To get through to Shangri-La, we'd have to get past them. We fought them once before and they had a lot of RPGs. These are LAVs we're driving, which stands for light armored vehicles. *Light* armored vehicles. They're not tanks and they're not designed to absorb RPG hits."

"What is an RPG?"

That surprised Hakala. "Rocket-propelled grenade. You don't have any?"

Qadim shook his head. "No."

"You'll have to take my word for it then, but we can't shoot our way through that many people armed with weapons that can destroy us. Even counting my crews, corpsman, and mechanic, I've only got thirty men. Thirty against thousands doesn't work. I should know. I've done it before."

"Why not go around them?"

"I thought you said they were moving down that other highway from the west."

"There are other roads than highways. There are small roads and game trails through the desert west of Shangri-La, then all we have to do is go over the Western Ridge and we're there."

"Any water barriers?"

"What do you mean?"

"Lakes, rivers, that kind of thing."

"There is the Jemez River, but there are many fords. I have crossed it many times on foot."

"Could the Sevens know about all this?"

"I don't think so."

Hakala made an instant decision. He checked his watch and then, half walking, half running down the slope toward the parked LAVs, he barked out orders. Three minutes later, First Platoon, Dog Company, 1st Marine Recon Battalion, pulled out heading north.

#

Chapter 69

The Marines are like my West Highland Terrier. They get up every morning, they want to dig a hole, and they want to kill something.
Thomas P.M. Barnett

Gallup, New Mexico
1547 hours, April 30

Captain Martin Sully tilted the old Rand McNally road map so that the glare from the afternoon sun didn't wash out the details. He'd already memorized the routes east that Dog Company might need to follow, but it never hurt to identify alternate roads just in case. Besides, he'd been napping when First Platoon called in a sitrep and that shot of adrenaline had made going back to sleep impossible. But since Dog Company's other four platoons stood ready to carry out whatever orders he issued, either to stand fast against attack, withdraw, or advance, like everybody else Sully had little left to do. Unlike everybody else, he couldn't be seen wasting time, thus the map.

First Sergeant Meyer found him holding the map close to his face just outside the company command post, in an old wooden barn. Using his peripheral vision, Sully noticed the sergeant's limp seemed better.

"Colonel Berger again, Captain," Meyer said. "He wants that sitrep... he doesn't sound happy."

Sully lowered the map. He knew he could only play the 'radio problems' card for so long before it became insubordination. In his pre-Overtime career, Sully would not only never have sent out a deep recon against the spirit of his orders, even if not the actual letter of them, but feigning technical issues to stall for time would have been anathema. All of this ran through his mind before he answered. "Are you certain that wasn't garbled in transmission? It sounds odd, considering I spoke with the colonel late last night."

Meyer carefully weighed his words. "There *was* a lot of interference. Should we request they resend?"

"No! We have to maintain radio silence for the security of our mission. Let's wait and see if they send again."

The corners of Meyer's mouth twitched and Sully knew he was trying not to smile. "Aye, sir."

"You need to watch yourself, Meyer."

"Sir?" Meyer said, confused and suddenly worried.

"Keep this up and you'll be a butter bar." *Second Lieutenant.*

Meyer replied past a grin, "Wouldn't want that, Cap."

"On the other hand, you might be looking up at PFC."

"Wouldn't want that, either."

1549 hours
Shangri-La

Men and women of all ages scurried to and fro on errands before the Sevens reached them. As he stood behind the last barriers on Highway 4, directing final preparations, reports came to Johnny Rainwater from all over Shangri-La about the fighting. None of them were good. Despite suffering heavy casualties, the Sevens advanced on all sides. On the east they'd advanced past the old Valles Calderas National Preserve in a running gun battle against the withdrawing soldiers of Shangri-La, and his people had been forced back to Los Griegos Peak, a mountain overlooking Highway 501. Any minute he expected to hear that the last line of trees blocking the road were under attack. He'd put most of the available defenders there, because if that position was overrun, the Sevens could pour into Shangri-La and destroy them.

Things were even worse on the west side, where his people reported a woman in charge. From what Rainwater knew of the Sevens, that wasn't possible, but those who had seen her swore that a heavy-set woman with black hair drove the enemy forward without mercy. One of the messengers swore she'd seen the woman shoot one of her own soldiers in the back while he appeared to be running away, and then execute two captured Shangri-La defenders as they begged for mercy on their knees. One of them had been Trinka Mathis.

"Trinka's only eleven," Rainwater said to the messenger. "What was she doing there?"

"Helping her dad load his rifles. He was killed before they caught her. I saw him fall."

"And this woman killed her?"

The messenger nodded. "Stabbed Trinka in the throat and watched her die. She laughed the whole time."

"Thank you," Rainwater said. The viciousness of his enemy left him stunned and sick. Vengeance was a stranger at Shangri-La, which was generally a peaceful and cooperative community, but Rainwater felt an unfamiliar anger boiling inside. That woman needed to die. She didn't just deserve to die; she *needed* to die, and preferably in the slowest, most painful way.

Then he heard gunshots and felt something sting his right ear. Touching it, he felt something slick and looked at his fingers, now red with blood. It took a second for his brain to register his danger before he fell into a squat. Bullets zipped overhead like angry wasps.

Muhdin's new plan seemed to be working. He'd lined up three regiments beside each other and attacked due north. The Pir Baba Regiment, his best troops, attacked up Highway 4 and the ridge to its west. Beside it, over the eastern ridge flanking the highway, came the Nathar Shah Regiment, and on the right flank was the Kaaba Regiment in the open desert. Unlike the previous year, his men didn't simply run forward as fast as they could. Over the winter they had learned fire and advance tactics. Part of a unit would advance to cover while the rest provided suppressing fire. They weren't all that good at it yet, but already it was proving far more effective than simply attacking in human waves. The RPGs and mortars he kept in reserve.

Also unlike the previous summer, Muhdin stayed close behind his advancing troops, so close that when two men fell into a pit near the left shoulder of the highway, he had heard their screams when the cougar trapped inside tore them to pieces. When his men tried to shoot the animal, it had vanished. Only when they had dropped to the bottom of the pit to check on their comrades did they see the tunnel in one wall of the hole, closed off by a retractable gate.

Despite mounting losses, his men kept moving forward. Rumors said that the infidels had erected a tall flagpole from which flew the American flag, surrounded by four stone towers. Standing atop his command Bradley using his prized Leica binoculars, Muhdin saw a small flag attached to a metal pole flapping in the breeze, with four shorter structures around it. As he watched, the flag lowered and disappeared, replaced moments later by one more than twice as large. The colors on this one shone in the sun so there could be no mistake of what they represented; they were the hated red, white, and blue of the old United States.

The defiance of the infidels knew no bounds, and so their punishment had to be equally severe. Emir el Mofty, the Superior Imam of the Caliphate of the Seven Prayers of the New Prophet, would demand nothing less, and Muhdin would be glad to give him what he wanted. Shangri-La and all of its infidel citizens would die.

1557 hours·
Shangri-La

Johnny Rainwater couldn't be everywhere at once, so when Abigail Deak volunteered to help wherever he needed it, he detailed her to stay at Highway 4 and hold their position no matter what happened. The Sevens had made it to the bur oak, the last defenses before Shangri-La itself. Built on the bones of the old Jemez Springs town, the common buildings of Shangri-La were long and centered on the highway, with no place to make a stand until the final stone wall sanctuary around the flag and towers. Regardless of cost, the barriers had to be held.

Leaving her in charge there, he galloped to what the citizens of Shangri-La called the Valley of Death, two miles to the south. Over the decades, a great deal of defensive work had been done there to devastate any attackers, which the people had always assumed would be Sevens. The two sides of the valley were low, but sharply sloped hills rose about forty feet high on one side and eighty on the other. On the outside of those hills, the ground tended to be flat with no cover, a perfect killing ground. Facing that approach, the defenders had constructed an elaborate stone wall ten feet high and three feet thick, with firing ports; nothing less than heavy artillery or air strikes could destroy those positions.

The valley, on the other hand, offered an enticing alternative. It looked like an old, dry riverbed two hundred yards across. The ground rolled a bit, offering cover except for the last fifty yards in front of a much lower stone wall, about four feet high, sited at the top of a gentle ten-foot slope. To the eyes of those who didn't know better, it appeared to be the weak point in an otherwise stout defensive position.

It was, of course, another trap, or rather a series of traps.

When Rainwater dismounted one hundred yards behind the lower wall, he tied his horse to a scrub red elderberry tree. The soldiers of Shangri-La, a mix of both genders and ages from 16 to 80, clustered thicker at the head of the valley than on the two flanks, where the wall was higher. Likewise, the few available semi-automatic rifles that had been converted to full automatic capability covered the valley, while everyone outside the valley carried single-shot rifles. Most of those had been forged at Shangri-La and comprised a mixture of muzzle- and breech-loaders, but a few were pre-Collapse bolt-action hunting rifles. One man had a Garand M1 that had once belonged to his grandfather.

After inspecting the position and encouraging those manning the wall, Rainwater loaded his own rifle, taking thirty seconds to pour powder, slug, and patch down the muzzle and tamp it down with a rod made for the purpose. He found a place along the valley wall, leaned his rifle against the rocks, and sat with his back to the stones. On his left was a seventeen-year-old girl named Koho, and to his right was her mother, Brenda. Both of their faces seemed to fold inward with anxiety, although each tried to smile. Nothing would relieve the tension now except sight of the enemy.

They didn't have long to wait.

#

CHAPTER 70

If some of them wanted to stay back and eat breakfast, I reck-on I'd be all right with that.
Alleged quote from Davy Crockett before the last attack on the Alamo

Southern fringe of Shangri-La
1612 hours, April 30

Peering through one of the rifle slits in the stone wall, Rainwater saw knots of men 300 yards away run forward and then disappear behind cover. Seconds later, other groups did the same thing, advancing slightly further than the first group. Those who couldn't find a boulder or rise in the ground to hide behind simply fell to their stomachs. A third group came, and then a fourth. And then the first group jumped up and ran toward the wall again. Within a short time, the leading groups had closed within two hundred yards. He watched enrapt, knowing what was coming.

Four groups of ten men each advanced at a crouch with rifles at the ready, spread out over the two-hundred-yard front. On the far left side of the riverbed, the southern side, he heard a cry of pain followed by screams. One hundred twelve ankle-deep holes pockmarked the valley floor, each one covered by a thin wooden board with topsoil and pebbles scattered on its top for camouflage. Each hole contained sharpened stakes, but seventeen also contained rattlesnakes

STANDING BEFORE HELL'S GATE

placed there a few hours earlier. Shangri-La had a designated team of snake handlers who removed rattlesnakes from areas where they could endanger the citizens. When the objective of the Sevens had become obvious, those experienced snake wranglers had captured as many of the serpents as they could find and then placed them into the pre-dug holes. The terrified screams echoing in the still afternoon air made it obvious one man had been bitten.

The others immediately stopped in their tracks. The injured man rolled in the dirt and screamed. Even at that distance, Rainwater could see the other Sevens hesitate and look at each other. Few things struck fear into a man's heart like the bite of a venomous snake, particularly rattlesnakes. The defense of Shangri-La depended on terrifying attackers and it appeared to be working. Dragging himself backward, the wounded Seven yelled to his friends for help, and then stood up and wobbled backward with arms outstretched. Rainwater couldn't help smiling.

A single shot rang out in the distance. The staggering man fell to one knee, and then toppled sideways.

Muhdin handed the rifle back to its owner without changing his expression or speaking a word, although he said a silent prayer of thanks that he hadn't missed. Every eye in his army stared at him in disbelief. All of his men knew the penalty for retreat. Likewise they all remembered the previous summer's battle, when Muhdin had tried to turn machine guns on men who fled from the fight. A few men had fallen from the guns' fire before the gunners had also fled. Now they'd all been reminded that cowardice in the face of the enemy betrayed lack of faith in their prophet, who promised immediate salvation for martyrs who died fighting infidels. Followers of the New Prophet should crave death in battle, not fear it.

The advance continued.

As the Sevens resumed their leap-frog advance, Johnny Rainwater's smile faded. He'd been told by the only Muslim who'd volunteered to infiltrate the Caliphate and returned that the commanding general of the Sword of the New Prophet was Moodeen or Moodinn or something like that, and that he terrified the Sevens. Now Rainwater could see why. Much of Shangri-La's defense had been dependent on instilling fear in attackers, but it seemed the Sevens feared their own commander more than they did sudden and painful death.

To their west, gunfire broke out, and from the sound he knew the positions at the highway were under assault. Along the wall, some of the defenders grew antsy. Squatting so as not to make himself a target, he duck-walked and crawled all along the line, whispering encouragement and reminding them not to open fire until he did. He knew them all and had grown up with many of them and knew who needed a hand on the shoulder and who would respond to bravado. But to all of them he repeated the same line. "No matter what you hear somewhere else, don't shoot until I shoot."

While talking to a particularly frightened 17-year-old boy, he heard screams coming from the valley and knew the Sevens had found the trench.

Muhdin sensed this was the moment when all of the training and the intimidation would pay off. His men would appreciate his harshness when they celebrated victory among the spoils of their sacrifices, spoils that lay just beyond the low wall of stone ahead. He harbored no doubts that many rifles pointed at his men, even if so far no defenders had shown themselves. Soon, though, it wouldn't matter. Once they closed within one hundred yards, he felt confident they couldn't be stopped.

Another harbinger of victory was the gunfire coming from the highway. That meant his men had targets to aim at, and so must have closed on the defenders. Everything seemed to be going well... until the first explosion came from the west, closely followed by another and then a third. They weren't black powder blasts, though, which had a sound all their own. They sounded like RPGs going off, and that wasn't supposed to happen unless something had gone very, very wrong.

Leaning into the command Bradley, he told the driver to head west at maximum speed. No sooner had the vehicle turned and started down the slope of the ridge where they'd parked than four groups of men moving forward toward the wall disappeared from sight.

#

CHAPTER 71

*What is more rare in war is a general who can learn from ex-
perience.*
paraphrased quote from Shelby Foote

Two miles west of Shangri-La
1638 hours, April 30

The old Forest Ranger road climbed a hundred-foot-high
hill and ended there. The cracked and crumbling pavement
brought them through the ravines and forest to a point due
west of Jemez Springs, with only a short expanse of prairie
and a long, high ridgeline to get over. From his vantage
point, Lieutenant Hakala knew that was easier said than
done. Turning to the four vehicle commanders assembled
around him, he laid out the plan. "Bravo Two, you remain
here. This will be our rally point."

"She can make it, Lieutenant."

"No reason to risk it. And if you see us coming back over
the mountain at high speed, you'll know we need fire support. Now, see that over there, next to that sheer cliff? Our
two guides, Qadim and Billy, both say that ground is solid
enough to hold the LAVs. If you look right there, that black-
ish-looking line about halfway up, that's where the slope's
angle up changes, but to the right of that is another, lower-
angle slope that will get us to the top. Under no circumstances are you to continue if you believe your vehicle is in

danger of sliding or falling. The safety of you and your LAV are of paramount importance, clear?"

They all nodded.

"Once we top that ridge, be ready to engage the enemy. We don't know their exact location or strength, so expect the worst. Any questions?"

"What are the ROEs, Loot? Do we fire only in self-defense?"

Hakala paused. Until that point, everything he had done was on the direct orders of his commanding officer. Whether or not that violated orders from up the chain of command wasn't his problem; it was Captain Sully's. But the answer he gave now could change all of that. The company had been given direct orders not to initiate combat with the Sevens, and indeed not to return fire if fired upon, but instead to retreat. Giving his men orders to fire first, while knowing that it was in direct conflict with orders from higher command, was a court-martial offense.

"Negative. If we are separated, you may fire on the enemy at the moment you judge it tactically sound. Otherwise, wait for me to fire first. But let me repeat that the safety of your men and your vehicle comes before all other considerations."

They all grinned. "So in plain language, we're good to send those motherfuckers to hell," said the commander of Alpha Two.

Hakala gave him a thumbs-up. "With extreme prejudice."

New Mexico Highway 126
1647 hours

During a short break in the fighting northwest of Shangri-La, Tracy Gollins heard several distant explosions followed by small arms fire. She also thought, but couldn't be sure, there was more firing in the east. That meant both Sati Bashara and General Muhdin might beat her to the big prize, just as they'd always said they would. She'd sworn she would prove her worth in battle, but the infidels had fought harder and died harder than anyone had given them credit for, and her losses had been high. Even with single-shot rifles, they'd taken a heavy toll on Mecca Regiment and the most obvious lesson so far was that accuracy trumped volume of fire. The infidels rarely missed while her people rarely hit anything, even with automatic weapons. And now the ammo was running low.

Ahead, the road curved out of sight to the southeast. Beyond that was supposed to be a last stretch of Highway 126 before it merged into Highway 4 north of Jemez Springs. From there it was about five miles into Shangri-La. Gollins pulled up the picture of the map in her mind... if Bashara was still pushing through the opposition on the east, then she had a chance of getting onto Highway 4 before he did. And if she did that, anything was possible.

"Get moving!" she yelled, stalking down the highway through the debris of battle. Branches, leaves, pine needles, spent cartridge casings, flies circling and lighting in puddles of blood and on corpses, none of them mattered to her in the least. "Get your Allah-loving asses in gear, you worthless dogs! Move out!"

In a ditch near a steep hillside, a young girl crawling onto the pavement trailed a smear of blood. She reached out to Gollins, tears staining a face that couldn't have been older than sixteen. "Help me," she said in a weak voice. Gollins shot her in the head.

Her men saw it. The ones who'd been resting stood up and started moving. Some didn't move fast enough and earned a kick in the ass. When she told one man to get up, he showed a bloody left hand and stayed in the grass. She touched the rifle barrel to his forehead. Eyes wide, he got up and joined the others moving forward.

She'd be damned if the boys would beat her to Shangri-La.

#

CHAPTER 72

I knew that if the feat was accomplished it must be at a most fearful sacrifice of as brave and gallant soldiers as ever engaged in battle.
General John Bell Hood

Los Griegos Peak, 6 miles as the crow flies north of Shangri-La
1654 hours, April 30

Bullets ricocheted off the Bradley's armor as it moved up the north slope of Los Griegos, the 10,000-foot peak overlooking their travel route on the south. APCs weren't built for climbing rugged mountains and Sati Bashara ordered it stopped a few hundred feet up. Three hundred yards ahead, an infidel bunker had his men pinned down as they tried to clear the mountain of enemy forces. Most of Rashū Regiment and all of Ayyub continued down Highway 4 as it headed for the ninety-degree turn from an east-west axis to one heading due south.

Bashara was eager to get back to the highway, but he couldn't leave infidels on his flank, and if his men could capture the summit of the mountain, they'd have a full view over the battlefield. He hadn't yet had to expend any 25mm ammunition, but the bunker had to be taken quickly and it was the only heavy weapon they had. The fortification was nothing elaborate, like so many of the other traps they'd encountered that day, just a stack of small tree trunks laid out in a triangle with an unknown number of enemy behind it. There was no cover, however, so when his men charged, they'd be cut to pieces and casualties had already been high. He ordered the Bushmaster brought to bear.

"Blessed General," said the gunner in Arabic, "I don't think the cannon will cut through those trees, unless, perhaps, we use all of our ammunition."

Bashara's initial instinct was to tell the man to shut up, but he stopped himself. Ammunition *was* precious and the gunner knew his weapon's capabilities far better than Bashara. "What do you suggest?"

"We have two missiles left."

"Those are our last two. There are no more."

"Yes, General."

Bashara thought about it. He didn't know much about TOW missiles, except that they were deadly. And the afternoon sun was beginning to wane... "Very well. Prepare to fire at the direct center of that fortification. And Tamid... do not miss."

"I will not, Blessed General."

Five seconds passed and then Bashara heard a loud *thunk*, like someone hitting an old plastic bucket, followed less than a second later by a loud explosion that sounded like a massive shotgun blast, followed by a *whoosh*. A red dot sped from the Bradley's TOW missile firing mount on the left side of the turret and raced away. Bashara watched it impact the bunker, but if the explosion was smaller than he'd expected, the effect was greater.

His men charged forward from a tree line 100 yards from the bunker and met no resistance. Instead the defenders fled up the slope, where they would be no danger to his attack. It was the previous year in reverse. Then, his men had been the ones unblooded against modern weapons, and when the artillery strike had hit them, they'd broken and fled. But now he commanded the combat veterans and it was his enemies who ran from a missile strike.

After turning the Bradley around, it was mere minutes before they were back on the highway, where Haleem met him with the latest news.

"There is a roadblock ahead, Sati, made from large trees and rocks. Many infidels are there. I believe it to be the last defensive position on this road. You should also know that we hear small arms fire coming from the east. It appears Mecca Regiment may have broken through."

"No!" Bashara barked. "That... *woman*..." He said the word like it tasted bad. "...will not beat us to the prize. Follow me!" He turned and called to the men passing by on both sides. "Follow me! Our next stop is the infidels' camp!"

The Bradley roared off toward the roadblock. Bashara told Tamid to be prepared to fire the last TOW missile and then use the Bushmaster to break through. Nothing was going to stop him from beating Tracy Gollins to the prize.

Nothing.

1700 hours

Would it work? Johnny Rainwater wondered, staring through a rifle port in the stone wall. The explosions and increased shooting at Highway 4 worried him, but he couldn't leave the wall until he knew the latest trap had worked. It should buy them time, at the least. But had they designed it correctly? *Would it work?*

Seconds later, he got his answer. Twenty of the enemy approached in five groups, spread out over a hundred-yard front. One hundred thirty yards from the wall, the group in the center ran forward, crouched and with rifles at the ready, and then disappeared into the ground. The group to their left and the one on the far left flank also vanished. A fourth group stopped and knelt, and Rainwater could tell they had been lagging behind and hadn't yet reached the trench. The fifth foursome kept coming beyond it, only kneeling once they had passed the danger zone. By sheer bad luck, they'd found the narrow causeway across the fire trench.

He turned his head and shouted behind him, "Light it!"

An older man fifteen feet back put his head into a hole in the ground and repeated the order. Rainwater heard the next man in the tunnel leading to the trench also yell the command, but not the ones after. He said a silent prayer that this would work.

The trench stretched across the entire valley floor for nearly one hundred fifty yards. It was eight feet wide and eight feet deep, and had taken three years to dig. At the bottom were the usual sharpened stakes, with the recent addition of a flammable mixture based on a formula found in some old books that called it Greek fire. The ingredients had taken a long time to find and assemble. Small-scale tests had showed that it worked, but spread across a long trench filled with dry grasses and anything else that would burn was a different matter. He pictured the men at the bottom either skewered or standing in puddles of the tar-like substance, sunk to their knees in branches and grasses. Those who weren't killed by the stakes or the fall would be calling for help.

"Come on," he said, staring for the slightest wisp of smoke. Three tunnels led to the trench. The last two feet of each one narrowed so a man couldn't crawl through without extensive digging, but would allow an outstretched arm to light the mixture with a torch.

Without warning, a sheet of flame erupted from the trench with a roar. Even so far away, Rainwater could hear the screams of men being burned alive. *Let's see them attack through* THAT!

Every rifle behind the wall concentrated either on one of the two narrow causeways over the trench, where flames licked at the edges, or the strips of land on either end of it. They didn't have long to wait. Four-man teams ran forward at all four spots and got hit by a wall of bullets. The homemade mortar started firing its homemade rounds, filled with old shards of glass, porcelain, and stones, chiefly quartzite, whose edges had been chiseled to a lethal sharpness. Flame rippled from the muzzles of the single-shot muskets, bolt-action hunting rifles, and the few semi-automatic rifles modified to automatic capability.

Of the first wave of Sevens, fifteen out of twenty fell before crossing the trench line. The survivors immediately dove to the dirt on the other side, the side closest to the wall, and opened fire at the rifle slits to cover another four groups. Rainwater took aim at one of the prone riflemen and pulled the trigger. He had the satisfaction of seeing the man's head knocked backward, after which the body twitched for a few seconds before lying still.

He pulled away from the rifle port at exactly the right moment. A bullet struck the inside wall of the slit and ricocheted harmlessly past him in a spray of rock splinters. Had he been peering through while reloading, the bullet would have hit him in the face. A glance down the wall showed two people lying in unmoving heaps, and a third crawling backward using one hand as blood poured from the other shoulder.

Once he'd reloaded, Rainwater didn't hesitate to stick his rifle into the slit. Bullets smacked around the outside wall as he took aim at one of the causeways, waiting for a target to appear. He only waited seconds and then fired at a large man in a flapping white robe and with something tied across his face, most likely to block the smoke. The heavy lead slug struck him dead center in the chest, right under the sternum. He jerked upright, and a man running behind hit him in the back. As Rainwater watched, both men toppled into the trench, and seconds later the flames there flared higher.

The next time he'd reloaded and sought another target, the leading Sevens had closed within sixty yards of the wall. Hundreds had now passed the trench. A sudden nausea twisted his stomach as he realized they didn't have enough firepower to stop them.

Highway 4, near Shangri-La
1507 hours, April 30

The trunk of the giant tree blocking Highway 4 had resisted efforts to blast a way through, even using one of the three TOW missiles carried by Muhdin's Bradley, one of which was a reload. Whatever the tree was, two RPGs and a TOW missile had blown a chunk out of its five-foot girth but hadn't come close to blasting a passage out of the dense wood. Now, instead of pushing forward, an intense firefight raked the highway and surrounding woods with a murderous buzzsaw of bullets. On the road, the infidels reloaded behind the impenetrable tree, popped up, aimed, and fired before his men could take aim. They did the same thing from the ground on either side, using piles of rocks or large boulders for cover. It didn't matter whether they hit his men or not; it kept them pinned down.

Muhdin stood behind his command Bradley about four hundred yards south of the main fighting. One of the crew loaded the third TOW into the empty launcher. A messenger from the stone wall told him about the fiery trap and how his men had charged into the intense rifle fire. Currently they were exchanging fire at a range of fifty yards and gathering for a final charge on the wall. Elsewhere, other messengers had brought him up to date on the progress made by Sati Bashara and the hated woman Tracy Gollins. Both seemed on the verge of breaking through to Shangri-La. Victory was at hand.

"Blessed General," called the Bradley's commander, "the Emir wants a report on our progress."

He wanted to swear. *He* was supposed to capture Shangri-La, not one of the others, and here he was held up by a damned tree! Going around wasn't really an option, either. On the southern side, the ground fell away in a sharp fifty-foot drop, and the northern side, while flatter, had a field of boulders left over from an ancient landslide. No, the only way was through that tree or over it, and that meant firepower.

"Commander, be ready to support an infantry push with the chain gun."

"What about the other missile?"

"No, it's time to bring up something bigger. Radio the Abrams to move forward and blast that thing out of our way."

#

CHAPTER 73

No man is an island entire of itself; every man
is a piece of the continent, a part of the main;
if a clod be washed away by the sea, Europe
is the less, as well as if a promontory were, as
well as any manner of thy friends or of thine
own were; any man's death diminishes me,
because I am involved in mankind.
- John Donne, MEDITATION XVII
Devotions upon Emergent Occasions

Mojave Desert, southeast of Groom Lake Air Force Facility
1642 hours, April 30

From ground level, the hiding spot for Angriff's Humvee meant it might as well have been invisible. Nobody could spot it clustered in the small opening in the jumble of boulders that had spilled from a low hill, not unless they followed the same path he had in parking it there. Between three walls of stone lay a bare patch large enough not only for the Humvee itself, but also to turn around. A short tunnel-like opening about fifteen feet long allowed access through an entrance to the west, which was why the two Rednecks setting up camp to the east hadn't seen him yet.

For the past two days, he'd seen helicopters in the distance, presumably hunting him. He'd also seen another contrail from something moving very fast, but too high for him to make sure it was a jet airplane, much like the night before he'd left with Colonel Young. So while it would be much more dangerous, Angriff had decided to travel only at night from then on out as he tried to find a way back to Arizona. With daylight fading and dark clouds in the west, it seemed the perfect time to pull out, except when he climbed to a point where he could scout the desert to the east, in his path he'd seen the two Rednecks building a fire.

He considered waiting to see if the storm hit that area, but there seemed little doubt. A dark cloud wall stretched from horizon to horizon. He could leave as it raged, but visibility grew dimmer with each passing minute; under such a storm, it might well be reduced to zero. Or he could wait it out and leave after it passed, except there was no way of knowing how long that would be. The only other option was to take off right away and get as far east as possible before it hit, except that meant getting past the two Rednecks.

His brain automatically ran through the plusses and minuses of each choice, the way it always did during combat, and within seconds he'd picked number three. He'd leave now. But what to do about the Rednecks? If he simply sped past them, they might pursue and, if they were dogged enough, catch up tomorrow after he stopped again. Or they might lead a patrolling helicopter to his trail. And what about those strange other flying things he'd seen way off in the distance, the ones that looked like men standing on top of a tiny flying saucer?

There was really only one choice.

Getting into the driver's seat, he checked both of his Desert Eagles to make sure each had a chambered round, strapped on his helmet, slipped on his sunglasses, started the Humvee, and pulled out of the natural revetment. The two horsemen's camp lay about five hundred yards east and the ground between them looked as flat as could be hoped for. Without hesitation or second thoughts, he pushed the gas pedal and accelerated past sixty miles per hour.

At such a speed, even small holes sent the Humvee bouncing and bottoming out. Something skittered out of his path, but Angriff was too focused on holding the vehicle straight to notice what. It took all of the immense strength in his wrists and forearms to keep it from flipping over, but slowing down wasn't an option; even doing sixty, he only closed the 1,500-foot distance at 88 feet per second, which left the Rednecks twenty seconds to react. The helmet softened the blows when his head slammed into the roof.

The wind had increased in promise of the coming storm, so neither man heard him until he'd closed within 200 yards. From the corner of his eye, he saw the horses jumping and pulling at their reins, and that distracted the men for another two seconds. They grew larger in his sight, the dirty red scarves standing out against their light clothing.

Five seconds out.

Both men saw him simultaneously and reached for their rifles. The one closest to his weapon grabbed it, pulled back the bolt, and got off a single shot as the Humvee hit a two-foot-high rise and bounded into the air. The shot went wild a microsecond before the right front tire landed on his chest and smashed it to jelly.

The Humvee bounced and spun to a stop in a swirl of dust and pebbles. Spinning tires sent a wave of rocks and dirt into the other Redneck's face. Blinded, he tried to keep his eyes open but couldn't, and lost orientation. With his rifle set to full automatic, he emptied it into a creosote bush to the northwest.

Angriff stepped out and drew an Eagle. As the Redneck stood in a pall of dust and tried to blindly change his empty magazine, Angriff closed within ten feet, aimed at the left side of the man's back, and fired. The huge bullet ripped through his heart and out his ribcage. Death was instantaneous.

Searching among their possessions, he took all the food and water, one M-16 — the other having been crushed under his tires — a total of nine loaded magazines, plus the empty one. He searched for and found his own ejected shell casing. He wanted to take the saddles with him, but he needed to move east before the storm hit so time didn't permit. Instead he cut the straps and untied the horses to fend for themselves. The fire he kicked out, scattering the ashes, while he dumped the bodies in a shallow depression and threw some stones on top. From running over the Redneck to getting back into the Humvee took no more than five minutes.

Angriff thought about lighting a cigar, but only had four left and decided to wait. It seemed callous somehow. He'd killed a lot of people in service to his country, but the stoic face he showed the outside world was just a façade. In truth he hated taking lives, regardless of how necessary their deaths might have been. It wouldn't slow him down, though; America's enemies chose their path, and once you chose an action you chose the inevitable equal and opposite reaction.

"Don't send to know for whom the bell tolls, Nick. It tolls for thee."

A minute later, he changed his mind and brought out a Habana Cubano Monte Cristo Number Three Especiales, inhaled the aroma of the unlit tobacco, and determined to light it the instant full darkness fell. He always mourned the enemies he was forced to kill, just not for very long.

#

CHAPTER 74

I'm hunting wabbits.
Elmer Fudd

Over the Mojave Desert southeast of Groom Lake Air Force Facility
1717 hours, April 30

The thunderstorm at their back towered dark gray and black, with lightning flashes high in the towering clouds. It was less of a problem as long as they flew east, although the closer it got the worse the downdrafts became. But unless they hurried, when they turned back they'd have to fly right through it and that would not be fun.

"Dust cloud at two o'clock," Pra Sakoya said into her helmet mike. "Bearing one three five." She lowered the binoculars and turned toward the pilot, Ted Wang. "It's gotta be him."

"I've got it," Wang said.

Tank Girl responded to his touch like a lover, the bank to the southeast done so gently that he didn't feel his body tighten against the minimal G-forces. Wang had to admit that Rossi and her crew knew their way around an AH-72. He'd never had one of the flying tanks feel so responsive, so... *right*. He wondered if Randall had modified it somehow and made a mental note to find out. After all, if Randall and Carlos never came back, *Tank Girl* would be his and he was already picking out potential new names. *Asian Avenger* was leading so far.

Despite the storm to their west, sunlight poured through the Comanche's overhead canopy and would have blinded them if not for their anti-glare visors. But while they could see, even with the air-conditioning cranked to max, the UV radiation heated the cockpit until he felt sweat running inside his flight suit.

When Wang's right hand touched the throttle, Sakoya spoke up. "Do you wanna do that?"

"If I don't, we might lose him. That storm's movin' fast."

"If you say so."

They turned heads toward each other, despite being unable to see past the dark helmet visors. He and Cochran had only been a team for six months and he didn't want her to misread his deeper voice tone, or that it signaled his disagreement with her analysis. He wanted her to tell everybody back home how mission-oriented he was, how determined, just in case somebody else tried to make a case for taking over *Tank Girl.*

Then he glanced at the instrument panel, more to mollify Cochran than anything else. Fuel showed a hair under half full. Air speed indicated one hundred forty knots. He knew instantly how much flying time they had left at their current speed, factoring in altitude and weather, and how much they would lose by increasing to maximum. She had a point.

He finally responded to her last statement. "It's a good call, Pra. We've got less time than I thought we did, but I still want to check out that dust cloud."

"Thank you," she said, and he heard the surprise in her voice. He didn't hand out compliments very often.

Wang smiled, even though she couldn't see it. *Perfect.*

———

Fine yellow dust coated the Humvee's windshield despite the wipers moving at full speed. Although his run at the Rednecks had topped sixty, Angriff otherwise tried to maintain a steady forty miles an hour speed lest he break an axle or blow a tire, but over the rough terrain even that was too high to be realistic. He'd slowed to twenty when a deep hole appeared ten feet to the front. Jerking the wheel left, he barely missed going front-first into the depression. For a few bumpy yards he steered due north, and that was when he saw it — the glint of sun off a distant helicopter.

The left rear tire hit another hole, and pain lanced through his buttocks and up his spine. He squinted through the swishing wipers and tried to see the helicopter again, but while driving there was simply too much dust, so he stopped and left the engine idling. Fresh winds drove the dust cloud to the east, a sign of the storm coming out of the west. Standing on the door frame, he blocked the overhead sun as best he could and used his hands as sunscreens. This time he got a better look at the aircraft, which was unmistakably an AH-72.

Shit!

Had they seen him? It was hard to tell the helicopter's attitude at that range, but within ten seconds he knew, without a doubt, that it had changed course directly for him. Without wasting another second, he jumped back in, turned around, and headed back the way he'd come, directly at the towering black clouds.

Within fifty yards he stopped. The winds screamed over the desert, throwing rocks and dirt against the windshield like a giant badger burrowing underground. He couldn't see anything and the Comanche had to be closing in. With no other choice, he turned around a second time and sped east. With any luck, the winds would be too much for the Comanche.

———

When Sakoya had first spotted the telltale cloud of something fast moving over the desert, it had been eight or ten miles distant. As they flew toward it at an increasingly dangerous speed, however, it vanished, dissipated by the increasing winds ahead of the thunderstorm. Four long minutes later, they flew over the spot where both of them estimated it should be.

"I've got negative visual," she said.

"Winds are increasing. We've only got a few minutes left. Look for tire tracks."

"I can't see much through all that blowing dust."

Wang throttled down to eighty knots and dropped to one hundred feet altitude. Increasing winds buffeted the giant helicopter and Cochran felt herself first thrown upward and then sideways, but she never stopped scanning the desert floor.

"I'm heading for Creech."

"No, there, look!" The dust cloud thinned enough to see the desert below and Sakoya pointed to fresh tracks in the dirt on the leeside of a hill. Wang turned *Tank Girl* sharply to the left, then eased back on the throttle. They picked up an immediate tailwind, and then it swirled, coming first from the southwest, then the northwest, then the west, and back again. Keeping the Comanche trimmed took all of Wang's concentration. If they didn't spot Angriff within two or three minutes, they'd have to *gitfoh.*

———

Angriff's shoulder hit the doorframe as the Humvee lurched left, bouncing and jostling him like rattling dice before throwing craps. He followed no road, only the curves and undulations of the moonlike landscape of the eastern Nevada desert. After hitting a deep hole, he crested a small hill and slammed on the brakes. Thirty feet directly ahead of where he stopped, a fifteen-foot-wide ravine cut the desert floor like cracks inside an overripe watermelon.

Climbing out of the Humvee, he felt something running down his left temple and touched a sticky, dirt-covered streak of blood running from a shallow cut. He didn't know when it had happened and didn't at that moment care. Running to the edge of the crevice, he looked down, hoping it was shallow and might offer a hiding place. Swirling dirt got in his eyes, but instead of being ten feet deep, as he'd hoped, the bottom was at least one hundred down.

He heard the *whump whump whump* of helicopter blades even over the wind, and he knew his time was nearly up. They'd caught him. But as he looked at the ravine's walls below the lip, filled with holes and cracks, and then estimated the distance across the yawning gap to the other side, a desperate plan formed.

The slackening of winds didn't last long and dust clouds again made it feel like flying under the waters of a muddy river. Wang keyed his mike to tell Pra they were turning for home when he glimpsed something to one side. "Tire tracks at one o'clock!"

"Roger that. I've got 'em," she said as Wang added thrust. *Tank Girl* moved that way even as the gust front buffeted her. They'd gone half a mile when the tracks led over a fifty-foot-high dune... and straight into a ravine beyond. Flying over at three hundred feet, they both stared into the darkness at the bottom and saw yellow-orange flames billowing upward from a wrecked Humvee.

"Oh, shit," Sakoya said. "Oh, shit, oh, shit."

"Keep it professional, Pra."

She'd forgotten that her mike was on. "Sorry. I can't see much, but there's no way a man could survive that fall. It must be at least a hundred feet. Not to mention the explosion."

"I agree that nobody could survive that. And even without this weather, the ravine's too narrow for us to get down there to verify. It'll take grappling gear. See if you can raise Prime and tell them what we found."

"Overtime Prime, this is Ripsaw Real," Cochran said. There hadn't been time to change call signs. "Over."

Hovering in high winds was dangerous. They were reminded how dangerous when a strong downdraft drove them from 200 feet to 50 in less than three seconds. Wang said nothing as Sakoya told Prime what they'd done and seen. He was too busy trying to keep the helicopter in the air. Finally stabilized and back up to 500 feet, he firewalled the throttle and headed due east. Once far enough ahead of the storm, he turned south, then west back to Creech.

"Ripsaw Real, this is Prime, copy three." Their signal was understandable, but only with difficulty. Cochran thought she knew all of the comm. people who usually dealt with the attack squadrons, but this one was unfamiliar. "Be aware that radio protocol two is in place."

Sakoya looked up at that, to see if Wang reacted the way she did. Protocol two meant imminent threat of a compromised transmission. Even so, the emotions of the moment choked her and Sakoya had to clear her throat before continuing the radio call. "Whiskey tango foxtrot, Prime. Over."

At that, Wang's helmet snapped around to look at her. Sakoya could almost hear both his and the woman's teeth grinding in anger, but for some reason, in that moment, she didn't care. She'd only met Angriff once, but that had been enough. He was a man whose death was worth grieving.

The radiowoman's voice was curt. "Maintain radio discipline, Ripsaw Real."

"HVT found," she said, with as much *fuck you* flavoring in the words as she could muster. "Target is no longer operative. Over."

"Say again, Ripsaw Real."

"The target's Humvee is on fire at the bottom of a hundred-foot-deep ravine. No survivors were observed. Do you copy that, Prime? No survivors. I'm sending map coordinates. Over."

"Target is... destroyed?"

"Affirmative. Ripsaw Real out."

Neither she nor Wang spoke for a few seconds. Once they'd cleared the immediate danger zone of the fast-moving storm, they both raised their visors.

"I never thought I'd see this day," she said. "It's like a legend is gone."

"Yeah," Wang said. "Him and his son-in-law both. It's a damned shame."

Even inside his helmet, she could see his smile, and wanted to hit him.

#

CHAPTER 75

Therefore take up the whole armor of God, that you may be able to withstand in the evil day, and having done all, to stand.
Ephesians 6:13

Shangri-La
1718 hours, April 30

From atop the ridge, Lieutenant Hakala saw the battlefield spread out below. Using the binoculars, in the far distance he could make out some sort of attack against a fixed position, but up close the picture was much clearer. Half a mile away, a huge tree blocked the highway. On one side were people in civilian clothing shooting all types of weapons to try and hold back a large number of men wearing white robes, men he recognized from the previous year: Sevens. The fighting spilled into the land on either side of the road. What he didn't see were RPGs. Hakala felt certain they had some, but not seeing them brandished made him think there might not be too many.

Then he heard a sound that was unmistakable to the ears of Americans who drove armored vehicles: the hammering sound of an M242 Bushmaster chain gun. Trees blocked his view of part of the highway, but only a few vehicles mounted such a gun and all of his were accounted for. Was it somehow another Marine LAV-25? Or any Army vehicle? In his heart, he knew it was neither.

"Anybody got a line of sight on what's shooting that Bushmaster out on the highway?" he said over the inter-vehicle frequency.

"Trees are in the way," replied his EO, the commander of Bravo One, situated fifty feet to his right. "But I've got a partial sighting on a military vehicle. Stand by, Alpha One, am dismounting for a better look."

As he waited, Hakala could make out more details of the battle. The Sevens had rushed the big tree and were trying to get over it, while the people of Shangri-La fought them off. He swept the glasses up and to the north and there, flying in the breeze like something out of a movie, was a giant American flag, colors shining so bright they seemed iridescent.

Over the screams and gunshots of battle, a deep and distant *boom* rolled over the fields. Once again the sound was known to every American soldier.

"Alpha One," called the commander of Alpha Two, "did you hear that?"

"I heard it."

"That was a tank cannon, Loot."

"I know."

"Didn't sound like one of ours."

"It wasn't. That's a one-oh-five."

"Shit, what carries a one-oh-five?"

They both got their answer before Hakala could respond. "Alpha One, there's a fucking Bradley down there with Arabic scribbling on its side. It looks to be supporting an infantry attack."

"We can take out a Bradley if we have the element of surprise."

"Yeah, but we can't take out the tank that's five hundred yards south and closing."

It only took Hakala seconds to recognize the situation, and what had made the explosion they'd heard a few seconds before. "That's an M1 Abrams, boys. Carries a 105-millimeter rifled cannon, enough to tear these cans apart."

"That thing'll blow that tree out of the way in no time. What do we do, Loot?"

"All right, Bravo One, you head north on that highway and see if anything's coming this way. Alpha Two, station your vehicle behind that tree blocking the highway and assist the defense."

"What about you, Loot Hack?"

He knew they used the term out of fondness, but he still hated that nickname. "I'm gonna radio a sitrep to Kicker and then deal with that Bradley and the Abrams."

"You can't fight an Abrams with an LAV."

"So I've been told."

#

Chapter 76

Let me go now into the land where only dwell the lost,
For I have done my duty as I saw it, but at fearful cost.
Tomb along the Appian Way outside of Rome

Near Gallup, New Mexico
1722 hours, April 30

For what seemed like the fiftieth time, Captain Sully started to have their field radio operator request a situation report from Field Goal, the radio call sign for Lieutenant Hakala's First Platoon, and for what seemed like the fiftieth time he stopped himself. You either trusted your subordinates to report at the earliest possible time or you didn't. So outwardly he kept a stoic demeanor while inwardly wanting to scream.

"Kicker, this is Field Goal, do you copy?"

Finally! "Roger that, Punter. What does the smart bird eat?"

"The early worm, over."

"Affirmative, over to you, Field Goal."

Hakala reported their position and the battle unfolding below them in succinct detail, including the presence of the Bradley, the confirmation of at least one M1 Abrams, and the likelihood of a second. Sully folded his arms and closed his eyes as he listened, trying to visualize the scene for himself. Distortion wasn't too bad, which he owed to Punter being on a high ridge.

When Hakala finished, Sully took the receiver from the operator. "Roger that, Field Goal, sitrep received." He wanted to say *out* and end the conversation there, but he couldn't. That would be hanging Hakala out to dry. "What are your proposed courses of action? Over."

He knew what was coming even as he repeated a plea in his mind: *don't say it, don't say it, for God's sake, please don't say it.* But he knew that Hakala would say it, and right on time, he did.

"Request permission to engage hostile forces."

"By hostile, do you mean Sevens?"

"Affirmative."

Sully figuratively lifted his boot and stepped into the Rubicon. "Permission granted, on my authority. This is a direct order for you to intervene on behalf of citizens flying the American flag. Do you copy?"

"Affirmative. Field Goal out." Without his noticing, every single person with a reason to be near the CP, and some who didn't, had listened in. When Sully spotted First Sergeant Meyer, he gave the order. "Assemble the company," he said. "At least..." He let a faint crease to the corner of his mouth serve as a smile. "...those who aren't already here."

More than one hundred people surrounded him, so many that Sully had to climb on the back of his LAV-25 to be heard. Once there, he didn't have to ask for quiet. As the waning afternoon sun lit him like a spotlight, nobody else spoke, or even whispered.

"First Platoon is at this moment actively engaged in the defense of the place called Shangri-La. This community lies more than one hundred miles to the east and flies the American flag over its compound, which to me indicates that it falls under our mission of liberating and protecting anyone with allegiance to the United States of America. To that end, First Platoon asked for and I granted permission to use any means necessary to accomplish that mission. I will soon pull out to support them.

"However, as you may have heard, General Steeple has taken command of Operation Overtime in place of General

Angriff, and has ordered us to stand down in the face of our enemy. We are not to engage in combat with the forces we refer to as Sevens, not even in self-defense. My orders to First Platoon violate that order from the commanding general. To put it bluntly, I'm disobeying a direct order because I believe that order is morally wrong and possibly illegal.

"But I can't order any of you to do the same. If I do, and you obey me, then all I will have done is throw the onus onto you of proving why you obeyed my orders. That's not fair. Anyone who wishes to accompany my crew and I, we will accommodate as long as space allows. For those who wish to stay behind, no ill will or stigma will attach to you, since you will actually be the one in compliance with orders from above. Are there any questions?"

Only one man raised his hand. "Is time of the essence, Cap?"

Sully nodded. "It is."

"Then with all due respect, sir, why are we still standing around here?"

#

CHAPTER 77

When you're slapped you'll take it and like it.
Sam Spade

Overtime Prime
1729 hours, April 30

With Master Sergeant Schiller's help, Amunet Mwangi had set up a makeshift office in the Crystal Palace's small conference room. She was busily leafing through a report from Chain Saw about the state of readiness of Overtime's spread-out forces when a priority message popped up on the computer monitor. She scanned it, printed it, and took it into the office of the commanding general, where Steeple leaned back reading something on his tablet. He looked up with a questioning expression she knew very well.

"Sitrep from Task Force Kicker."

Steeple closed and rubbed his eyes. "All of these code names give me a headache. Who is Kicker again?"

"Dog Company, 1st Marine Light Recon Battalion. They're over in New Mexico."

"Make a note to change their designation to Delta Company, not Dog. This isn't 1950. Now, what about them?"

"One of their platoons on a long-range reconnaissance has met and engaged in combat with an army of Sevens."

Steeple stiffened, laid the tablet aside, and leaned his elbows on the desk. When he clasped his fingers as if in prayer, Mwangi knew what would come next — narrowed eyes and a soft, dangerous voice. "Did I not order them to avoid conflict with the forces of the Caliphate regardless of the circumstances?"

"That you did, Tom. That you did."

"And they acknowledged receipt of the message?"

"They did."

"So this is direct disobedience."

"It gets worse. The remainder of Dog Company is on the move to support First Platoon."

"So a whole company is in mutiny?"

"That's about the size of it."

His face turned so red she thought he might have a stroke. "Warn them that unless they comply with my orders immediately, they will be considered a rogue unit and enemy of the brigade. As such, they will be open to any and all possible retaliatory actions, including artillery and air strikes."

Mwangi hesitated. She'd never seen her boss that angry before. Usually she could talk him out of his more damaging orders issued during a tantrum, but this time she wasn't sure that she could. "Is that really a good idea?"

"That is an *order*, Colonel! Have two Golden Eagles fuel and arm themselves with anti-armor packages, and order the artillery battalion to ready its fastest road machines to prepare for movement."

"Okay," she said, stunned by his vehemence. This wasn't the Tom Steeple she knew. "They'll need escort."

"See to it."

"Yes, sir."

"We're going to put the fear of God into those bastards, do you hear me? Better yet, the fear of Tom Steeple... I want to crucify them. God, I hate Marines. Do we have any other units in the vicinity?"

"We do, Tom, another Marine company. Echo, not far north of Dog Company."

"Would they respond to my order to oppose their fellow Marines?"

Mwangi paused and ran a tongue over her lips. "They're also marching to the sound of the guns."

<hr />

1730 hours

Muhdin knew the M1 with him on Highway 4 had nine rounds of ammunition left, while Bashara's only had eight. Five of those nine rounds were armor-piercing, largely useless against most non-fortified targets, but an excellent choice for smashing through a massive tree. It took a little while for the tank to clank its way forward, and he used the time to clear the highway of men and debris, offering a clear target ahead. Five hundred yards from the fallen bur oak it stopped, rocking back and forth on a worn-out suspension.

Once the gun had stabilized, it fired. The round raced past hundreds of men lying in roadside ditches with a *shoop* sound. In less than a second it passed over the tree, over the heads of the people behind the tree, and out of sight. Muhdin cursed. How could they miss at that range?

The second round struck dead center on the bole and blew the tree in two. Wood splinters cut down defenders in a fifty-foot swath around the blast site. The Abrams fired a third round before Muhdin could stop it and that one struck to the right of the first hit, completely blasting one half of the tree off the road and opening the highway to traffic.

With a roar, the Pir Baba Regiment rose and charged the opening. Two defenders showed themselves in the gap between the two halves of the tree and were cut to pieces by the Bradley's chain gun. Here and there an infidel stood up and fired, and a few of his men fell, but the vast majority didn't. They poured through the opening and began to spread out. Muhdin climbed aboard his Bradley and ordered it forward. The turret rotated this way and that, looking for targets.

———

Muhdin was thirty yards before the shattered tree when his men began streaming backward, *away* from Shangri-La, with tracers zipping past and through them. One man had his left leg vaporized by a direct hit, collapsed to one side, but used his remaining leg and arms to pull himself forward until a second shell shattered his head like a pumpkin. Images of the previous year flashed through Muhdin's mind, when his men had disappeared over a hill only to come

426

streaming back in the face of cannonfire from American AFVs. Surely Allah could not be cruel enough to allow that to happen again?

"Ready your other TOW missile," he commanded. "Load the main cannon with armor-piercing rounds."

"Armor-piercing, Blessed General?"

"Do it!"

Ten seconds later, an eight-wheeled armored vehicle sped past the tree so fast it nearly rolled over to the left. Several of his men were run down before they could move. Clearly seen on its side was a white star.

"Fire, fire!" Muhdin screamed.

The gunner fired the TOW, which theoretically shouldn't miss since it was wire-guided. But the new machine moved too fast directly toward them, as if it intended to ram, and the missile flew harmlessly past it on the right. Nor could the Bradley's turret track fast enough to take aim. But ten yards from the Bradley in the two o'clock position, the American machine opened fire with its own Bushmaster.

At point blank range, the 25mm armor-piercing rounds easily penetrated the Bradley's defensive armor, exploding and chopping up the men inside like a butcher grinding meat and fat for sausage. Standing in the commander's hatch, Muhdin felt a searing pain across his stomach, and then something hot and wet drenched his pants. The Bradley shuddered under repeated hits and smoke curled up from within the hull.

The strange enemy vehicle circled and fired more rounds into it from the left side. Muhdin pushed up with his arms to get out as red hot steel splinters peppered his arms. Flames licked at his feet, but he felt a weight holding him down. Reaching down, he felt the body of the vehicle commander leaning against his legs. By touch, Muhdin realized the big shells had blown off half of the man's head.

Bleeding and with agony radiating from the wound in his upper groin, the general gritted his teeth and pushed himself free of the mangled turret. The eight-wheeled enemy vehicle had come around and stopped. He'd swung his legs over the side and was about to jump down when two things happened within microseconds. The enemy Bushmaster tracked toward him and stopped, and Muhdin looked down its barrel. Then something supersonic zipped by the fatally wounded Bradley and struck the enemy directly in the glacis plate. It blew up with such violence that the turret flew into the air, and kept blowing up as secondary explosions rent the twisted metal.

Sitting on the now flaming Bradley, Muhdin stared at the equally flaming mass twenty yards down the highway, trying to understand what had just happened. Then it dawned on him: the M1! A 105mm shell had crushed the American. Limping away from his own burning AFV, he realized with a start that there was still ammunition there to cook off, including the remaining TOW missile and most of a load of fuel.

Two of his men let him loop an arm over their shoulders, and they helped carry him fifty yards down the road before internal explosions began to wrack the Bradley. Only after they helped him sit did Muhdin see the drying blood and gobs of gray stuck to his pants from the vehicle commander's brain.

Horrified, all he could think was to get the pants off. He stood to unbuckle his belt when new cannonfire erupted. A dust trail from down the ridge at his back followed a second enemy vehicle which had come up behind the M1 and fired into its vulnerable rear with its Bushmaster. With his pants halfway down, Muhdin could only stare in horror as the Abrams absorbed hit after hit.

#

CHAPTER 78

Duty is the essence of manhood.
Lt. General George S. Patton

Shangri-La
1732 hours, April 30

Even at a range of thirty feet, Lieutenant Hakala couldn't be certain his rounds would penetrate the Abrams' rear. It was, after all, a main battle tank, and the LAV-25 was distinctly defined as *not* being an AFV. But the one most vulnerable area of an M1 was the rear and his gunner put round after round into the engine and fuel area. The grinding whine of the tank's engine increased, like someone hitting the gas while in first gear, and then abruptly shut down. Smoke curled from cracks in the hull.

Nearby Sevens opened up with rifles, spraying the thinly armored LAV from close range. Worse, instead of bailing out of the injured tank, the crew decided to fight it out. While the Bushmaster kept hammering its rear, the big turret began to slowly rotate. Hakala knew the Abrams had emergency hand cranks to operate the turret in case it lost engine power. He could only stay in place for a few more seconds. Either the gun would do to them what it had already done to Alpha Two, or the Sevens would bring up an RPG. Fortunately for him and his crew, the gun had been aimed directly forward and it took a long time for it to rotate one hundred eighty degrees so it could bear on the LAV. It made it to about one hundred twenty degrees before fire reached the Abrams' fuel tank.

Both Hakala and his gunner had been inside the turret, so when the tank exploded the rain of shrapnel and flaming fuel didn't kill them instantly. The blast wave shook it like an angry mob overturning a police car.

"Back up, back up!" Hakala yelled into the intercom mike, trying to keep his voice calm. Through the periscope, he made sure nothing obstructed their rear, and saw stunned and injured Sevens scattered everywhere from the Abrams' blast wave. Several of them lay in the highway. He watched one man on his hands and knees, in their path, look up and see the LAV speeding toward him. Instead of scrambling away, he raised an arm. Hakala watched his face stretch in terror and then felt the *bump bump bump bump* of the LAV's eight big tires flattening him into the asphalt.

One hundred yards south of the still exploding Abrams, he called for a stop and climbed out onto the turret, holding the fire extinguisher. Burning gasoline had shattered both headlights, and the two spare tires slung under the downward-angled front had caught fire. Hakala inhaled smoke filled with bits of melted rubber and coughed. Then, as if things weren't bad enough, two Sevens between them and the Abrams started firing at him. They missed and the bullets ricocheted into the woods, but it would only take seconds for them to correct their aim.

Then the hammering chatter of their M240 7.62mm machine gun added to the general chaos. Both Sevens flew backward under multiple hits. While his gunner gave him cover, Hakala put the fires out, even though he had to dismount to finally extinguish the tires.

Once he'd climbed back into the commander's seat, the driver got on the intercom. "We're sittin' ducks, Loot!"

He took two seconds to decide between going back up the ridge, where they'd make a perfect target for an RPG, or racing down the highway into Shangri-La. His brain instantly decided there was enough room to get by the Abrams, although with ammunition still cooking off it was risky. But the smoke palls from the Abrams, the Bradley, and Alpha Two's LAV-25 worked as well as smoke grenades for blocking vision.

"Go!" he said. "Straight down the highway past that tree!"

Without hesitation, the driver hit the gas and the LAV accelerated past forty miles per hour. At that speed they couldn't avoid any unexpected dangers, but hitting them without an RPG was nearly impossible. Swerving in and out of smoke clouds and squishing bodies, they rocketed past the tank, the Bradley, and their own comrades in the flaming LAV without incident, and made it past the tree into the relative safety of Shangri-La.

1738 hours

Abigail Deak sat with her back against the bole of a still-standing bur oak as explosion after explosion threw shrapnel into the other side of the tree. The last thing she'd seen was a second one of those strange green... she didn't know what else to call it other than *tank*... show up and start shooting at the other tank, the one that had blown up the tree thirty feet from where she now sat. She peeked around the tree and watched flames come out of the big one until a sheet of flame rose high into the sky and sent some huge piece of the tank flying skyward. Hot pieces of metal fell like hail as she pressed against the oak in a tight ball.

She didn't realize she was panting until the green eight-wheeled tank with the white star roared past the tree and stopped thirty yards up the highway. Somebody screamed in pain and Abigail saw others rushing to help someone who lay on the pavement, a jagged piece of metal sticking out of his leg.

Some switch in her brain clicked into place and she ran toward the green tank, waving her arms and shouting for nobody to shoot. The people in the tank could only be the Americans they'd heard rumors about and she didn't want any of her people firing at them by mistake.

When she stopped beside it, a hatch on the top opened and a man wearing some sort of rounded helmet appeared and looked down at her. "You need to get back under cover, ma'am. This isn't over yet."

"Are you the Americans?"

"Better! We're the Marines."

431

1751 hours

Like the Texicans at the Alamo, Johnny Rainwater and the defenders of Shangri-La stood fast trying to defend the five-foot-high wall blocking outlet from the Valley of Death. The Sevens had rushed over the bodies of their own wounded to get at the infidels and reached the wall. Some climbed and made it over to grapple with the defenders on the other side, while most got a rifle butt or bullet in the face. Several held their rifles over the wall and shot down without looking, until the infidels learned to snatch the guns out of their hands.

Both sides shot through the rifle ports in the wall. In one case, a young girl aimed at the knee of a Seven, but before she could fire, he dropped to a crouch and pointed his own gun at her. They fired simultaneously and both fell backward, dead.

Sheer numbers had pushed the Sevens over the wall and the defense was near collapse when reinforcements arrived.

The ten-foot-high walls on either side of the valley had not been attacked, so the defenders gathered there left a skeleton watch guard and ran to assist at the valley wall. With the new infusion of energy, the fight became a melee of rifle butts, pistols, knives, teeth, and fists. Cannonfire coming from the west went unheard over the tumult.

One boy of sixteen tried to choke a Seven, but wasn't strong enough. Thrown onto his back, he stared as the Seven swung his rifle around to fire, but a lifetime in the desert had given him reflexes a normal teenager wouldn't have. He rolled to his left as the shot plowed into the dirt where his head had been, pulled a knife from his boot, and threw it from his knees. It dug deep into the man's side and blood immediately stained his dirty robe. Screaming in pain, he climbed back over the wall.

A tremendous blast from the direction of the highway echoed over the desert, followed by more explosions. Within a minute, shouts of *Tarajue! Retreat!* sent the Sevens flying back over the wall and down the valley. A few defenders sent shots after them, but most simply bent over and gasped for breath.

Johnny Rainwater rose to hands and knees, then stood, wobbly, and felt blood running from a cut over his right eye. He wasn't sure exactly what had happened, except that somehow they'd driven back the Sevens.

#

CHAPTER 79

My prayer is that when I die, all Hell rejoices that I am out of the fight.
C.S. Lewis

Sulphur Creek, New Mexico
1803 hours, April 30

Shadows covered half the old parking lot of a single-story motel. The firefight to capture the place had been short and violent. Now, having a wide space gave the Mecca Regiment a chance to rest, regroup, and treat their wounded. Tracy Gollins hated the delay, but even she realized that her men had been fighting all day and needed the break. So she gave them fifteen minutes and then the attack would continue. Twilight came early under the forest canopy, after which further attacks would be too risky.

She didn't show the worry she felt. The explosion they'd heard earlier hadn't been close, yet even at such a distance she knew it had been huge, which could have been either good or bad. Being a pessimist, she assumed it was bad. The closer small arms fire wasn't such a mystery; it could only be Sati Bashara with the Rasūl and Ayyub Regiments.

Less than a quarter mile ahead, Highway 126 joined the leg of Highway 4 running east-west from Los Alamos, and both turned south toward Shangri-La. The Y-shaped crossroad had the largest barrier yet of boulders and felled trees, which no doubt had infidels behind it in strength. Flanking it through the dense woods would require more men than she had left, thus the need to join with Bashara's two regiments. Between them they would have at least 2,000 men, more than enough to smash their way through.

But damn, did she hate sharing credit with that pompous little shit Bashara. It was a good thing they'd taken a prisoner during the fight for the motel. Torturing him would be a little bit of fun before she had to be nice to the Caliph's asshole nephew.

1804 hours

"How did that vile *woman* beat us to the crossroads, Haleem? How did she do it?"

"I would not dishonor your uncle by answering that question, Sati."

"Dishonor him? Do you think she is a servant of Satan?"

"I did not say that."

Sati Bashara rubbed his chin. "Perhaps you should," he said in a low voice.

"What?"

"Nothing. It is not important. The day grows late. We will let the men rest ten more minutes and then we will capture this accursed place. It has cost too much blood already. Bring up the tank."

1805 hours

Johnny Rainwater wanted nothing more than to soak in the hot springs and then sleep. Everything in his body hurt, every muscle and joint and especially his head. Drying blood got into his eye and he'd wiped it away with his fingers, but that only replaced the blood with dirt. Sweat had turned the dust coating him into a paste. He only cleared his vision by pouring water from his canteen into the affected eye.

Once the daze wore off, he staggered around trying to help the wounded. Everywhere, the people of Shangri-La knelt beside the bodies of their friends and loved ones, some dead, some dying, and some wounded, binding their wounds with whatever was at hand and getting them off the battlefield.

"Go to the sanctuary," he said, walking among them. "Women, stand to the wall in case the Sevens come back. Men, help the injured back to the sanctuary. Hurry!"

He helped a middle-aged woman named Harriet to her feet. Her simple white shirt had a big red stain on one side. Looping one of her arms over his shoulder, he began to help her walk back to the main compound called the Sanctuary, but she shrugged him off and told him to help someone else.

But as his head cleared, Rainwater remembered he was in charge of the entire defense, not just the wall. His anxious horse was still tethered, so he climbed into the saddle and rode to Highway 4. Most of the shooting had stopped and he needed to find out why.

1812 hours

Sati Bashara didn't like eating or drinking in sight of his men, in case he spilled something. He was their leader and refused to show weakness to them in any form. While awaiting the arrival of his fellow general, the despicable Tracy Gollins, he retreated up a heavily wooded hill with a canteen of water and some corn cakes and dried beef. The canteen was U.S. Army surplus and made of metal, so the water bordered on being hot and had a metallic taste. Fried in corn oil, the corn cakes left a greasy residue on his fingers, while chewing the leather-like beef made his jaw hurt. After he'd ripped off the third chunk of meat, he took a swig of water and chewed the mixture just enough so he could swallow.

Bashara heard the Bradley before it rounded the curve 200 yards to the west. The pitch of the engine's roar was higher than the supply trucks of his army, and much higher than that of the Abrams. General Muhdin had split the available tank ammunition evenly, so his Abrams had the same nine rounds as the one Muhdin had kept with his own command. But neither his Bradley nor Gollins' had a full load of ammo now, and he assumed that Muhdin's did.

Without him realizing it, his lip curled when her Bradley came to a stop in front of his. She stepped out and approached Haleem, directly below where he ate. Her walk reminded him of a well-used whore, stiff and bow-legged, and he thought she looked more like a cow than a woman. Nor did she have any reason for being there; war was men's work. A woman had no place on the battlefield.

But the Emir had made it crystal clear that this hideous female was the exception, the *sole* exception, to that law as laid down in the New Prophet's supplement to the Koran. He didn't know the Caliph's feelings on the matter and knew that asking would have to be done very carefully. Bashara had worked hard to earn his uncle's trust, and with no male heirs, the Emir recently had begun treating him like his successor. Now this bitch had showed up. It seemed unlikely that she would ever ascend to a religious rank such as Superior Imam or Emir, but she wasn't supposed to be a general, either, and yet here she was. And he had to cooperate with her to achieve their mutual goal.

Having finished eating, Bashara crossed his arms and waited for her to walk up to him, because he'd be damned if he'd go to her. Under lowered brows, he watched her speak with Haleem, until one of the Bradley's crew called out and waved for Haleem to come over. From the look on the man's face, Bashara thought, *This does not look good.*

Moments later, Haleem looked up the ridge and waved. "Sati!" His voice barely carried up, but he heard it clearly. "We have new orders!"

"Not a moment too soon," he said, as all around him the shadows deepened under the trees. Once down the slope and standing beside Haleem, he crossed his arms again and said one word to her by way of greeting. "General."

"Hello, Sati," she said, with the barest hint of a smile at one corner of her mouth. Women were not supposed to address men by their given name unless they were a relative, but among men of equal status it was common. It was her way of reminding him that a woman held rank equal to his.

"My generals," Haleem said before either of them could insult the other, "General Muhdin has new instructions. We are to hold in place and prepare for further attacks, but *not* to attack until specifically told to. It seems the forces under the command of General Muhdin were ambushed by some- thing none of us expected... the Americans."

"How can that be?" Bashara said. "We are hundreds of miles from the last place we encountered them."

"I cannot say, Sati. The man operating the general's radio said they lost both the tank and their Bradley."

"Was it the big man with his pistols? Did they say?"

"No, only that Americans were now inside Shangri-La."

"We cannot let this stop us," said Gollins. "We have rest- ed and are ready to attack, Sati. You have an Abrams and between us we have three Bradleys and three regiments. The only thing left between us and the home of the infidels are some trees piled on the road. We can blast through them and win this fight before nightfall, but we must act now."

Something inside Bashara knew she was right, which triggered the opposite response. If they attacked and won, she would get half of the credit or more. Even failure was preferable to that, particularly since he would only be follow- ing orders. "I cannot disobey Muhdin."

"Sati, listen to me. How do we know that more Americans are not on the way? If we attack now, before they have orga- nized, we can still achieve victory. But now is the time, not later and not tomorrow. Now."

He wanted to say *yes*. He *knew* he should yes, that Muhdin was wrong. But capturing this Shangri-La place was only one stepping stone to his ultimate objective and both Gollins and Muhdin could be obstacles to achieving that. "No," he said. "I will obey orders."

"Then give me the Abrams. Or have it fire two or three times to blow up those logs and leave the rest to me. You know it's the smart move; you *know* it."

Yes, he thought. *I do. It's a brilliant move... for you.* "No!"

She motioned Bashara a few feet away, leaned in close, and lowered her voice so that only Bashara could hear. "I can read your mind, you little shit, but I never thought your ha- tred of me would let you endanger what's good for the Cali- phate. You know as well as I do that the longer we wait to restart the attack, the more blood we shed."

"I wouldn't expect a woman to understand these things, but an honorable man obeys the orders of his superiors."

"Honorable man, my ass." She wheeled and stalked back to her own command Bradley. Bashara watched her, and thought the ass she spoke of looked like two bags of wet sand swaying back and forth.

#

Chapter 80

In the Marine Corps, your buddy is not only your classmate or fellow officer, but he is also the Marine under your command. If you don't prepare yourself to properly train him, lead him, and support him on the battlefield, then you're going to let him down. That is unforgivable in the Marine Corps.
Chesty Puller

Shangri-La
1828 hours, April 30

Rainwater found Abby Deak standing beside a large green tank-like vehicle, speaking with a man in a camo uniform who held something that looked like the old football helmets they used when working in tunnels. To his left, the bur oak lay in two pieces, with the ends of each half shattered by something powerful. Bodies and puddles of blood lay scattered in the dirt and on the highway. Three distinct columns of black smoke rose from beyond the tree, and a quick glance showed dozens more bodies interspersed with burning armored vehicles.

"Not that I'm not grateful," he said as he approached Deak and the man she stood beside, "but who are you?"

Dirty streaks lined the man's face. He shifted the helmet to his left hand and stuck out his right. "Lieutenant Onni Hakala, First Platoon, Dog Company, First Marine Recon Battalion."

"Marine?"

"Yes, sir."

"Lieutenant Hakala is part of the Americans we heard about," Deak said. "He saved us, Johnny. Without him, they would have rolled over us."

"It wasn't just me," Hakala said. He nodded with his head in the direction of the tree. "Those are my friends out there."

"I am very sorry for the loss of your friends, but I am very glad that you are here. My name is Johnny Rainwater. May I ask you why?"

"Why what?"

"Why you're here? Why risk your life for us?"

"I didn't exactly do it for you, Mr. Rainwater." The lieutenant pointed toward the flag half a mile in the distance. "I've spent my whole life pledging allegiance to that flag, sir, and the country it stands for. It's why I became a Marine. I'll defend it to the death, and anyone who stands in defense of it is my brother or sister in arms."

"What sort of man still thinks that way?"

Hakala smiled. "We do."

Sara Snowtiger's Cave
1832 hours

"Skip, wake up."

Dennis Tompkins squinted in the semi-darkness of the cave. It took a second for him to remember where he was, or that his arm lay around the shoulders of the slim woman sleeping at his side.

Framed against the twilight outside the cave mouth, John Thibodeaux crouched on his right side holding two paper packets. "Creamed wheat or oatmeal with raisins?"

Tompkins cocked his head but didn't need to ask the question. Thibodeaux had known him too long for that.

"We're splittin' them MRE things up so's they last longer. No tellin' how long we'll be here."

"Did somebody say oatmeal?" said Sara Snowtiger in a sleepy voice. "With raisins?"

Thibodeaux glanced at her and back to Tompkins. He knew that Tompkins hated creamed wheat and loved oatmeal.

"You like oatmeal?" Tompkins said.

"Oh, my... I did when I was a girl, but I have not had it in probably sixty years."

"We can fix that right quick. I'll take the creamed wheat, John. Please bring Sara the oatmeal."

"You sure, Skip?"

"Yes, Dennis, please. I'm fine eating anything. If you prefer the oatmeal, then please eat it."

"Nah, I love creamed wheat. This is perfect."

Thibodeaux wasn't good at hiding what he really felt, but he tried. Rising to go add hot water to the mixes, he stopped when Tompkins asked another question.

"Our friends still outside?"

"Yeah, they's still there. Had a few join 'em."

"How many?"

"Not real sure... best guess is twenty or thirty. I figger there's sixty out there all told, maybe a few more."

"I'll be out for my watch in a minute."

"We's okay, Skip. You stay here wit' the lady an' I's bring your dinner, me."

When he'd gone, Sara Snowtiger looked up at him while still clutching his arm. "It is not good, is it, Dennis?"

He patted her hand. "We'll be fine. You wait and see."

When she smiled, Tompkins thought she looked thirty years younger. "You are a terrible liar."

─────

Lying on one side of the ledge, well away from the others, Piccaldi lowered the binoculars and glanced west, where a semi-circle of the sun still shone above the mountains. "If you wanna grab some chow, I'll stay here 'til you're done."

"I'll wait until you can join me," replied Lara Snowtiger.

"Yeah?"

"Yes." She did something then that she rarely did; she smiled.

"You sure?"

"Yes, I'm sure."

"Why?"

The smile faded and she shook her head. "You know something, Zo? You're a real dumbass."

#

CHAPTER 81

On whom does the cheetah prey? The old, the sick, the wounded, the weak, the very young, but never the strong. Lesson: If you would not be prey, you had better be strong.
G. Gordon Liddy

EP1
1833 hours, April 30

Leaning against the outer wall near the bunker's entrance, arms folded, Joe Randall pretended to watch the single flitter moving toward him at a steady pace, but in reality he was looking past the one-man aircraft toward the south, where the dark clouds of a thunderstorm were lit by streaks of lightning. They'd planned on heading that direction and Randall had been fretting about the storm, but it looked like it might have already passed to the east.

He'd assumed that Bondo and Roe would return to pick them up, but the figure on the platform had a cloth wrapped around its face and, from its size, could have been either one or even someone else. There was no way to tell, nor did it really matter; they had to go through with the plan no matter what happened.

As it turned out, the pilot was Bondo. Landing far enough away that backwash didn't coat Randall with dust, he walked over and wiped his hands on his pants. "How'd you boys like day two out here? Talking to the snakes yet?

444

Hey, where's Carlos? We need to get going before that storm hits."

"In the wind."

"What?" Bondo glanced over each shoulder. "It's not even blowing that hard yet."

"He's gone," Randall said. "Bunny's gone. He's out there somewhere." He waved his hand toward the desert.

Bondo squinted and examined his face as Randall stared back at him. Randall assumed he was looking for signs of deceit, but he doubted that fooling a man who'd never played poker with pilots would be hard. It *was* hard staying focused on Bondo when Carlos rose from the shallow trench they'd dug that afternoon. Dirt and sand poured from his body in yellow clouds. They'd agreed that if Bondo heard him, Randall would stop him from reacting by using his own rifle, but the big man showed no sign of being on alert.

"You mean gone, like into the desert gone?" Bondo said.

Randall ignored Carlos raising his rifle toward the back of Bondo's head. "That's it. He couldn't take it any more and took off that way." He pointed east.

"He'll be back."

"Why's that?"

"There's a crack in the desert out that way, really wide and deep. Runs a long way north and south and there's no going around it."

"Then I guess it's a good thing we've got these flitters," Randall said. With that his eyes flicked to Carlos.

He pushed the muzzle of his rifle against Bondo's head. "Don't make any sudden moves, big boy."

Bondo stiffened. "I knew you fuckers couldn't be trusted..."

A sudden wind gust filled the air with dust and pebbles, the last gasp of the storm.

"You're a regular Einstein," Randall said. He stuck out his hand and waggled his fingers. "The relays?"

Bondo handed them over and Randall clicked them into place without trouble. Unlike most military gear, the hovercraft had a modular assembly that simplified both production and maintenance. Both powered up immediately. He then went to Bondo's flitter and removed the identical relay.

"Here's what's going to happen," Randall told him. "We're gonna take your rifle and this relay and leave them a few hundred yards out from here on a big boulder. That way you don't get stuck out here." Another gust blew his hat off. He retrieved it before continuing and put the strap around his neck. "Don't get in our way and you won't get hurt."

Bondo looked over his shoulder, met Carlos' eyes, but then looked beyond him. When Randall followed the direction of his gaze, he had to cup hands around his eyes to keep out debris stirred up by the coming storm. Through the haze of dust, he spotted multiple somethings moving their way. "Shit!"

Bondo smiled.

"What?" Carlos said, still focused on Bondo.

"Second wife time! Move!"

They were on their flitters and moving within seconds. Randall checked his power levels, which registered fifty-three percent. How was that possible? He knew he was missing something but didn't have time to figure out what.

Despite the turbulence, they both accelerated toward maximum speed until the wind nearly flipped Carlos. The platform vibrated like an out-of-track rotor blade on a helicopter. He struggled to keep from impacting the ground at seventy miles per hour. With no other choice, both men slowed to less than forty. As the desert raced away under them, it seemed like they blazed along, until a glance behind showed their four experienced pursuers closing fast.

A black line ahead had to be the crack that Bondo spoke of. Flying over it wasn't a problem, but that wouldn't shake the posse on their tail, and there didn't seem much doubt about what would happen if they were recaptured. Without goggles, they couldn't keep going much longer, as more and more dust swirled upward. Another look back showed their pursuers had closed to about four hundred yards.

Although the craft was different, the situation was an environment Randall and Carlos knew well. Randall's brain did the calculations automatically between the maximum speed they could make without crashing, about forty in the current wind conditions, and that of their more experienced pursuers, at least sixty. That meant their closing rate neared thirty feet per second, which only gave them forty seconds until they were caught. He and Carlos either had to increase speed and risk disaster, or evade them somehow. But how could they evade when the people chasing them had more experience in flitters?

They raced toward the ravine and Randall saw his chance. He couldn't risk taking a hand off the controls to get Carlos' attention, so he risked disaster and sped up. When he nosed ahead of Carlos, he veered hard right into the darkness of the crack and hoped Carlos would follow.

It was a tight squeeze, but to the two gunship pilots the violent maneuvering seemed like they were at home in *Tank Girl*. It was the kind of flying that came naturally to Randall, and inside the sheltering walls the wind had dropped to near zero.

The width of the crevice didn't exceed twenty feet. Each side varied from ninety degrees sheer down to the bottom, which appeared to be at least two hundred feet down, and less than sixty degrees in a few places. As they flew along, the width in places narrowed to less than ten feet. The safe play was to slow down, but instead Randall zipped through without reducing speed.

The ravine bent to the right. Randall's last glance behind showed they were opening the distance. As experienced as they might be in flying over the desert, their pursuers weren't trained pilots. Randall's plan was working.

Until he looked at the power gauge: twenty-one percent.

Damn!

Whatever they did, they'd have to do it fast. Scenarios flashed through his mind. The ravine bottom offered no solace and would only get them shot from above. He considered going back up into the desert with hopes that the winds might bring some chance to escape, but he nixed that, too, as the chasers had already proven they were better in the turbulent air left over by the storm. Nor did going straight help; he couldn't be sure how accurate the power gauges were, and if they ran out of juice so far up, the fall would be fatal.

Desperation brought an idea. As the ravine bent right at an acute angle, a number of collapsed areas showed up on his right. These were effectively caves created by whatever stresses had triggered the fault in the first place. Most were small, but if one were big enough for them...

And just like that, he spotted one ahead. The air around it was hazy and he got a brief glimpse of something burning on the ravine floor below, but had no time for a look. Risking losing control, he used his left hand to signal Carlos. Zooming toward the black mouth, he decelerated and hovered by the mouth. Five feet wide at the bottom, tapering to less than three feet at the apex, the cave roof stood about six feet high. In other words, it was a tight fit.

There was no way to know if the cave connected to the surface twenty feet above. There could be rattlesnakes inside, or scorpions, or even a coyote den, but with no other choice, both men gently steered their flitters into the narrow opening, dismounted, turned the machines sideways, and went back thirty feet. Then they crouched and waited.

#

Chapter 82

I'll Sleep When I'm Dead
Warren Zevon

Sierra Army Depot
1834 hours, April 30

"Sir, I hate to do this again, but I need you to wake up."

Green Ghost had an arm over his face so that his mumbled response also came out muffled. "What time is it?"

"It's nineteen fifteen hours."

"Did Vapor put you up to this?"

"I wouldn't do that, sir. Junker Jane says it's urgent."

Green Ghost moved his arm, hoping to see the face of the man leaning over his makeshift bed. Instead all he saw was a black outline against the slightly less black night. "Tell her I'm coming."

When he dragged himself awake, he followed the man to Fleming's office, where the only illumination was a battle lamp. The shadows made an obviously exhausted Norm Fleming look worse than Green Ghost felt. Fleming's entire body seemed to sag. But then he got a good look at Jane, who in the wan light looked closer to sixty than forty.

He hadn't even sat down when she blurted out her news. "There's a big force of Americans to the south of Carson City."

"Maybe they've got coffee."

"Nick, listen up," Fleming said. "This is bad."

Ignoring the use of his first name, Green Ghost rubbed his eyes. "How's that, Socrates? Don't they have fuel trucks?"

Fleming turned to Jane and lifted his eyebrows in question.

"Yes, four of them. And lots of those AFV things, but—"

"Wheels or tracks?" Green Ghost interrupted.

"Ummm... tracks like tanks, you mean?"

He nodded.

"Tracks."

"Bradleys," he and Fleming said simultaneously.

Green Ghost added, "This is all stuff we expected."

"There's one thing we didn't expect, and it's the bad part." Fleming pointed at Jane and Green Ghost followed his finger to look at her.

"There's Chinese with them."

Doyle, California
1850 hours, April 30

For his part, Major Dieter Strootman wasn't surprised by the roadblock at the tiny cluster of ruined structures beside Highway 395 marked by a sign that read DOYLE, CA. The old road map which acted as their only guide showed a secondary road marked only 322 leading from the hamlet to the desert south of Sierra Army Depot, so a checkpoint of some kind was not only to be expected, it would have been negligent had there not been one. What he hadn't expected were men forbidding them to advance further under threat of being fired upon.

The column's lead Bradley idled in front of what passed for a barrier across the highway, being an old wooden plank laid across two rusted-out fifty-gallon drums. Standing behind this flimsy demarcation line stood an unshaven sergeant holding a Carl Gustav, an unmistakable threat. In response, the gunner directing the Bradley's M242 Bushmaster chain gun aimed it right at his fellow American, while its commander leaned out of the turret to bring Strootman up to speed.

450

"Says we can't go any further, Major, unless General Angriff himself comes up here and orders them to allow us to pass. I thought you might want to explain the situation."

"Thank you, Staff Sergeant Immeritt."

Strootman walked to the barrier while observing the sergeant standing guard and the five men in firing positions around him, some of them also holding Carl Gustavs. He only had a few seconds to decide how to play it, but the man's tired and dirty face didn't seem the least bit intimidated by having a cannon pointed at his chest.

"What's the meaning of this, Sergeant? We've been on the road a long time, and we're tired."

"I'm sorry, Major, but my orders are that only General Angriff in person can order this barrier taken down."

"Who gave you these orders, Sergeant?"

"My C.O., Major Ball. He indicated the orders came from General Fleming, and the only one person who could override that order would be General Angriff. I *am* authorized to allow one officer through as a liaison."

Strootman took a moment to study the men at the roadblock before wheeling and moving back down the column. He stopped and turned back when the sergeant called him.

"Major! I wouldn't try entering the base by going cross country. Anticipating another Chinese attack, we've spent every spare moment burying mines we found in the bunkers here. Must be thousands of 'em out there."

"Do you believe him?" asked Captain Chen Yi of the People's Liberation Army. The Chinese liaison officer stood to his left rear, but Major Strootman didn't turn even a little bit. Instead he focused all of his attention on Colonel Young.

"It's a pertinent question, Dieter. Do you think he's running a con or could he be serious?"

"I have no way of knowing, Colonel. All I've got is what my gut tells me."

"You Americans and your *gut*." That time it was the other Chinese captain, Xiao Ki, the intelligence officer. Strootman couldn't help staring at him sometimes because while his round face certainly appeared to be Chinese, his hair was pale blonde. "The man is obviously lying."

Colonel Young rubbed his mouth and stepped away, thinking. What he really wanted to do was order the two Chinese officers shot and his regiment to rebase to Sierra, but logistically that was impossible. Within a fortnight, they'd all be starving, nor would four tankers of gas last forever. "I'm sending the officer," he finally said. "But not you, Dieter. I need you here. Find me Lieutenant Ruiz. I want her for this mission."

"Why Ruiz, Colonel?"

Young smiled as though at a memory. "She once told me she'd never gas me."

"What does that mean?" said Yi.

"It means she won't bullshit me."

"And you believe her?"

"Yeah," Young said. "I do. My gut tells me she's not lying."

———————

"This is not how things are done in my army!" Yi said. His orderly, Lieutenant Li Da, stood nearby. The screech of a passing prairie falcon momentarily diverted his gaze skyward.

"I'll take that under advisement," Colonel Young said.

"It is an inefficient way to run an army, trusting your instincts instead of enforcing discipline. My report to General Steeple will reflect my disagreement with your decisions."

"That's your prerogative, Captain."

"I will also express confusion at how you were assigned this mission."

"I can answer that for you," said Major Strootman. "It's because this regiment kicked your ass at Prescott last year. And those people up at Sierra kicked it again this year."

Young held up one hand in a *stop* motion. "Enough—"

Yi nodded and scowled at Strootman. "Thank you, Colonel, for—"

"And *you*, Captain Yi, are a guest in my headquarters." Young gave the Chinese captain his best commanding officer's glare. "So instead of chewing you out for interrupting me, I will politely ask you not to do it again, lest you force me to take measures to ensure it *doesn't* happen again."

Sulking, Yi stalked off just as Lieutenant Ruiz approached Colonel Young's command vehicle. Small, with quick brown eyes, Ruiz had been instrumental in the previous year's battle as part of the regimental headquarters. She had impressed Young with her calm demeanor even during the height of the battle.

He wasted no time before taking her aside and explaining her mission. "I need you to make General Fleming understand our situation, Maria. You are authorized to tell him that General Angriff is no longer in charge of Overtime, and that General Steeple is. You must impress upon him that we are under strict orders to occupy Sierra one way or another, and that includes suppressing any opposition, by whatever means necessary. You are not authorized to conduct any negotiations or to reveal more than I have told you. Are these orders clear?"

The critical nature of what Young asked of her showed in deep lines cut into her youthful face. "Ummm... yes, sir. Colonel... am I allowed to mention our new... *arrangement* with the Chinese?"

Young thought about it. "Dieter, didn't you serve under General Fleming once?"

"Briefly."

"What do you think?"

"General Fleming is one of the most meticulous officers I've ever met, sir. He and I played chess some, and he killed me every time. He can see five moves ahead of the rest of us. I think you have to tell him, Colonel, you have to let him know how bad the odds are against him."

"Very well. All right, Maria, you can tell him that a second Chinese force is approaching from the west and that we are now allies. He's not going to like it one little bit, but you've got to convince him that resistance will just mean futile casualties. He can't win this one."

"I'll do my best, Colonel."

"All right, but look, it's already late today. Let's just wait until the morning. Negotiations are always better when all parties are rested and thinking clearly."

Ruiz's relief was palpable in her loud exhale and smile. As they watched her half walk, half run toward the front of the column to inform Sergeant Immeritt of the delay, Strootman leaned closer.

"For the record, I don't like it, either."

"Eh? What's that?"

"This alliance with the PLA."

"Oh. Me three. I'd just as soon wipe out the lot of 'em, starting with that arrogant prick Yi."

"Do you think General Angriff will make it? To someplace safe, I mean."

"He won't go somewhere safe. From what I know of General Angriff, he's on his way back to Prime, and when he gets there, somebody's gonna get an ass whoopin'."

"Hope you're right, sir."

"Yeah, me, too."

#

Chapter 83

Every government degenerates when trusted to the rulers of the people alone.
Thomas Jefferson

Overtime Prime
1834 hours, April 30

Tom Steeple stared at Károly Rosos' back as his unwanted visitor stood admiring the view of the desert beyond the blast windows. The presence of the least pleasant of the Rosos trio had not been his idea, although he did understand Károly's influence with the Chinese had been invaluable. At some point, he might be able to risk purging the Rosos clan from his plans, but that time was still far in the future.

"To paraphrase the unwashed masses," Rosos said without turning around, "you done good, Tom. Our money was well spent. Father tends not to prefer such modernistic surroundings for his workspace, but I do. I am well pleased."

It took a truly shocking occurrence to leave Tom Steeple gaping in disbelief, but that was his reaction to Rosos' statement. Pointing his finger despite the younger man still not having turned around, his angry response to Rosos' arrogance died on his lips and he looked toward the door at a rap on the frame. Amunet Mwangi stepped into the room and shut the door. By the look on her face, he knew something momentous had happened. "What is it, Amy?"

Grim-faced, she laid a message on his desk from the radio room. Then a smile put a deep crease into her cheeks. Rosos had finally half-turned at her entrance and she smiled at him, too. "They got him. We might one day find what's left of him. Maybe."

"General Angriff is dead?"

"Burnt to a crisp at the bottom of some ravine. I took the liberty to ice some vodka."

"Why are you so happy? This is not good news. Angriff inspired loyalty, and now all of those people are going to think that we killed him on purpose and burned the body to cover it up. Having him alive would have allowed us to control the narrative."

"I didn't think of that, Tom."

"Which is why I am sitting in this chair." He leaned back. "Things are *never* as clear cut as they seem. Thank God for our new allies."

She giggled. That brought a scowl. The one thing that angered Tom Steeple enough to break his façade of calm was being ridiculed. He even had a rarely used, teeth clenched tone of voice for such moments and used it now.

"Care to share what is so funny?"

Mwangi knew him better than most, however. Instead of being intimidated, her laugh softened into a gentle smile. "Don't be angry, Tom. Think about the irony of what you said. You thanked God for sending us allies who officially and by government policy don't believe in Him."

At that he smiled; it was why he valued her so much. She sometimes saw things that he missed, such as ironic situations. And Steeple loved irony. "You are right, Amy, that is funny. And do they not say that He works in mysterious ways?"

"That's what I learned in Sunday school."

"And me as well. And now I know exactly how to break the news to the Seventh Cavalry. How does this sound... most of us thought of General Nicholas T. Angriff as a superhero, and superheroes are not supposed to die. We may not understand God's plan, but we must all have faith that He is in control."

"Are you really going to say that?"

"Is there something wrong with it?"

"Only that your cynicism knows no bounds."

"How do you know I do not actually believe that?"

For a short moment she cocked her head, trying to decide if he was serious. He stared back at her with his best I'm-being-totally-honest expression. But he could only hold it so long before they both started laughing.

Rosos joined in. "My father will be very proud."

#

EPILOGUE

Inside the ravine, the western side had slipped into deep shadow as the sunlight fell in the west. Two flitters sped by the cave mouth. One slowed, looking inside, and the rider pointed his M-16 into the yawning black mouth. Randall leaned against the wall, deep enough in the cave to be swallowed in the darkness. He gulped down the moldy tasting air and stifled the urge to wipe away sweat with his shirt sleeve.

"If he opens up," Carlos whispered into his left ear, "we're meat."

"Ssshhh!"

The hoverboard slipped and slid in mid-air as the rider tried to control it. Craning his neck to see inside for at least ten seconds, he finally sped off down the ravine after his buddies.

Minutes later they felt safe enough to talk.

"This place creeps me out, Joe. I mean, there could be all kinds of snakes and scorpions in here."

"If you'd rather leave, be my guest. But the hoverboard stays here."

Both men fell quiet for a moment. "I thought caves were supposed to be cool. This ain't cool, this is hell."

Before Randall could answer, another voice did it for him.

A hoarse, familiar voice with a Virginia accent. An orange dot flared in the darkness and the scent of burnt tobacco trickled through the small cavern.

"This ain't hell, but you *can* see it from here."

The End

If you enjoyed *Standing Before Hell's Gate*, I would appreciate it if you'd help others enjoy it, too!

Recommend it! Please help other readers find this book by recommending it to family, friends, readers' groups, libraries, and discussion boards.

Review it! The best way to support an author is to leave a review. Please take a minute to review *Standing Before Hell's Gate* on Amazon or Goodreads!

Thank you again and happy reading!

About the Author

He's the world's oldest teenager. Reading, writing, and rock & roll make for an awesome life. The occasional beach doesn't hurt, either.

Bill grew up in West Tennessee, riding his bike on narrow rural roads lined with wild blackberry bushes, in the days before urban sprawl. He spent those long rides dreaming of new worlds of adventure. Childhood for him was one interesting activity after another, from front yard football to naval miniatures, but from the very beginning reading was the central pillar of his life.

Any and all military history books fascinated him, beginning before age eight. By his teenage years, he had discovered J.R.R. Tolkien and Robert E. Howard, Robert Heinlein and Fritz Leiber. Teachers ripped comic books out of his hands during Spanish and accounting classes. Oops!

College found him searching for his favorite rock groups, smuggling beer into his dorm room, and growing his hair long. He read a book a day back then, sometimes two, and always SFF. He even went to class sometimes.

After college, he turned to writing history and nonfiction and was published a number of times, including in *World War Two* magazine.

In September of 2014, he wrote the first pages of what would become *Standing The Final Watch* and its direct sequel, *Standing In The Storm*, plus the fill-in work *The Ghost of Voodoo Village*. That was followed in 2017 by the launch of a brand new fantasy series **Sharp Steel and High Adventure**, starting with the novella *Two Moons Waning*. Who says you can't teach an old dog new tricks? And if you like his work, a whole slew of new books are on the schedule for 2019 and 2020.

Bill is an Active (voting) member of the Science Fiction & Fantasy Writers of America, the Society For Military History, and the Alliance of Independent Authors. He writes exclusive stories for those on his mailing list at his website, www.thelastbrigade.com.

Also by William Alan Webb

The Last Brigade
Standing the Final Watch
The Ghost of Voodoo Village
Standing in the Storm
Standing at the Edge
The Hairy Man

Sharp Steel and High Adventure
Two Moons Waning
The Queen of Death and Darkness
A Night at The Quay
Sharp Steel

The Time Wars
Jurassic Jail

Nonfiction
The Last Attack
Killing Hitler's Reich
Unsuck Your Book

LifeEnders, Inc.
Kill Me When You Can

Thanks for reading! Dingbat Publishing strives to bring you quality entertainment that doesn't take itself too seriously. I mean honestly, with a name like that, our books have to be good or we're going to be laughed at. Or maybe both.

If you enjoyed this book, the best thing you can do is buy a million more copies and give them to all your friends... erm, leave a review on the readers' website of your preference. All authors love feedback and we take reviews from readers like you seriously.

Oh, and c'mon over to our website:
www.DingbatPublishing.ninja

Who knows what other books you'll find there?

Cheers,

Gunnar Grey,
publisher, author, and Chief Dingbat

δ